Praise for *Simmer Down*

"Fantastic writing, great characters, and sizzling chemistry make this contemporary romance a *must read*."
— Samantha Young, *New York Times* bestselling author of *Much Ado About You*

"This food truck romance serves up an enemies-to-lovers story that is spicy, salty, and sweet. Delicious!"
— Mia Hopkins, author of *Trashed*

"*Simmer Down* is full of love and food (which is love), and you're sure to crave more with each page."
— Tif Marcelo, *USA Today* bestselling author of *In a Book Club Far Away*

"While the enemies-to-lovers romance is irresistible, it's the sincere, well-developed characters and heart-tugging family dynamics that make this fulfilling love story stand out. This is a winner." — *Publishers Weekly* (starred review)

"Fun, flirty, finger-licking-good." — *Woman's World*

"A powerhouse romance with a perfect mélange of spicy banter, lush scenery, and passion!"
— Charish Reid, author of *(Trust) Falling for You*

"This book had everything: a heart-melting hero, laugh-out-loud moments, family drama, and delicious food all wrapped up in a lush, tropical setting. Fresh, fun, and utterly addictive."
— Sara Desai, author of *The Dating Plan*

Praise for *Faker*

"A funny, charming, and thoroughly entertaining debut. I couldn't put it down!"

—*New York Times* bestselling author Samantha Young

"A fresh, sweet, and funny story about how the people we think we know can surprise us in the sexiest way. Full of swoony kisses and heartfelt honesty, *Faker* is like a warm, reassuring hug."

—Lyssa Kay Adams, author of *Isn't It Bromantic?*

"I loved every page of Smith's wonderful debut! The romance was sweet and heartwarming, but it was Smith's ability to write a main character who embraces all of her power that had me cheering throughout this book."

—Alexa Martin, author of *Mom Jeans and Other Mistakes*

"Written with insight and humor, Sarah Smith's *Faker* is a charming, feminist, and diverse romance that will have you hooked until the very last page."

—Sonya Lalli, author of *A Holly Jolly Diwali*

"A sweet, slow-burn romance between rival coworkers at a power tool company makes for a promising debut." —*Kirkus Reviews*

"Smith brings the heat in more ways than one in this enemies-to-friends-to-lovers story with a splash of humor. . . . Perfect for fans of Tessa Bailey and Christina Lauren." —*Booklist*

Also by Sarah Echavarre Smith

Faker

Simmer Down

ON LOCATION

Sarah Echavarre Smith

JOVE
NEW YORK

A JOVE BOOK
Published by Berkley
An imprint of Penguin Random House LLC
penguinrandomhouse.com

Library of Congress Cataloging-in-Publication Data

Names: Smith, Sarah, 1985– author.
Title: On location / Sarah Smith.
Description: First edition. | New York : Jove, 2021.
Identifiers: LCCN 2021008052 (print) | LCCN 2021008053 (ebook) |
ISBN 9780593201657 (trade paperback) | ISBN 9780593201664 (ebook)
Subjects: GSAFD: Love stories.
Classification: LCC PS3619.M59298 O5 2021 (print) |
LCC PS3619.M59298 (ebook) | DDC 813/.6—dc23
LC record available at https://lccn.loc.gov/2021008052
LC ebook record available at https://lccn.loc.gov/2021008053

First Edition: September 2021

Printed in the United States of America
1st Printing

Book design by Ashley Tucker
Interior art: © Shutterstock / Vector Tradition

For Joanne. You rule.

NEVER THOUGHT BRIE CHEESE COULD BE SO INFURIATING.

But infuriated is exactly how I feel as I watch the man sitting in front of me in this packed New York City subway car pull a wheel of Brie from his jacket pocket.

He takes noisy, sloppy bites, like he's eating an apple.

I bite back a curse and try not to gag. On any other day, I'd take this scene in stride. This is the subway during a Friday evening commute, after all. Weird stuff is bound to happen, and normally I'd be down to people watch.

But after the day I've had, witnessing a stranger noisily devour a round of soft cheese as I stand one foot away is the last straw. My well of patience is depleted, and I've got no more fucks to give.

"You've got to be freaking kidding me," I mutter to myself, not caring one bit if he hears.

My phone buzzes in my pocket between stations.

Haley: Want me to slash Byron's tires? Just say the word and it's done.

I crack a smile. It's the first time my mouth has curved upward ever since this morning's failed pitch—the reason for my current sour mood.

Me: As long as you're okay with taking the heat. I'm currently on the subway headed home. I don't have the energy to make my way from Brooklyn to Manhattan to bail you out.

Haley: You won't have to. I won't get caught ☺

I chuckle. This text exchange with my coworker and best friend is the perfect distraction.

I glance around the car, packed to the max with commuters eager to get the hell home, just like me. I inhale, then promptly wrinkle my nose at the smell of BO, smoke, urine, and stale fast food.

"This is Brooklyn Bridge–City Hall," the automated voice announces through the speaker system as we shudder to a stop.

The doors fly open and a wave of people push their way onto the car while a handful try to walk out. I close my eyes and sigh. Every. Single. Time. Everyone knows that you're supposed to let people get off the train first before you walk on. It's such a simple rule.

But this city is riddled with rule breakers. Like the Brie cheese guy, who is now eating a giant, smelly egg salad sandwich and washing it down with a can of beer. He lets out a loud belch that doesn't seem to faze anyone else sitting or standing in this packed-to-the-brim car.

I hold in a groan. Isn't it enough that we're permitted to consume food on crowded mass transportation? Why does he have to eat one of the stinkiest foods imaginable *and* drink alcohol? I'm in the mood to guzzle copious amounts of liquor after the day I've had, but I'm not about to down a bottle of whiskey on the subway.

I wonder if network executive Byron would think that's risky enough—openly consuming alcohol on the subway in direct defiance of mass-transit policy.

I shake my head and look away, annoyed that I can't seem to

shed my awful attitude. But I can't help it. Because today I had
a shot at my dream—the dream I've been working toward ever
since I graduated college and started working in television. And
I lost it. That's why Haley is texting me—to comfort me because
she knows just how much this kills.

As someone who works in TV production, I'm used to being
disappointed. I've spent my entire career working for Expedition
TV, the most popular travel-themed channel on cable. When I
started as an intern and production assistant, I worked long hours,
often having my ideas shot down because they were too ambitious or because I was too inexperienced. But the disappointment
of rejection was easy to brush off, because I got to spend the bulk
of my twenties traveling all over the US, working on shows that
documented the most beautiful parts of the country. I also
learned an important lesson early on: the TV industry isn't for the
faint of heart.

If I didn't have it in me to keep trying, keep working hard,
keep amassing years of experience while learning the industry
ropes, then I wasn't cut out for this business. So that's exactly
what I did—for nine years, I slept in tents and cars while on
shoots, took countless red-eye flights, pulled all-nighters to re-
write scripts scheduled to shoot the next morning, and rode in
rickety puddle-jumper airplanes across rugged terrain to capture
their remote beauty. But this was my passion, and I couldn't
imagine doing anything else.

It was my dream to work for Expedition when I was a kid. I
couldn't get enough of the nature programs about odd-looking
animals with cool-sounding names or the shows featuring hosts
backpacking all over the world—places I had dreamed of visiting. I watched with wide eyes, dreaming of when I would grow
up and make shows like this.

That's how I got to where I am now—a producer for Expedition TV. Today I was as close as I've ever been to making my dream come true: I pitched my very own outdoor series.

It's inspired by a childhood road trip through Utah that I took with my brother and our *apong* to visit all five national parks in the state. Even now I still remember how awestruck I was at the endless adobe-hued rock formations, the fiery colors of the sand and dirt.

Beautiful, Apong Lita whispered as she held my hand, her smoky topaz eyes wide as she scanned the scenery around her. *I've never seen anything like it before. I'm so glad I get to see it with my grandbabies.*

I don't think Apong Lita, my brother, or I blinked once the entire two-week trip. There were too many stunning sites: impossibly red cliffs lining the horizon, eye-popping rock formations that could have come straight out of a sci-fi movie, and desert shrubbery that I'd never seen before.

"I want to highlight the national parks in a way they haven't been before," I said this morning to Byron during my pitch. Buzzing with excitement, I described my idea for a twelve-episode series called *Discovering Utah.* Each episode would follow a host as they explored not only the most popular trails and attractions, but hidden gems in each park as well. Breathtaking shots of the landscape cut with modern music would be the backdrop.

"It would be the ultimate outdoor adventure program," I said.

All Byron did was stare at the paper handout in front of him. It included all the data I could compile on viewership, ratings, and our audience's interest in hiking and national parks, and explained how it related to my series concept. All those numbers, charts, and graphs I put together showed how *Discovering Utah* was sure to be a hit with viewers.

When he finally looked up at me, an unimpressed frown was all he had to offer. And then he dove into the million reasons why my series could never work.

An overdone concept . . . the national parks are antiquated . . . there's no real hook.

My chest aches recalling how he tossed the papers I printed out for him onto the conference table, like all those months of researching and rehearsing this pitch meant nothing.

"It's a cute idea, Alia," he said while flashing his trademark condescending expression: a raised eyebrow and pursed lips. "But if you want to succeed here at Expedition, you gotta be willing to take risks. This pitch is too safe. And you won't get anywhere in this business if you keep playing it safe."

I release my death grip on the metal pole and shake my hand out, careful not to hit the person next to me in the subway car. I should have known better than to feel optimistic. Byron is notorious for being the hardest sell of all the execs. And his tastes are damn near impossible to discern. He's rejected groundbreaking concepts and given the green light to boring ideas that are canceled after a few episodes.

In the back of my mind, I wonder if I should have pitched my idea for an international travel show that popped into my head years ago. I called it *Hidden Gem Island Getaways*. I wanted to start in Palawan, my mom and *apong*'s favorite place to visit in the Philippines when they lived there. I grew up hearing them rave about the island's white-sand beaches, emerald lagoons, lush rain forests, and rocky cliffs, and the endless secret coves that were a blast to explore. When I got into TV production, I knew it would be the perfect lesser-known international getaway to highlight. We'd film in other locations in the Pacific that are often overlooked as tourist destinations. It would be more than just a show about pretty beaches, though; with the exposure of Expedition, it would also hopefully bring an influx of tourism and recognition to those lesser-known areas.

Pitching it would have been a long shot . . . but maybe it would have appealed to unpredictable Byron. I'll never know.

I bite the inside of my cheek, devastated that playing it safe cost me my own show.

Maybe if I had just sucked it up and—

"This is Wall Street," the automated voice announces, jolting me back to my evening commute.

The car halts once more, and once more passengers around me exit. A whole new wave of people files in. Everyone moves like a frenzied school of fish, vying for any and all available spaces.

A small elderly lady clutching her purse slowly makes her way near me as the train car lurches forward. I offer a polite smile, then scoot over as much as I can to give her room without body-humping the person behind me.

She reaches for the metal pole next to me but then loses her balance as the car takes a turn. With my free hand, I steady her.

"You all right?" I ask.

She offers a weak smile. "Fine, dear. Thank you."

She manages to grab hold of the pole as the car picks up speed. I gaze around, hoping by some miracle to find a free spot for her to sit, but every single seat is taken by someone in a staring contest with their phone.

I huff out a breath, frustrated. Most of the people sitting are at least half this woman's age, and not a single one of them seems to realize or care that the decent thing for them to do would be to offer their seat to the elderly lady with the cane.

She leans against the pole, frowning. I can't tell if she's tired or in pain.

"I can ask someone who's sitting to trade spots with you," I say to her.

She gazes up at me, her gray eyes behind her glasses hopeful. Then she scans the full seats lining the subway car and her face falls.

"It's all right, dear," she says.

I nod at her. Just then a shadow appears in the corner of my eye.

I look up and see a very tall, very broad, and very handsome bearded stranger approach the elderly lady. "Ma'am, why don't you take my seat?"

Her brow raises as she smiles. "Oh my. Thank you."

The six-foot-plus strapping stranger with an impressive head of golden-brown hair gives her a gentle smile, then leads her with a hand on the arm to sit down.

My heartbeat flutters out of control. This single act of decency performed by a guy who could be the stand-in for Alex O'Loughlin in *Hawaii Five-0* is the highlight of my day.

My insides go mushy at the scene of him hunched over, holding her hands to support her as she sits down. A dozen heads turn to take in the visual. This dude. This dude has no idea what a panty-dropping move he just pulled. I fully expect every single person in the vicinity to swarm him like bees to honey the moment he finishes assisting the elderly woman.

For a second I contemplate taking a photo and texting it to Haley. She would definitely appreciate seeing a hottie pulling an aww-inducing move like this one.

And then, like a weirdly timed flashback, Byron's words from earlier echo in my mind.

You gotta be willing to take risks. You won't get anywhere if you keep playing it safe.

I pull my phone out, snap a photo of the hot stranger smiling down at the elderly lady, then post it to my Twitter.

This hottie just gave up his seat to an elderly lady on a crowded subway car #aww #subwaygentleman

I shove my phone back in my pocket.

How's that for taking a risk, Byron?

I deflate when I realize that I'm conducting an imaginary scolding of my boss and that I will likely never have the balls to say any of that out loud to him. How very, very sad.

Closing my eyes, I sigh and take a breath.

"You don't mind that we've traded places, do you?"

My eyes snap open and I'm greeted with the image of the hot and helpful stranger standing next to me in the exact spot where the elderly woman was just a minute before. He displays a heart-melting half smile.

I offer a flustered smile at him in return. "Not at all."

He nods once at me before checking something on his phone. It's a few seconds before I realize I'm staring at his deliciously thick neck. I quickly look down at my shoes and silently admonish myself for gawking at him. It's rude to stare at someone you don't know like they're a dish you're dying to taste.

You gotta be willing to take risks.

The words tumble in my head once more. Byron may be a jerk, but I bet he's never too shy or intimidated to talk to anyone. He walks into every room like he owns it, even though he spends most of his days playing solitaire on his office computer and is still employed only because his dad started Expedition TV years ago.

If someone as unqualified and untalented as Byron has zero problem taking risks, I shouldn't either.

So I swallow back all the nerves that typically swirl through me when I'm chatting with a hot guy. I wouldn't normally ever think to flirt with someone on the subway. But it's time to take a risk.

I glance back up at the hot stranger. "That was really sweet, what you did."

He looks back at me. "Sorry?"

"What you did—giving up your seat for that lady."

I jut my chin at the elderly woman, who's sitting with a small smile on her face while looking through her purse, clearly more comfortable than earlier.

"Oh." He smiles and runs a hand over his face.

My gaze snags on his forearm, which is exposed nicely by the rolled-up sleeves of the gray sweater he's wearing.

"It's nothing, really," he says.

I raise an eyebrow at him, feeling more emboldened by the second. "It is, though. No one else was willing to give up their seat. You did."

A smile tugs at his lips, and his light complexion flushes. He scratches at his short-trimmed beard. "Actually, if you were to find out the real reason I gave up my seat, you'd think I was a dog. Guaranteed."

I let out a snort at his phrasing. "What, did you have some nefarious reason for doing it?"

He shrugs, a sly smile on his lips. The way his brownish-hazel eyes shine warms me from the inside out. I'm instantly mesmerized.

I take a half step over so I can be closer to him. Chatting up a stranger is risky. You don't want to bother someone or make them feel creeped out. But all of this guy's body language and conversation cues are on point. He's positioned his body to face me. He's keeping steady eye contact and smiling. He's joking along with me and engaging in conversation. All clear signs he's into this interaction.

And the best thing? He's letting me lead things. In a city where women are bombarded with catcalls and unwanted advances daily, it's demoralizing to constantly have to fight that attention off. Now that I've conquered my nerves, it's refreshing to be the one initiating for once.

He bites the corner of his lip, which makes his smile look the slightest bit wolfish. I like.

"I wouldn't say it was a nefarious reason," he says. "More like half-selfless and half-selfish."

"You've gotta tell me now."

Chuckling, he glances down at the leather boots he's wearing and smooths a hand over his tattered jeans. He locks eyes with me once more, then raises his eyebrow. "You sure?"

"Positive."

"I gave up my seat because it was the right thing to do, of course. But getting to stand next to you was a nice bonus."

His eyes fall to the ground once more as he blushes. A grin splits my face at his compliment.

"Didn't see that coming," I manage to say without sounding like a complete dork.

When he glances back at me, there's a glimmer of hesitation in his eyes. "Sorry, maybe I shouldn't have said that."

The car shudders to a halt, and the automated voice announces the stop for Bowling Green station. For a second, I worry that this is his stop and that's the last I'll hear from this sexy stranger. But he stays put as people around us shuffle in and out.

"Don't be sorry. I'm glad you said it," I say while locking eyes with him once more.

"Really?"

My hand twitches with the urge to take this interaction to the next level.

Take a risk.

I reach toward him and set my hand on his forearm. "Really."

The car moves as he eyes my hand on his forearm, his smile widening. A beat later I drop my hand back to my side. I've made my move. Now we'll see if he's into it or wants to just leave things at that.

"Hey, so . . ."

I turn back to look at him. He scrunches his lips for a second.

On the inside, I let out a silent squeal. He's nervous and it's extremely cute.

"I don't normally do this, but . . ." He rubs the back of his neck.

My ears perk up at what I hope he's going to say.

"My stop is the next one, Borough Hall," he says in a low, quiet voice. "I don't know where you're headed or what your plans are right now, but if you're free, would you want to grab a drink? It's been fun chatting with you, and I really don't want it to end just yet."

The pointed way he looks at me makes my stomach flip and my skin heat all at once.

"I'd love to . . ."

"Drew." He sticks his hand out for me to shake.

"Lia."

I shake his hand after giving him my childhood nickname. Not only is it easier for most people to pronounce—even though my full name is only one letter longer—it's safer this way. Yeah, he's sweet and sexy and giving off all the good vibes, but he's still a stranger. Despite our flirty exchange, things could go south when we sit down for a drink. If that's the case, it's best he doesn't know my full name so he can't Facebook stalk me or anything like that.

"Lia." The corner of his mouth quirks up, like he's relishing how it sounds on his tongue. "That's a beautiful name."

"Thank you. Just one rule."

"What's that?"

"No work talk. It's been a dumpster fire of a day for me, so I'd like to avoid all things work related."

"I can handle that."

The intercom announces the next stop, and we ease to a halt once more.

Drew flashes an easy smile at me. "Shall we?"

"Definitely."

2

DREW EYES ME OVER THE RIM OF HIS GLASS. "NOT POSsible."

"Oh, it's possible."

"You've never had a hangover? I call BS."

My head falls back as I laugh. We're on our second drink—bourbon for us both—at the Brazen Head, and our first hour of conversation has been a blast. I've never hit it off this quickly with anyone before.

Sitting at the far end of the bar, we've moved from topic to topic, answering an array of questions about each other ranging from what we were like in high school to what is our favorite drunk-bingeing food. I've learned that Drew is an avid mountain biker who has traveled to every state and loathes pineapple and mushrooms. I've divulged that I prefer audiobooks to print books, can't sleep past eight in the morning, and would rather do hot yoga for an hour every day than do a single push-up. Still the fun-and-flirty vibe remains.

"Of course it's true," I say. "I've made it to thirty-two without enduring a single hangover in my life. I refuse to start now."

He sets his empty glass on the smooth wooden bar top and asks the bartender for another. "What's your secret?"

"Pickle juice."

He coughs on the sip he takes, covering his mouth. I pat his back while covering my own mouth to keep my giggling under control. The hard feel of his body under the fabric of his sweater elicits a low hum in my throat. I swallow to cover up the sound.

"Pickle juice? Is that a joke?" he asks, wiping his mouth with a cocktail napkin.

"Nope. I always keep a jar of dill pickle juice in my fridge. And then before I go out or have a drink at my place, I drink a cup of it. I read it in an article. Apparently the salt from the pickle brine replenishes the electrolytes you lose when you're drinking, which helps prevent that god-awful headache most people get the morning after a rough drinking session. Or something like that."

"Well, damn." Drew's stare turns thoughtful. "You're just full of surprises, Lia. It's pretty sexy. And a little weird. But mostly sexy."

I roll my eyes while laughing. "You're one to talk."

He raises an eyebrow. It gives his expression a playful edge.

"Am I?"

"You and your 'let me give up my seat on the subway for an elderly lady just so I can stand next to you' move? Insanely sexy. That combined with how you look . . ."

He leans in closer and licks his lips. "How do I look?" His tone is a whispered growl that makes my knees weak and my mouth water. I blink and imagine his lips all over my body, that soft growl whispering all the unspeakable things he plans to do to me.

I steady my breathing, my mantra for the night sounding in my brain.

Take a risk.

"You're sex on a stick, Drew."

He makes a stuttered noise before clearing his throat; then he flashes a flustered grin. "I haven't heard that one before. I'm flattered."

The parts of his cheeks that aren't covered by his beard turn pink. His eye contact doesn't waver for even a second. That hungry look in his eyes sets off that newly formed risk-taking segment in my brain.

Take a risk.

"I'm just speaking the truth," I say. "You're insanely attractive."

My gaze falls along the length of his body. I can't stop gawking at his long and muscled legs, his lean torso, those broad shoulders, those meaty and veiny forearms that I hope will be pinning me to a bed at some point this evening.

My skin heats at the thought. I fight the urge to look away.

Take a risk.

"Insanely attractive," I mutter again, almost to myself.

"Funny. I was just about to say the same about you." His hand lands softly on top of mine. He turns it over so that my palm is exposed and starts tracing my skin with his index finger.

My breath catches, and I have to bite my lip to get my sounds under control. Never has such minimal contact driven me so wild.

Take a risk.

I lean forward and lay my signature first-date kiss on him. I wouldn't normally kiss a guy less than two hours into knowing him—but this impromptu date is inspiring me to throw out the playbook. Might as well pull out all the stops.

The kiss I press on Drew lasts just a couple of seconds—but it's the end that counts. Because when I start to pull away, I lick my bottom lip, and my tongue skims his mouth. It's a way to give him a taste of the good stuff while leaving him wanting more.

When I settle back on my barstool, he doesn't blink for a few seconds. He looks like he's been shocked by an electrical current. Then he shakes his head slightly, seeming to refocus. A shy smile spreads across his face.

His gaze falls to my palm, then back to my face. There's a new intensity behind his eyes. "Look, I don't mean for this to sound as crass as it does, but . . ."

I hold my breath, wondering what he's about to say.

"It's taking everything in me not to ask you back to my place right now."

"For the record, I'd say yes."

He runs a hand though his hair, his face flustered as he chuckles. "Believe me, I want that more than anything. But my aunt is visiting me," he says through a groan.

The hopeful bubble inside me bursts, but I laugh it off. "It's okay. That makes me like you even more—that you're not willing to ditch your aunt for a hookup."

"It's a tough call, believe me." He sighs, the struggle on his face playing out as he asks the bartender for the check. I bite my lip, it's so adorable.

He leans forward, gently grabbing my hand in his. "Please tell me you're free tomorrow. Her flight leaves in the morning, and I'd like to see you again."

"I'm free."

Fire ignites behind his hazel-brown eyes as his lips tug into grin.

He pulls out his phone and we exchange numbers.

"Can I call you tomorrow?" he asks when he finishes signing the check.

"You'd better."

"Then it's a date." The smile he flashes is one for the record books. It makes me weak in the knees *and* sends my stomach flipping *and* has my heart fluttering. No smile has ever had that effect on me before.

He stands up and helps me off my stool, then pulls that deliciously sweet move of leading me with soft yet firm fingers on the small of my back while walking out of the Brazen Head. Seconds later we're standing on the sidewalk facing each other, grinning like goobers.

"Thank you for the drinks," I say.

"Thank you for the company."

Drew takes a step forward and pulls me in for a hug. When we pull apart, I lean up and press my lips against his for first-date kiss number two.

But this time he doesn't let me leave so quickly. This time, he leads me in a teasing kiss that lasts long enough to illicit whistles and car honks from passersby.

When he finishes, my ears are ringing. I'm so dizzy I stumble a bit. He steadies me with a hand on my arm.

"You good?" he asks.

"Really, really good."

"How are you getting home?"

My senses pull back into focus at the concern in his voice.

I flash my phone at him. "Ride-share app."

"I'll wait until your car comes."

A minute later a car pulls up next to me. He opens the back passenger door for me, shuts it, then leans down so he can still see me. Through that killer smile, he mouths, "Bye," then stands on the sidewalk, watching as I pull away. I grin the entire ride home.

I TAKE A long sip of coffee as I sift through the mountain of Monday morning emails at my desk, still reeling from this letdown of a weekend.

Actually, "letdown" isn't even the right way to describe it. "Soul-crushing" is more like it.

Because I was utterly crushed when Saturday came and went and I didn't hear a peep from Drew. No call, no text, nothing.

I wince as I take another long gulp of coffee, remembering how I spent the day running errands and cleaning my apartment, checking my phone every few minutes. But nothing.

And then Saturday evening when I sent him a "you alive?" text, still nothing.

That's as clear a sign as there ever was. Drew just wasn't that into me.

And I think I know why—because I might be responsible for it.

I take a quick glance at my Twitter account and see that the photo I took of Drew on the subway helping that elderly lady has officially gone viral.

A thousand retweets—and thousands of comments, most of which are thirsty proclamations for Drew.

Who is this #subwaygentleman?? I need a name! And Twitter handle! And a phone number!

Damn, #subwaygentleman is a hottie for sure and is seriously making me consider scouring the streets of New York to try and find him.

Hot damn gimme some of that #subwaygentleman.

I have to resist a full-on cringe when I think about how I teed him up for man-hungry New Yorkers. When he left me Friday night, I have no doubt there were people prowling the streets for the subway gentleman.

I let out another sigh when I think about how close I was to tears Sunday morning when I checked my Twitter account and saw how Drew's photo had blown up. There were hundreds of notifications on my phone—too many for me to sort through. So I decided to ignore them and haven't checked Twitter since. That's why he never contacted me. He must have crossed paths with one of his admirers and decided that she was more enticing. Or maybe he saw the tweet, realized I was responsible for it, and thought I was a freak for ogling him and making him go viral—then decided not to contact me.

I tried everything to get myself out of the rejection funk. I indulged in some wine and Netflix, then hit up a kickboxing class. Then Haley came over to my apartment Sunday evening and cooked her mom's *longanisa* recipe with rice and eggs because it's my ultimate comfort meal—and hers too. Ever since sophomore year of college when we became friends, we would cook that yummy spicy sausage for each other every time one of us was feeling down after a bad date, and it's a tradition we've kept up. Now that it's Monday morning, I'm more than ready to move on and pretend like Drew never happened.

I glance up and spot Haley through the glass wall of my office. She's standing in one of the cubicles chatting with the new graphic designer, whose name I can't remember. When he hunches over to check something on his computer, she looks away, catching my eye.

"You okay?" she mouths, the concern in her deep-brown eyes crystal clear, even from several feet away.

I nod, plastering a professional smile on my face.

She raises an eyebrow while retying her ponytail. "You sure?" she mouths.

I roll my eyes and mouth a silent "yes" in return.

But on the inside I'm still a mess. I connected with Drew in a way I haven't experienced in ages. He was sweet and funny and charming. I've never felt that at ease that quickly on a date. That spark with him was special.

You've thought that before . . . Remember what a disaster that was?

I shove the thought away with a shake of my head.

When Haley's focused stare finds me again, it's a signal that she doesn't buy it. Because she's the one person who knows what a toll that particular disaster had on me.

I look away and squint at my computer screen. Just then my office phone rings. I look and see my boss's extension.

"Hey, Brooke. Happy Monday."

"Happy Monday indeed." Judging by her chipper tone, it sounds like she's smiling. That's a first. Usually Brooke loathes Monday mornings with a passion. She's my favorite producer turned show-runner here and has become a mentor and a friend after our years of working on shoots together. But we also get along because we have similar work styles when we're in the office. She usually holes up in her office most mornings, slowly sipping a giant mug of coffee and a green smoothie to energize herself while refusing to answer the phone until at least 10 a.m., just like me.

"I have some news," she says. "Can you come to my office? Like, now?"

"Oh. Sure."

I hang up, confused about whether I should be happy or nervous. The fact that Brooke was so chipper is encouraging . . . but it's not usually a good sign when you're called into your boss's office to receive some mystery "news" with zero explanation.

As I walk down the hallway toward Brooke's corner office, I mentally leaf through every recent project I've done and what I've got on the docket, but I come up empty by the time I make it to her door.

Brooke's typing when I walk in, but she immediately stops and beams up at me before asking me to shut the door. The muscles in my shoulders relax a tiny bit. Wide smile is definitely a good sign.

She gestures for me to have a seat, then turns her chair to face me. She runs a hand through her wild blond curls.

"So you said something about news?" I ask, trying to keep my tone light and professional.

She nods while pushing up the sleeves of her green paisley-print wrap dress. "Really, really good news, Alia. Your Utah series just got the green light. And you're gonna be the showrunner."

"What?" A wide grin nearly splits Brooke's delicate and fair face in half. "But I thought Byron passed on it."

"The other network execs changed their minds."

This time when I say, "What?" my voice ticks up in excitement. "But I thought Byron—"

Brooke lifts an eyebrow, her smile morphing into something smug. "Byron can suck on a lemon."

I stifle a laugh. It's no secret that Brooke loathes Byron. He's the old-fashioned, boring counter to the open-minded and free-spirited concepts Brooke comes up with.

"That ancient-ruins show the network planned to air this fall fell through," she explains. "The execs rallied over the weekend and chose your series to replace it."

My jaw falls open. "Are you serious?"

She nods, beaming wide once more.

Shedding all professionalism, I jump up and round the corner of Brooke's mahogany desk to hug her. She doesn't seem to mind, though, since she returns a tight hug and pitchy squeals of excitement that rival mine.

I pull away, my head spinning.

"Brooke, thank you. For whatever you said to them to make them choose my series as the one to go with."

"Don't thank me. They made this decision on their own—I'm just relaying the good news because they're all in meetings and conference calls today and apparently can't spare a minute." She rolls her eyes before that bright smile returns to her expression.

I cup my hands over my cheeks. "Oh my God, my own series!"

Another ear-to-ear smile splits my face. We sit back down and chat logistics, how the network wants a dozen twenty-one-minute episodes shot over six weeks on location in Utah starting at the end of March, which is just a week away. The budget is tight, but I don't even care. As showrunner, that means I'm in charge of the entire shoot, from every aspect of production to script writing to the creative side. Butterflies soar inside my stomach.

"You get to handpick your crew," Brooke says. "Whoever you want, as long as they're free for the scheduled shoot time, they're yours. And, look, I know six weeks is kind of tight. And I know that the weather in Utah in March and April is iffy. I would have fought for you to have longer and at a more convenient time of year, but they honestly just sprung it on me, like, twenty minutes before I called you in here. And from the way everything fell apart with the first option, they're not in the mood to extend the filming time."

I shake my head. "Don't even worry. I can work a miracle with six weeks. I've been on shoots that were half as long where it was just you and me, and we did everything from writing the script to scouting the locations," I say. "Besides, the good thing about shooting in March and April is that I'll avoid the worst of the busy tourist season. This is going to work out perfectly. I promise."

Brooke gives me budget details, then looks at me once more, pride dancing in her blue eyes. "Congrats, Alia."

I cover my face in my hands once more. "I just . . . I can't believe it."

"Let it sink in for a bit. And then hit the ground running,"

Brooke says. "Byron insisted that he pick the host, since this is all last-minute, but you should know tomorrow who it is."

I nod, then stand up to leave her office. Before I walk out the door I turn back to Brooke. "I couldn't have done this without you."

Her expression turns warm. "Thank you for the kind words, but all the credit goes to you. You earned this, every bit of it."

Brooke's words echo through my head as I make my way back to my office. I finally got my shot—my big break. I'm finally where I've wanted to be for so long: my own travel show, set in one of my favorite places in the world.

When I make it back to my office, I shut the door behind me, draw the blinds over the glass wall that overlooks the floor, and then I jump up and down, silently cheering.

Seconds later I'm breathless and leaning against the door. I grin to myself. "I did it."

3

REFRESH MY WORK EMAIL INBOX. STILL NOTHING. ONE DAY after I got the best professional news of my life, I'm a ball of nerves. I still have no idea who's hosting the series.

Brooke and I have been calling and emailing the casting department nonstop since I got the news Monday morning, and we've gotten nothing other than noncommittal hemming and hawing.

And with Brooke gone today for the preproduction of an upcoming series she's producing about sailing in New England, that leaves me to panic all on my own.

When my phone rings with a call from Brooke, I answer it right away.

"Hey." The way she breathes through her greeting, I know something's up. "You busy?"

"Always free for you. What's up?"

"Okay, well . . ."

My heart pounds as she hesitates for several more seconds. This is so unlike confident and decisive Brooke. Ever since I've known her, she speaks with certainty—and I don't think I've ever heard her hesitate.

"Is everything okay, Brooke?"

She sighs. "I finally got word on the host."

I start to smile. Finally. But then she once more falls into a few seconds of silence and stumbling.

"I guess there's no way around this," she finally says. "Check your email. And I just want to say I'm sorry in advance."

Half an hour later my eyes are bulging as I stare at the screen of my computer. It doesn't matter how many viral videos I watch featuring the soon-to-be host of my series. My reaction is always the same. Disbelief. Disgust. Confusion.

When Brooke told me an hour ago that the network cast Blaine Stephens to host *Discovering Utah*, I didn't react. I had no idea who he was—and I had no idea why Brooke was so upset about it. But then I clicked on the video links she sent me.

Blaine Stephens is a former reality star and D-list celebrity. He's also a train wreck in human form.

That thought repeats over and over in my brain as I watch yet another video I found online when I searched for his name. There's Blaine standing on top of a car that's parked on a busy street in San Francisco, his hands in the air as he's screaming something unintelligible, totally nude.

People walk past while staring and pointing. A few parents cover the eyes of their children. A handful of people stop to film him on their phones.

"What the . . ."

I don't even finish my sentence before Blaine starts jumping up and down on the car, denting the roof. Then he loses his footing and plummets to the sidewalk, hitting his head on the cement.

I whip my head to Haley, who's hunched over and watching along with me while eating the gluten-free breakfast bar I brought her this morning.

"How the hell is this guy still alive?"

"He apparently dropped acid that day," she says between bites. "Must have been one hell of a trip."

The moment I realized who this Blaine person was, my internal panic began. How in the world is a guy like this going to host a show? Brooke apologized while on the phone with me, saying that she initially told the execs that no way would he work as host, but it was a done deal. The contract was already signed, and Byron said Blaine was a nonnegotiable. He claimed that since Blaine already has an established fan base, it would translate into guaranteed viewership for the series.

I emailed Byron stating my case for a new host, but he wouldn't budge. Once I realized I wouldn't be able to fight him on this, I texted Haley to come to my office ASAP. I need help gathering as much info about Blaine as possible so I can prepare myself to deal with him.

Haley leans over to do another search on my computer. "Why did they tell Brooke the news about the host and not you? It's your show."

I let out a slow hiss of breath while remembering what Brooke said to me. "They want her to oversee things for me during the shoot."

Haley stops typing and turns to look at me. "So, like, micromanage you?"

"Yup. They don't think I can pull it off on my own. They assume I'll need help from someone more experienced."

Haley shakes her head, clearly annoyed. "Buncha dicks."

"Brooke had my back. She told them I don't need to be micromanaged and that I can pull this off as the one in charge."

"Good. I mean, I'd expect nothing less from Brooke. She's amazing and so supportive of you. I just can't believe how insulting the execs are being."

"All the more reason why I need to just accept this host casting. I need to show that I can handle whatever they throw at me without needing my mentor to babysit me."

Haley mutters a curse word as she turns back to the computer screen while I scroll through the links.

"How is this guy so famous? I've never even heard of him."

"We're too young," I say. "He's some big reality star from the early nineties who was in a bunch of straight-to-video movies. And his agent is Byron's golfing buddy."

"Of course," Haley mutters.

I click on another video. This one shows Blaine shouting profanities at a valet who didn't bring his car out fast enough. The poor young guy in the maroon vest looks like he's about to cry.

"Jesus," Haley mutters.

"Wait until you see this one."

I lean over to click on another video. In this one, Blaine's walking out of a courthouse wearing sunglasses and dressed in jeans and a shirt that says "Save the Whales." Next to him is an older mustached guy in a three-piece suit holding a briefcase. They stop at the bottom of the stairs, where there's a podium and a microphone.

"Due to a court gag order, Mr. Stephens will not be taking questions at this time," the fifty-something mustached man says. His lawyer, I assume. "He's asked me to express his deepest regrets and apologies for his behavior on the night of January 7."

Behind his sunglasses, Blaine frowns and lowers his head.

"Mr. Stephens wants to reiterate that even though he takes full responsibility for breaking into the San Diego Zoo and releasing various animals from their enclosures, he was under the influence of both illegal and prescription substances and was therefore not in his right mind," his lawyer says.

Haley's jaw drops once more. "Wait, he's the guy who broke into the San Diego Zoo last year?"

I nod.

I remember distinctly that story circulating on the news. How some inebriated guy climbed a fence along the perimeter of the San Diego Zoo and started randomly breaking into animal cages. Then he climbed the gate of the big cats exhibit, and one of the pumas mauled him. By some miracle—and a few hundred stitches—he survived.

"Apparently Blaine is trying to clean up his act after the zoo incident because he's lost a bunch of sponsorships," I say. "Three alcohol brands and a delivery service for keto snacks."

Haley mumbles, "What the fuck."

"All he's got left is an energy drink brand deal, some new app I've never heard of, and a reality show in the fall."

Haley straightens the blouse she's wearing, then crosses her arms. "You know, I'm so sick of Byron getting whatever he wants just because his dad started this network. He's pushing sixty and still useless. He does zero work and collects a paycheck. He's the dictionary definition of 'entitled dude who is so beyond undeserving of every privilege he possesses.'"

Even though at five foot three she's a handful of inches shorter than me, Haley's energy is fierce.

I lean my head back against my office chair, groaning. Then I glance back at the computer screen, which is paused on his press conference. "So . . . this is the host of my show, huh? An insufferable man-diva who's constantly high and behaves like a delinquent child."

"Afraid so." Haley gives my shoulder a soft squeeze.

I lean my elbows against the edge of the desk, then cup my face in my hands. "I knew this was too good to be true."

Haley rubs that spot between my shoulders that always tenses up when I get stressed out.

"Look, maybe we can petition for a new host," she says. "If we show the other execs what this guy is like on video, maybe then they'll reconsider."

I sit up straight and shake my head. "If Byron put him up for it, the execs already know what he's like. And they obviously don't care."

I click on Blaine's Instagram account, which popped up when I googled him. Half a million followers.

"Besides"—I point to the massive number on the screen—"I'm willing to bet that Blaine's follower count trumps all and is why everyone agreed to hire him. No one who has any pull at this network is going to care that he's a crappy person, because he's got more than five hundred thousand followers that might translate into viewers for the series."

Haley crosses her arms. Her shoulders slump.

I sigh, even though I want to scream. Blaine is going to be impossible to manage as a host—but he's my only choice. And right now, I have to accept it and move on if I want to make this series happen.

Haley offers a sympathetic smile, her deep-brown eyes understanding. "The bright side is the rest of the crew is going to be killer. You've got me as production manager, so you know it's going to be dynamite."

I laugh and pat her arm.

"I'm your right-hand woman," she says. "I'll do whatever you need me to do. Writing scripts, scoping out locations, getting permits, setting up interviews, managing the lighting, going on coffee runs, whatever. I'll support you in every way possible. You've done the same for me on a million shoots before."

"Thank you. Seriously."

"Wyatt and Joe will be on camera. They're the best you could ask for."

I nod along, thankful that I've worked with them both multiple times. They have stellar work ethics and are willing to go from sunup to sundown for days in a row if necessary. And they're both laid-back and easygoing, which will be crucial for this series with a host as unpredictable as Blaine.

"We'll need an intern or a PA too," I say. "How about Rylan? She's been here since the fall and she's been great. Always eager and willing to take on work. Brooke said she did a good job as PA on that documentary about oyster farms in the Pacific Northwest."

Haley smiles. "She told me a while ago that she's dying to work with you."

I can't help but feel flattered. Rylan is a recent college graduate who interned for the network her senior year.

My phone buzzes with a text from Brooke. I look back up at Haley and smile. "Tell Rylan she's hired."

Brooke: Just want to say sorry again. I fought them tooth and nail, but those ball sacks refused to budge.

I let out another loaded breath. Of course the execs don't listen to Brooke and me. We're not relatives or golfing buddies.

Me: It's okay. Thanks for fighting for me.

Me: Don't think that I'm letting one man-child host bring me down. I'm going to kick ass on this project.

Brooke: My girl!

Brooke: Before I forget, here's the email for a freelancer you're gonna want to hire. I've worked with him on international shoots. He's officially a field coordinator, but this guy's done it all. Camera operator, sound guy, intern, production assistant, script supervisor, catering, set assistant. He'll be clutch on a shoot like this.

Brooke: I already emailed him to tell him you'd be reaching out

I text Brooke thanks once more, wish her good luck on her shoot, and check back in with Haley.

"Just messaged Rylan," Haley says, eyes on her phone screen. "We'll see what—"

Just then there's a soft squeal from down the hall, then hurried footsteps that stop right outside the door. Then there's a soft knock.

"Come in," Haley calls.

When the door opens, there's Rylan standing with the biggest smile I've ever seen. She wrings her hands for a second, then takes a breath and walks in.

"I'm so sorry. It's probably unprofessional to be so . . . ex-cited." She bites her lip before fiddling with her blond hair, which is swept over one of her shoulders. "But I honestly am so thrilled to work with you, Alia." Her blue eyes dart to Haley. "And you too, Haley."

"There's nothing unprofessional about being excited," I say. "I'm really looking forward to working with you too."

Rylan starts wringing her hands again, but then quickly stops and folds them in front of her. Then her chest heaves once when she takes a breath. "I just really admire the way you work," she says. "You're so encouraging and hardworking. You don't just dump me-nial stuff on us PAs and interns, like some other producers do."

I nod in understanding, recalling how when I was young and eager to learn on a set too, all anyone would let me do was fetch coffee or run their errands.

I stand up and take a step toward her. "Thank you, Rylan. I really admire your work ethic too. You're focused and committed to whatever project you're working on, and that's definitely the kind of person I want to work with on *Discovering Utah*."

She beams wide once more. "I'm going to start packing the minute I get home tonight."

She says good-bye, then walks out of the office, shutting the door behind her.

"Damn," Haley says, staring at the closed door. "I miss being that excited and optimistic."

"It's sweet. And honestly, her enthusiasm helped me forget about Blaine for a bit."

Haley leaves to refill her coffee while I type out a message for the field coordinator Brooke referred me to—some guy named Andrew Irons.

I briefly introduce myself; then I dive into the concept of the series and the tight shooting schedule.

You came with a glowing review from Brooke, my mentor, and I'm hoping you'll be able to work with us on this project. Hope to hear from you!

I hit Send, then answer an email from the office manager about booking plane tickets for our trip to Utah next week. Then I email Joe, Wyatt, Rylan, and Haley to set up a meeting to go over the schedule for the shoot. I want to prep in advance as much as I can. We're going to have an unruly and unpredictable host to contend with, so the more we can plan out, the better.

I send it and then see a reply from Andrew pop up in my in-box. I click it, eager for his response.

Hey Alia,

Please tell Brooke thanks for saying such lovely things about me. That was bribe money well spent.

I snort out a laugh.

But in all seriousness, this sounds like an incredible series. I've always wanted to visit Utah, but haven't gotten the chance. I'd love to sign on. I'm shooting in Nova Scotia until Tuesday, so I can't make it out there till Wednesday evening. Will that work for you? Sorry, I don't mean to kick things off by being the last crew member to arrive, but that's the earliest I can wrap up. But I'm hoping you'll say yes because this sounds like a blast and you sound like a pleasure to work with.

I'm beaming at his response. Sure, I'm disappointed that I won't be able to meet Andrew until we're all actually in Utah. But then again, this happens. People who work on travel shows are all over the place at any given time and fly to whatever job they've been hired for. On any past job, I wouldn't blink twice at this—but that's because I've never been a series creator before.

I silently acknowledge that I'm going to have to dial back my expectations in order to shoot this series. And at the very least, Andrew sounds like a funny and accommodating person, which will be refreshing to work with.

I quickly type out my reply.

No worries at all. I'm thrilled to have you on board. I'll email you the hotel and flight info later today, then the script and shooting schedule this weekend. Looking forward to meeting you and working with you.

I send the message, relieved that I have the best crew possible for this series. Haley walks back in and sets a mug of coffee in front of me.

"All the Blaine nonsense aside, I'm so pumped for this," she says. "Your own series, Alia. You're going to kick ass."

I smile despite the uncertainty whirring inside me. I hope she's right.

4

A WEEK LATER, I'M PULLING A RENTAL CAR INTO THE PARKing lot of a local chain motel in Moab, Utah. When I jump out, I scan the massive red-rock formations surrounding us.

"Damn," Haley says as she climbs out of the front passenger seat.

Rylan says the same as she climbs out of the back seat.

I turn around and beam at them both. "I know a motel isn't the most glamorous of digs, but I swear this one is good. Plus, the view."

I gesture to the landscape once more, which is practically on fire in the sunlight.

Rylan shakes her head. "A motel is perfect!"

She runs to the back of the SUV and starts pulling out the luggage and camera equipment. Even after a 5 a.m. flight, a three-hour layover, and hours on the cramped plane, she's *still* smiling and chipper.

I walk over to her and help her unload. "Your attitude is a breath of fresh air, Rylan."

She flashes a thumbs-up while beaming. We sling the bags over our shoulders right as Wyatt and Joe pull up in a rental van.

They park in the slot across from our rental. Wyatt climbs out and ruffles a hand through his jet-black hair. He blinks, his eyes puffy.

"Doing okay?" I ask.

Closing his eyes, he nods. I almost laugh. He looks half-asleep. Joe nudges his shoulder, then hands him a cup of coffee.

Wyatt takes a long sip, then turns to me. "My mom called to pray the rosary with me before our flight this morning. I'm dragging."

I wince and nod in sympathy. "A lot of my aunts do that. My grandma used to do that with my mom every time she transferred to a new post in the air force."

Wyatt rubs his eyes with the heel of his hand. "She had me on the phone for an hour. That's an hour I could have spent sleeping." He groans. "She's freaking out that I'll get bit by a rattlesnake or fall into a canyon and get pinned by a boulder for days and that I'll have to chop my own hand off, like that guy in that one movie. Or that I'll accidentally ingest something that I'm allergic to. I mean, I'm allergic to vodka. That's it." He rolls his eyes.

Haley and I laugh.

Joe pats him on the back. "You gotta give us parents a break. It's in our blood to worry."

"Your kid is in kindergarten, Joe. It's understandable that you'd worry about him. I'm a thirty-year-old man."

"Gotta love those overbearing parents," I say. "Tell your mom I've got a fully stocked first aid kit with an EpiPen just in case a rogue vodka bottle attacks you."

Joe and Wyatt laugh as they unload their van. Haley, Rylan, and I walk into the entrance to check in. I quietly admire how clean and uncluttered this motel is. When I think back on all the road trips I took with my family growing up, I recall that we often ended up in run-down motels because they were cheap and convenient. This place is a definite step up. All the surfaces are sleek and shiny, with blond-colored engineered wood on the floor. There's a neutral color-block theme in the décor, which is a definite upgrade from the retro floral aesthetic I always saw growing up. This one even has a small gym along with a pool and hot tub.

"This is actually pretty decent," Haley says, gazing around. "I can definitely live with this."

I walk up to reception and wait while the person in front of me is checked in.

"You act like we're staying here forever," I say. "This is just for the first two weeks of the shoot. Then we're off to Springdale to film at Zion."

When the person in front of me finishes up, I step forward and check in. Wyatt and Joe come in soon after, and I hand everyone their room key cards.

"Okay, so how about we do a quick preproduction meeting in an hour? That way you guys can all get settled in your rooms for a bit, we'll have the meeting, and then you can rest up for tomorrow."

Everyone agrees, then heads to their rooms. I follow Haley through the hallway.

Haley turns her head back to look at me. "Will our star be joining us tonight?" she asks in a sarcastic tone.

I groan. We haven't even started shooting and already Blaine Stephens is a thorn in my side. Apparently washed-up reality stars with a penchant for breaking the law are too good to stay at a chain motel. His agent emailed me a few days ago to say that Blaine will be staying at some off-the-grid glamping spot that costs thousands of dollars per night, an hour outside Moab. I silently stew once more over how he gets rock star accommodations while I'm running an entire series on a shoestring budget.

When I emailed his agent the schedule and mentioned the importance of Blaine's attendance at our preproduction meeting, he refused, saying how important it was for Blaine to rest up until the last possible second before shooting actually begins.

"Blaine will not be attending tonight's preproduction meeting, sadly," I say, the bite in my tone clear.

We stop at the doors of our rooms, which are side by side.

"Apparently he needs to meditate or nap or be one with nature or some ridiculous shit right up until shooting starts," I say. "His agent said he'll be ready to go tomorrow morning when we start shooting at Arches. I guess we'll see."

Thankfully Arches National Park is only a handful of miles from Moab. That will hopefully mean quick transit times to and from shooting, so we can spend as much time as possible filming and corralling Blaine.

Haley flashes a sympathetic smile as she grips her room key card in her hand. "Promise you won't be battling this guy on your own. I've got your back. We all do."

"Thanks."

Despite her reassurance, I can't help the anxiety surging through me already, manifesting in my knotted muscles. Whenever I remind myself that I'm going to have to spend a good chunk of these next six weeks handling a man-child pseudo-celebrity, my stomach churns. Because if things go wrong with Blaine, if he pulls some insane stunt that compromises the shoot, it could cost me the entire series.

Haley seems to sense the stress I'm trying so hard to hide, because she quickly changes the subject. "How is our field coordinator? Andrew, right?"

I nod, relieved that everything I know about Andrew—from Brooke's glowing recommendation to the emails we've exchanged—has only proven he's going to be easy to work with.

"He's due to arrive in a couple of hours," I say, then check the time on my phone. "He's still midflight, so I'll text him that I left his key card with the front desk. And if he gets here on time, we'll see him in the meeting."

Haley yawns. "I'm going to catch a quick nap, then. See you in a few."

I walk into my room, pleased to see a queen-size bed in the middle. The bright-green hue of the accent wall pops against the light color scheme of the rest of the space. The floors and furniture are made of the same engineered wood. The furnishings are minimal—just a smallish desk, a chair, and a flat-screen TV that hangs from the wall. It almost reminds me of a hospital, which is comforting in a way. Normally motel rooms are dingy and stuffy. The fact that this one borders on sterile and clean is a pleasant surprise.

When I plop on the bed, I text Andrew the info, then roll over and fall asleep.

AN HOUR LATER, the crew filters into the meeting room located on the first floor of the motel. We sit at a long rectangular table. Rylan hands out the shooting schedule I've printed out.

"So we're starting at Arches tomorrow?" she asks. "So cool! I've always wanted to see the Delicate Arch."

Wyatt frowns at Rylan's unbridled enthusiasm as I go over the call time and what shots we need to get tomorrow in order to stay on track for the week. Everyone scribbles notes on their papers.

"For the first day of filming, I want to get an early-morning shot of Blaine at the Delicate Arch," I say. "Most shows opt to do a sunset shot there because the sun sets right behind the arch, but I want to do something different."

I explain how I want to capture the sun as it rises from behind the gigantic sandstone mounds right next to the Delicate Arch.

"The sunlight will illuminate it from the side. It'll look amazing, almost like a painting."

I mention that the hike to get there from the trailhead is about a mile and a half and that it's rated as strenuous.

Wyatt lets out a groan, then shoots me a mock glare. "You know we're going to be hauling camera equipment, right?"

"Yes, I know. But we'll all pitch in to carry stuff. And since we're starting before dawn, it'll be cooler. I promise you won't be sweating your face off—much."

He points out the call time listed on the sheet.

"I know, I know. You're not a fan of early call times," I say. I've worked with him enough times to know that. "But seeing the Delicate Arch at sunrise is going to be worth it, I promise."

He groans but nods. This is textbook Wyatt, which I've come to love through our years working together. He whines all the way up until the actual shoot, which is when he becomes all business. He'll put in long hours day after day and consistently delivers stellar work. I can put up with a bit of whining in exchange for that.

Joe takes a giant bite from the bagel he brought with him, then tightens the bun holding his golden-blond hair. "Come on, man." He gestures wildly as he speaks. "It'll be exhilarating to be at one of the most stunning natural wonders in the country."

Joe is an outdoors enthusiast, always camping and backpacking with his girlfriend and son when he's not working. In the last few years, he's also taken up running ultramarathons in the mountains. It's one of the reasons I wanted him on this series—in addition to his stellar camera skills, I knew he'd counter all Wyatt's whining.

"Yes. Exactly what Joe said," I say. "Okay, so for the—"

The door to the meeting room whooshes open and I look up—and choke on the saliva in my mouth.

Because standing in the room just a few feet from me is Drew—the guy I had the most epic first date on planet Earth with, who then stood me up the next day.

And then my brain puts it all together.

Drew is Andrew. He's the field coordinator I'll be working with side by side for the next six weeks.

I almost say "duh" out loud. Such an obvious nickname.

His eyes widen as he stares at me. I'm guessing he's equally shocked that I'm here.

I spend a few seconds stammering before a dizzy spell hits me. I instinctively try to inhale, but that kicks off a coughing fit. Haley thumps my back, then hands me my water bottle.

"You okay?" she asks.

I nod, clear my throat, then look up at Drew. "You're Andrew?"

It only takes him a second to rein in his shock. He shoves his hands in the pockets of his jacket and purses his lips. "Uh, no one really calls me that anymore. Call me Drew." There's a short pause. "You must be *Alia*?"

The pointed way he says my name makes the muscles in my neck tense. He's probably putting together now that I gave him a nickname when we met.

"Um, yes. That's correct." I try for a professional tone, but my voice is still squeaky with shock.

Before this moment can get any more awkward, Wyatt, Joe, Haley, and Rylan all stand to shake his hand and introduce themselves. Drew's shoulders relax and he smiles. When they ask how his journey was, he chats easily about his flight. Rylan hands him a copy of the schedule, and he takes the seat across from me.

Focusing on the paper, I take a slow, silent breath. Then I

look back up at him. "We were just going over the shooting schedule for tomorrow."

Drew stares at the paper like it's the most fascinating document ever printed. "Awesome."

I refocus and get through the rest of the meeting. Ten minutes later, we're done. Everyone leaves as I gather my papers, and I wonder how quickly I can dart back to my hotel room. But when I look up, I see Drew standing next to the doorway, staring at me.

"Can we talk?" He shuffles his feet and frowns.

"About what?" I bite the inside of my cheek at hearing how affected I sound. I hate that it's obvious in those two words just how much him ditching me still hurts my feelings.

"I just want to explain what happened the other week. I don't want you to think that I intentionally stood you up."

I tilt my head at him, frowning. "But that's exactly what happened."

He runs a hand through his hair, sighing. "No, I . . . I'm sorry. I swear to you, it wasn't on purpose. It was like every possible bad thing that could happen to me happened the day after we met. After I took my aunt to the airport, I was getting off the subway in my neighborhood in Brooklyn, and my phone fell from my pocket onto the track and it took for-fucking-ever for the transit police to come get it. It was totally shattered; even the SIM card was cracked in half. I couldn't even get it to turn on. So then I had to run to the store and buy a new phone, and I swear to God, I tried to look for you on Facebook, but I couldn't find you when I searched for 'Lia.' I didn't have your last name and after that I kind of just gave up."

The way he shrugs his shoulders when he says "gave up" stings.

He's probably lying to save face. You know what that's like better than anyone.

I swallow the lump in my throat along with the memory that Drew's frantic explanation brings up.

He opens his mouth like he's going to say more but quickly clamps it shut.

"Lia was my nickname as a kid," I finally say after a long moment of silence. "I gave it to you because we barely knew each other, and I wanted to be safe."

Drew blinks, worry glistening in his eyes. "I get it. Drew's not my full name either. Obviously." The chuckle he lets out lands like a rock on cement.

"Brooke called you Andrew."

"There was one shoot where there were two Drews on the crew. I told her to call me Andrew just to make it easier. It kind of stuck."

"Oh. Cool."

We stare awkwardly at each other for a few seconds.

"So . . . is that all you wanted to say?" I ask, determined to end this cringey-as-hell reunion.

Drew's brow lifts the slightest bit. "I guess. I mean, I just wanted you to know what happened."

The urge to shrink into myself takes hold, but I stand up straight, fighting it. It's probably best that it didn't work out. Dating a coworker can be all kinds of trouble.

You know better than to do that again.

"Apology accepted," I say. "We can just pretend like it never happened."

His eyes widen the slightest bit before he swallows. "Okay, yeah. Sounds good to me."

I turn to walk out the door, brushing past him, but then he says, "Wait."

I still as I register the skin-to-skin sensation of my arm touching his arm. The memory of the night we met jolts to the front of my mind. I remember it all perfectly. The hard feel of Drew's body under my hands. The way he traced his finger along my palm. How yummy his bottom lip tasted.

I look up at his face and try not to focus on how sharp his jawline is even under that sheet of stubble.

"What should I call you? Alia? Lia? Dunn?"

"Whatever you feel like."

"How about Dunn? Fresh start, new name. And I promise I won't stand you up this time."

He laughs like he's joking with a friend. I resist the urge to roll my eyes and purse my lips instead. I guess Drew is the kind of guy who likes to move on from cringey moments with annoying humor.

When I don't laugh in response, he swallows and clears his throat. "I was, uh, joking."

"I know."

He tugs a hand through his hair once more and sighs. "So I, uh, guess I'll see you bright and early, Dunn."

I walk past him and out the door. "Sounds good, Irons."

5

H OLY SHIT." HALEY STARES AT ME FROM THE PASSENGER
seat.

When I turn to look at her for a moment, her eyes are
wide. "Drew's the guy who stood you up? And the guy in your
photo that went viral?"

I glare at the darkened road ahead. It's the middle of the
night, and we need to make it to Arches National Park before
sunrise. "Yup. Except he says he didn't mean to stand me up."

Out of the corner of my eye, I see her shaking her head. "Oh,
please. That story he concocted is more scripted than an episode
of *The Bachelorette*. Why didn't you tell me last night after the
meeting?"

"It was a mind-fuck seeing him. I needed time to process
everything. Like, out of all the people in the world—out of all the
people in New York City—he ends up being my coworker for the
next six weeks."

I take the turn off the highway into the park entrance, pass
the visitors' center, then head on in. Behind me are Wyatt, Joe,
and Rylan in a van with all the camera equipment, then Drew in
his truck at the very end. Thanks to all the planning we did, we
managed to gain exclusive access to the park in the middle of the

night, allowing us to set up for our sunrise shoot at Delicate Arch.

"I just . . . God, what are the odds?" Haley mutters to herself.

"My exact thoughts."

I drive along the curving road that cuts through the park and glance out the window. It's too dark to see the fiery-red rock dotted with purple sage, blackbrush, and pinyon-juniper woodlands that make up this park, but in a few hours sunlight will illuminate every gorgeous inch of Arches. I smile to myself remembering how Apong Lita drove my brother and me along this same road, and how giddy we were gazing out the window at the scenery, which looked like it belonged on Mars rather than Earth.

Haley removes her glasses and mutters a curse about how smudgy they are. I lift the center console to reveal a travel-size bottle of glasses cleaner and a microfiber cloth.

"You're a lifesaver," she says.

"I wouldn't dream of going on a shoot with you without plenty of glasses cleaner and microfiber cloths. Or gluten-free snacks, which there are loads of in the cooler in the back whenever you get hungry."

"This is why I love you," she says while wiping her lenses. "I've got your back. If Drew does anything to fall out of line, I'll set him straight."

Haley's fierce defense of me makes me smile. "I appreciate that. But hopefully that won't be necessary. I'm going to behave like a professional, and he said he will too."

"But if he doesn't . . ." Haley makes a squelching noise while swiping her hand across her neck. I let out a laugh.

Minutes later we're at the parking lot at the Delicate Arch trailhead. Everyone hops out of their vehicles and starts unloading equipment.

When I see that there are no other cars around—meaning

Blaine hasn't yet showed up—there's a slow drop in my stomach. If he doesn't turn up, the sunrise shot is toast.

Half an hour later, we're all almost ready.

Wyatt gazes around. "So is this Blaine guy ever going to show up?"

His question sends panic to the pit of my stomach.

"I hope so," I mutter, then turn to gather the rest of the equipment before we kick off our hike.

I called Blaine's handler last night before bed to remind him of the early call time and to make sure he'd make it on time. The jittery personal assistant assured me that he would without a doubt be there from whatever mystery glamping grounds he's staying at.

I silently curse Blaine. Sunrise is less than three hours away. If I want to capture the sun rising along the horizon, slowly bathing the Delicate Arch in sunlight—the shot I've been planning this entire first part of filming around—we need to start hiking soon.

In the darkness, my eyes adjust. Everyone is milling around, equipment strapped to them. Rylan and Haley look at me with concern in their eyes.

"Everyone ready?" I announce.

Drew's voice cuts in from my right just a few feet away. "Shouldn't we wait for Blaine?"

I button up the front of my jacket as he walks up to me. It's a Herculean task to keep my eyes from bulging out of my head. Because Drew looks good enough to devour. His tall, lean-muscled frame is adorned with a puffy gray jacket, worn jeans, hiking boots, and a gray knit beanie. He looks like a male model showcasing outdoorwear for a clothing catalog.

Thankfully it's still dark enough to conceal the flush that's currently taking over my entire body.

It takes a long second, but I get ahold of myself and answer Drew's question.

"Blaine was informed of the call time well in advance," I say, fiddling with the strap of the bag that I've slung over my shoulder. "He can catch up when he gets here."

"He's kind of an integral part of this shot, don't you think?"

Drew's tone borders on sarcastic. I bite the inside of my cheek to keep from going off. I've already endured a sleepless night stressing about the first day of shooting. I don't need to be undermined in front of my crew by its newest member.

"I'd rather have a sunrise shot without the host than no sunrise shot at all. I'm not missing that to wait for him. We have multiple shots to get today that don't involve him. We'll film his segments whenever he decides to come, and Frankenstein it all together later on in editing."

I try to keep my tone as free of bitterness as possible, but judging by the hard look on Drew's face and the wide-eyed look Haley shoots me, I didn't do a very convincing job.

When I walk over to lock the car, Drew glances at his phone to check the time. "Maybe I should wait here for him while you all go on up. Then the two of us can meet up with you."

I clench my jaw, annoyed that Drew is going against the plan for today. "I hired you as the field coordinator for this shoot. You're here to assist me on this series. Is that correct?"

Drew opens his mouth, then sighs. "Yeah," he mumbles.

"I didn't hire you to be a babysitter who hangs out in the parking lot when I need you for the full day of shooting. Blaine is an adult. He knows how to read, and I'm sure he'll be able to read the trail signs to find his way here when he finally gets around to arriving. Understood?"

There's a pause when Drew stands in silence, staring at me. "Understood."

I turn on my heel and make my way up the trail.

"Damn," Haley says under her breath from behind me. "What a way to set the tone."

I roll my eyes, shaking my head. "I've already got one impossible crew member to tangle with on this shoot. I don't need two."

WE REACH THE Delicate Arch, the most popular arch and trail in the entire park, with an hour to go until sunrise. I wipe the sweat off my brow with my jacket sleeve and take in the massive, fifty-foot-plus sandstone arch that looks more like a shadow than a rock formation in the predawn darkness. Even though some guides rate this trail as moderate, hiking the mostly uphill path with packs of camera equipment slingshots it into the strenuous category, especially during the middle third of the hike, which is a steep section of slickrock. I stomp my feet onto the smooth rock below, thankful that I sprung for the hiking boots with excellent traction and ankle support. I would have wobbled and tripped without them.

Catching my breath, I gaze around as the jagged horizon to the east begins to glow periwinkle. Sunrise will soon turn the sky cotton-candy orange and yellow, then blue. I inhale, relishing the earthy scent. Almost like the soil is wet, even though it hasn't rained. It's a smell I remember well from the first time I visited this park as a kid.

When we visited Arches with Apong Lita, we didn't have time to hike to Delicate Arch. Despite the stress from arguing with Drew and an MIA host, this moment in this natural wonder is pure tranquility and nostalgia. Apong Lita would have loved it.

Joe and Wyatt quickly set up their cameras while Rylan helps them. Haley drops her bags on the ground and goes through the shot list for today. Wyatt mentions something about a busted boom

mic and a missing tripod and battery pack, which threatens to an-
nihilate my momentary calm. Is this first day of shooting cursed?

Joe says fixing wonky boom mics is his secret specialty, and
a smidge of my anxiety eases. I walk off and take a deep breath
while scoping out various spots and angles near the arch, when
Drew comes up to me.

"Hey. Can we talk?" He stands with his hands in his gray
puffer jacket.

"Please make it quick; we've got a lot to do."

"I didn't mean to come off like I was questioning your authority back there."

I cross my arms and look up at him, my lips pursed as I say
nothing.

His expression turns sheepish. "But I guess that's exactly
how it came off. Sorry."

He trails off. I raise my brow at him. "Is that all you wanted
to say?"

He nods.

"Great. Now can you please help Haley work out the shot list?"

His jaw set tight, he nods and walks over to her. Minutes
later, Wyatt and Joe are set up and ready to go. Sunrise starts as
a sliver of luminescent orange along the rocky terrain. The glow
intensifies as the sun eases slowly into the sky.

"Damn," Wyatt mutters from behind the camera.

I look up to where Joe is set up, which is high atop the rock
formation that sits about fifty feet from the arch. He's getting
panoramic shots of the sunrise and the entire area. Since Blaine
no-showed, my new idea is to use the sunrise footage in a sped-up
time lapse for the episode intro.

For the next couple of hours, Joe and Wyatt record multiple shots.

"This is just incredible," Wyatt says for the millionth time,
his brown eyes wide and disbelieving.

Joe chuckles while pausing to chug from his water bottle in

the middle of a short break. "Told you, man. Sleep is trivial when it comes to natural beauty like this. You should come out with me one of these days for a predawn jog."

Wyatt rolls his eyes, which makes Joe laugh.

"No way in hell, man," Wyatt says. "You're the only person who didn't break a sweat climbing up this trail and you had the heaviest pack. You think I can keep up with you on a run?"

While Joe and Wyatt engage in a friendly argument about fitness, Haley saunters up to me, hesitation written all over her otherwise youthful face. "You think this guy Blaine is gonna no-show the whole day?"

I sigh, scrunching my face as I glance back at today's shooting schedule. We've already had to scrap him in the sunrise shot. We have a handful of other spots in the park to film, and we'll need to leave in the next ninety minutes to stay on schedule. If he's not going to show up at all, I'm not sure how in the world we're going to salvage today's shoot.

Pursing my lips, I take another breath as I try to calm the doubts whirring inside me. "I guess we'll just have to—"

Loud profanity steals my attention. We turn our heads behind us and spot a guy in tight black biker shorts, tall hiking boots, and a blue parka trotting toward us.

Blaine Stephens in the flesh.

"Pardon my *français*, but holy shit is that a pretty sight." He gawks at the Delicate Arch while snapping photos with his phone.

Relief and annoyance collide in the form of my chest tightening. I'm glad he's finally here, but what the hell is he doing taking photos like an awestruck tourist when he should be apologizing for his inexcusably late entrance and jumping right into work?

Biting my tongue, I take a moment to glance over at the Delicate Arch, hoping its majestic beauty will calm me. It doesn't. I remind myself just how much sentiment and memory this spot holds. That doesn't help either.

I muster a breath and plaster on a smile, hoping I look and sound professional. As much as I already can't stand Blaine, I need him in a cooperative mood.

I walk over to him and stick out my hand. "Blaine. I'm Alia, the showrunner of this series. We're so glad to have you on board."

He shakes my hand while flashing a smirk that makes my skin crawl. He's lithe and only a couple of inches taller than my five-foot-nine frame—not physically threatening at all. But the creepy way his smirk lingers unsettles me. I quickly pull my hand out of his and introduce him to the crew, who all wave from their posts.

"Can you please go stand over there so we can film the first few scenes?" I point to the Delicate Arch.

He frowns at me like he has no idea what I'm talking about.

I fight with every muscle in my face to keep smiling. "All you have to do is say your lines a few times, we'll film it, and then we can move on to the next scene."

His overly tanned face scrunches in what I assume is confusion. His eyes dart between me and the arch.

"What lines?"

"The lines from the script the network sent your agent weeks ago. Didn't you read it?"

His expression turns irritated and he waves a hand. "Psssh. I don't bother with scripts. Too formal."

"What?" It comes out like a sharp scolding, even though I don't mean it to.

Blaine frowns. "What's with your face? You mad about something?"

My chest expands as I summon yet another deep breath to deal with him. Yes, I know I should probably be kissing this guy's ass—he seems like the type who enjoys being fawned over—but I don't have it in me. Not when his laziness is the reason why we've blown today's key shot.

I start to talk, but Drew cuts in. "Blaine Stephens? Oh man, I'm such a huge fan!"

All semblance of irritation disappears from Blaine's face the moment Drew grins and shakes his hand.

"I know these shots can be kind of overwhelming," Drew says, his voice at a weirdly cheery register. I wrinkle my nose at how superficial it sounds. "Why don't I just demonstrate for you?"

Blaine runs a hand through his shaggy dyed-blond hair. "Bro, you read my mind." He glances at me. "Why didn't you offer to do that?"

My jaw drops at Blaine's comment. And then I gawk in disbelief as Drew jogs over to the mark right under the Delicate Arch, then recites Blaine's lines perfectly from memory. The way he walks and gestures leaves me in awe. If I didn't know he was a behind-the-scenes guy, I would have thought he was born to host. He holds natural eye contact with the camera and transitions smoothly whenever he looks away to the horizon and to point out the massive Delicate Arch that stretches to more than fifty feet in the air.

When he finishes, I'm speechless. Brooke was right. He really is a jack-of-all-trades.

Drew then points at Blaine and says, "You're up, superstar."

Blaine saunters over and mimics what Drew did. He messes up a few of the words, but overall it's a solid run.

I walk over to where Wyatt is filming everything on his camera. Then I swallow my pride, take a cue from Drew, and showcase a bit of false charm. "Blaine, that was fantastic. Can you run through it again?"

Blaine runs through the scene twice more. When I yell cut, he yells, "I need water. Now."

From behind the camera, I roll my eyes.

"Yo! Blondie!" Blaine calls to Rylan. "I said I need water."

"Jesus fucking Christ this guy," Wyatt mutters from behind the camera.

As Rylan scrambles to dig out a water bottle from her backpack, a bewildered look on her face, I make my way over to Blaine to tell him that he'd better not ever call her that again, but to my surprise Drew beats me to it.

"Her name's Rylan, not Blondie. Understand?" Drew booms at Blaine, who looks shocked.

Blaine nods once, his expression mildly annoyed as Rylan hands him the bottle. But then when he looks at her, he flashes another smug smile that sends a chill through my spine. She barely makes eye contact with him, then quickly turns and walks away. Blaine's gaze stays locked on her as he sips. I ball my fists at my sides, enraged that he's eyeing her so openly.

I walk over to Rylan.

"Sorry he called you that," I say.

"It's okay. It's not the first time someone's made that comment to me," she says quietly.

"Hey." I put my hand on her arm and gently turn her away so that Blaine isn't in her line of sight. "I don't care who this guy is. He doesn't get to speak to you that way on my set. Okay?"

She nods, a sad smile on her face.

"If he ever makes you uncomfortable again and I'm not around to see it, please tell me."

"I will," she says quietly.

Just as I walk over to Drew, Blaine announces that the blast of water has helped him feel reenergized and he wants to do one more run-through.

"Fantastic," I say sarcastically, which he clearly doesn't pick up on because he flashes a thumbs-up before running through his lines again.

I pull Drew aside so that the camera and microphones don't pick up our sound.

"Thanks for calling out Blaine like that."

"Of course."

"That being said, please don't interrupt me the next time I'm talking to him one-on-one. It undermines me as the producer in charge."

Drew frowns, clearly confused. "I was just trying to help. You looked like you were going to strangle the guy." He chuckles. "How would we have filmed this series with our host deceased on day one of shooting?"

I purse my lips. He's not wrong about that.

"I'd prefer to be the one telling Blaine what to do," I say. "And I'd also prefer not to have to pander to him in order to get him to do his job," I say pointedly.

Drew raises an eyebrow, like he's offended by what I've said. "I've worked with enough entitled jerks in my career to know that sometimes you have to appease guys like Blaine to a degree—because we've got a job to do."

"That's great. But this is my series and I'll make the final call on how to handle the host."

Drew tilts his head at me. "Wait, you're not still mad about what happened between us . . . are you?"

I bite down, annoyed that he would accuse me of letting my emotions get in the way of my job. Yeah, I'm still hurt about that, but that has nothing to do with today.

"Do you honestly think I'm the kind of person who would let my personal life affect my professional conduct?"

Drew opens his mouth but shakes his head, looking off to the side rather than saying anything.

"It's real simple, Drew. Please don't interrupt me the next time I'm having a conversation with Blaine or anyone else on this shoot."

Drew clenches his jaw and nods once. I spin around and walk away. A few seconds later, behind me I hear Drew clap and praise Blaine for completing his latest subpar take.

I look on, my arms crossed and my insides on fire, fuming

that Drew is so willing to play to Blaine's ego—and also that he might be right about it.

As I lightly kick the red clay with my boot, doubt creeps in. For the first time in my career, I wonder if I've got what it takes to do this job.

"BUT, I MEAN, can you really, truly promise me that I won't die?" Blaine gazes at me with wide eyes.

I take a breath and try not to scream. It's been ten full minutes of complimenting and coddling while trying to convince him to do this shot, the last shot on our second day of shooting.

Usually that's all it takes to deal with a difficult host. Sometimes a few extra perks work too, like a luxe car service or gourmet catering.

But Blaine is a different animal entirely. None of that is going to help right now because what's holding him back is a completely illogical fear.

As I stand in front of him, I glance above at the Double Arch, one of the most visited spots in the park. It's a jaw-dropping formation of two arches that share the same massive stone foundation as their outer legs. The opening of the two stretches nearly a hundred and fifty feet and stands more than one hundred feet high, making it one of the biggest arches in the entire park.

"Blaine." I say his name with forced patience in my tone. He doesn't seem to notice as his gaze darts around at the massive arches that surround us. He takes a step and nearly trips over one of the green desert shrubs that dot this area of the park. For a second I'm afraid he's going to lose his balance and trip down the uneven sloped rock face, which is riddled in boulders and leads up to the Double Arch like an earthen staircase, but he steadies himself.

"This rock formation has stood here for millions of years," I say. "It's not going to suddenly collapse onto you."

Behind me Wyatt mutters, "Unfortunately," as he waits with his camera setup several feet away. I bite my lip to stifle a laugh.

"How can you be so sure?" Blaine asks, his eyes darting all over the arches.

Day two of shooting and it was another morning of Blaine showing up three hours late, then screwing up his lines a dozen times for the first scheduled scene of the day. And then I lectured him about professionalism, which led to him rolling his eyes at me, which led to an argument. Drew then stepped in from that point on and modeled that scene for him, and each one after that, just like he did yesterday. It was the only way Joe and Wyatt could film halfway-decent takes.

And then Blaine insisted on a two-hour lunch break because my arguing with him was so upsetting that he needed to meditate to recenter himself for the rest of the day's shoot. And then he claimed he needed to take his "medicine," which in actuality was just a bong. That pushed our shooting schedule behind two hours. Plus, we had to wait out an unexpected rainstorm that lasted nearly forty minutes, yet another unexpected setback. And now, on our last shot of the day, we're less than an hour from losing the sunlight we need to wrap things up.

My face twists as I take a breath and muster that last iota of patience I've dug up from some mystery reserve I didn't know I had. Mother Nature and Blaine are conspiring against me today, and I don't know how much longer I can take it.

"Blaine. I promise you're not going to die," I say.

He frowns, his bloodshot eyes still darting all over the place. Great. He's a paranoid stoner in addition to being completely unqualified for this job.

He mumbles some incoherent comment about earthquakes

and erosion as I turn around to check on the rest of the crew. Both Wyatt and Joe are set up and ready to go. Haley looks at me, tapping her bare wrist to indicate that we're losing time.

Closing my eyes, I clench my jaw for the millionth time today. Yelling at him again isn't going to move this along. I glance to my right and spot Drew standing twenty feet away, observing the shit show with pursed lips and his arms crossed over his chest. He props a leg on a nearby rock and shrugs at me.

And that's when I know I need to take a page out of Drew's book. No more scolding Blaine—not if I want to get this shot done.

I grab Blaine by the shoulders and jerk him to look at me. "Do you realize you're making history with this segment, Blaine?" I hitch my voice up so that the words sound extra-urgent.

Confusion clouds his face. He shakes his head no.

"You are. Because the Double Arch—this very arch you're standing under—was where the opening scene for *Indiana Jones and the Last Crusade* took place." I make my eyes go wide and give his shoulders a shake.

"Whoa . . ." He gazes up again, muttering about the streaks of red that cover the Double Arch. "It's like God dumped giant buckets of red paint all over them. I mean, look at those colors! Reds! And oranges! And browns too!"

"Yes. That's exactly what it looks like, Blaine. And you're making history by filming here. No other travel show host has ever shot a scene in this very spot—this spot that Indiana Jones made famous."

Even though every word is absolute bullshit, I speak them with conviction. And Blaine seems to buy it, judging by his awestruck expression.

I nod my chin to Drew. "Drew is gonna show you how it's done. But then *you* have to do it—you have to nail this, Blaine. We're counting on you to make this episode we're shooting today a worthy homage to Indiana Jones. You can do that, can't you? You can be the Indiana Jones of this travel series, right?"

His leathery, tanned face turns pointed and serious. "I can do it." He turns to Drew. "Drew, my man! Show me how it's done!"

With that, Drew jogs up to the top of the Double Arch. He stands, the rich adobe-hued arch serving as a wondrous frame for this shot. Drew runs through the lines while I stand next to Blaine at the base of the rock formation. He gawks at Drew, his eyes sparkling with wonderment. When Drew finishes, I call cut, then smack Blaine on the back to take his turn. It takes five takes, but by the end, I'm confident we have enough footage to cut into a solid intro.

"That's a wrap!" I yell. Rylan claps, then everyone starts to pack up just as the sun begins to dip below the horizon.

Blaine blows kisses and waves to an imaginary crowd of on-lookers, then declares that he's going to take a nap in this spot under the Double Arch to fully absorb the spirit of Indiana Jones so he can channel his aura for the rest of the shoot.

"Great idea!" I yell, then turn around and roll my eyes. I start packing up the equipment with everyone else.

"You've got the patience of a saint dealing with that guy," Wyatt says to me quietly as he coils up a cord.

"Not really. The only way I got through this shoot is by fanta-sizing about the arch actually collapsing on him like he feared so we'd be rid of him once and for all."

Wyatt chuckles, then reins in his expression. "Do you want me to pull Blaine aside and have a talk with him?"

"What do you mean?"

"Joe and I were talking earlier and said maybe one of us needs to set him straight about proper conduct on set. It shouldn't just fall on Rylan or you to set boundaries. As screwed up as it is, maybe it would hit harder if another guy called him out."

I flash a small smile at Wyatt. "I appreciate that. Truly. But I've got it under control. You shouldn't have to deal with this. It's my job to do the unpleasant stuff like that. I promise I'm going to have a talk with him."

Inside I'm annoyed that I even have to navigate this. Normally I'd have no problem reporting harassment to the execs, but seeing as his agent is chummy with Byron, I highly doubt they'd be receptive to it. Especially over a word like "blondie." It's not technically an offensive word, so I can just imagine the eye roll the execs would give me if I tried to call attention to it. It's best if I just handle it myself.

I thank Wyatt, grateful to have his and Joe's support. Just then Joe runs up to grab a gear bag, but Wyatt stops him.

"We've got your back one hundred percent when it comes to dealing with Blaine. Right, Joe?"

"Absolutely. We're not going to let his behavior slide."

I'm heartened at their support. But I also want to show that I can handle this Blaine issue independently. I don't want to be known as the showrunner who gets my crew to do my bidding for me.

I thank them both before they continue packing up the gear. I turn and spot Drew walking toward me, the look on his face hesitant.

"Hey," I say, shutting the back door of my car after loading it. Inside I brace myself, just in case he feels the need to rub it in my face that I broke down and used his technique of appeasing Blaine instead of arguing with him in order to finish the last scene.

He rests his hands on his hips. "I just got a call this afternoon from the ranger's station out at the Needles section of Canyonlands. It looks like filming there is a no-go."

"What?" I say sharply.

The Needles shoot is the shoot I've been looking forward to the most during this entire six weeks of being in Utah—it's my favorite episode of the season. I wrote it because visiting the Needles was my favorite family vacation of all the ones we ever took. When my brother was in middle school and I was in elementary school, we lived with Apong Lita for the summer because our parents traveled constantly for their military jobs. She took us on summer road trips to Utah, and we spent one of the days driving to the Needles district of Canyonlands National Park. It was one of the last vacations she took with us before getting diagnosed with cancer a handful of years later. She passed away when I was in high school.

I don't think I blinked even once while staring at the endless sandstone spires that dominate that section of the park. It was like being in a children's fantasy picture book brought to life. The rock formations were in various needle and dome shapes, in every shade of red and orange. Apong Lita held my hand as we hiked around the viewing spots, pointing out every odd yet beautiful rock form we saw. I still can't believe only a fraction of tourists visit this section of the park compared to the other more popular attractions, like Arches, Zion, and Bryce. I've always thought it was the most beautiful.

The next time we come here, we'll have to see if we remember which ones we pointed out, she'd said, smiling down at me.

My chest swells. We never had the time to plan another trip before she got sick. That was the only time I ever visited the Needles. My goal with this episode of *Discovering Utah* is to shine a light on this area so that hopefully viewers of the series will feel compelled to visit it. But more than that, I want to be able to revisit the place that was so special to my grandma that she never got the chance to see again.

I swallow back the lump in my throat and refocus on Drew. "What do you mean shooting is a no-go?"

His brows furrow together, like he's annoyed that I'm questioning him. "The ranger said there was a mix-up in the scheduling. Apparently they're closed that week for park maintenance and aren't admitting any visitors."

I tug at my ponytail. I guess nothing on this shoot is going to go as planned. "Well, that's just fucking great," I mutter.

"Nice choice of language there." Drew's expression turns sour.

"I'm sorry, does swearing offend you?"

He glares down at me. "A little. We're on the clock, Dunn. Shouldn't we try to be a little professional?"

"Interesting. I mean, we're currently dealing with the most unprofessional host on the planet, who seems hell-bent on driving this series into the ground, but I haven't heard you complain about that. But cursing, that offends you? Good to know."

I walk to the driver's side of the car and start to open the door, but Drew's voice stops me.

"Calm down. It's no big deal, okay? Canyonlands is huge. We'll find some other section of the park to film for those days. At least we have enough notice that there's time to rework the script and the schedule."

I bite the inside of my cheek at his irritated tone. An angry sort of heat flashes through my chest. "You don't think this is a big deal. Noted."

He scoffs at my obvious sarcasm. "This is the nature of this business. Stuff happens and you roll with it. Here, we can set up a shoot in the Maze section of Canyonlands or something."

"Not a chance."

He jerks his head back at my sharp response. "Why not?"

"What a great idea, filming in the least accessible and most dangerous section of Canyonlands. You know that the Maze is consistently ranked as one of the deadliest places to hike in the US, right?"

I don't wait for Drew to answer.

"First of all, any vehicle we take out there has to be high clearance and four-wheel drive, otherwise we're guaranteed to get stuck or get a flat tire because none of the roads are maintained. They're all littered with jagged rocks and potholes. The trails there aren't well marked. They're difficult even for expert hikers to follow. And there are zero services in the Maze, not even water. We'd have to haul literally everything from drinking water to toilet paper with us. And if we get lost or stranded, it'll take rangers days to find us, the area is so remote and vast. That's a disaster waiting to happen, especially with someone like Blaine."

Drew spits out a bitter laugh. "Wow, okay, Dunn. Way to go full throttle to every worst-case scenario possible."

I bite my lip to keep from going off.

"We can figure something out," he says, rubbing his hand over his face. "Butch Cassidy had his hideout in the Maze, I think. We can just go there. That could be cool to film."

"Drew, the entire point of this series is to showcase *safe* attractions in Utah's national parks, not glamorize the illegal hideouts of dead criminals."

I'm about to turn away, but I stop when he speaks.

"I don't understand why this is such a touchy subject for you."

I twist so I'm fully facing him. "Of course you don't understand. You're not the one who planned this series from every angle—from the shot setups to the scene breaks to every last word in the script. You're not the one whose blood, sweat, and tears and heart and soul went into developing this series." I swallow just as my voice starts to shake. "This is just a job to you, and that's fine. But this is my dream. So you'll allow me a goddamn minute to be upset when you inform me of how it's all falling apart."

I know I'm overreacting, but I don't care. This shoot is personal—it's a tribute to my grandma for never being able to take that second vacation to Utah with her grandkids. Knowing that I won't be able to film at her favorite part cuts me to the core.

Just as my eyes start to water, I hop in the driver's seat and slam the door. From the corner of my eye, I spot Haley in the passenger seat, eyeing me.

"What happened?" she asks gently.

I shake my head, start the car, and leave Drew standing in the dust that my tires kick up.

I focus on navigating the unpaved pockmarked road that leads to the highway. "Just another change in the shooting schedule," I say in a quiet, defeated tone. "It's no big deal."

6

DON'T CARE HOW MANY TIMES YOU SAY OTHERWISE." HALEY frowns at me from behind her coffee mug. "It *is* a big deal."

I open my mouth to refute her claim yet again, but instead of telling another lie, I sigh. I gaze around at the main street that runs through downtown Moab. This is the first day off for the crew since we started filming a week ago, and Haley convinced me to take a break from editing and reviewing footage to explore downtown with her.

Sipping my drip coffee, I peer up from the outdoor patio where we're seated. I glance at the restaurants, breweries, coffee shops, galleries, bookstores, and souvenir shops that dot this side of the street. Normally I'd be *aww*-ing at the quaintness of this tiny desert tourist town, but I don't have it in me. Not when I'm still reeling from the disappointment of losing the Needles shoot.

"Okay, you're right," I finally admit. The coffee shop employee stops by our corner table right next to the nearby alley and asks if we need anything. We politely decline.

"It really, really sucks that the Needles episode isn't happening. But what can I do?"

I hate how dejected the tone of my voice sounds. But after seven days of long hours, limited sleep, and handling Blaine's unpredictable antics, I'm exhausted. And the sting of losing the most sentimental part of this series is impossible to shake.

Haley offers a sympathetic nod. "I can call up the ranger's office and ask them to open it up even for just a few hours. Or maybe we can ask Brooke to help us think of something."

I shake my head. "This series is my one shot to show the network that I can put a show together, no matter the circumstances. I don't want them thinking I have to call my mentor to hold my hand every time I run into a problem."

"Do you want me to talk to Drew and ask him to give it another go?"

I scoff. "No way. He thinks it's ridiculous that I'm so upset."

Haley stares back at me, her deep-brown eyes sincere. "Maybe if you told him how much it meant to you, he'd understand. And then he can approach the ranger's office again. It's his job to help secure the shooting locations, after all."

"He very clearly doesn't appeal to sentiment," I say, remembering the disinterested look on his face when I explained to him how upset I was at losing the Needles shoot. "Besides, according to Brooke, Drew's the best of the best. If he couldn't talk the park into letting us shoot there, no one will be able to."

"Alia," Haley says softly, reaching to place her hand on my arm. "I know how special the Needles is to you. And honestly, I was so excited to see it. When you talk about visiting there with your grandma, it always makes me smile. Every time you reminisce about it, it's like it just happened yesterday. That memory is vivid and so special to you. You can't hide that."

I glance away, hoping I don't tear up yet again at the thought of losing the opportunity to film an episode as a tribute to my grandma.

My nose stings as I sniffle. "I was even going to put a credit at the end of the episode. 'Dedicated to the memory of Lita Santos.' It was going to be a surprise for my mom when she watched the series, seeing that tribute. I just feel like I let them down . . . even though my grandma's not here anymore and my mom didn't even know about the surprise."

I clear my throat to keep my voice from breaking.

Just then Haley gives my arm a gentle squeeze. "Hey. Don't you dare feel bad. You didn't let anyone down. None of this is your fault. The fact that you even thought to do something so thoughtful in her memory is what counts. Your mom and your grandma would tell you that, I promise."

I take a breath, then blink away the burning tears in my eyes. I glance up at Haley. "Thanks for saying that."

"Always."

"Hey, you guys."

We twist around to see who's speaking to us. I deflate immediately when I see it's Drew standing a few feet outside the wrought iron fence that marks the outdoor seating area of the coffee shop. A concerned frown paints his face. I wonder what he's so worried about.

"Shopping on your day off?" Haley asks.

Drew clears his throat and his expression eases. "Uh, yeah. Just exploring a bit." He raises his arm and points to the trio of small shopping bags he's holding in his left hand. "Souvenirs for the family."

Haley smiles, then makes a "gimme" gesture with her hands. I roll my eyes. Shopping fanatic Haley always wants to see people's hauls.

Drew's face turns red, but he walks up to the waist-high fence and hands her his bags. She digs out a few mugs with various red-rock formations and the word "Moab" on them, some hand-painted pottery, key chains, a bunch of postcards, shot glasses, coasters, and a Christmas ornament that's made of red stone, carved in the shape of a Santa.

"Wow," Haley says. "Impressive haul."

"I've got a lot of family to buy for." Drew's eyes dart to me; then he quickly looks away. "They sent me a list of stuff they wanted since they've never been here."

There's a temporary break in my hostility toward him. It's really sweet that he's spending his one day off scouring the town for gifts.

Just then Haley lets out a whistle as she pulls out a black velvet jewelry box. When she starts to open it without asking him, I scold her.

She rolls her eyes, then looks at Drew. "May I pretty please open this?"

A grin breaks free and he nods yes. My stomach drops. His flustered smiles are the most adorable I've ever seen.

I turn my stare to the jewelry box to keep from gawking at him like a creep.

"Oooh, pretty!" Haley says as she studies the teal droplet earrings in the box.

"That's a gift for my niece," he says quietly. "She's going to her first middle school dance in a couple of months. Turquoise is her favorite color, and I thought they would look nice with her dress."

Haley says, "Aww," just as my heart swells. A tender expression takes over his face. It's obvious he adores his niece, and damn if that's not the sweetest thing I've heard in a while.

"You want to join us?" Haley asks as she puts his items back.

He opens his mouth to answer just as my phone rings. Wyatt's calling me.

"Hey, man," I answer. "Couldn't bear just one day away from us, could you?"

"Hey," Wyatt pants, then says nothing for a few seconds.

"Are you all right?"

"I need you to come to the McDonald's in town. Now."

"What? Why?"

He yells something unintelligible to someone in the distance. "I just—I can't explain it, you need to get here. It's an emergency."

He hangs up. I glance up and see Haley and Drew staring at me, confusion marring their faces.

"Is something wrong with Wyatt?" Drew asks.

"I have no idea." I stand, coffee cup in hand. "But he said there's an emergency at McDonald's."

"Here. I'll drive us," Drew says and gestures to his truck, which is parked right in front of the coffee shop.

We make the drive, which is just a couple of minutes on the main street of town. When Drew pulls his car into the parking lot, all of our jaws drop.

"Holy . . ."

"Motherfucker."

"Shit."

We climb out of the car, our gazes glued to the roof of the McDonald's building. Because on the roof stands a naked Blaine shouting while gesturing randomly.

Wyatt waves to us, and we jog over to where he's standing. Around us a small crowd has formed.

"What the hell happened?" I ask Wyatt.

He takes off his baseball cap and rubs his forehead with the heel of his hand. "I . . . have no idea. I was driving down the street looking for a place to grab some lunch. Then I saw some naked dude waving from the roof of McDonald's. And then I realized it was Blaine."

Wyatt explains that he pulled over to try to coax Blaine down, but he wouldn't listen.

"I think he's on something," Wyatt mutters.

"You think?" Haley stares wide-eyed at Blaine.

"You're beautiful!" Blaine hollers, eyes closed and arms motioning like he's conducting an invisible symphony. "You're so, so, so, so beautiful! Every single one of you!" Then he opens his eyes and zeroes in on someone in the crowd. "Especially you, my man. Look at those calves! Woo!"

Blaine starts singing some song I don't recognize. My head spins trying to figure out what to do.

"I was going to call the police, but . . ." Wyatt turns his stare at me. "I figured he'd get arrested and we need him for tomorrow's shoot. I didn't want to screw up the schedule. I'm sorry, Alia."

Bailing out Blaine and dealing with a court appearance would most definitely ruin the rest of the shoot. But the fact that Wyatt refused to do the right thing—the legal thing—for my sake sends a wave of guilt through me. He shouldn't have to wrestle with doing the right thing on my account.

I pat his shoulder. "I appreciate that, Wyatt. I really do. I'm sorry you were in this position to begin with."

Just then an employee walks out of the store and glares up at the roof. Then she glances at the crowd, which is now fifty-some people deep. Every single one of them has their phone out recording the spectacle.

"Of course they would film the prick and not call the police," she mumbles.

When she pulls her phone out of her apron pocket, I rush over to her. "Hey! Please don't call the police. This guy . . . is our friend."

I gesture to Wyatt, Drew, and Haley, who are standing a few feet away, bewildered looks on their faces. Drew forces an awkward smile, then waves. I look at the name tag on her uniform.

"Amber." My voice is pleading as she turns back to look at me. "I know what he's doing is disrupting your business, but can you please just let us handle it? We'll get him down soon, I promise. Please?"

Amber's frown eases back a tad. "Fine. But if he's not down in five minutes, I'm calling."

I nod once, thank her, then rush back over to Drew, Wyatt, and Haley.

"We need to get him off of the roof in the next five minutes or they're going to call the police, he'll get arrested, and the shoot will be screwed."

They all nod in silent agreement.

"How did he even get up there in the first place?" Haley asks.

Drew points to a roofing van that's parked nearby. A ladder is propped up on top of the car, and it's angled to the roof of the building.

I rush over to the van, climb on top of it, then scale the ladder to the roof. Haley calls my name, but I ignore her.

I walk over to Blaine, who's now humming with his eyes closed, swaying to whatever tune is playing in his head.

Someone taps my shoulder and I jump, then spin around. Drew's startled face greets me.

"What the hell are you doing up here?"

Drew aims a pointed, indignant stare at me. "If you think I was going to let you come up here alone, you're nuts."

My chest heaves slightly as I rein in my breath. How patronizing, thinking I can't handle this on my own. I spin around to face Blaine, ignoring Drew.

"Blaine," I say firmly.

When he doesn't answer, I practically scream his name.

His eyes fly open. "Yo! It's you, Little Miss Showrunner or Producer or whatever you are!"

I grit my teeth at the obnoxious nickname. "You need to get off the roof. Now."

"What? Why?" It's like he's a toddler who's been told he needs to stop playing and go take a nap.

"Because if you don't, the police are going to come and arrest you." I take a step toward him. "You don't want to spend the night in jail, do you? You don't want to lose your job, do you?"

He scrunches his face. "No way."

"Okay. Then climb back down the ladder with me. We'll pretend this never happened."

When he starts nodding, I'm hopeful. But then he crosses his arms and frowns. "I don't wanna."

"Excuse me?"

He tilts his head up, indignant. "I don't wanna. And you can't make me."

Whatever drugs he's on must give him out-of-control mood swings . . . or this could just be more of his shitty natural personality shining through.

"Blaine. If you don't come down with me right now, you're going to get arrested. You'll have to post bail and go to court. We'll all lose our jobs because of you."

He tosses his head back. "I don't care." And then he turns his glassy stare back at me and takes a step toward me. We're just a foot apart now.

He points at me. "I'm done listening to you, you bossy little bitch."

I clench my jaw, balling my fists at my sides. All I see is red.

There's a flash at the corner of my eye. Drew appears at Blaine's side. His eyes are wild with an intense fury, his face and neck are flushed, and his chest heaves as he takes a rough breath. Then he claps a hand on Blaine's shoulder and backs him up to stand behind a tall, pillar-like section of the roof, near the edge. Blaine's eyes glaze over and he smirks at Drew. Then Drew wraps one arm around Blaine, grabs Blaine's arm, and twists it behind his back.

My eyes go wide. Blaine winces through gritted teeth. Drew leans his face closer to Blaine's.

"Don't ever call her that again," he growls. "Got it?"

Blaine nods.

"Alia is in charge and you will listen to whatever the hell she says from now on." Drew practically spits out the words in a snarl, like an attack dog ready to go for the throat. "Do you understand?"

Blaine groans but then nods.

Drew releases Blaine's arm, grabs him by the shoulders, and walks him toward me. Drew's eyes cut back to me. "Is there anything you'd like to add?"

My heart hammering in my chest, I turn to Blaine. "Climb down that ladder. Now."

Blaine rasps a barely audible "okay" before hobbling to the ladder while wringing out the arm that Drew grabbed. Drew and I stand next to each other and watch him make his way down. Even though we're not touching, I can feel the heat from Drew's body skim across my skin. I swallow, still thrown by what I saw . . . but also flattered. I can't help the satisfaction that surged through me when Drew came to my defense without hesitation.

What in the world should I say to him? Slowly, I turn to face him. But before I can utter a word, Drew walks over to climb down the ladder. Clamping my mouth shut, I follow him. Applause breaks out below me. When my feet are back on the ground, I hear the sound of tires screeching. I look up and see a black Audi pull into the parking lot. A redheaded guy who's Drew's height but skinnier and looks barely old enough to drink hops out of the driver's seat. Haley waves him down, jogs up to him, and says something I can't hear. The kid frowns, then rushes over to Blaine, who's wringing out his arm while walking.

The young redheaded guy holds a towel in his hand and drapes it over Blaine's lower half, then ushers him into the back seat of the Audi. When he shuts the door, he looks up, then pivots his stare back and forth across the crowd, a panicked look on his face.

I walk over to him. "Hey. Are you okay?" I ask, my heart finally slowing from its frenzied beat.

"Yeah, I'm fine. I'm Colton." He smooths his hand over the front of his striped dress shirt. "I'm Mr. Stephens's personal assistant."

I let out a breath. Then I stick out my hand for him to shake. "I'm Alia Dunn, the one in charge of the show he's hosting."

Recognition flashes through his blue eyes and he runs a hand over his face. "Look, I'm sorry for how . . . difficult he's been. His agent, his manager—we're all trying to get him under control."

As annoyed and angry as I am, Blaine's actions are not the fault of his personal assistant. Judging by the fatigue in Colton's eyes, he's exhausted. I can't imagine what it must be like handling Blaine twenty-four seven. All the money in the world wouldn't be enough for me to do that job.

"Thanks for getting him down," Colton says.

I glance over at Drew, who's standing just a few feet away talking to Wyatt. There's still a tad bit of strain in his expression.

"It was mostly my colleague's doing." I nod in Drew's direction. "He's pretty convincing." I clear my throat. "I'm sorry you have to put up with Blaine."

Colton shrugs and smiles weakly. "We all pay our dues, right?"

He promises that Blaine will be rested and ready to go for tomorrow's scheduled shoot. Even though I have zero faith in his promise, I thank him anyway. He rounds the car and jumps back in the driver's seat, then speeds away.

Haley, Drew, and Wyatt walk over to me.

"Damn," Wyatt says to Drew. "Whatever you two did up there to get him down, nicely done."

I let out a breath, relieved that there won't be a viral video of Drew twisting Blaine's arm. We already have Blaine's naked disaster to sort out once these spectators inevitably upload the videos and photos they took online.

I glance over at Drew. "A bit of strong-arming did the trick."
He clears his throat.

I suddenly feel exhausted. That must be the adrenaline of witnessing this fiasco leaving my body.

Haley peers around. "We'd all better get out of here just in case any police end up stopping by."

Wyatt peels away in his van, and Drew drives Haley and me back downtown.

"I could use a drink after that," Haley says from the back seat. "How about you guys?"

"Count me in," I say.

Drew says thanks but declines. "I would, but I promised my sister I'd FaceTime with her and my little nephew this afternoon. Don't wanna be buzzed for that."

Haley chuckles, shaking her head. "You're something else. One minute you're gushing over your niece and nephew and the next you're wrangling D-list celebrities."

She hops out of the car. I roll down the window and call after her.

"I'll be there in a minute. Get us a table?"

Haley nods yes and walks through the door of the brewery.

I turn to Drew. "Hey, um, thank you," I say.

He frowns. "For what?"

"For defending me back there, when Blaine insulted me."

My face heats when I recall the vitriol in Blaine's voice and expression. His opinion of me means less than nothing, but still. It always hurts to be called a bitch, no matter the circumstance.

Drew scoffs, shaking his head. "Come on, Dunn. I would have done the same thing if he had insulted a stranger on the street."

"Oh."

My face heats yet again, but not because I'm angry—because I'm embarrassed. I thought Drew's defense of me marked a turning point—that he reacted that way because he cared about me in some small way. But no. There was nothing special about his response. He does it for everyone—he said so himself.

My eyes fall to my lap as I gather my bags. "Thanks for the ride," I mutter as I stumble out of Drew's car, slamming the door behind me.

I make a beeline for the brewery entrance, annoyed that I thought for even one second that things between us could be different.

7

WHAT KIND OF SHOW ARE YOU SHOOTING THERE, Alia?" Richard, one of the network executives, asks. His disapproving frown makes up just one of the tiny squares on my laptop screen.

Gritting my teeth, I try to keep my annoyance at bay. "It's a show about the national parks in Utah. You gave me the go-ahead two weeks ago, remember?"

Richard's frown furrows deeper at me. I don't think he was expecting me to be a smart-ass when I answered him.

The half dozen other executives stare back at me from their respective tiny squares on my screen. Blaine's naked takeover of the Moab McDonald's yesterday made the rounds on social media. He's now known as #NakedMoabMan on Twitter and Instagram. Photos and videos of Blaine have been circulating online overnight, which of course made their way to the network. And the executives aren't happy about this unflattering publicity, to say the least. They decided to hold an emergency Zoom call with me to scold me for my poor management of Blaine.

And now I'm stuck inside my motel room at five in the morning enduring a meeting where every executive is taking turns grilling me on how I let the host of my show get this out of control. I glance at the clock, annoyed that this virtual meeting is how I get to kick off this long day of shooting. I could have caught an extra hour of sleep before heading to the scheduled shoot if I didn't have to do this.

"You really think you're going to solve this with that kind of an attitude?" Richard says in a pointed tone.

"There's nothing to solve," I say. "The crew and I took care of it. Shooting wasn't disrupted. We have a full day ahead of us, actually, so if we can wrap this up—"

Byron interrupts me with a gruff sigh. "We gave you the chance of your career, Alia. Your own series. And this is what you do with it? You let your host run around naked?"

Byron's biting criticism sets me off. I'm sick of taking responsibility for something that wasn't my fault.

"Hold on," I bark. Six pairs of eyes go wide. "As happy as I am for the opportunity to shoot this series, what happened with Blaine is not my fault. Byron, you're the one who made Blaine a nonnegotiable. You refused to hear any other option as host. So technically that means yesterday's fiasco is *your* fault. So don't for one second try to pin any of the blame on me. I asked for a different host. But appeasing your golfing buddy is apparently more important than employing quality talent." I pause for a quick moment to catch my breath. "You should be thanking us. If we hadn't intervened as quickly as we did to get him off that roof and back to whatever secret desert oasis he's staying at, he would have been arrested, and that would have been a much bigger disaster."

When I finish speaking, all sets of eyes are wide. Except for Byron's. He's frowning, his lips pursed. He's clearly pissed at me.

"So unless you're willing to do what I wanted to do from the get-go—fire Blaine and get an entirely different host who's actually professional and doesn't have a drug or attitude problem—there's really nothing more I can do."

"That's not happening," Byron says quickly. "Do you have any idea how much Blaine's contract is? To hire someone else at this point would put this project way, way over budget."

I bite the inside of my cheek to keep from lashing out at Byron for okaying Blaine's ridiculous salary while I'm expected to run this show on a tight budget.

I breathe in, hoping one of the other executives will chime in and say that they'll at least consider a different host. But as the seconds pass, they remain silent. A couple of them shake their heads in disappointment. A couple are clearly looking at their phones off-screen, not caring one bit about my series or this meeting.

I will myself not to scream in frustration. "Are we done here? I have a series to shoot."

Gruff yeses echo through the speakers of my laptop.

"In the future, if any of you have any other qualms about Blaine's behavior, I suggest you take it up with Byron. Have a nice day."

I leave the call, then stomp to the bathroom to take a shower. I've never once gone off on a superior before in my career—ever. Fitting that the one time I break, the one time I let my frustration boil over, it's aimed at the most powerful people at the network.

After a blazing-hot shower, I'm only slightly less worked up. Then I check my phone and see a missed call from Brooke. I call her back.

"Hey, Alia," she answers. "I just got an email from the execs."

My heart sinks. Did they call her to chew me out too? To remind me who's really in charge and put me back in my place?

Or maybe they're firing me. Maybe my little show of strength and anger pissed them off and they're pulling the plug—or maybe they now want Brooke to take over things since I'm sure they now consider me a hostile loose cannon.

"I'm sorry you got dragged into this," I say.

"Don't be sorry. They're just being their typical pompous

selves. They created this situation by allowing Byron to choose the worst person possible to host the series. And now they're upset about it and trying to blame everyone other than themselves."

I swallow, waiting for her to drop the bad news.

"It's okay, Alia," she says, seeming to sense my nerves over the phone. "They called to see if I could talk some sense into you." She scoffs. "I told Richard and Byron to shove it."

My mouth falls open. "You did?"

"You bet I did. And I told them exactly what I'm sure you told them too. That it's their fault Blaine's naked antics happened and that you're doing the best you can—the best anyone could in this situation. And that I'm the wrong person to call to attempt to get you in check because I'm on your side. Always."

I let out a relieved sigh and run my fingers through my wet hair.

"The nerve of those guys. I mean, they don't peep a word when a male producer legitimately screws up." Brooke scoffs. "Remember when Dale lost thirty thousand dollars in equipment after he left the grip truck unlocked during that shoot in the Everglades? The next morning it was cleaned out. Someone just came along and stole everything out of it. Or when that executive producer left his lit cigarette in one of the company cars and it caught on fire. Thousands of dollars in damage due to their negligence and the network execs didn't bat an eye. And you get yelled at because the guy *they* hired is out of control."

I huff out a breath of frustration remembering both of those instances.

"Thank you for sticking up for me, Brooke."

"Always. I told them to back off and leave you alone unless they had something legitimate to complain about. I know what it's like to have a group of all-male execs breathing down your neck for the most asinine stuff—problems that they caused because of their own crappy decision-making skills. You don't need to put up with that."

Once again I'm grateful to work with someone who is such an advocate for me.

"I just don't want you to get in trouble because you defended me," I say.

"Don't worry about me," she says, the confidence in her voice clear. "You just make the show you've worked so hard to earn. Okay?"

"Okay."

"How are things working out with Andrew?"

It takes a minute before I realize she's talking about Drew.

"Oh. Things are great. I mean, he's as great as you said he'd be. He knows how to do everything on set. And everyone loves working with him. I can't thank you enough for recommending him," I say, hoping that she doesn't pick up on the hitch in my voice when I talk about him. "How are things with you? How's Maine? Are you a sailing enthusiast yet?"

There's a pause where she chuckles, then stammers.

"I . . . may have met someone while on location. A pretty great guy who loves sailing . . . so you could say I've become an enthusiast for sailing in a way."

I grin as she tells me she hit it off with a guy named Greg, one of the sailing guides she's been collaborating with and filming for the series.

"I like him. A lot," she says, the smile in her voice clear.

"Brooke, that's awesome. You deserve a stud."

I think back to all those times when the two of us complained about how difficult it is to maintain a relationship, with our unpredictable work and travel schedules. We've killed downtime during shoots exchanging endless dating horror stories—bonding over that helped us shift from just colleagues to friends. And I'm so happy that my mentor and friend has met a guy that gets her this excited.

"I never thought I'd meet someone and hit it off while on location." She laughs. "But listen, if anything else comes up—if the execs try to hassle you about some other ridiculous thing, don't be afraid to call me, okay?" Brooke says.

"Promise I will." I huff out a sigh. "We really need more female execs."

"So very true." She lets out a sigh and we say good-bye. I quickly get ready, then head out to the shoot, determined to kick ass.

"OKAY, GUYS. THAT'S a wrap," I say.

I smile to myself and look up at the sun shining bright in the late-afternoon sky. We've finished shooting at Arches and are two days into filming segments at Canyonlands National Park.

"I totally thought we'd be here until nightfall," Haley says, standing next to me and fixing her gaze on the tablet she's holding. "Glad we're done ahead of schedule."

"You and me both," I say.

Yesterday ran long thanks to Blaine's usual antics of showing up hours later than the call time, forgetting his lines, and needing Drew to demonstrate every scene for him.

But today Colton somehow got him to the set on time, and then an even bigger miracle happened: Blaine actually performed well for once. He nailed most of his lines and oozed charm while filming. Drew only had to coach him through one scene. As much as I can't stand Blaine, I finally realize how he's made it this far in his career—he's a compelling performer when he's willing to put in the effort. That's probably how he keeps getting jobs—for every few times he screws up or no-shows, he delivers one day of top-quality work.

But underneath the relief, frustration simmers. A forty-something man shouldn't be this hot and cold. He should be able to deliver consistent performances. And he shouldn't have to be babysat by a personal assistant half his age. It's clear I'm going to need to have a talk with him about professionalism and his work ethic.

I glance over at Blaine as he stands several feet away at the lookout point for Upheaval Dome, which is where we ended today's shoot. It's one of the most popular attractions at the Island in the Sky section of Canyonlands.

He pulls a pack of cigarettes from his back pocket, lights one, then takes a long drag. Of course he's openly flouting the park's no-smoking policy.

For the millionth time, I think about just how many hours of the day we waste accommodating him. I clench my jaw in frustration, still bitter about the roof incident. Then I take a breath and start to walk over to tell him to put out his cigarette.

But then Drew marches up to him with a frown so fierce, it stops me dead in my tracks. I can't hear what he's saying, but it causes Blaine's eyes to widen. Then he rolls his shoulders, sulks, and hands his cigarette to Drew, who puts it out in the almost-empty plastic water bottle he's holding.

Drew turns around, catching eyes with me for a moment before I quickly look away.

We haven't spoken a word about what happened during the roof incident with Blaine. Whenever we talk, it's only about filming. There's never any mention of how he twisted Blaine's arm when he insulted me—or his dismissal when I thanked him for defending me.

My skin heats, and not just at the memory of that embarrassing letdown. But because every night since then, I've thought about Drew . . . specifically that feral look in his eye when he unloaded on Blaine.

Every night in the shower, specifically.

My breath hitches at the image of Drew's long, muscled arm as he overpowered him. At how the veins in his forearms bulged. At how his jaw muscles twitched through the stubble on his exquisitely square jaw. At that caveman grunt he let out. At how lethal he sounded when he ordered Blaine to never, ever speak to me like that again.

It all replays like some sort of slow-motion action-movie montage.

I swallow. Yes, it is very, very unenlightened of me to entertain such a fantasy—and I especially shouldn't do it when I'm naked and hot water is running all over my body.

But it's been years since my last relationship, which was a dumpster fire. Months since my last date, not counting the one with Drew. He's my most recent kiss too . . . and I can't even remember the last time before that. I guess this is what the dirty part of my brain gets off on when it's been a while: a hot guy defending my honor.

A beat later, when the heat starts to subside, a new wave of humiliation tumbles through me. Drew isn't the slightest bit interested in me in that way, and here I am replaying my ridiculous hero fantasy.

I walk up to Blaine, whose eyes are glued to his phone. "Can I talk to you for a second?"

"Huh?" He doesn't even glance up from the screen.

"I'd like to talk to you. About your work performance."

Seconds later he finally looks at me. "What about it?"

I lightly ball my fists at my sides. He sounds so indignant that it's taking everything in me to keep a patient, professional tone. But I need to approach this topic with a level of pleasantness.

I force myself to smile at him. "We really appreciate you being the host of this show."

Crossing his arms, he lets out a sigh.

"Your performance today was excellent," I say.

"Thanks."

"That's the level of work I'd like to see from you consistently for the rest of this shoot. That's exactly what we need for this series to be a hit. And I really think you can deliver it."

Holding my breath, I make myself smile once more. I'm hoping my encouragement will be the boost Blaine needs to get himself into gear for the next handful of weeks.

He scrunches his face, like he's thinking deeply about something. Then he lets out a laugh. "Okay."

I know I should just brush it off, but there's a cruel edge to his chuckle that I can't ignore.

"Is something funny?"

He shakes his head, still chuckling. "Come on. This is a series about the desert. Let's not pretend it's anything more than that."

"What?"

He turns back to his phone. "It's dirt and sand and some pretty rocks. Whether or not I bring my A game isn't gonna make much of a difference."

"Actually, Blaine, your performance makes a huge impact. Every time you're late or forget your lines, it compromises the integrity of the series. A compelling host can make even the most boring subject engaging. Besides, aren't you trying to clean up your image with this show? You're not accomplishing that with your recent behavior."

He shakes his head and squints at his phone screen. "I'm doing just fine. I don't need to change anything."

I open my mouth but quickly clamp it back shut. Because nothing I can say will change his mind. Based on his attitude, Blaine isn't the least bit interested in making this series a priority.

But there's one thing I still need to make clear to him.

"You clearly don't care about your performance on-screen, but you need to care about how you act around the crew. Specifically the female crew members."

When he glares at me, I look him straight in the eye.

"You know what I'm talking about. I haven't forgotten what you said to Rylan the first day of shooting—or the way you looked at her. Watch how you act. If I catch you doing anything inappropriate, there will be hell to pay. Understand?"

He purses his lips. The overly tanned skin around his mouth explodes into a million wrinkles. "Yup."

I spin around and walk back to the rest of the crew, my heart pounding out of sheer anger. I stare at nearby Upheaval Dome to distract myself. I fixate on the three-mile-wide expanse of grayish rocks pushed up into multiple cone-like formations, mesmerized. The landscape sticks out from the hundreds of miles of red desert like a sore thumb.

Rylan walks up to stand by my side. "This is the single coolest thing I've ever seen in my life," she says, her blue eyes sparkling as she stares at it. "But you know, I think it's so much cooler that geologists and scientists don't know how it was formed." She turns to face me. "I think the theory that a meteorite hit this spot millions of years ago makes the most sense. I mean, I've seen photos of Upheaval Dome from outer space and it looks like such an obvious meteorite impact. To me, at least."

I smile at her. Witnessing her genuine excitement melts away the frustration in me.

Then she laughs and blushes while cupping her cheeks with her hands. "Sorry," she says softly. "I'm a huge geology nerd."

"Don't be sorry, Rylan. I love how enthusiastic you are about this. Actually, would you want to put your geology knowledge to use? I've been kicking around the idea of including bonus content online to go along with the series, and it sounds like you'd be the perfect person to help with that. I think Upheaval Dome would make a great mini-featurette."

Rylan's mouth falls open. She cups a hand over it before nodding yes. "Oh my gosh, I would absolutely love to do that!"

She leaves to help Joe and Wyatt pack up the camera equipment while I help Haley pack up. When I look up for a moment, I catch Colton hurrying up the nearby trail to the lookout point where Blaine is scrolling through his phone. When Colton reaches and speaks to him, Blaine frowns up at him.

"What do you mean they don't have camel milk? This is the desert, isn't it?" Blaine yells.

Wide-eyed Colton starts to say something, but Blaine holds up his hand and stomps in the direction of the parking lot.

"Poor kid," Haley says.

"Whenever I get annoyed at all the Blaine-related bullshit we have to endure, I remind myself that Colton has to put up with way worse."

"That makes you feel better?" Haley asks.

"No. It makes me feel worse. Colton shouldn't have to put up with being mistreated. But then I fantasize about all these creative ways of taking Blaine down."

Haley chuckles before typing something in her tablet. Colton starts to walk back to the parking lot, but Rylan runs up to him and stops him. I nudge Haley to discreetly take a look. They both smile shyly as they chat for a minute. They give each other identical timid waves, their hands lingering low and by their sides, before Colton walks off, a giant smile on his face.

"It seems like he found a way to cope with the stress," Haley says.

An hour later we're at the parking lot packing the equipment into the cars. Joe and Wyatt take off in their van right as Drew walks up to me.

"You still planning on scouting locations in the park today to film for online content?"

"Yeah, with Haley."

"Just wondered if you needed some help." He scrubs a hand over his face. Judging by the furrow of his brow, I thought he had something more serious to say.

"I think we'll be okay."

"Goddamn it!"

The back door of the SUV slams shut, rattling the car. Haley stomps over to us, venting about how one of the web-content editors at Expedition just accidentally deleted the raw footage from her recent shoot in the Adirondacks.

She tugs at her ponytail. "I have to run to the hotel now to get my laptop and email everything to him again tonight if we're going to make the editing deadline." She rubs her eye with the heel of her hand. "You'll have to location scout on your own. Sorry, Alia."

I start to say it's no big deal, I've done it a million times before, but Drew interrupts.

"I can stay and help you scout." His lips are pursed like he's aching to spill something.

I'm about to tell him that I can handle it just fine on my own, but Haley flashes a thumbs-up at us. "You're a lifesaver, Drew," she says, her eyes glued to her phone as she speaks.

She jumps in the car, Rylan hops in the driver's seat, and seconds later they're gone.

He turns to me. "Looks like it's just me and you, Dunn."

I let out a quiet sigh, bracing myself for what is sure to be an awkward few hours. "Looks like it."

8

WE WALK TO HIS CAR AND HE ASKS WHERE HE SHOULD drive to.

"Whale Rock."

I buckle my seat belt and brace myself for a few minutes of awkward silence.

As he pulls out onto the main road, he glances at me. "I want to apologize."

"For what? You did a great job reining in Blaine today. If you hadn't told him to put out his cigarette, I was going to shove it down his throat."

A chuckle bursts out of him. It's so goofy and joyful-sounding.

"No, that's not . . ." He clears his throat. "I mean, thanks."

Another few seconds of silence follow. I swallow.

"I want to apologize for how dismissive I was when we were talking about the Needles shoot getting canceled."

"Oh." On the inside I deflate just thinking about it.

"I didn't realize you had such a history there. And that you wanted to honor your grandma."

I turn to look at him. "How did you know that?"

He rubs the back of his neck. "I was walking up the alley near the coffee shop and heard you and Haley talking the other

day. I'm sorry for eavesdropping, but I want you to know that I
think your idea of memorializing your grandma with an episode
at the Needles is really thoughtful."

When he turns to look at me, I see there's softness in his
eyes too.

"And I'm sorry for saying it wasn't a big deal," he says. "That
was an asshole thing to say."

He turns back to the road. I stay quiet for a bit as he pulls
into the parking lot at the trailhead for Whale Rock. We park
and I glance up at the massive, long, dome-shaped, sandstone
rock half a mile away. It looks like a beached whale jutting out of
the orange-red dirt.

"Thanks for saying that. I appreciate it."

Drew clears his throat as he unbuckles his seat belt and
turns to me once more. "I was able to call the ranger's office at
the Needles and get them to reschedule."

I whip my head to face him. "You what?"

"I booked an overnight shoot there for this weekend. Saturday night into Sunday late morning," he says. "If you're okay with
moving things around in the schedule, the Needles is yours."

I gawk at him, speechless.

"I know it throws off the shooting schedule a bit. These first
two weeks were supposed to be in Moab, and then we'd move on
to Zion, then Bryce, then Capitol Reef. We'll have to cut things
short in Moab to make it work, but then we could tack on a
couple of days back in Moab at the end of the shoot, if you're
cool with that. We'll be going back and forth across the state,
which I know isn't ideal, but—"

I reach across my seat to hug him. I squeeze him so hard that
he makes an "oof" sound.

"Oh my God!" I squeal softly into his left pectoral muscle.

He chuckles above me, and I take a breath. He smells like

mint and pine needles. It makes my heart beat just a tad bit quicker.

A few more seconds of hugging him and it hits me just how inappropriate it is that I'm touching Drew like this. I lean back into my seat, embarrassed. But I'm too hyped up on excitement to stay embarrassed for long.

When I look at him, he's fighting back a grin.

"How did you . . . I mean, you said . . . I thought it was impossible at this point . . ."

"I called in a favor."

I let out a laugh. "A favor?"

"I promised the ranger I talked to that we'd put his name in the credits as a consultant for the series."

I exhale and fall back into my seat. I'm smiling so wide that it starts to ache behind my ears. "You have no idea what this means. I've been dreaming about filming there ever since I got into travel production. I just . . ." I face him. "Thank you for making this happen. It means everything."

A smile stretches across his face. "If I had known how special the Needles was to you because of your grandma, I wouldn't have let the ranger's office cancel it in the first place."

"You've redeemed yourself. You really are as incredible as Brooke said you'd be."

We jump out of the car, and I sling my hiking pack over my shoulder.

He raises an eyebrow. "Brooke said that?"

"Her exact words. She sang your praises."

He flashes that flustered smile I remember seeing when he ran into Haley and me at the coffee shop. It sends a tingle from my fingers to my toes.

My phone buzzes with a text, and I sneak a quick peek. It's a slew of messages from my parents in our family group text chain.

I beam when I see that they filmed a short video of themselves.

"Hi, *anak*!" my mom says while grinning. She holds a giant mug with a picture of Zion National Park on it. "We just wanted to say a quick hello and wish you luck while you film your series! We're so proud of you!"

"Hope filming is going well, honeybun." My dad waves and then tugs on the bill of the baseball cap he's wearing, which has the word "Utah" stitched on it in bright orange letters.

He hunches down to be at the same height as my mom, who's a foot shorter than him. He wraps an arm around her, pulling her against him before kissing her cheek. She beams up at him. That obvious look of love between them makes my chest ache. It's the best feeling knowing that my parents are still in love with each other after more than thirty years together.

"We love you! Call us soon, okay?" Mom says in her singsong voice.

Underneath their video is a text from my older brother, Chase.

You two are ridiculous LOL. Way to go, sis. Proud of you.

Behind me I hear Drew's low chuckle. "Your parents are sweet."

"They really are."

I make a mental note to call them tomorrow after we finish filming for the day.

"I don't know if my parents would ever have the patience—or technological know-how—to film a video and text it to me."

I laugh as I slather sunscreen on my face and neck. "Oh, it took them ages to figure out FaceTime. But once they did, it's their preferred way to communicate with my brother and me."

"My parents favor yelling on the phone because they still haven't figured out that they can actually adjust the volume on their phones."

We laugh, and I hand him the bottle of sunscreen.

He shakes his head no. "I think I'll be okay. I've got a hat." He slips on a baseball cap and I frown.

"I know that this is a short trail, but there's zero cover so we're completely exposed to the sun. Believe me, you'll burn quicker than you think. And a baseball cap is terrible sun protection."

I place the sunscreen in his palm and pull out an extra collapsible sun hat that I always keep in my pack. "This is way better. Your neck and the sides of your face are completely uncovered in a baseball cap."

Drew sighs through a smile as he takes the hat, then applies sunscreen. "Damn. I didn't know I'd be contending with the sun-protection police," he jokes. "Especially someone with a tan like you've got."

"My tan is all natural, thanks to my mom," I say. "And protection from the sun is no joke on a wilderness shoot like this. I know better after years of working on outdoor shoots."

He secures the hat on his head and looks at me, his face scrunched. "God, I bet I look like a grandpa wearing this."

Even in the unglamorous design of a giant, floppy sun hat, Drew still looks dynamite—the exact physical opposite of a grandpa. All the unflattering protective gear in the world can do little to dampen his rugged handsomeness.

I do a quick once-over of him, hoping it comes off as casual and not at all like I'm struggling to process just how impossibly hot he is. "You look great. You want a snack or anything before heading out?"

"Nah, I'm good." He chuckles.

"What?"

His hazel-brown gaze fixes on me. "It's cool how you look after the crew. I notice you've always got plenty of snacks for everyone, and you're always reminding us to drink water while we work. You're such a den mother. It's so cute."

I lower the brim of my hat just a tad bit more so he can't see, I hope, just how much I'm blushing at the sound of him calling me cute.

"You ready?"

We walk to the trailhead. As we make our way side by side along the red dirt path, I feel myself loosen. That same comfort and ease I felt when we chatted over drinks on our date comes over me.

Drew pulls a package of Snoballs from his pocket, rips open the plastic wrap, and chows down. "See? I've got snacks covered," he says around a mouthful of that cream-filled snack cake. "You want some?"

I make a face and shake my head. I don't see how he can eat that.

"What? It's delicious." Two bites later the first Snoball is demolished and he's digging into the second one. "It's yummy chocolate cake and cream inside of a coconut-dusted marshmallow. What's not to love?"

"The processed flavor. And the chemically enhanced color."

Drew lets out a laugh, then kicks a small rock off the trail with one of his sneaker-clad feet.

"What happened to your hiking boots?" I ask.

"Thought I'd give them a break."

"Give your sneakers a break. If you want to survive this shoot, wear hiking boots. And moisture-wicking socks. Your blister-free feet will thank you."

"Yes, ma'am."

I laugh at his playful tone. "I wore only sneakers during a shoot at the continental divide. A million blisters and two destroyed pairs of sneakers later, I learned my lesson."

"I've done a bunch of wilderness shoots, but never for this

many weeks. I've got a lot to learn from you, Dunn." He wags his eyebrow at me.

I smile down at my hiking boots. "So what's your story? How did you get into this line of work?"

"It's a long one," Drew says with an exaggerated exhale.

I gesture to the half-mile-long trail ahead of us. "We've got plenty of time to kill, and we're the only people on this trail."

Drew explains how he started out working as a caterer and an extra for low-budget movies a couple of years out of high school.

"Wait, you wanted to work in films?"

He shakes his head. "Not really. I had no idea what I wanted to do when I was twenty. I didn't do great in school, like a lot of other kids. I was good at sports, but not good enough to make it a career. I was living at home, working endless dead-end jobs while taking college classes, which I hated. And then one day I saw an ad on Craigslist looking for extras on a random indie movie. I made friends with another extra, whose cousin worked on a travel series. That show needed a production assistant, and that's what kicked it all off."

"So that PA job hooked you?"

"Yeah, believe it or not. So many other people I met over the years hated starting out as a PA. And I mean, parts about it definitely were rough, but overall I liked it. Every day was different. I never got bored. I think that was my problem in school and my other jobs. I'm not good with routine. It's tough, but I like all the random things that pop up when you're filming. Every day is a challenge. I like having to problem solve and put out all the fires that come up."

"That explains why you're so good at handling Blaine."

He shakes his head while rolling his eyes and grinning.

"Seriously. Brooke said you're a jack-of-all-trades and she was right. You can do everything."

"Not everything."

The way he softly mutters his words makes me curious. "What do you mean?"

He stares at the ground, his footfalls getting heavier with each step. "I'd make a terrible host."

I scoff. "Do you not remember how slick you've been every time you've had to spoon-feed Blaine his scenes? You're a natural. A million times better than him."

I glance at him, admiring his profile as he focuses on the trail ahead of us. My eyes follow the smooth, strong lines of his nose and jaw.

"It's a different story when the cameras are rolling." He pauses and for a few moments the only sounds are from our shoes hitting the dirt and rock. A crow flies above us and caws.

I want to ask him to say more, but I don't want to pry.

"I actually auditioned to host a show years ago," he says as we close in on the rock formation.

"You did?"

He nods. "It was for some online gaming series. I don't even remember the name of it. But I do remember how badly I blew the audition."

"I'm sure it wasn't that bad." I try to laugh to lighten the mood, but he purses his lips and says nothing as he stares straight ahead.

"It was that bad. I have pretty severe stage fright. I've had it ever since I was a kid."

"Oh." I stop in my tracks. Drew stops too and turns to look at me. "I'm sorry. I didn't mean to make light of that. I wouldn't had I known . . ."

"It's okay, Alia. If people were to watch my tape and see how I froze up and stared wide-eyed into the camera for almost a solid minute, they'd probably have a good laugh. I mean, I spent weeks memorizing those lines. Hosting was something I'd wanted to break into since I started out in this business. But one look at that camera, all those producers and the casting director staring right at me, and poof. I forgot everything. I just stuttered, then ran out of the room." He groans and rubs a hand over his face. "Kind of embarrassing to suck at something you wanted so badly."

He starts to walk ahead, but I grab his hand, stopping him.

"Drew, no decent person would laugh at that. That was an incredibly high-stress moment. I mean, would you laugh at a person having a nervous breakdown or bursting into tears? You have nothing to be embarrassed about."

Instead of answering me, he looks down at our joined hands. I immediately let go. "Sorry," I mumble, my face fiery. Why did I think it would be okay to grab him?

But when I glance up, a small smile tugs at his lips. "No worries, Dunn."

I continue walking forward, stopping right where the gigantic sandstone starts to jut up from the earth and form the whale formation.

"I'm sorry to hear how your audition went."

Drew shrugs. "It was years ago. It just goes to show I'm not meant to be a host. I should have known given what a hard time I have controlling my nerves sometimes."

The urge to argue with him hits my tongue. I've been on countless shoots, with more hosts than I can remember, and none of them possess the natural ease and charm that Drew has.

"I hope you change your mind someday," I say. "I think you'd be amazing at it."

Drew's stubbly cheeks flush red as his mouth curves up. He gestures to my pack. "Here, let me carry that. It'll be easier for you to scramble up the rock without it weighing you down."

I thank him, quietly giddy at how he gestures for me to go first after explaining how much safer it is for him to be behind me.

And then he taps the small of my back and I get a flashback to that night at the Brazen Head when he pulled the same move as he walked me out, right before we shared that knee-wobbling kiss on the sidewalk.

I swallow as his hand falls away and he gestures to the rock.

"In case you lose your footing, I can break your fall," he huffs behind me as we scramble up the steepest part of the rock face.

"If anyone's losing their footing, it's you in those sneakers," I tease as I make my way ahead of him.

Behind me Drew's low, throaty chuckle sounds. The rest of the way up we say nothing, just huffs of air and grunts. When we reach the top of Whale Rock, we stop to catch our breath.

"Damn, that's pretty," Drew says through an exhale. Canyons stretch in every direction. Bright green shrubs pop from the orange-red desert surrounding us.

"If we can convince Wyatt and Joe to hike up here with the camera equipment tomorrow, we could get some gorgeous shots to use as online clips," he says.

"Joe will be all over it, but Wyatt might be a harder sell. I'll probably have to bribe him."

We walk along the top of the rock all the way to the other side and stop several feet from the edge.

Drew wipes the sweat from his brow with his forearm, then looks at me. "Wanna sit?"

"Sure."

He lowers himself into a sitting position, then pats the spot next to him. For a long moment, all we do is sit and stare at the endless canyon in front of us.

"Tell me about your grandma," Drew says.

"I owe my love of Utah, traveling, and nature to her. Both of my parents traveled a ton for work when my brother and I were little, so we stayed with her a lot."

"What did your parents do for a living?"

"They were both in the military. We moved a lot because of it, so I was used to never staying in one place for very long. But there were a couple times when they were stationed overseas for months at a time, and they didn't want to take us out of school, so we'd live with our grandma."

"That must have been hard," he says softly. It makes goose bumps flash across my skin, how gentle and caring he sounds.

"Saying good-bye was always so hard. I always cried when they left—they did too. But staying with my grandma was the best. She would take us on road trips almost every weekend. One time they were stationed out of the country for an entire summer, so Apong Lita took us on a road trip. We hit up as many national parks as we could in one summer. Utah was my favorite state that we visited."

I pause, thinking about the first time I ever laid eyes on the Needles.

"It's like being on a whole new planet," Drew says while gazing ahead.

"It's so different from New York. Everything from the landscape to the weather to the lifestyle. I mean, don't get me wrong. I adore the city and how bustling it is with people from all over the world. And the fact that you can get any type of food at all hours of the day and night. You definitely can't get that in Moab. But living in a crowded city can feel so stifling. I love being able to travel all over the place for work, and when I get to come to places like this, where it's all open spaces and the landscape is practically endless, it's like a reset. Even the air here is different. It smells like shrubbery and dirt . . . but in a good way." I take a breath. "I get to miss New York for a bit while basking in this openness." I scrunch my nose. "God, that sounds corny."

"Not corny in the slightest, Dunn. I totally get what you mean."

He turns his head to me, a sweet half smile tugging at his mouth.

"It's probably weird that I dreamed up an entire travel series because of one vacation with my grandma."

"It's not. At all," Drew says. "Honestly, I get so sick of working on shows where the only objective is to appease advertisers or executives. This series actually has sentiment and meaning."

His words settle at the center of my chest, like a warm hug. "That's a nice thing to say."

"Just speaking the truth."

"Well, truthfully, I wanted to pitch something else entirely—something a lot more ambitious."

"Which was?"

"An international series in the Philippines." Excitement bubbles in my stomach at the mention of the idea. "When I was little, my grandma would show me pictures of Palawan. She and my mom are originally from Northern Luzon, but their family loved vacationing on Palawan Island. The white-sand beaches there look so gorgeous. And there are all these rocky cliffs covered in this lush, vibrant greenery. She would talk about how growing up she had a blast exploring all these hidden coves and lagoons. When I was little I'd ask her to tell me about her adventures there over and over. We always said we'd go there for a family vacation, but we never got around to it. My parents were always busy with work and traveling. And then my grandma passed away when I was in high school."

"I'm sorry," Drew says quietly, his eyes fixed on me.

"That's life. You don't always get to do what you plan." I clear my throat. "Producing a travel show in the Philippines would be another dream come true. Actually, having a travel series where I can highlight lesser-known vacation spots there and around the world would be the ultimate dream."

Drew frowns. "So why didn't you pitch that?"

"International travel shows are expensive. The network wasn't going to give me, a producer who's never been in charge of a series before, a generous budget and just let me have at it. They tend to only do that if you've proven yourself. And this Utah series is how I'll hopefully prove myself."

That excitement in my stomach turns to anxiety. If only I had a different host, I'd be one thousand percent confident of producing a killer series and blowing away the network execs. But Blaine is such a wild card. We're not even two weeks into shooting and he's already derailed so much. So far we've all been able to contain it . . . but can I really do damage control for almost five more weeks?

I push the thought aside just as Drew speaks.

"Don't take this the wrong way, because I think what you're doing with this Utah series is brilliant. Not only will the national parks in Utah get a boost from this show, but I think all the national parks across the country will too." Drew pauses to clear his throat. "But you shouldn't sell yourself short. You should have pitched your international idea to the network. I think they would have gone for it."

"You don't know the network execs."

I think back on the patronizing lecture that Byron gave me the day I pitched *Discovering Utah* on the importance of taking risks.

"You'll never know what will work out if you don't try, Alia."

"That's nice advice in theory. But when your ideas constantly get shot down, you start to pick up on what will work for you and what won't. But that's par for the course in this business. The network executives—the people who say yes or no to everyone's pitches—are all old white dudes who don't seem to want to try anything different. They almost always say yes to the male pro-

ducers' pitches, though—more often than they do to female producers' pitches."

I mention the reality TV series that a male colleague pitched
where a dozen people signed up to work at a horse-racing stable,
then competed to see who was the best at breeding horses.

Drew squints at me. "Wait, what?"

"There were multiple episodes filmed where the contestants
had to collect sperm from stallions and then inseminate the
mares. That was the whole hook of the show."

He stammers, then shakes his head when he gives up on trying to say anything.

"And then there was the documentary that another producer
pitched about squirrels. Like, just following around squirrels all
day, every day, for weeks. That was a snoozefest. And a ratings
bomb. But he got another series idea green-lit because the execs
thought he deserved another chance." I swallow, trying hard not
to sound too bitter. "Brooke has had to fight for almost every series she's pitched. She's won awards for her work and still her
ideas get rejected a lot of the time. And she's not the only woman
at Expedition who goes through that. I'll have to go through that
too if I want to keep producing my own shows. I accept that. I
mean, I'm not happy about it, but I'm not surprised that I have to
do it either."

Drew looks at me. "I'm sorry they've stifled you and made you
feel like your ideas aren't good enough. But believe me when I
tell you that this series is one of the best I've worked on. The
script is tight and well written. The ideas you come up with for
opening and closing shots are brilliant. You have an artist's eye.
And the crew loves working with you."

I stammer as I try to say thank you, blown away at the caliber
of his compliments.

"It's upsetting that you haven't been given the opportunity to showcase your skills before this," he says. "I know we haven't worked together for very long, but I could tell right away how talented you are. You're one of the best I've ever worked with. And when you finally get to make your international series, I'm certain people will love it."

It takes a second for me to process his words. But when they finally register, I feel heartened in a way I haven't before whenever I've chatted with guys about the frustrations of being a woman in this industry.

"Thank you," I say. "That means . . . honestly, it's hard to put into words how much that means."

He flashes the most beautiful smile. For a minute we share another comfortable silence while taking in the scenery. Then we decide to hike back.

Drew pops up, offering his hand to help me up.

"Such a gentleman, even in the wilderness," I joke as we walk back down to the other edge of the rock to meet up with the trail.

"I think it's fitting that the subway gentleman be a wilderness gentleman too."

I stop dead in my tracks and turn to look at him. He wears a smug grin.

"Wait, you . . . you saw that photo?"

"Yup."

"Shit." I cover my face with my hands and groan.

Just then I feel Drew's hands on my wrists. He gently pulls my hands down. "It's okay, Dunn. I was flattered."

"That's a relief. But still . . . kind of embarrassing for you to see it."

"Is it?"

He offers me his hand again as I make my way down the side of Whale Rock to the trail on the ground.

"Well, yeah," I say after my feet hit the dirt and we head back to the parking lot. "When I took that photo, I didn't think anything would come of it. I didn't even know your name."

"I saw it the night after we met up," he says.

"You did?"

He nods. "When I saw the original tweet, I figured that was you. I was psyched. I thought I'd be able to message you, but your DMs were closed. So then I thought if I tagged you in a post, you'd see it and then I could get ahold of you . . ."

"You did?"

"Yeah, but you never responded. I'm guessing your notifications were blowing up."

"Um, yeah, actually. I turned off the notifications on my phone and stopped checking my Twitter account because there were so many."

"I figured. When I never heard from you, I was pretty crushed." His expression turns sheepish.

"Why didn't you mention this when we saw each other at the hotel again?"

"I was going to, but you seemed kind of upset about it still. I didn't think you wanted to talk about it more than you had to."

"Right." I glance down at the ground. "I was crushed too," I say softly. "I had such a great time with you. I was eager to pick up where we left off."

I'm blown away at how candid we're both being with each other right now. But that's the beauty of hiking with someone. You're either walking side by side or one person in front of the other. You don't have to make direct, unnerving eye contact. It's like being in a makeshift confessional out in nature. It's so much easier to be honest when you don't have to look someone in the eye.

"It was the biggest letdown when you never called," I admit.

I pick up the pace, walking ahead of him. We reach Drew's

truck, he unlocks it, and we climb in without another word. We're on the highway when he finally speaks.

"You don't believe that I actually shattered my phone on the subway tracks, do you?" His tone isn't accusatory. More like inquisitive.

"I didn't at first," I say, looking out the passenger window. "I believe you now, though."

"What made you change your mind?"

"How you acted during the first day of filming. The way you stood up for Rylan and called out Blaine. A truly good person who gives a crap about those kinds of things wouldn't stand someone up."

"You're right. I wouldn't."

"I guess I've just gotten burned one too many times in the dating and relationships department. I always jump to the worst conclusion until proven otherwise."

It's weird admitting that out loud to Drew just now. I've thought it a million times to myself over the past few years, but I've never said it.

I turn my head to look at him; he's nodding along like he can relate to what I've said. Even though our conversation has taken a slightly serious turn, the comfort remains.

The next several miles to Moab pass in silence. Then as we pull into town, Drew clears his throat.

"You know, when I walked into the hotel meeting room my first day in Moab, I was shocked to see you. More than shocked, actually . . . I thought that maybe . . ."

I hold my breath, my heart pounding as I wait for him to finish his sentence. He pulls into the hotel parking lot and turns the engine off. He turns to me and opens his mouth, but nothing comes out. A long second passes; then he shakes his head and turns away.

I have no idea what to say in this awkward, tension-riddled moment, so I grab my pack from the back seat. "Okay, well . . . thanks for scouting with me. And, um, for the ride too," I say quietly. I open the door and hop out, but before I can close it, Drew stops me.

"Dunn, wait a sec."

I stand just outside the passenger seat. He stares at me with a new kind of intensity. The longer I look at him, the more I question it. Intensity doesn't seem like the right word. Maybe regret?

My stomach does a backflip, and I swallow. Damn. Just his gaze is doing things to me.

"I should have done everything differently the night we met." The edge of his jaw bulges, and he rasps a breath.

"Like what?"

He's twisted in his seat to face me, his arm braced on the top of the steering wheel. "I should have said screw it and gone home with you."

His chest heaves, and he runs his tongue along his bottom lip. I have to bite my lip just to keep myself from diving across the seat and taking his mouth for myself.

My gaze fixes on his eyes and how wild they look when he speaks. "What would you have done when we got to my apartment?"

He swallows, his neck flushing red. "I would have waited until you shut the door behind you. Then I would have pressed your—"

A car honk interrupts us. We turn our heads in the direction of the sound, which is a few spaces away from the spot where Drew's parked. Rylan waves at us as she hops out of Wyatt's van. Both of them hold stacks of pizza boxes in their arms.

"Surprise!" she says. "Dinner! Haley's treat. So nice of her, right?"

My mouth opens, but I say nothing. I step back from Drew's

truck and shut the door. On the inside, I'm a mass of invisible flames and arousal. I have to blink twice to get my bearings back.

A few seconds later I nod at them and holler "Oh great!" to Rylan. The smell of garlic and cheese hits my nostrils as she and Wyatt walk into the hotel.

But even the prospect of yummy food after a long day of shooting doesn't hold a candle to the prospect of Drew finishing his thought about what exactly he wanted to do to me the night we met.

And maybe, just maybe, he'd be up for showing me now.

I turn around, ready to ask him, but he's gone. Then I spot him walking into the hotel entrance without a second look back at me.

THREE SLICES OF PIZZA, ONE CAN OF BEER, AND TWO hours later, I'm sitting on my hotel bed, staring at my phone.

It's driving me nuts the way Drew left things earlier. He skipped out on pizza with the crew in Haley's room. Wyatt said he texted him to say he couldn't join because he was FaceTiming with his niece and nephew.

I try to focus on the cute image that conjures up, but that only distracts me for a minute. I can't stop thinking about Drew and what he said to me earlier. How we flipped from coworkers with a weird and strained history to coworkers who were flirting up a storm.

For the umpteenth time this evening, I contemplate texting him . . . but I don't want to interrupt if he's visiting with family. But I also don't want to show up to the set tomorrow morning with this unresolved tension. It will make it impossible to focus.

I cover my face with my hand and I groan. I'm thirty-two years old. Why am I acting like some insecure tween? How beyond embarrassing to be agonizing over a text message.

I straighten my posture, drop my hand from my face, and smack the bed. No more second-guessing myself. All I need to do is send one simple text message.

So I type one out.

We should talk about what happened earlier.

But before I can send it, Drew texts me.

My stomach takes a tumble. And then I take a breath and read his message.

Drew: Hey. I think I owe you an explanation.

Me: You think?

When I send the message, I immediately regret it. That sounded way, way too dismissive. I quickly send a goofy face emoji, then cup my face in my free hand and groan. God, I am so, so bad at this.

But he replies with a "haha," and I let out a relieved exhale.

Drew: But srsly . . . sorry for what I said earlier. Kinda inappropriate.

I frown at my phone screen. Inappropriate? Now I'm confused as hell. Because thinking back on our interaction, I feel like I was sending a million positive signals to him that I was into what he was saying. How I hung on his every word, how I couldn't take my eyes off him, the ragged way I was breathing when we talked about the night we met.

I start to type a message asking him to clarify, to tell him that he doesn't have anything to apologize for because I loved everything he said—but he texts me first.

Drew: I got caught up in the moment, talking about our date. That shouldn't have happened, especially now that we're coworkers. We agreed to forget it . . . so that's what I'm hoping we can do with my slip up.

Drew: Can we move on as colleagues?

His change in feelings hits like a bucket of cold water to the face. I guess this afternoon of scouting and riding together didn't mean nearly as much to him as it meant to me.

I dry swallow the lump in my throat, then take another breath before I reply.

Me: No worries! Already forgotten.

And then I place my phone on the nightstand and stumble to the bathroom to get ready for bed, feeling like the biggest loser on the planet.

"I KNOW I'VE said this about five thousand times since we arrived this morning, but holy hell, this is gorgeous." Haley gazes around the trailhead of the Narrows.

This trail is the most popular one in Zion National Park. It's actually a river—the Virgin River, which cuts through a section of the canyons at this end of the park. Visitors wade through the water, which varies in depth from ankle-deep to chest-high, to admire the slot canyons that surround them.

Everyone in the crew has stopped to gawk about a million times during our first day of shooting. I haven't set foot here since I was a kid. Every few minutes I catch myself staring openmouthed at the endless red canyons that make up this park.

Haley stops to snap some photos on her phone. "When shooting is over, I'm going to come back here like a proper tourist."

I smile as I refocus back on today's shot list.

"This place is something else, isn't it?" Drew comments from nearby.

A handful of days after he rejected me via text, and I can count on one hand the number of times we've had a conversation— always work related.

Judging by the neutral expression on his face every single time he's spoken to me, he's forgotten about our conversation while hiking Whale Rock. There's not one smidgen of awkwardness in his interactions with me . . . which makes all those times I blush and stammer in front of him all the more humiliating.

Because he's clearly moved on from our flirty interlude . . . while I can't stop thinking about it.

I sigh and stare unblinking at the tablet until Drew walks over to Joe.

Haley comes up to me. "You think Blaine is going to show up today?"

I check the time. He's already an hour late. I shrug and shake my head, then let out my breath in a slow, silent hiss. "I'm sure Blaine has more important things to do. Like drop acid and try to free-climb a random rock face totally naked."

Haley lets out a chuckle, then sobers. "Sorry, I don't mean to dwell on him. I know he's causing enough stress for you already."

I offer a weak smile. "It's okay. It's part of the job."

Just then Rylan walks up, her phone in hand. "Colton says that he's on his way with Blaine. And he apologizes for the late start, but I guess Blaine was impossible to wake up this morning. Plus, the drive from that exclusive resort he's staying at is over an hour away."

The stress knot in my neck eases the tiniest bit knowing that Blaine is at least headed here.

"Thanks for the update," I say.

"How are things going with you and Colton, by the way?" Haley asks.

She grins wide. "Really good. He's the sweetest. He's taking me to some hidden hiking spot next week."

"Aww, puppy love," Haley teases as she gently nudges Rylan's arm.

Rylan blushes. The smile doesn't budge from her face. She fidgets, then folds her hands in front of her. "I just can't believe I randomly met someone while shooting this series—and that we hit it off so well!"

Haley studies the schedule for today. "Well, given that our diva douchebag host is only an hour and a half late today, we'll wrap up shooting at the Narrows sometime in the late after-noon." She looks up at me. "You sure you don't want to at least get a shot of him trying out Angel's Landing? It's the most popu-lar hike in the park."

I shake my head. "Positive. As breathtaking as the Angel's Landing hike is, it's incredibly dangerous. People have died hik-ing it. And as much as I despise Blaine, I don't want him to die."

Rylan whips her head to me, her eyes wide with terror. "Are you serious? People die on that trail?"

I nod. "There's a part where you have to scale the edge of a cliff and the trail is super narrow. Like, less than two feet wide. There's a chain bolted to the rock that you hold on to, but still. If you lose your footing or your grip, you fall. And I mean, Blaine would definitely fall."

Haley and Rylan nod in agreement. Just then I hear the sound of chanting. I turn to where the dirt path leads from the Narrows hike to the parking lot and see Blaine marching, wear-ing nothing but tight yellow boxer briefs that highlight the un-sightly bulge between his legs and tall hiking boots.

"Jesus Christ," Haley mutters. "Where is his shirt? And his pants? It's barely fifty degrees out right now."

A handful of tourists stop and stare at Blaine while he sings some song I don't recognize. As insane as it is that he's showing up to a shoot dressed like a maniac, it could be worse. Today there are only half a dozen people around to witness this spec-tacle. If we were filming this in the summer when Zion is packed to the max with tourists, there would be hundreds of people observing this freak show.

He marches up to me, heaving a breath through a wide smile.

I'm aching to take him to task over his wholly inappropriate attire, but I bite my tongue. Best to just ignore it, get him into his gear for the shoot, and start filming.

He holds his arms out like he's presenting himself. In the position he's in and the way that he's dressed, his highlighter-yellow crotch is the focus. A couple of tourists gasp. A man nearby covers the eyes of the small child he's with.

"Since I have to wear a wet suit and all that sponsored gear, I figured I'd show up on set ready to dress," he announces proudly.

I force a smile that probably looks more like a grimace. Blaine doesn't seem to notice or care, his chest puffed out and his hands on his hips.

"Great idea," I say through gritted teeth, trying my hardest not to look at that godforsaken hump in the front of his fluorescent underwear. "Drew will show you where the gear is so you can get set up. Hey, Drew!"

Drew jogs over to us. His brow flies up to his hairline as he stares at Blaine, but he reins it in a second later. He takes Blaine to the spot where we've set up the equipment and gear under an open tent.

"Thank God we've got a wet suit sponsor for this episode. Can you imagine if we had to film him hiking the river in that getup?" Haley shudders.

I press my eyes shut. "Please. I don't need a mental picture of that."

When I glance over at the open tent, Blaine is almost dressed. I overhear him suggesting to Drew that he leave the top of his wet suit open so he can display his chest at "maximum aesthetically pleasing levels."

I close my eyes and take a breath. "Give me strength," I mutter to myself. Then I walk over to the river.

Three hours later, we've only filmed half the number of scenes scheduled for today. Blaine started strong, nailing the first scene. But now he's stuck flubbing his lines like usual, even with Drew spoon-feeding each one to him.

Blaine stands at the beginning of the trailhead, where the water in the Virgin River is the shallowest and the calmest. It's a stunning shot with the river snaking all the way to the horizon flanked by the massive brownish-red slot canyons. The crisp blue hue of the sky is the perfect backdrop.

"Join us next week when we explore the unique and mesmerizing beauty of Br . . . Brinson . . ."

"Bryce Canyon National Park!" we all say in frustrated unison.

Blaine frowns. "Jeez. You don't have to yell."

"Okay, cut! Let's take five, okay? We'll set up some B-roll shots while you take a break. Keep practicing saying 'Bryce.'"

As I throw on a pair of neoprene socks and lace up my waterproof hiking boots, I hear Blaine mutter something about not needing to practice. Then he announces he's going to do tai chi in the water in order to prepare for the next take. I bite down until pain shoots through the back of my neck. I'm going to shatter my teeth because of this guy.

Wading through the water, I scope out the surroundings. I notice there aren't any tourists near us anymore, which means we could get a clean panorama of the river and surrounding slot canyon.

I tell that to Wyatt, who takes the camera off the tripod and props it on his shoulder. A nearby boulder jutting out of the water about fifteen feet into the air catches my attention. If we could get a camera shot from up there, we could do an overhead shot here too.

I turn around and relay my idea to Wyatt, who studies the boulder in response.

I walk ahead to the rock with Wyatt splashing behind me. I scramble up the jagged rock face and stand up, gauging the steadiness of the rock.

"Yeah, it's totally solid up here," I say, stomping my boot on the boulder to test the sturdiness. I look up and try to gauge the position of the sun behind that wall of clouds.

I spot Drew and Joe making their way through the water in this direction, several feet behind where Wyatt stands.

"Be careful," Wyatt calls. I look down and see him staring up at me, a terrified frown on his face.

"I am. Promise." I squint at the clouds. "Okay, while we're waiting for the sun to come out, let's at least get some footage of this part of the river."

I turn around and scan the jagged rock face on the other side of the river. I point to an area where the water rushes over a cluster of boulders, then spin around to address Wyatt and Joe. "Joe, can you get—"

I stumble on the edge of the boulder and lose my footing. Instinct tells me to plant my feet on the rock to steady myself. But then when I stomp down, there's nothing. And that's when I realize I'm falling.

WHEN I HIT the icy-cold water, I gasp. I choke on a mouthful of water as I struggle to gain my footing underwater. This end of the Narrows is barely waist-high, but because of how I fell, I land back-first and am completely submerged.

The frigid water feels like a million ice picks plunging into my skin. I kick my feet until I hit solid ground below, then shoot above the surface.

Around me all I hear are shouts: "Are you okay?" and "Holy shit!"

My heart is pounding and my chest heaves as I struggle to breathe. Every inhale is a stab to my chest. It's like someone is squeezing their fist around my lungs.

Every time I try to stand up, I wobble and fall back into the water. I attempt to wipe away the soaking wet hair plastered across my face, but my hands and face are so numb I can barely feel anything.

Just then I hear splashing. I look up and see Drew barreling toward me. He stops in front of me, his brow furrowed and his eyes sharp with worry, then bends down and grabs me. "We gotta get you out of this water."

He scoops me up and starts walking. I mutter something about how I can manage, even though I know I can't. It's like a reflex, saying I'm okay when I'm not, or saying I've got this when I know I don't.

A gust of wind whips around me and turns my soaking-wet skin to frost. My teeth chatter.

"It's fine," I mumble. "I'm fine."

Another reflex, another reassurance I know isn't true.

"It's okay," Drew says through a breath. "I've got you."

I try to focus on my surroundings, but my vision goes blurry.

I clutch Drew's shoulders. "Can't see . . . very well," I slur.

"Well, that's because you fell in icy-cold water, Dunn." Drew grunts, then stops walking to tighten his hold around me. "Just hang on. We're almost to land. We'll get you warm and dry. Promise."

I close my eyes and lean my head against his chest until the splashing sound stops. I look down and see that instead of rocks and water, there's rocks and red dirt. We're back on land.

Drew yells something before speedily walking us to the tent setup. Then he sets me on the ground and props me up to lean against something giant and sturdy. He crouches down so that we're face-to-face, then presses his hands against my cheeks. The slightest hint of panic flashes in his eyes. Then he heaves a breath, scoops me up into his arms once more, and takes off.

I close my eyes, still feeling cloudy-headed. There are hurried footsteps behind us, then Haley asking something I can't make out.

After what feels like seconds, I open my eyes and see that we're back at the parking lot. Drew sets me down so I'm sitting on the concrete, my back against Wyatt and Joe's van. He disappears, yelling something I can't understand to someone I can't see. I open my mouth to say "thank you for helping me out of the water and carrying me all the way from the river to the parking lot," but my lips won't stop quivering. My teeth won't stop chattering either.

A beat later Haley comes running over and tugs my jacket off. "Let's get rid of those wet clothes, okay?"

I nod and try my best to shrug out of the sleeves, but I'm shaking so hard that I can barely bend my arm. "Sorry," I slur again.

Haley grips my face in her hands. She's frowning, her brown eyes wild with worry. "It's okay. Just try to breathe slowly, okay?"

I stop forcing my arm to move. Haley grabs me with gentle hands and tugs off my jacket, then my shirt. I move to try to unbutton my jeans, but my hands are still shaking so hard that I can't get a steady grip on them.

Just then a giant pair of hands cover mine. I look up and see Drew's face twisted in concern.

"Why don't you let Haley do that," he says gently.

I nod. He scoots me forward, then settles behind me, his arm wrapping around my torso. It's not until I realize how warm his skin feels on mine that I register what's happening. Drew's shirtless torso is now shrouding my shirtless torso. My eyes go wide at the realization, but then I remember that I'm still wearing my bra. I close my eyes for a long second and try to ease my racing heart.

Haley pulls off my boots and jeans; then Drew stands and lifts me up. Then he sets me inside the van. I land on something soft and slick and plush. A sleeping bag. Drew is crouched over me wearing only the worn jeans I saw him in this morning. He tucks me inside the sleeping bag and I hug my arms around myself, gritting my teeth at just how cold my skin feels.

He turns around and jumps out of the van. "Someone's gotta jump in there and warm her up."

Behind me I hear Blaine say, "I'll do it." Even in my shattered state I cringe at the eagerness in his voice. I'd rather succumb to hypothermia than let Blaine get anywhere near me.

"Back off," Drew growls.

"Why don't you go smoke a bowl of something," Haley says.

I close my eyes to the sound of Blaine muttering something unintelligible, then stomping away.

"You get in there and warm her up," Haley says, her voice softer.

"You sure that's a good idea?" Drew asks.

"Are we seriously going to have an argument about who is going to warm her up? You're the biggest dude here other than Blaine, and there's no way in hell I'm letting him go near her. You're our best bet at warming her up in the fastest amount of time. There's no way we can get an ambulance out here to help before her internal temperature drops to dangerous levels. Do it."

There's a thud, then the whooshing sound of the van door shutting. Then tugging at the sleeping bag. Then instant, comforting warmth.

Eyes still closed, I let out a hum.

"I'm jumping in the sleeping bag to warm you up, okay? I know this'll be weird, but we have to. To get your core temperature back up."

I let out an "mmm" noise and nod. There's the sound of fabric rustling, then the tug of the zipper. He snakes his arms around my torso once more, then presses his legs against the backs of mine. I curl my toes, relishing how toasty his feet feel. His entire body shrouds mine. *How is he so warm? It's like cuddling into a heated blanket.*

I let out a sigh. Slowly, as I start to warm up, my brain clears up. My heartbeat steadies, and I open my eyes. All I see is Drew's arm braced over me.

"You're gonna be fine," Drew says softly.

When I blink, my eyelids grow heavy. It's like the rush of adrenaline has left me. My muscles loosen. It's a struggle to stay awake, but I manage to say one more thing before I fade.

Against my back his heart thuds. "Sorry about this, Dunn," he says in a low voice.

"Don't be sorry." I don't slur this time. "Thanks for being so warm."

10

I WAKE TO THE SOUND OF THUDDING.

I immediately push myself to sit up, but my head feels as heavy as a cinder block. I brace myself with both hands on the floor, hunched over.

"Easy," Drew says from behind me.

The thudding persists. It's coming from outside, I realize.

"What's that noise?" I ask.

With his arms on my shoulders, he slowly helps me back to a lying-down position.

"My truck got a flat. Wyatt and Joe are putting on the spare," he says.

"God, this shoot really is cursed," I groan, pressing the heels of my hands against my eyes. "Busted equipment, a nightmare host, me falling into the river. Now your truck."

"Come on, now, Dunn. Let's not get dramatic." Drew's playful tone rings softly in my ear.

Goose bumps flash across my shoulders as he extracts himself from the sleeping bag. He crawls over to the far end of the van and crouches next to a large black backpack. When my eyes focus, I blink twice, then stare, appreciating for the millionth time just how built Drew is. I do a slow once-over of him as he searches for something inside his bag. Everything from his back to his arms to his chest to his stomach is lean, hard mass. My mouth waters. I swallow as I fixate on his sculpted rump and thighs. *Damn, damn, damn.* He's got one of those strong, functional physiques that isn't hairless or oiled to hell like some preened and primped underwear model. Drew's look is the rugged counter to that. He's like a strong and manly lumberjack with a stylish haircut and stubble. I decide right then and there it's my favorite aesthetic on the planet.

Blinking furiously, I force my stare to a random spot on the floor. I absolutely shouldn't be checking out one of my crew members. That's an ethical and professional violation if I've ever heard one.

"Aha." He turns to me, a grin plastered on his face as he holds up a thermos.

Then he crawls over and kneels next to me. My face heats and a bevy of inappropriate images swirl through my brain involving Drew on his knees.

I frown at nothing in particular. "What's that?"

"Hot tea." He unscrews the lid of the thermos and pours some out into the lid, which serves as a cup. Then he brings it to his mouth and blows on it. "Are you able to lean up?"

I nod, propping myself up on my elbows. I move slowly this time so as to not give myself a head rush. Then Drew cradles the back of my head with his free hand while slowly, carefully bringing the cup to my lips.

"Careful. It's still pretty warm," he says.

I hum while taking a sip, the hot liquid soothing my throat. All the while my heart races in my chest at Drew's doting gesture. But I know better than to get carried away. I heard what Haley said earlier. She practically commanded him to warm me up. He's just carrying out her orders.

"You need to drink this whole thermos," he says softly, bring-ing the cup back to my lips. "It'll help you warm up on the inside."

I let out a moan after another swallow. "I'll do my best."

"And after that, we should get you checked out at a hospital."

I shake my head while gulping. "No way."

Drew frowns at me. "Dunn, you probably had hypothermia. You still might."

I shake my head, cutting him off. "I don't. I'm not shivering anymore. My skin is warm. I'm not slurring my words or foggy-headed. Clearly my core temperature is back up."

I lean my back against the interior of the van. He sets the thermos to my side, then sits cross-legged in front of me.

His eyebrows crash together as he sighs; then he reaches over and presses the back of his hand to my forehead. Then he turns his hand over and cups my cheek for a long second as he stares at me, his expression easing. If anyone else tried to pull that move on me, I'd shove them away. But there's something so sweet and doting in Drew's gesture.

"Drew, I'm fine. I promise, if I still felt off, I'd tell you. I wouldn't put myself at risk like that."

He pulls his hand away. "Okay," he says softly.

I shift and the sleeping bag slips down, exposing my bra. I quickly pull it up, my face heating.

"Thank you for everything you did," I say.

"Of course."

There's a long moment of silence where we just look at each other while I drink more tea. I sigh. I need to say this. Now's as good a time as any.

"Look, I know . . . I know we've had kind of a weird start with each other so far. And we've had some awkward moments during this shoot . . ."

Drew looks off to the side while rubbing his jaw.

I clear my throat. "I really do like working with you, Drew. And I just want to say, you're the best field coordinator I've ever worked with. Thank you for all your hard work and for having my back so many times."

His eyes brighten the slightest bit at what I've said. "Of course. And thanks."

He sounds taken aback, like he's surprised I would say any of this.

"And I'm sorry you had to jump half-naked into a sleeping bag with me," I say. "I'm sure that counts as some weird kind of hostile work environment."

"Don't say that." He frowns, like it's absurd I would even think to apologize.

I run my finger along the rim of the plastic cup. "I just don't want to cross any professional boundaries. If you felt like you had no choice, like you were coerced into doing that with me . . ."

"Hey." His firm tone compels me to look up at him. "I didn't feel that way at all. Don't be ridiculous. It was an emergency."

I sigh, both relieved that he feels that way and disappointed in myself that I'm clearly the only one who got the tiniest bit of enjoyment out of it.

"Okay. Thank you," I say softly.

I drain the last of the tea in my mug, and he leans over to pour more. "I would have done the same for anyone on the crew, so please don't even worry about it."

"Even Blaine?" I say as I hold the cup to my mouth.

"Nope. I'd let him freeze to death."

I laugh just as I sip, which causes a coughing fit. Drew leans over to pat me on the back.

"You good?" he asks, his brows furrowed together.

I nod and clear my throat.

He sits back, resting his elbows on the tops of his bent knees.

"You know, cuddling you for the last hour wasn't the worst thing I've ever had to do on the job, Dunn."

I could swear I see a glimmer in his eyes when he admits that. The corner of his mouth twitches up, like he's trying to keep a smile at bay. Inside I grow warm, and my stomach goes giddy.

"Really?" I shake my head, chuckling.

"Really. The things I had to do as a production assistant make today look like a spa getaway," he says.

I chuckle again. "What did you have to do?"

"The usual. Coffee runs, lugging all the gear by myself, crowd control, locking down locations, all the grunt work every PA has to do."

I nod along, remembering how I did those exact same jobs when I first started.

"One time, the cinematographer on a nature documentary I was working on texted me in the middle of the night to buy him socks," Drew says.

I cover my mouth as I swallow so I don't do a spit take.

Drew runs a hand through his hair, grinning. "Apparently he had been up for three days straight editing while wearing the same pair of socks and didn't have time to run home or to the store and get himself fresh ones."

"Jesus," I mutter, thankful I never had to do that.

"Then there was that one time a director asked me to pick up condoms on my way to set because he had a hot date that night and was sure he was going to score," Drew says. "He demanded that I buy four boxes of magnums. I had to drive to three different drugstores to find enough boxes."

My head falls back as I laugh.

"So don't even worry about what happened, Dunn." His expression softens to a sweet smile. "It was essentially like taking a nap in the middle of the day. It was pretty nice, actually."

My heart thunders at just how sincere he sounds. Maybe he did like it a little bit, after all.

"Do I get to hear any of your awful PA stories?" he asks.

"God, there aren't enough hours in the day. Okay, you want to hear the most outrageous thing I had to do?"

"Yes."

"I was working on that *Planet Earth* spin-off Expedition did, like, ten years ago. One of the head producers got arrested for drunk driving when we were shooting for a few months in the Pacific Northwest. She got a fine and community service, which she was pissed about. She swore up and down she wasn't going to do the community service because she worked fourteen-hour days and just didn't have the time."

"Wow." Drew grimaces. "She sounds like an entitled jerk."

"Oh, she was. Very much so."

"How did she get out of her community service?"

"She didn't. She was best friends with the executive producer—they were film school buddies, I think. So the EP told me to report to her community service, lie and say that I was her, and do it for her so the producer wouldn't have to."

Drew's jaw drops. "Are you kidding me?"

"I wish I were."

"And you just went along with it?"

"I was barely twenty-two and determined as hell to impress the EP because I wanted her to hire me on her next shoot. It was two weeks of picking up garbage off the side of the road. Totally miserable—but it paid off. The EP and producer were appreciative and hired me on as a production coordinator for their next series."

Drew's expression turns bewildered. "That's really fucked up they made you do that. And illegal."

"I wouldn't ever be okay with something like that now, of

course. And I would never, ever even think to ask that of anyone I work with. I was young and naive and eager to impress. A dangerous combo."

Young and naive and eager to impress . . . a dangerous combo.

That also perfectly describes how I got into the single worst relationship I've ever been in and why I'm the jaded dating and relationship cynic I am today . . .

I down the rest of the tea in my cup, then refill it. Just then I notice how energetic and lively I feel.

"I'm feeling a lot better," I say. "Thank you. For everything."

He raises an eyebrow at me and smirks. "Don't get sentimental on me, Dunn. It's unprofessional."

I tilt my head at him. "I like you a lot better like this."

"Like what? Me in my underwear serving you tea?"

I roll my eyes while chuckling and looking off to the side. When I lock eyes with Drew once more, there's a sparkle I recognize immediately. It's the same hungry stare he flashed at me that night at the Brazen Head.

I run my gaze over his bare chest and legs. "You in your underwear serving me tea is definitely a plus."

He wags an eyebrow at me, and my stomach does a flip. I swallow to keep myself in check.

"But what I meant is I like that we're getting along now," I say. "It feels a million times better than clashing with you."

His expression softens. "I gotta admit that I like this too. I like you a lot, Dunn."

His pointed look sends goose bumps all over my skin.

Just then there's pounding on the door, jolting me. Drew grabs a white T-shirt from the van floor, throws it on, then opens the door.

A frowning Wyatt stands there, his worried gaze flitting between us. "I've got some bad news."

I brace myself. "What is it?"

"Blaine took some edibles and passed out in the bed of Drew's truck." Wyatt looks off to the side, presumably where the truck is parked. "I don't think he's gonna be getting up for a few hours at the very least. And judging by that wall of dark clouds coming in, we've only got about two hours of shooting left."

"Fuck," Drew and I mutter at once.

Wyatt points his defeated gaze at me. "I'm sorry, Alia."

I shake my head. "No, I'm sorry. If I had been more careful when I was climbing around, I wouldn't have fallen into the river and we could have nailed this segment an hour ago."

Just then Drew gently grabs my shoulder and gives it a soft, encouraging squeeze. "Don't apologize. That was an accident. And it's not your fault Blaine is an unreliable flake."

I nod and say thanks, taken aback by how fiercely he attempts to comfort me.

Just then an idea hits. It's wild and completely reckless—but it just might work.

I sit up and turn to Drew. "I just thought of something."

TWENTY MINUTES LATER, the crew and I—sans Blaine—are back in the Narrows getting ready to film. In Blaine's place is Drew, standing in the knee-deep water several yards away from the start of the trail in a wet suit and ad-sponsored gear.

In the van, when I pitched the idea of Drew filming Blaine's remaining scenes for today, Drew hesitated. But then I explained that I just needed him as a sort of digital stand-in. We already had the episode intro filmed with Blaine. All we needed were some demo shots of the sponsored gear. In editing I could go back and lay over Blaine's face and voice. Drew was on board after that.

"Okay, guys!" I holler, standing in the water just a few feet away from him. "We've got exactly ninety minutes of sunlight and good weather left. That means we need to nail this segment as quickly as possible."

I gaze up at Drew, who's decked out head to toe in gear from BetBet Activewear, our sponsor for this episode, including a hat and sunglasses. I silently thank the heavens that they sent a size too big by mistake. Drew has about fifteen pounds of lean muscle on Blaine, so the gear fits him like a glove.

From a distance, with this much of his face covered, he looks similar to how Blaine looked when he had the gear on while filming earlier in the day.

For a split second Drew looks straight into Joe's camera with a deer-in-the-headlights look. I walk over to him.

"You sure you're okay with this?" I ask him.

He blinks, then nods. The color starts to return to his face. "Yeah. I'm good. I just had a bit of a flashback for a sec there."

"That's understandable. Take as much time as you need."

The focus in his eyes slowly returns the longer he looks at me. "I'm ready, Dunn."

"Wanna practice saying the intro just to warm up your voice?"

"Good idea."

I pat him gently on the arm and give him what I hope is an encouraging smile. Then I tell Wyatt and Joe that Drew is going to practice the intro to get comfortable.

"Hey, everyone." He beams wide, showcasing his perfectly straight white teeth. "On today's episode of *Discovering Utah*, we're hiking the Narrows at the stunning Zion National Park."

He goes into the short explanation of the park and this trail that he memorized to coach Blaine earlier. I'm blown away at how natural and charismatic Drew is on camera. His smile is inviting, not smug. When he talks, it's like he's having a one-on-one conversation with the viewer.

He raises his eyebrow, tilting his head ever so slightly while leaning on the walking stick. "Since it's springtime in Utah, that means the water is still pretty frigid. Wearing a wet suit is a must."

Wyatt gets a close-up as Drew explains the safety, clothing, and equipment recommendations before aiming that killer smile of his into the camera. "Now, let's get hiking."

He turns and starts hiking down the river, balancing himself with his walking stick.

"Cut!" I yell, then immediately start cheering. "That was amazing! Drew, you rocked it. Seriously."

Haley, Joe, Wyatt, Rylan, and the rest of the crew cheer and whoop. Drew's face turns bright red as his trademark flustered smile appears.

I walk up to him, grinning like a madwoman. "You knocked it out of the park."

"You sure? I thought my voice wobbled a bit at the beginning. I was kind of nervous."

"No way. I couldn't even tell. You were a natural. Funny, charismatic, engaging." He blushes once more, and I give his arm a squeeze. "I'm really glad you said yes to this."

"I don't think I could ever say no to you, Dunn." Again that cheeky look flashes in his eyes.

I smile at him, then quickly look away to the rest of the crew. "Okay, let's do the actual hiking shots." I turn back to Drew. "That okay with you?"

"Absolutely."

I walk back to my observation spot and watch as Drew nails multiple hiking shots along the river. We finish just as that wall of dark clouds rolls in.

"That's a wrap!" I yell.

Everyone claps and praises Drew while he once again adorably blushes. Then we all pack up the equipment and head for the van.

Haley walks up to me. "I think Drew just saved our asses."

I nod at her while skimming over tomorrow's shooting schedule on my tablet. Haley flips through a page on the script. "Too bad he can't be the host, right?"

"Ha. Right."

She walks over to Joe while I let the idea of Drew as the host take hold. Drew would be a million times easier to work with than Blaine. But no way would the network go for that. They hired Blaine because of the audience he'll bring to the show. So even though he's the most unpleasant and difficult human being I've ever worked with, I have to figure out a way to make it work with him.

Unless . . .

I look up and spot Joe and Wyatt loading the truck around Blaine's snoring body. Then I spot Drew hopping into the van and closing the door to change.

I pull out my phone and text him.

Free for a drink tonight? There's an idea I want to run by you.

11

SPOT DREW JUST AS HE WALKS INTO THE ZION CANYON
Brew Pub in Springdale, the town right next to Zion National
Park. I wave him down from my spot at the bar.

And then he pulls that delicious hand-on-the-small-of-my-back
move as he stops and stands next to me, and I nearly topple over
from the delicious shivers that tiny bit of contact gives me.

His hand falls away, and he flashes a smile. I do a quick once-
over while I pull myself together as he takes the stool next to me.
He's changed into dark jeans, a plain long-sleeved shirt, and a
lightweight jacket.

His eyes drift up and down. "Damn. You clean up nicely, Dunn."

Blush creeps up my chest and neck and all the way up my
cheeks. I smooth a hand over the burnt-orange flowy top I'm wearing with skinny jeans.

"These are the only clean things in my suitcase," I admit.

He lets out a low whistle. "I approve. You ought to put off doing laundry more often."

He raises an eyebrow at me, and I shove him lightly on the
shoulder. He rests his arm on the edge of the bar top, sitting just
inches from me. "If I didn't know any better, I'd say you were dressing up for me."

I laugh at the smug undercurrent in his tone. "Jeans and a top are not dressing up."

"They're not?" he jokes.

I shake my head. "Sorry. This is travel TV life. You don't dress to impress anyone—you just wear what's clean."

I could swear Drew's expression falls just a tad, but he quickly smiles. "How did you know I was craving a beer?"

The bartender walks over and takes Drew's order.

"I guess I have a sixth sense about these things." I take a sip of my own beer. "I figured we could both use a drink after today, and this place is the closest to our hotel."

Drew glances around, presumably to take in the lodge-like décor. Dark wood makes up the bar, the stools, the tables surrounding us, and even the floor. On the dark-hued walls are framed photos of nearby Zion National Park.

A server sets down Drew's beer and Drew takes a sip.

He grimaces. "Wow. That's weak."

"It's Utah. It's illegal to brew and sell beer higher than four percent alcohol."

"Jesus, really?" Horror clouds his expression.

"You didn't know that?" I chuckle.

"I didn't. Damn. I wouldn't have signed on to this project had I known I'd be spending six weeks drinking this stuff."

"Oh my gosh, such a baby. Six weeks of drinking something other than pretentious microbrews. It's a hard life you lead." I laugh and enjoy the teasing banter we've got going.

"So." He twists to me. "What did you want to talk to me about?"

I take a breath and prepare my pitch. "How would you feel about pulling a coup?"

His brow jumps. "That's a hell of a way to start a conversation."

"Okay, yeah, maybe that's not the best way to sell it. Look, the gist of it is that Blaine is a nightmare to work with. Wouldn't you agree?"

"To say the least." Drew sighs before taking another long swallow of his beer. "I can't believe the network wanted to sign him as host. The guy has the work ethic of a cranky toddler."

"He's a reality TV star with a huge social media following. They think his audience will translate to a viewership with the series. And the network heads aren't the ones who have to deal with him on a day-to-day basis. We are."

I take another sip of weak beer to ease the irritation creeping up inside me once more.

Concern paints Drew's face as he looks at me. "Does that bother you?"

"Does what bother me?"

"How they finally let you run your own series but refused to let you call the shots on such an important part of it?"

I stay silent for a moment, remembering all the shit I've had to eat working in this industry. How over the years I've put in longer hours than a lot of my male counterparts just to be noticed. How I've had to speak up twice as loud to get some of my bosses to pay attention to ideas I've come up with, because they always just deferred to their peers.

How it was pure luck that this opportunity for my own show worked out in the first place, because someone else's show fell through. How if just one exec had been feeling off that day, they probably would have said yes to someone else's pitch.

Every time I think about this, it always hits like punches to my gut. I'm getting my big break not because of my work ethic, but because of pure chance.

I glance at him. "Honestly? Yeah, it does bother me. But that's the industry. That's the opportunity I've been given. And all I can do is deliver a kick-ass project that makes the higher-ups at the network want to keep giving me jobs like this. That's the only way I'll ever get to make that series in Palawan. Someday. Hopefully."

"You will, Dunn."

In the quiet moment that follows as we sip our drinks, I'm heartened by his support.

After a bit I turn to him and refocus on why I asked him here in the first place.

"So. How are you feeling about what I've said?"

"Staging a coup on Blaine?"

I let out a breath. "Yes."

"And you want me as the host, I'm guessing?"

"I know this is unconventional."

"Unconventional?" he says incredulously.

"Okay, fine, it's akin to throwing out the playbook entirely. But honestly, Drew, you were amazing today. You lit up the screen in a way that I haven't seen before."

He squints at my hands, and I realize I'm gesturing wildly, I'm so enthusiastic.

I fold my hands and set them in my lap. "I mean it. Even the times when we actually got Blaine to give a shit and do a decent run-through of his lines, he still wasn't half as good as you. You have this natural charisma that translates so well on camera."

He purses his lips and glances at the floor. I can't tell if he's soaking in my compliments or he's turned off by the prospect of upending the show.

"Here's my thing: unless some miracle happens and Blaine magically develops a moral compass and a work ethic overnight, he's going to keep sleeping through call times and showing up to locations hungover, drunk, or high. We can't film a show with a host like that. The network execs are convinced Blaine is their guy and refused every time I've asked to replace him."

I pause to take a breath, then another sip of beer.

"But if I go to them with footage—with episodes already cut of you as the host, running lines and demoing scenes, I honestly think they'll get on board. I'd have something to present to them as a way, way better alternative than Blaine."

He sits up straight and squares his shoulders. "Sorry. I can't."

The hard set of his jaw tells me he doesn't want to say more. But I can't help but try to plead my case. I know without a doubt Drew is the perfect host for my series. I just need to convince him.

"Can you at least consider it? I honestly think this is the right thing to do. I can't imagine anyone else hosting this series. You're it."

The way he looks off and rolls his eyes sends a punch to my chest.

"You don't get it." He looks down at the bar top.

"Get what?"

He turns to look at me. "How hard this kind of stuff is for me."

"What do you mean? Drew, you did an incredible job today. You made it look so easy."

"Easy?" The sharp way he speaks makes me jolt back on my stool. He stares at me for a long second, like he can't believe what I've said.

"I'm sorry, I didn't mean to—"

Drew stands up and digs his wallet out of his pocket, then slaps cash on the counter. When he looks up at me, his jaw is tight and his eyes are hard.

"I can't shove aside my nerves just because you want to switch things up on a whim for your show."

"That's not how I feel at all. I know it must be difficult for you—"

"Do you? Do you really know how it feels to have your heart race like it's going to burst out of your chest? Or feel like you can't catch your breath no matter how deeply you breathe? Or feel like every cell in your body is freezing up while everyone around you is watching you fuck up?"

I stay quiet because he's right. I can't relate to any of that. So instead of saying yet another insensitive comment, I put my hand over his hand that's resting on the counter and hope that conveys the empathy I feel for him. He jerks away from my touch immediately.

All of a sudden he looks tired and beaten down. "When I told you about my stage fright, I thought you understood. I thought you were different from everyone else who told me I just needed to suck it up and get over it. But I guess I was wrong."

When Drew walks off, I slump in my stool and sip my drink, but it tastes bitter on my tongue. I push away the glass, feeling like the biggest, most insensitive jerk in the world.

How could I have misjudged this so badly? I remember so clearly the dread and pain on Drew's face when we hiked Whale Rock and he opened up to me about his stage fright.

I was so focused on my idea to switch hosts that I didn't stop and think about how it could affect Drew and his stage fright.

As I walk out of the bar, I hold my breath, hoping like hell I can at least make it outside before I let any tears fall.

I GAZE UP at the night sky. A zillion stars sparkle above me.

This is what I remember best about the Needles section of Canyonlands—how the night sky glitters. It's ten o'clock and we're setting up for the nighttime portion of our overnight Needles shoot. The sky is a deep black-blue hue, the most captivating color I've ever seen. Each of the stars bursts from the darkness like a tiny exploding diamond.

When I visited with Apong Lita, she held my hand as we counted the stars together. The memory warms me from the inside out, like an invisible hug.

It's a pleasant distraction from the quiet tension between Drew and me. Ever since our argument two days ago, we haven't spoken to each other except to chat briefly about work stuff on set. I texted him an apology the night he stormed out on me, but he never responded. I figured that means he wants to move on and never mention it again.

A scream jolts me back to the present. I whip my head around and see Blaine standing several feet away from me, his face to the sky, neck bent back at a weird angle, his mouth open.

"Hot damn these stars!" he announces. "Billions of them in the sky. Billions! Holy shit! And those rocks!" He points to the pitch-black horizon. "Those rocks over there are shaped like huge, giant dicks. Beautiful!"

I do my best to tune him out and hope that there aren't any mule deer nearby. They're sometimes spotted in the park and will most certainly freak out at Blaine's shouting.

I glance over at the crew. Joe, Wyatt, Haley, Drew, and Rylan are finishing setting up the gear for the shoot while I go over the shot list on my tablet.

A quarter mile away, all our tents are set up. We arrived a couple of hours before sunset to set those up first in the daylight so we could hike here, film, and then go straight to our tents and sleep for a bit before capturing the sunrise.

Holding my breath, I hazard another look at Blaine, who is still gawking up at the sky. He arrived hours late, chauffeured by Colton as usual, and has spent the fifteen minutes he's been here staring at the sky with his mouth wide open.

I say a silent prayer that he actually does his job with zero issues tonight.

From the corner of my eye, I watch as Drew approaches. "Hey." Seriousness paints the knit of his eyebrows.

"Oh. Hey."

I quickly glance back down at my tablet, the muscles in my

neck and shoulders tense at his approach. I don't have it in me to have another emotionally charged conversation with him right now.

"I just wanted to say that I'm sorry I never replied to your text." A heavy sigh rockets from his mouth. "And I'm sorry for how upset I got at you the other day."

"It's okay, Drew," I say quickly. "We don't need to rehash things."

"But I just wanted you to know that . . ."

I hold up a hand, cutting him off. "I said it's okay." I swallow, hoping the pause dials back the conviction in my tone. "I was the one who was out of line. And I think it's best if we just try to move on and not talk about it again. I've got an overnight shoot to focus on and Blaine to keep an eye on, and I don't want to lose track of him because then he might accidentally fall off a cliff or ingest a cactus and then the whole shoot will be—"

Just then Wyatt screams, "No!"

Both Drew and I whip our heads around and see Wyatt sprinting toward Blaine.

"What the . . ." Drew trails off the second Wyatt tackles Blaine.

Drew and I run over to them. The rest of the crew takes off for the scene too. A few seconds later we all reach Wyatt as he tries to pry open Blaine's mouth.

"What is going on?" I ask.

"He just ate a whole bag of edibles!" Wyatt grunts.

Something shiny catches my eye. I turn and see multiple empty mini vodka bottles next to Blaine. He's been drinking too. Panic surges through me. Joe and Drew squat down and grab either side of Blaine while Wyatt tries to pry open his mouth. My eyes go wide as I stand off to the side, breathless and waiting, hoping that Blaine hasn't ingested them.

A second later his mouth is wide open and my heart sinks. It's empty. Blaine swallowed the whole bag, which means he's drunk *and* high, and he's going to be completely out of it for the rest of the night—which means he will be utterly useless for filming. We'll probably have to take him to the hospital too.

"Shit, is he gonna OD? Should we call an ambulance?" Haley asks.

Joe shakes his head. "No, he'll be fine. He'll just pass out for the night and have some crazy-ass dreams."

Everyone turns to Joe, who shrugs. "I consumed a lot of edibles in my twenties."

My eyes water as dread and frustration fill me.

Wyatt gazes up at me, his brown eyes sorrowful. "I'm sorry, Alia."

I shake my head. "It's not your fault." I let out a sigh, thankful that I'm holding it together enough not to cry in front of everyone.

Blaine starts giggling. Wyatt, Joe, and Drew all stand up.

"I tried to get to him as soon as I saw him pull something out of his jacket pocket," Wyatt says.

"It's okay, Wyatt," I say softly. "I was keeping an eye on him. I just got distracted—"

"It's my fault." Drew rubs a hand over his face. When it falls away, he looks utterly dejected. "If I hadn't distracted you, this wouldn't have happened."

"Well, there's not a whole lot we can do about it now," I mutter.

Blaine gyrates against the dirt as he starts to chant something I can't understand. Rylan walks off into the darkness, returning later with Colton, whose youthful face breaks into a worried expression after Rylan tells him what happened.

He darts his stare to me. "Crap, Alia. I'm so sorry. Blaine went off on me about finding his lucky pukka shell necklace. He said he couldn't film without it. He swore it was in one of his packs by the tents so I was trying to find it. I should have been keeping an eye on him."

I repeat what I said to Wyatt—that it's not his fault and that it's okay. On the inside, my gut is curdling with anger and frustration. All of us have been working so hard to keep this shoot going—to babysit a grown man who continues to ruin everything.

But more than that, I'm angry at how the Needles shoot is now ruined—and angry at myself for the role I played in this. Instead of trying to reason with Drew, I should have just walked away and kept Blaine on my radar. And now because I didn't, the single most meaningful shoot in the whole series—the tribute to my grandmother—is ruined.

I almost let out a bitter, angry laugh. Because if I can't even nail this one overnight shoot, I have no business thinking that I can someday be in charge of an international series. Maybe it's a good thing I didn't have the guts to pitch *Hidden Gem Island Getaways*. Because ruining that, an entire series based on a place that was so special to my *apong* Lita, would hurt a million times worse than this.

"I'll host." Drew's sudden words jerk me out of my silent pity party.

"What?"

"I'll host. I did it before at the Narrows. I'll do it again now."

There's such certainty in his voice. It makes my head spin. Just a couple of days ago, he was adamantly against the idea of playing host ever again.

The rest of the crew look at Drew with confused yet intrigued expressions.

"Drew, even if you host this segment, it still wouldn't work," I say. "We need at least a couple of shots of Blaine standing in the landscape or saying a few lines. It can't just be you."

"We'll fake it," he says. "We'll do another quick nighttime shoot just outside of the park one of these nights when he's sobered up. We'll get some shots of him against the darkened sky with all the stars. Then we can have him do a voice-over later for the intro. It'll work. I promise."

His words settle into my brain. That's actually doable.

A relieved smile flashes across Wyatt's face. "I really think this could work, Alia."

Joe nods just as Haley says, "That's a great idea." Rylan voices her agreement, and Colton offers to walk Blaine to the tents so that he's out of the way.

Joe starts to compliment Drew, but he stops him. "It's not my idea. It's Alia's."

My shoulders loosen at how he makes sure I get credit. Joe flashes me a thumbs-up as Wyatt tells me "well done."

I check the time, then clap my hands once. "Okay, guys. Let's do this."

12

JOE AND WYATT TAKE PANORAMIC SHOTS OF DREW AS HE stands on the edge of a mushroom-cap-shaped rock formation.

We're hours into the shoot, and we've got this panorama shot to finish, then the outro.

Standing next to me, Haley looks ahead at the scene, then smiles at me. "This episode is going to be incredible, Alia. Apong Lita would have loved it. And your mom is going to burst into happy tears when she watches it."

I'm beaming. "Thanks, Haley."

The panorama shots wrap up and we start to set up the outro. We don't technically need it since we're going to come back and do the makeup shoot with Blaine later, but the planner in me thinks it would be good to have the extra footage. We could use part of the audio in a voice-over for online content too.

Like before, Drew nails the lines on the first try. We probably don't even need multiple takes, but because I'm such a control freak, I want them just in case. And every time he delivers with the same enthusiasm and that same killer smile.

"The Needles are beautiful in the daylight, no doubt," he says to the camera. "But honestly, I think I prefer them at night.

It's a whole new kind of beauty. Do yourself a favor and take a trip to the Needles district of Canyonlands at night sometime. I promise it will blow you away. That's it for this episode of *Discovering Utah*. See you all next time. And until then, keep exploring."

I yell cut. Colton and Rylan clap and jump up and down before sharing a cute peck on the lips. I grin at how adorably in love they are.

"Now, that is disgustingly cute," Haley says. I laugh.

We spend the next hour packing everything up, then hike the quarter mile back to the tents. Colton walks ahead and pops into the tent where I assume he set up Blaine. A second later, he darts out, his face twisted in panic.

Rylan runs up to him. "What is it?"

He shakes his head, then darts from tent to tent. I'm about to ask what's going on, but he stumbles out of the two-person tent Haley and I set up to share this evening, a look of relief on his face.

He heaves a breath. "I guess Blaine decided he wants to stay in the big tent."

He explains that he put him in one of the single-person tents earlier, but Blaine must have woken up and walked to the bigger one. I try to suppress a groan.

"He's out cold," Colton says, a worried look on his face. "Do you want me to move him to one of the smaller tents? It's not right that he should have the big one to himself."

I shake my head no even though I'm annoyed. "I'm done dealing with him for one night."

Colton says he could get one of the guys to help move him, but I tell him there's no need.

"The fact that he was aware enough to find the biggest tent even in his inebriated state tells me we should just leave him there," I say. "He'll be a nightmare if he wakes up and is pissed that he isn't sleeping in the biggest tent here."

Colton nods, looking regretful. After Haley sets down her equipment bag, I break the bad news that Blaine has taken over our tent.

She rubs her eyes. "If I weren't so exhausted, I would strangle him."

Just then Drew sets down the two bags of equipment he lugged back right next to Haley.

She mutters something about grabbing our bags from the big tent. I tell her thanks, then turn my focus back on Drew. Arms crossed, I walk up to him.

"Hey," I say quietly, looking him in the eye. "Thanks for saving the shoot tonight."

"I didn't. You did."

My cheeks grow hot with his eyes on me. I look to the large tent once more and try my hardest to stifle a groan. I have to find somewhere else to sleep now.

Rylan runs up to me, a sheepish look on her face. "I'm so sorry about your tent."

"It's not your fault," I say. "You don't have to apologize for something you didn't do."

She shakes her head. "I told Haley you two can have my tent. I'll share with Colton."

Her cheeks turn pink as she glances past me to where Colton is standing.

"You sure?"

She nods, and I thank her, even though I'm bracing myself for what that means. Haley and I have shared camping and lodging countless times before, and she's a notorious space hog. I won't get a wink of sleep sharing a one-person tent with her since she'll be kicking me all night. I'd get a more restful few hours of sleep inside one of the cars.

I sigh, then walk over to Haley, who's digging through her pack just a few feet away from where Drew and I stand. "Hey. You take Rylan's tent. I'll sleep in one of the cars tonight."

She frowns. "You don't want to share?"

I tilt my head. "Have you forgotten just how violent you are in your sleep?"

Her expression turns sheepish. "Here, you take the tent and I'll take one of the cars. I'm smaller than you anyway."

"You can sleep in my tent with me," Drew interjects.

"Oh . . . um . . ." I stammer for another few seconds.

Haley glances at me, a mischievous gleam in her eyes. "Drew to the rescue again." She turns to face him. "Look at you, saving the day."

He rolls his eyes while fighting against a flustered smile, then turns to me. "I'm serious. I know it looks like a small one-person tent, but the design is roomy. There's plenty of space for two."

Haley walks off, giving me a thumbs-up before hopping into her tent. I glance around and see that Joe and Wyatt have tucked away in their one-person tents. Colton helps Rylan into their tent, then zips the closure shut.

"I know this is an awkward situation for us to be in. Again." Drew rubs the scruff along his jawline. "But the prospect of sharing a tent with me can't be that awful. Can it?"

He lets out a chuckle, which helps loosen the tension within me. I clear my throat. "It's not that. I just . . . how would it look if the showrunner forced a crew member to bunk with her?"

Drew tilts his head. "Come on, Dunn. It's not like that, not even close. You're not forcing me to do this. *You* know you're not forcing me to do that. I'm the one offering."

I glance at the darkened trail ahead, the one that leads to the vehicles. The last thing I want to do is hike all the way back to the parking lot, get a crappy few hours of sleep, then hike all the way back to make it in time for the sunrise shoot. I'm sure to wake up with a million aches and pains, groggy as hell, and in the worst mood.

I glance up at Drew, concern painting his face. "If it makes you feel more comfortable, I'll sleep outside and you can have my tent."

I shove my hands in my pockets and wrinkle my nose, noting how cold my face is in the freezing overnight temperatures. "There's no chance I'm making you sleep outside in this cold." I swallow. "You sure you're comfortable with sharing?"

"Positive. This is a strictly professional situation. Promise I'll treat it that way."

I swallow and nod once. "I will too."

The idea of a roomy tent with cozy blankets and an air mattress pad sounds more and more enticing by the minute.

"Lead the way," I say.

I follow Drew to his tent, silently telling myself that it's just one night—one night of a very awkward sleeping arrangement . . . with a guy I picked up on the subway and shared a hot kiss with who turned out to be my coworker, whom I've been flirting and fighting with these past two weeks.

Get it together.

I take a breath and shove away all those thoughts from before. Drew unzips the tent flap and tells me to go ahead. When I step forward, the soft feel of his hand on the small of my back, guiding me in, sends my nerves haywire in the best way.

God, I like that way the hell too much.

I crawl into the tent, drop my bag on the ground, plop down next to it, and tell myself it'll all be fine.

Drew comes in after me, zips the closure shut, and glances at the center of the tent.

His eyes go wide. "Shit."

"What? What's wrong?" I ask, taking in the flustered look on his face.

He hesitates at first. "There's only one sleeping bag."

"So?"

He frowns. "So you're . . . okay with sharing a sleeping bag?"

"Drew, we shared a sleeping bag in our underwear a few days ago. How is this any worse than that?"

"I guess you're right."

"Besides, that looks huge. That's for one person?"

Drew nods while chuckling. "It was a Christmas gift from my aunt. She ordered it from some big-and-tall catalog. She's barely five feet and thinks anyone taller than her is a giant. You should see the clothes she bought for me when my growth spurt during puberty hit. I'm six foot three and I still can't fit into them."

I laugh, then open my bag, pull out some clothes, and then turn around with my back to him. I start stripping off my coat, gloves, and jeans so I can change into the oversize T-shirt I brought to sleep in.

Behind me I hear the soft sounds of zippers and fabric rustling. Drew must be changing too.

A minute later, I turn around and do a double take at Drew's bare back. His bare, perfectly cut, perfectly tanned back.

I thought since I've seen it before it would soften the blow the second time; it doesn't. I'm still just as speechless as the first time I saw his exquisitely chiseled, broad expanse of man-flesh. A second passes and my face is on fire. He leans over to reach something, which makes all that flawless skin and muscle flex. My eyes grow wider. *How the hell am I going to relax enough when I'll be sleeping next to that?*

I divert my gaze to the hem of my shirt, pretending to fuss with a thread as he turns around. I glance up and see he's wearing only a pair of navy-blue gym shorts . . . and they're doing an abysmal job of properly covering his built thighs.

I swallow. This night. Goddamn, this night is going to be sweet torture to get through.

"Cute." He smiles, pointing to the oversize, gray, tattered shirt I'm wearing with Mickey Mouse's faded face on it.

"Oh. Thanks." I pat my palms on the tops of my thighs as I kneel. "Shall we?"

He nods just as his smile fades. "So, um . . . Should I get in first? Or do you . . ."

"You first." I say quickly, crossing my arms over my chest, hoping he can't see my very erect, very hard nipples through the flimsy fabric of this ancient T-shirt.

He clears his throat, then crawls inside the plush, gray material. His eyes cut to me. "You're up, Dunn."

He lets out what sounds like a nervous chuckle, which makes a nervous chuckle spill out of me too. But then I take a breath, steadying myself before I crawl over to him.

My heartbeat thuds in my ears. All the blood in my body rushes to my face, pooling at my cheeks. Not even my tan can save me because judging by how hot I feel on the inside, I can guarantee my skin is fire-engine red—and Drew is close enough to see it.

Take a chill pill, Alia. This isn't the first time you've ever shared a sleeping space with a man.

And then my inner voice—the voice that sometimes tells me to do risky things . . . like flirt with that hot guy on the subway—pipes up.

Are you kidding me? This is NOT the same. You're sharing a sleeping bag, not a bed. And this is not a guy you're dating. This is your coworker . . . your mega-hot coworker who is the sexiest man you've ever laid eyes on.

Clenching my jaw, I force a polite smile at Drew. Then I quickly avert my gaze as I climb in. This is definitely roomier than any other one-person sleeping bag I've ever slept in . . . but it's going to be a snug fit with the both of us.

"We're going to have to spoon," he says softly. "That okay with you?"

"There's really no other way to do it," I mumble as I settle against his chest. Then I realize just how dismissive I sound. "I mean, of course it's fine. Sorry."

A low rumble sounds from above my head. "I knew what you meant," he says softly, the smile in his voice clear.

I let out a slow hiss of breath in relief and still against his body. It's a few seconds of silence where we only make the slightest movements. It's like we're trying to politely stay as still as possible so we don't touch each other more than we have to . . . even though we both know that's impossible.

Settling on my side, I tuck my hands under my cheek and close my eyes. I inhale and relax against him. Slowly, the tension in my muscles melts. With my neck against his naked chest, I have to bite back a moan. His body feels so, so good against mine.

He clears his throat. "Sorry, I, uh, I guess I should have put a shirt on."

"It's fine." My voice hits that pitchy tone it always falls into when I'm flustered.

"I'm just so used to sleeping without one in this sleeping bag because it's thermal and actually gets kind of hot if you're wearing too many clothes . . ."

"Drew, it's fine." *More than fine. It's actually goddamn exquisite to have you cradle your naked chest against my body. Don't you even worry about it.*

I swallow back the words, willing my inner thoughts to shut the hell up.

He lets out a breath, the moist heat blanketing the back of my neck. "You're comfortable?"

"Very," I say without thinking.

I bite my tongue at just how creepy that sounded.

"I mean, I feel fine. Thanks for asking." I let out a nervous cough. "How do you feel? Am I . . . hurting you or anything?"

"Not even close. But can I move my arm up? Like, um . . ."

He hovers his deliciously bare, deliciously veiny, deliciously thick arm along the length of my body, careful not to touch me.

"You can rest your hand on me, Drew," I say after a few seconds. "I'm fine with it."

You know you're more than fine with his arm on you, you thirsty little minx.

I roll my eyes at my inner monologue gone rogue, thankful that Drew is behind me and can't see my face.

"Um, where would you like it?" he asks, his tone tentative.

Reaching up slowly, I softly grip his hand between my fingers and set it on my hip. "How about here?"

"Perfect."

The soft, gentle way he says it makes me smile.

He twists around and turns off the lantern. Everything goes dark.

I close my eyes, but then he speaks. "I know you're probably exhausted and want to go to sleep, but . . . can I say something really quick?"

"Sure."

"I want to say again how sorry I am for lashing out at you when you pitched that idea of me taking over as host."

I let out a slow breath, my face growing hot again. "It's okay. You were right to be mad. I didn't mean to sound so dismissive of your stage fright. I still feel horrible about that."

"Don't. Please don't." He pauses. I can hear the soft sound of a swallow behind me.

"Alia, I had no right to get upset with you. I was jolted by the idea and it brought up all those awful feelings from my failed audition years ago. I didn't even let you talk or explain yourself. I just flipped out."

"It's okay."

"It's not okay. I'm so sorry. I wasn't even upset at your idea . . . it was more like I was scared of failing again, and just the thought of that was what upset me. But when you're the one guiding me, like you did tonight and during the Narrows shoot, I feel so at ease. And . . . if you're still willing, I'm up for it."

I twist my neck around to look at him, even though I can't see clearly in the darkness. "Wait, what?"

"You're right. Blaine is a disaster. The entire crew agrees. Even his own personal assistant can't stand him. But more than that . . . I really like hosting. Love it, actually. When I get past my nerves, I enjoy it so much."

I shift around completely so that I'm facing him. "You're an amazing host, Drew. You're perfect for this series. But I just have to make sure that you really want to do this. You want to take over as host? I'm one hundred percent on board, but I want you to feel comfortable."

"I'm one thousand percent on board if you're the one directing me, Alia."

The soft rumble in his voice as he says my name makes me hum from the inside out.

"We'd have to tell the crew what we're doing so they can be in on it," I say. "We'd have to keep shooting footage of Blaine in addition to filming you. It could get exhausting doing double duty like that. But we need to so he doesn't catch on."

"Given the way the crew responded during tonight's shoot, I think they'd be an easy sell."

"We can't tell anyone outside of the crew what we're doing."

"Absolutely. It's gotta be under wraps until the big reveal."

"And you'd have to start posting regularly on Twitter and Instagram. It's the best way to build up a fan base and eventual viewership for you."

"I can do that. And I probably already have a bit of a following thanks to your subway gentleman photo." The grin he flashes dazzles, even in the darkness.

"I promise I'll make you as comfortable as possible while filming. Anytime you start to feel overwhelmed or nervous, all you have to do is tell me. I promise we'll take a break. We'll take as much time as you need. I'll do everything I can to support you and make you as comfortable as possible during filming."

"I know you will, Dunn. You're the only person I want to do this with."

In the darkness, I smile to myself. "Okay. Let's do it."

His hand on my hip gives me a soft squeeze.

I resist the pleasant shiver that makes its way through my body at his touch. "We'll tell the crew tomorrow."

"Sounds good."

Eyelids heavy, I let out a tired moan and roll back over so that my back is to Drew. "After all that excitement, I'm tempted to call it a night.

He lets out a soft laugh. "Good night, Dunn."

"Good night, Irons."

I close my eyes. Before long, I doze off.

WAKE, MY EYES STILL CLOSED. I'M IN THAT TEASE OF SLEEP your body does right before you fall into a deep slumber. For however long I've been dozing, I must have shifted a bit because now only one arm is cradling the side of my head.

And the other is . . .

Oh no . . . Oh my God no . . .

I start to gasp in horror because my other hand is cupping Drew's dick.

My eyes snap open, but all I see is pitch-black. It's been so long since I've shared a sleeping spot with someone that I forgot just how handsy I get in my sleep. In the haze of almost-sleep my brain is operating on a five-second delay. I command my hand to release Drew's penis, but it takes a few seconds before my hand actually lets go. When I finally do, my body's response is reflexive. I jerk my arm back, forgetting that Drew is cradling me, and promptly elbow him in the gut.

He grunts, then coughs himself awake. As he hacks, I scoot around so I'm lying on my other side facing him. My eyes adjust to the darkness, and I'm able to make out his face. It's twisted in agony as he winces through the pain.

I cup my hand over my mouth. "Oh my God, Drew. I'm so, so sorry," I mumble against my hand.

"Did you hit me in the stomach?" he wheezes. "What the hell was that for?"

"I'm so sorry!" At least I'm alert enough to know to keep my voice down. Our tents are clustered just a couple of feet apart from one another. I don't want to wake anyone with the commotion happening in our tent. "I . . . I . . . um . . . I kind of freaked out in my sleep."

Drew lets out a soft groan. "Damn, did you have a nightmare or something?" he asks, eyes closed.

He presses his hand to his lower abdomen—where I'm guessing I hit him.

"Um, not really. Here." I press my palm against his stomach and rub in small gentle circles. "I . . . um . . . what happened was . . ."

I hazard a glance up at him and see that the agony of his expression has melted away completely. His eyes are puffy, but he's looking at me with softness.

I blink and then come clean.

"I know this is going to sound weird . . . but . . . I get a little handsy in my sleep sometimes . . . when I'm cuddled with someone. And I—I grabbed your junk while I was sleeping, and then when I woke up and realized what I was doing, I was so freaked out about it that I immediately jerked my hand away to let go. That's when I elbowed you. By accident. God, this is so embarrassing."

I don't even look him in the eye when I whisper my confession. Because if I did, my brain would melt. It would be too humiliating. Just the fact that I'm trapped in a sleeping bag with Drew while confessing that I've groped him is horrible enough.

I wait a beat, then direct my gaze back up at him. I fully expect him to glare, to recoil, to throw me out of his tent. But all I see is amusement in his expression.

The corner of his mouth moves up slowly. "It's okay, Dunn."

"What?"

He lets out a soft chuckle. "It's totally fine."

"It is?"

"God's honest truth? That's kind of hot."

"Sorry, what?" I can't help the whispered chuckle of disbelief that falls from my lips.

"Dunn, I'm super attracted to you. Didn't you realize that?"

I shake my head.

"Well, I am."

"But . . . what about when you texted me after our hike at Whale Rock? You said it's best to just be colleagues and nothing more."

He shrugs a shoulder. "That was bullshit. I was super attracted to you then and wanted to be with you, but I lost my nerve when Rylan interrupted us. That text was me trying to save face."

Even though the volume of his voice is low and soft, he can't hide that growl. That feral, guttural noise that signals pure want. For me.

Now that Drew has made it crystal clear that he's into me, the nerves dissipate.

My hand stills against his stomach. "So . . . you like the way I'm touching you right now?"

He grunts another yes.

Slowly, I run my hand up his stomach, relishing the way each hard line feels under my palm. I stop on his chest, just over his heart, which is thundering inside him. A quiet pant falls from his mouth.

He swallows. "You can do whatever you want to my body, Alia. Asleep, awake. Anytime, anyplace. You have my permission."

I tilt my head up until our faces are barely inches apart. "I'm so attracted to you, Drew. Like, you have no idea."

His half smile turns full. It's so bright it cuts through the darkness.

"It's been a struggle not to drool over you while we're shooting." I tap my fingers against his chest, quietly delighting in the way his hard mass barely budges.

"It's been the same for me. You're beautiful, Alia. Every time I look at you, I feel like a creep because I can't stop staring. I still can't believe we ended up here."

My heart melts in my chest. Whatever blip in the universe resulted in us seeing each other again, I'm thankful for it.

He cups my cheek with his hand. Closing my eyes, I hum.

"I've been trying my hardest not to pull you aside so we can finish that kiss we started that night we met."

"We can finish it now."

I hover my mouth over his for a hot second, taking his declaration from minutes ago to heart.

You can do whatever you want to my body, Alia.

So I do. I press my lips against his, moving slowly. I run my tongue along his bottom lip, savoring the flavor of salt and mint. It's just a few slow seconds, but it sends a bolt of lightning to my chest. The last time I had my mouth on Drew's mouth was almost a month ago. Since then I've spent so much time trying to forget the glorious feel of his mouth on my mouth.

Now I know why I couldn't get it out of my head. Because it was insanely, insanely good.

He kisses back, his lips firm against mine. Then he swipes my tongue with his. It's a teasing game we play. He takes the lead for a bit, lapping at my tongue with an exquisitely slow rhythm until he can hardly breathe; then I take over. Then he catches up, our tongues tangle, and we switch off who leads once more.

It goes that way until we're both gasping for air. My hands claw at his hair; his hands grab at my waist.

He pulls away for a second. "Fuck—kissing you is the best."

"Is it?" Biting my bottom lip, I grin at him, then pull his mouth back to mine before he can answer. I tease him with my tongue and he groans softly.

My hands slide down to his chest. His hot skin and firm muscle pulse under my palms. Once again I'm silently thankful that Drew crawled into the sleeping bag bare-chested. That's one less step I have to take to get his skin on mine.

He runs his hand under my shirt, cupping my breast in his massive, warm palm. I moan into his mouth as he circles my hard nipple with his thumb.

When he pulls his mouth away from mine, I let out a whispered whine. Even in the darkness, his smirk dazzles. I can make out his glistening lips, his pearly-white teeth, that mischievous glint in his eyes. My head spins from his kiss. My lord is he good with that tongue of his. For a split second I wonder if he'll go where I hope he will, in that spot between my legs that's currently throbbing like crazy from just his kiss.

But then he hovers his mouth over my T-shirt-covered breast and bites me lightly, his teeth scraping against the flimsy fabric.

"Holy sh . . ." I trail off as pleasure jolts through me. And then I remind myself that I need to keep my voice down. We're just a handful of feet away from the next tent, and I cannot risk anyone overhearing us fooling around.

Drew works me over with his mouth for several more seconds before pulling away. His eyes shine bright as he looks up at me. "Okay if I take this off?" He tugs at the hem of my shirt.

I nod so fast, I get dizzy. Or maybe that's an aftereffect of Drew's mouth.

I lift my torso up as he slides the shirt off and up my arms. I shake it off, and it lands somewhere behind me. And then he's back, running his magical mouth over my breasts once more, but this time he uses his tongue. Soon my eyes are rolling, my head falls back, and the silent breaths I'm forcing myself to take are turning ragged.

A split second later, he backs away and I catch my breath. It's like he can sense that if he continues, I may get too noisy.

I fall back so that I'm lying with my back flat on the ground. He leans up and stretches down to unzip the sleeping bag. Then he lies back down and snakes his massive arm up my back. He braces me so that I'm up on my side again before nudging my arm up.

For a second, I frown and wonder what he's doing, but then he presses his mouth on that supersensitive spot of skin between my underarm and the side of my breast.

He trails a few supersoft kisses down. I gasp and giggle at the same time.

"That tickle?" he whispers against my skin.

"Mmm-hmm. But . . ." My breath catches as his stubble runs lightly across that hot spot along the side of my breast, right underneath my upper arm. "I like it," I say through a sigh.

I squirm under his mouth, but he holds me steady with one hand on my hip and the other bracing my arm up. He slowly makes an invisible line with his lips along the side of my body. Closing my eyes, I savor the ticklish, teasing touch. It elicits a warring response from my body. On the inside, I'm all heat. My blood and my heart pulse fire. But on the outside? On the outside my skin is covered in a sheet of goose bumps. I shiver, groaning softly at the clash of sensations, how Drew's mouth and his gentle-as-a-feather kisses can leave me more turned on than any other kiss that every guy before him has given me.

"You're so . . . creative," I say, then bite my lip.

"Creative?"

I press my eyes shut as a way of enduring the teasing pleasure consuming my body. "Yeah. No one has ever kissed me there. I don't think they ever thought to."

"I couldn't help myself." He presses another kiss, this time near my hip. "Your mouth tastes so good. I want to taste you all over."

Just then my eyes fly open. I haven't had a shower since this morning. We've been hiking around most of the day. I'm covered in dust and dirt and sweat. Judging by the downward path he's making with his mouth along my torso, I know the spot he's aiming for—and I want his mouth there more than anything. But not when I'm as unclean as I currently am.

I reach down, grab him gently by the head, and pull him up to look at me. "As much as I'd love that, I'm just not very, um, fresh down there. Right now, I mean."

I'm not at all ashamed of my body, but this is my first time with Drew. I want my body to be in alluring condition, not swathed in BO.

Even though it's dark, my eyes have adjusted and I can see perfectly as a sly smile tugs at his lips. "So?"

He gently wraps his hands around my wrists and pulls my hand out of his hair. Then he dives back down, settling between my legs. His fingers skim the hem of my cotton panties. A low, soft, guttural sound rips from his throat right before his hot breath crashes against the skin of my inner thighs.

"I haven't showered," I plead through a whiny, whispered voice.

"I don't care," he grunts just before he presses a kiss to the inside of my thigh.

With one smooth move of his hands, my panties are gone and his mouth is on me.

I swear I try to speak, but all that comes out is a gasp, then a broken exhale; then I clamp my mouth shut. Noise. I can't be making any noise—there are people sleeping soundly all around us.

But . . . Drew's mouth. Holy goddamn hell, his mouth. Even though my eyes are closed, they're rolling back. Because Drew's mouth is divine—everything about him and what he's doing is heaven. The slow and steady way he moves his tongue, the wet heat he coats me with, the way he moans softly, like I'm the best thing he's ever tasted.

Heat flickers between my legs. It gets hotter and hotter by the second. Soon it spreads all over; I can feel it from the tips of my toes to the tips of my fingers, all the way up my neck. Inside my chest is squeezing with every breath I take.

My jaw drops, but no sound comes out—thankfully. It takes every brain cell I have to command myself to stay quiet. All I want to do is scream, to howl, to pant, to moan, to cry out Drew's name. This pleasure that he delivers from his mouth to my body is the best I've ever had. Yes, I've had satisfying sessions of oral sex in my life. But Drew is in a whole other league. He gauges my reactions with expert perception. He can seem to tell by the way I pant and tug at his hair what I like most, and to keep at it.

In my head, I pull up my secret test for every guy I've been with: the shower massager test. I've always asked myself if I'd rather have his mouth or my shower massager. Sadly my shower massager has beaten almost every guy. But I'd light my shower massager on fire and choose Drew any day of the week.

He swirls his tongue in a slow, steady, firm rhythm that jolts my entire body. He maintains the heavenly tempo, which intensifies the pleasure and heat building inside me. My mouth opens again, purely outside my control, and the beginnings of a yelp start to fall from my lips, but he reaches an arm up my body and presses his hand over my mouth, muffling the sound.

I moan softly against his massive, warm palm. Holy shit, that's a hot move.

Fire and pleasure intertwine inside me. I can feel it in every molecule of my body as it builds and builds. My chest heaves up and down and up and down, faster and faster, until I'm whining against his hand.

One of my hands clamps around the wrist of his hand that's on my mouth; the other stays tangled in his hair, pressing his face against me. Soon I'm grinding my entire body against his face. Every inch of me tingles, the pleasure about to boil over. A muffled moan escapes Drew's mouth. It's low and throaty and indulgent. It tells me that he's loving this so very much—just like me. And that's what sets me off.

My legs flail as a climax shatters me. My back arches off the ground as every muscle inside me tenses. The squeeze I feel inside is relentless. It's like I'm possessed by this orgasm; it's thrashing inside me, consuming me like a rogue wave that knocks me off my feet, engulfing me, then dragging me under the water. But I'm happy to drown in the pleasure. I don't care if I never touch land again. This mind-blowing, earth-shattering ecstasy is my new home now; I'd happily live here forever.

What feels like minutes later, my body starts to unfurl. My breath slows and evens out until I'm no longer panting like an Olympic sprinter. Drew presses impossibly soft kisses over my mound, then along my inner thighs once more. I cover my hands over my face as I lie on the ground and wait for my heart to stop thundering.

Then I lean up on my elbows, letting out a soft grunt when I feel the muscles in my body finally loosen. I'm going to be so, so sore tomorrow. Worth it.

When I open my eyes and look down at him, he's a blurry mass. After several blinks, his smug, satisfied smile comes into focus.

I let out a soft chuckle. "Okay," I pant-whisper. "You win."

"Win what?"

My elbows wobble so I lie back down, then coax him to crawl back up to me so we can cuddle.

"You win . . . the unofficial contest . . . against my shower massager. And every sex toy I've ever owned," I say between breaths. I swallow. "You are unquestionably superior. Like, hands down."

His head falls back in a laugh, but then he quickly covers his mouth. He cuddles me against his chest and nuzzles the top of my head. "I am beyond honored."

Closing my eyes, I smile into his bare chest. Then I feel that unmistakable hardness against my thigh. I tilt my head up to look up at him, wondering if he can see the grin spreading across my face.

"My turn?" I say before kissing him.

"I don't want you to feel like you have to," he says between slow, long kisses. "Like you have to return the favor or anything like that. I honestly just really wanted to do it."

I swallow back an "aww" noise. It's refreshing to be with a guy who is generous in bed instead of expecting things in return. It's also the biggest turn-on.

I press a kiss to the hinge of his jaw. "I want to. I want you in my mouth."

His eyes shine even brighter in the darkness, and I could swear I feel him get even harder. "Well. How could I say no to that?"

I leave him with a kiss on the mouth, then shimmy my way down. I push the sleeping bag aside, then settle between his legs and pull down his shorts. Even in the dark, I can discern Drew's impressive length.

My eyes go wide. "Oh . . . wow."

His amused chuckle sounds above me. "Good wow? Or bad wow?"

I wrap my hand around the base of him. He groans.

"Really, really good wow."

And then I lower my head down and begin teasing him with my tongue. He responds with a swallowed grunt, then shallow breathing. I let out a soft, satisfied hum.

It's been a long while since I've had the pleasure of using my mouth on a guy. My demanding job combined with my lack of enthusiasm for the shit show that is modern dating has resulted in very few opportunities to do this, which is a shame. I've always enjoyed it.

And now I remember why. Drew's sounds set me on fire. The way he pants and groans, the way he slides his hand into my hair and makes a gentle fist, signaling just how good I'm making him feel. The way his words fall from his mouth, desperate and pleading.

"Yes, like that." He pants. "Just . . . like . . . that."

I hum again as he turns to steel. With both my hand and my mouth, I pick up the pace.

He curses. "So good."

And then he tangles his fingers in my hair tighter, in that telltale way that signals he's close. With a grunt, he finishes. Above me I hear him take a few deep breaths.

I sit up, admiring the flustered look on his face. His eyes are wide and unbelieving. His chest heaves each time he inhales. Then he wipes his forehead with his arm before turning his stare at me.

He smirks. "Get over here, Dunn."

Grinning, I crawl back next to him. He wraps his arms around me, and my eyelids weigh heavy with each blink. I close my eyes, wincing inwardly when I remember that we're due to get up soon to film the sunrise.

I ask Drew what time it is and he checks his phone, which is lying off to the side.

"That means three hours until we have to be up," I whisper, then groan.

He squeezes his arms around me even tighter. Instantly I'm comforted.

I yawn. "So you're not annoyed all this fooling around means us missing out on, like, two hours of sleep?"

"I'd give up a week's worth of sleep for more naked time with you."

My entire body heats at how quickly he answers. Not a single trace of doubt in his tone. I can't remember the last time a guy made it so clear just how much he liked being with me. He really, truly means it. And I want to hear it again.

"So it was worth it?" I ask.

He backs up, then hooks his finger under my chin and tilts my face up to look at him. His eyes burn bright—brighter than I've ever seen.

He presses the softest kiss to my lips. "No question, Dunn. Very, very worth it."

I fall asleep with the biggest smile on my face.

14

T HAT'S A WRAP!" I CALL OUT AS WE FILM THE FINAL SUNRISE
shot at the Needles.

I glance over at Drew, who's the focus of Joe's camera shot, then look away. If I look too long, that giddy feeling I've been keeping at bay inside me this whole morning will certainly take over.

When everyone finishes packing up, I ask them to gather around for a quick chat. We huddle together in a small circle, and I commend them on the job they've done and thank them for their hard work.

"It's been a weird shoot, I know," I say. My eyes dart to Blaine's tent. I turn to Colton. "Blaine's still passed out?"

"Out cold. I checked on him earlier. He's breathing but sleeping very deeply."

"Okay, good. Because I need to ask you guys something."

I take a breath and dive right into my proposal to secretly make Drew the new host. I tell them everything Drew and I discussed last night—our plan for his social media accounts, our idea to continue filming Blaine so that he doesn't catch on, and how I'm going to pitch this change to the network execs once we wrap up shooting and have edited episodes ready to show them.

Everyone stares at me with slight frowns, except for Rylan, who's almost smiling.

"I know this is a really risky thing to ask you guys," I say. I glance at Drew before addressing everyone again. "And if anyone isn't on board with this, all you have to do is say so and we won't do it. We're a team. I'm not about to pull something like this without the full support of the crew. When we take this to the network, I'll tell them it was my call and my call only to make this switch. If the execs don't like it, fine. I'll take the heat for it. That's my responsibility as the one in charge of this project. But I don't want to do this unless you're all on board."

Haley holds up a hand before I can say more. "I'm in. I'm sick of Blaine's bullshit. I'm one hundred percent behind this."

I let out the breath I've been holding, relieved that I have Haley's support. After all the years we've worked together, she's never once held back on me. If I came up with a crappy idea, she'd be the first one to say so. But whenever I had a new idea that I was too unsure about to pitch, she was also the first one to encourage me. As nervous as I am to pull this off, she's the one person whose support I need most.

"That goes double for me," Wyatt says. "Honestly, I'm glad you thought this up. It's a great idea. The best way to handle this crappy host situation, honestly."

"I think so too," Joe says as he reties his wavy blond hair into a bun. "We're with you, Alia."

"We are too," Rylan says, standing tall. She grabs Colton's hand.

He nods. "I think that's the right thing to do. Honestly. I know . . . I know I'm his personal assistant, and I'm supposed to be loyal to him. But, God, he's the worst." He turns to Drew, who's standing at the other end of the semicircle we've formed. "You're a way better host. Seriously."

Drew smiles a thanks, then looks at me. "Obviously I'm in."

I grin and look at the ground. This is it. We're actually doing this—we're throwing out the playbook completely and it could totally screw me. But I don't care. This is the right thing to do. I can feel it in my bones.

"So this is what you two came up with in the tent together last night?" Haley says.

Even though her tone is professional, I can tell by the gleam in her eye that she's suspicious. I know she's wondering if Drew and I got up to something more.

I meet her knowing stare with a professional smile. "Yes. That's exactly what we did."

"We should throw you two together more often," she says. "See what other ideas you come up with."

"I'd be down for that," Drew adds.

I swallow and try my best to keep a straight face. Then I thank everyone, and we get back to packing up our equipment and tents to head back to Moab.

"Don't think I didn't pick up on that little look between you two," Haley says as I start to take down one of the tents.

"I don't know what you're talking about."

I keep my eyes on the bright orange material of the tent.

She rests a hand on my arm to get me to look at her. "I get it. You're keeping things quiet because this is a work situation. I respect it."

I let out a slow, quiet sigh, grateful that she's picked up on that.

She narrows an eye at me. "When you're ready to spill, I want all the details."

"Noted," I say, trying to keep my face straight.

She walks off to start tearing down her own tent. I spot Colton darting into Blaine's tent to wake him. Drew walks over to me.

"Need some help?" he asks.

I shake my head, then jut my chin at Blaine's tent. We both look over as Colton drags a very groggy Blaine out of there with his arm draped over him.

"Actually, could you help Colton take Blaine to his car?"

"Of course. But first, I just wanna say that I hope last night wasn't a one-off," he says quietly. "I'd like to see you again."

My cheeks are ablaze as I try not to smile, thrilled that he wants to see me again too. "You do?"

"Absolutely." He takes a step toward me. "I don't want to come off as a creep or weirdly eager, but I'm not a hit-it-and-quit-it kind of guy. I really like you, Alia. And I want to spend as much time as possible with you."

My stomach tingles as I bite my lip. "I'd like that too."

I'm about to tell him to meet me in my hotel room so we can shower off this trip together before going at it in bed, but I stop myself. This is my first-ever series, and I'm fooling around with one of the crew members. I need to be smart about things. Because the last time I did that, I blew up my life *and* my job.

"But I think we should talk about things first before we, um . . ."

I trail off when I notice Joe is about to walk by toward the tents, gear in hand.

A tad bit of the cheeky look in Drew's eyes fades. "Yeah, that's probably a good idea."

I take a step back from Drew, suddenly aware of how close we're standing. "We need to be careful about how we interact in front of everyone too."

He purses his lips, then nods. "Of course."

"Meet me at that smoothie place in downtown Moab? At four?"

"I'll be there," he says before jogging off.

I LOOK UP from my phone and spot Drew as he walks toward me. I'm seated at a wrought iron table on the side patio of the hipster juice bar a few blocks from the edge of downtown Moab.

I hand him the kiwi, kale, and banana smoothie I ordered for him.

He half smiles. "A green juice just for me? You really know how to woo a guy."

I sip my acai berry smoothie. "We've been eating like crap this entire shoot. I figured you could use something green. Especially after all those Snoballs I've seen you inhale."

"Snoballs are the food of the gods." He plops down next to me just as one of the workers drops off a plate of veggies, pita bread, and hummus.

We thank her, and Drew swipes a slice of pita bread, dips it into the hummus, then narrows his gaze at me as he chews.

"So what are we here to discuss, Dunn?"

I straighten up and then pivot my chair so that I'm facing him. We're so close our knees are almost touching.

"I'd like to keep seeing you during this shoot," I say.

"I'd like that too." Drew's expression brightens, which makes my heart flutter.

"I just think we should set some ground rules."

Drew narrows his gaze at me as he takes a sip of his juice. "Okay," he says slowly.

I chuckle and lean forward to rest my hand on his knee. "Don't look so suspicious. I just want to make sure we both know what we're getting into." I swallow and sit back. "I just . . . I don't want this to come off as unethical. Or like I'm taking advantage of you."

"Why would you think you're taking advantage of me? I thought it was pretty clear last night how much I wanted you."

"I'm in charge of this shoot. I don't want it to seem like I'm abusing my position over you as a freelancer on the set."

"You're definitely not doing that. It's not like you're pulling me into the elevator at the office and having your way with me." He tilts his head at me, smirking. "Although that would be a lot of fun."

I roll my eyes and start to look away, but then he grabs my hand.

"In all seriousness, I get it. You're the showrunner. But it's not like I'm your underling. I'm a freelancer hired by the network. I'm not an intern or a PA. There are no lines you're crossing with me. Promise."

I let out a breath. "Okay. Good."

"So what are your rules?"

I slide my phone back over and pull up the notes I typed out earlier while I was waiting for Drew to arrive.

"Damn. You made a whole list." He twists to read the screen.

My face heats. "Yeah, um. It's weird, but I write out lists every time I need help getting my thoughts together. It helps when I . . ."

I cut myself off before I say the rest, which will most definitely make me sound like a freak.

"When you what?"

"When I . . . can't stop thinking about something. Or someone." I pause, my face igniting. "Sorry, that came out wrong."

That warm smile tugs at his perfectly pouty mouth once more. "Don't be embarrassed. I like that I'm worth making a list for. And that you can't stop thinking about me. I can't stop thinking about you either."

I bite my lip, grinning. I focus back on the list. "First thing is discretion. I don't want anyone on the crew knowing about this."

"Of course."

"And I think we should keep our . . . private activities strictly limited to when we know we won't get caught."

He raises his brow.

"Okay, so you know how we're all sharing that house rental

the week we're filming at Bryce Canyon? And then we're sharing that condo rental while filming at Capitol Reef National Park? Since the whole crew minus Blaine is going to be staying in the same places, it's too risky for us to do anything with each other. Someone might see us."

He flashes a pointed look. "I don't know why you're so worried about people finding out about us. The crew likes you and respects you. I mean, I've only been working with you all for a couple of weeks and even I can see that. They're not going to think less of you for what you choose to do in your personal life."

I shake my head. "It's not like that; it's just . . . this series is my first big project. I want there to be as few issues as possible. And yeah, they probably wouldn't care what I'm getting up to in my off hours, but I don't want to take a chance. I want to keep my personal life as private as possible. I don't want anything to complicate this."

Drew spends a few moments processing what I've said. "I get it."

"So that means we'll have to abstain from hooking up while filming in Bryce."

"Fine," he says through a breath.

"And no sending sexy texts or naughty photos."

He coughs while sipping his drink. Grabbing a nearby napkin, he wipes his mouth. "Why not?"

I almost laugh at how whiny he sounds, like a kid being told he can't have ice cream before bed. "I don't want someone accidently seeing our phones. I know we both have passcodes, but sometimes when you send a text or a photo, it'll show up on your locked screen and someone might see that."

"Fair point."

"And if at any point one of us is uncomfortable or wants to stop this setup, we stop. Immediately. No questions asked."

Drew nods his head in understanding.

"And no talking about the future or putting pressure on each other about . . . expectations. I want this to be uncomplicated and fun."

He blinks, his expression neutral.

"That's okay with you, right?" I ask.

"Absolutely. Anything else?"

I shake my head and darken my phone screen. "That's it. Just being discreet and keeping it in our pants for the Bryce and Capitol Reef shoots."

He taps his empty cup while I start on the carrot sticks and hummus.

"Someone hurt you, didn't they?" Drew says out of the blue.

"What?"

"That's why you're taking this . . . approach with us."

I lean back in my chair, mildly surprised at how quickly Drew picked up on this.

I contemplate brushing it all off, but the way he looks at me, with sincerity and concern in his eyes, makes me want to tell the truth. So I do.

"Yeah. Big-time."

"What happened?" he asks softly.

I cross my arms and look off to the sidewalk in front of us, where tourists stroll up and down the street. "The usual. I was a typical naive twenty-something who fell for an older guy . . . and who didn't realize for the entire year that we dated that I wasn't actually his girlfriend. I was his mistress."

Drew's eyes go wide. "Shit. I'm sorry."

I shrug. "He was a director who showered me, a lowly PA, with loads of attention. I thought he was genuinely into me, but I was just his young and pretty thing he kept on the side. I should have known better."

When I look back up at Drew, his jaw muscle bulges underneath the thick scruff blanketing his cheeks. "Asshole."

"Reid was definitely that, now that I look back on things." Just the mention of his name after all these years turns the taste in my mouth sour. "But he was also charming and sweet. And I was sick of dating fuckboys my age. My twenty-two-year-old self thought that dating a guy in his forties was the answer. Little did I know then that forty-something men can be fuckboys too."

I take another long sip of my smoothie and give Drew a summary of my year dating Reid. How he never introduced me to his friends or family, how he never asked to meet my friends or parents. How he never planned a date in advance, always asking me out the day of. I didn't realize at the time what a red flag that was—he only made time for me on nights when his wife was working late or out of town.

How he never let me spend the night at his place, always paying for a taxi to take me back to my apartment.

How I can remember vividly the three times he stood me up when I insisted that we plan a dinner date a few days in advance—and the lies he told me to cover his ass.

"That's why it hurt so much when you didn't call me the day after we met," I say softly. "I figured you were standing me up, just like he did."

"Alia . . ."

I shake my head. "It's okay, I know you didn't. I just mean at the time, those were the feelings it brought up."

Drew leans forward and moves his arm like he wants to reach for me but places his hand on his leg instead.

"Can I ask how it ended?"

"Exactly how you'd think," I say, annoyed at how defeated I sound. "We were at my apartment. He was in the shower, and his phone kept buzzing. I thought it was an emergency, so I looked at his screen. And that's when I saw a slew of texts from his wife. I'll never forget the very last message she sent before I dropped the phone in shock. 'Are you with your little whore?'"

Drew reaches across the table to scoop my hand in his. "God, Alia. I'm so sorry."

"It's okay."

"It's not fucking okay."

There's a low-level anger in his voice that sends a flutter to my chest, like he's upset that anyone would dare hurt me.

"That guy was a piece of shit. He didn't deserve you. And you're not naive for what happened to you. You were vulnerable and trusting. Because why wouldn't you be? That's how you should be in a relationship. And he took advantage of it in the worst way."

The conviction in Drew's voice as he speaks, the way he doesn't dare blink as he holds my gaze—they're both like a warm blanket wrapped around my heart.

"That guy was a prick. He didn't deserve a single second with you, Dunn."

"I told him as much when I confronted him as he came out of the shower. And then I threw his clothes and phone out of my bedroom window."

The corner of Drew's mouth quirks up, and he gives my hand a gentle squeeze. "That's brutal. And exactly what he deserved."

I lean back in my chair, our hands still joined. "He fired me the next day at work."

"He what?"

"'Reassigned' is probably the better word, but he got me removed from the show I was working on and put me on that *Planet Earth* spin-off where I ended up doing community service for that EP I told you about. I felt so used."

Drew gives my hand another squeeze.

"I remember overhearing him on the phone right before I walked into his office the day he fired me. He must have been talking to someone who was in charge of the shoot he was reassigning me to. He was saying all these awful things about me.

How I was this obsessed girl who developed this weird crush on him and wouldn't stop pestering him to go out with me. How he needed to get me away from him as soon as possible and had to cash in on a favor to have the other series take me on. It was . . . humiliating."

I take a breath as that all-too-familiar wave of shame and heartache washes over me.

"He sounded like a totally different person. I remember that so vividly. His voice on that phone call wasn't the voice I knew, the voice I heard so many times telling me how beautiful I was and how much he loved my laugh. He spoke to me so sweetly before . . . but overhearing him on the phone, how hard and low and detached his tone was, it was like I was listening to a complete stranger. It killed me. And it made me realize that I didn't know him at all . . . and yet I had been so intimate with him. That made my skin crawl."

I pause to take a drink. Drew's eyes stay glued to me.

"I thought I was smarter than that."

"Alia," Drew says softly. He repeats my name when I don't look at him right away. "You *are* smart. He was exactly what you said—a manipulative jerk. Everything that happened was his fault, not yours."

"You're the only person other than Haley who knows about him. I was too humiliated to tell my other friends or even my family about what happened. I thought they'd be so ashamed of me, getting involved with a married guy and not even knowing it."

"Alia . . ."

"You know what the worst part is?" I say, ignoring him. "After all he did, I was still heartbroken. I was actually sad to lose him. I cried for weeks after things ended between us."

"Alia, look at me," Drew says calmly.

When I finally meet his gaze, I go breathless. He looks like a warrior ready to rip apart anyone who crosses my path.

"You have no reason to feel embarrassed or ashamed. What happened was his fault, not yours. You did nothing wrong. And crying over him is nothing to be embarrassed about. It shows how genuine your feelings were for him. He didn't deserve it, but that's not the point. You were in love and that selfish asshole broke your heart. Not one bit of it was your fault."

I let a small smile slip. "I know that now. It's just . . . made me skittish when it comes to relationships and dating—especially a coworker. I tried to do a couple of serious relationships since then, but nothing ever stuck."

Drew winces for a half second before nodding. "I get it. Completely."

He lets go of my hand, and we share a quiet few moments where all we do is people watch.

When I inhale, my chest feels looser. "Thanks for listening. And for all the sweet things you said."

"Of course, Dunn."

"So. Do you have any god-awful breakup stories you can share so I don't feel totally alone?"

Drew runs a hand through his hair. "I was engaged once."

"Oh. Crap, I didn't mean . . . I was only half-serious—"

"It's okay," Drew says, leaning forward and touching my hand once more. "I was in my twenties too. We were college sweethearts. We just weren't right for each other. Yeah, the breakup sucked, but better than marrying someone who isn't right for you."

"That's why I don't want to put any pressure on this, on us. I don't have the greatest track record. I just want something fun and easy."

Drew nods once. "Same."

He pulls me by the hand to scoot closer to him. "You ready to get out of here?"

The look in his eyes is positively hungry. All the tension from hashing out my failed relationship melts away when I focus on him. Instead I feel relaxed and comforted and content.

"Absolutely."

FIFTEEN MINUTES LATER I'm in Drew's hotel room, standing by the window.

"You're just a few doors down from me," I say as I look out at the view of the parking lot. A wall of red rock rests behind the concrete, cutting into the indigo sky of early evening. "You have a better view, though."

Just then I feel the warmth from Drew's body skimming mine as he walks up to stand behind me. His hands fall to my waist, and his mouth presses against the side of my neck.

"I think this is a better view," he growls softly against my neck.

My eyes close as I take in the sensation. The warmth from his lips and his breath. The firm press of his hands against my body. How I shiver with anticipation as he touches me.

He gently drags his mouth along the back of my neck. I let out a soft, shaky gasp as he lightly nuzzles his face right where the base of my neck meets my shoulder. A yummy shiver runs through me.

"Just say the word, Dunn."

I turn around to face him, cup his face in my hands, and kiss him until we're both aching for air. "On the bed, Irons."

A wide grin crowds his face. We walk the two feet to the bed, and then I gently push him to sit on the edge of it. Leaning over, I pull his T-shirt over his head. Just like in the tent, I'm speechless at the expanse of lines and firm muscle that cover his torso and arms. But it's even more glorious now because I get to see it in proper lighting. That patch of hair that runs from the center of his chiseled chest all the way down to below the waistline of his jeans makes me giddy with anticipation. I notice too that he's got a slight smattering of freckles along his shoulders. I run my fingers along his right shoulder. He closes his eyes and hums.

I place both hands on his shoulders, admiring their broad spread.

He narrows an eye at me, the expression on his face playful. "Is that a subtle cue for me to lie down?"

"Yup."

He winks up at me, and I smile. I start to push him to lie down on the bed, but he gently grabs my wrists with both of his hands, stopping me. He stays sitting up. "I thought of another rule," he says, his eyes shining.

"What's that?"

"Every time we're together when the situation allows, I want you to be loud." He lifts an eyebrow at me when I swallow.

I bite back a grin. "That . . . won't be a problem. I'm usually pretty loud. Like, I don't even mean to be. It's just natural. And a little embarrassing."

"Embarrassing?"

"When I lived with roommates, it was their most common complaint about me."

"We're a perfect match, then. I can't stand quiet."

He reaches to my waist to unbutton my jeans as I shed my top. And then I'm standing there in the only set of semi-matching bra and panties I brought with me to Utah—a black jersey-material bra and black cotton panties.

"I didn't think I'd be doing this while I'm here," I say, glancing at my bare feet. My face heats as I fiddle with my hands. "Otherwise I would have brought nicer . . . stuff."

Drew probably doesn't care that I'm not decked out in high-end lingerie, but I can't help but wish I had something a bit sexier to amp up this moment.

When I glance up, he has an awestruck look on his face. It's another couple of seconds of his hazel-brown eyes scanning my body until he makes eye contact with me again. "Are you joking?"

"I just mean—"

He grabs my hands in his. "Alia, you look incredible. Like, fucking incredible."

The way he speaks, it's like he's having a difficult time finding the right words to express just how much he likes seeing me nearly naked. It sends all the nerves and uncertainty inside me retreating.

He reaches up to unhook my bra and drops it onto the pile of my clothes on the floor. Holding my hips with both hands, he leans up and presses the softest kiss to my stomach. My mouth falls open as I inhale sharply. He trails feather-soft kiss after feather-soft kiss farther down my body until he reaches the hemline of my panties, then stops.

"Can I take these off?" he asks with his mouth against my skin.

I run my hands through his hair and moan. "Yes."

A beat later my panties are on the floor. I step out of them, and his hands fall away from me as he leans back on his elbows on the bed.

The smuggest grin I've ever seen fills his face. "Best view ever. Hands down."

He makes a come hither motion with his index finger, but I shake my head. "You need to be naked too."

He grins, then unzips his jeans. I lean over and help him slide out of them, leaving him in gray boxer briefs that perfectly highlight the generous bulge underneath. I slide those off and am once again appreciative of the excellent lighting in this hotel room. Now I can see Drew in his full, unobscured glory.

I climb onto the bed and gently palm his length.

He groans and leads me gently to rest over his face. My legs tremble on either side of his head, slightly shaky in anticipation.

He cradles both hands around my thighs. "Do you know how unbelievably sexy you are?"

The raw want in his tone shatters me.

"You're one to talk," I say.

He smiles, his cheeks blushing. Once I'm positioned over his face, I grip the headboard, close my eyes, and relax. Just like before, his expert tongue feels like heaven. He starts slow and soft, like he wants to tease me forever. Then his touch becomes firmer. The movements I make over him are small and slight. Drew is so, so good with the way he moves his head and his mouth and his tongue that I don't have to do much. I simply glide along with him, the warmth and pressure building and building.

My breath turns ragged as the minutes pass. My head falls back while both of my hands grip the headboard for balance. My head spins, the pleasure is so all-consuming. It hits everywhere inside me, from the tips of my toes to the top of my head. As the sensations intensify, I grow desperate. My gasps turn to moans, then screams. I grind against Drew's face like the world is ending. Everything inside me grows hotter and hotter until I finally burst.

I come with a shout and a gasp, my thighs quivering. Drew doesn't let up, though, not for a single second. He's got me with his hands wrapped around both of my thighs. His tongue works like some sort of magical sex toy that never, ever loses steam.

When it ends, I'm so shaky that I almost fall over, but he braces me with both of his arms, then slides me down his chest. I cuddle up against him, and he plants a soft kiss to the top of my head.

Chest heaving as I catch my breath, I close my eyes. When I

open them, my vision is blurry. I let out a giddy laugh as I glance up at him. It takes a few seconds before his grinning face comes into focus.

"That's the fastest and hardest that's happened in . . . honestly, I can't even remember." I laugh into his hot, slick skin. "That was . . . So. Freaking. Good."

His smile turns sly as he maneuvers so that I'm lying with my back on the bed as his body hovers over mine. He kisses me for a long few seconds before sitting up and leaning over the side of his bed to pull his wallet out of his jeans pocket. He swipes a condom from it and rips open the packet with his teeth, then slides it on him.

Then he turns that dangerously smug stare back to me. "Let's not be too quick to judge. I've still got a lot to prove."

15

THE MOMENT DREW SLIDES INSIDE ME, I'M GASPING. HE thrusts slowly, steadily at first, bracing his arms above my head. He gazes down at me, his eyes bright with concentration as he breathes, then leans down to kiss me.

"This feel okay?" he says, his rich voice like gravel.

I press my head against the pillow, trying not to let my eyes roll too far to the back of my head so I can at least attempt to look at him. But I fail. It feels too good.

"More than okay," I whine. "So, so good."

A throaty laugh erupts from him.

It's no surprise that Drew feels good. He's got the length and girth to satisfy. But *this* good? This is a very, very pleasant surprise.

He also seems to have an astute ability to observe. Every time I make an affirming sound or my body reacts positively to something he does, he immediately keeps doing it. I'm trembling and making unholy noises as a result.

"So very loud." He chuckles.

I turn my head up to look at him, admiring the light sheen of sweat beading along his hairline, then laugh. I start to babble an apology, but he stops me.

"No, no, no. Alia . . ." He laces his fingers in mine and positions my hands above my head, pressing them lightly against the bed. "I fucking love it."

His jaw tightens as he speeds up. Tingles shoot up from my chest all the way to my neck. My chest feels like it's going to burst and my head is spinning. This is an astounding level of pleasure—a level of pleasure I've never, ever experienced during the first time with someone.

And then Drew pauses, releases my hands, leans up, and pulls my legs tightly around his waist. When he hits a particularly deep and heavenly spot, my back arches, my mouth falls open, and I shout once more.

Pressure and heat collide in my core, spreading through the rest of my body. I slip my hand between my legs and circle around my most sensitive spot to intensify the feeling. The backs of my fingers brush against Drew's pelvis. His eyes go wide, and he slowly stills.

I glance up at him while still rubbing myself. "Is something wrong?"

He shakes his head. "No, it's just . . . seeing you do that . . . to yourself . . . I'm gonna lose it." He lets out a flustered chuckle. "I just, uh, need a minute."

I'm soaring on the inside. Because I'm driving Drew absolutely wild in this moment—so wild that he has to take a break and pace himself.

He leans up, slipping out of me. The loss of sensation is a disappointment, but then his gaze zeros in on my bare chest. It's like a fire is lit behind his eyes. He smirks, then lowers his head to my breast. His tongue, that nimble yet insanely strong tongue, runs over my nipple, then the other, causing me to lose all the breath in my body. He works me over for several minutes, sending tingles and jolts through my chest. I heave out a breath.

Biting my lip, I lock eyes with him and slow the circles that my hand makes. A shiver shoots through me.

"I really, really want you back inside of me," I say.

Drew's expression turns hungry once more. "How close are you?"

I swirl my hand faster and faster. "So . . . so . . . close," I whimper.

Gripping me by the hips, he thrusts back into me with one smooth, firm slide. And then he employs that steady rhythm my body loves so much already.

When all those tingles inside me turn to fire, that's when I know I'm on the verge. It's likely due to the winning combination of my hand and Drew's incredible technique. My insides, my skin, my bones, my brain—everything ignites. Stars cloud my vision.

"I'm not gonna be able to last much longer, Alia," he grunts.

"Me either," I yelp. And then I'm gone.

My legs splay out as orgasm levels me. It moves like a never-ending roll of thunder, sending pleasure everywhere inside me. I feel it in my every muscle; in my blood, which burns hot; in my chest, which feels like it's going to burst; in my lungs, which are on fire. It's absolute ecstasy, every part of this. This orgasm is grabbing hold of every single part of my body, and it's not letting go until it's finished with me.

With my free hand I grip his shoulder to steady myself, digging into that smooth skin and hard flesh with my fingertips.

"Fuck yeah," he grunts.

His raw reaction is everything. The gasp-shout that rips through me earns a satisfied grin from Drew. It's the last thing I see before my eyes roll to the back of my head for the millionth time. Then my head falls against the mattress and my vision goes black. My ears ring. And then I blink and look up just in time to watch Drew as he moves above me, groaning through one last thrust, his gaze positively feral. Those sparkling eyes of his are dilated and there's a hazy look in them, like he's drunk off this pleasure—just like me.

His body tenses above me; then he stills. A beat later he lowers his head, kissing along the side of my neck.

I moan, feeling heavy and light all at once.

"Goddamn it, Alia," he mutters, his mouth on my shoulder.

He leaves me with another light kiss, then sits up and slides off the bed to toss the condom in the bathroom trash can. Then he walks back over and falls into bed, cuddling me into him.

"So? What's the verdict?" he asks.

Frowning, I look up at him. "What?"

"Your sex toy drawer. I gotta know if I still measure up."

I press a kiss to his collarbone. "Oh, you more than measure up. There's not a sex toy in my apartment—on this planet—that compares to you."

Closing my eyes, I rest my head against his chest, his thundering heartbeat lightly tapping against my ear.

"I'm flattered," he says. "But I'm not done."

My eyelids fly open, and a giddy smile spreads across my face as I gaze up at him. "Already?"

"It's an old party trick of mine."

I burst out laughing, then push myself up and straddle him. I settle my legs on either side of his hips and start to slowly grind myself against his pelvis.

"How many condoms do you have left?"

I feel his hardness underneath me, teasing me that he's already ready for more. His jaw tightens as he takes a breath and that familiar look of concentration crosses his face.

"Two," he says, his voice strained. He digs his hands into the fleshy part where my hips meet my ass.

"We'll definitely need to do a drugstore run. But first." I lean over and lead him in a long, teasing kiss until neither of us can breathe properly. And then we do it all again.

"I . . . WHAT THE . . . Holy crap."

I chuckle at Drew. "You keep saying that."

He stands at the lookout point where we're parked in Bryce Canyon National Park to film a few panoramic shots of the hoodoo formations.

"I've never seen anything like this before," he says. Countless thin spires of rock in every shade of orange fill the basin below us.

"My *apong* said looking at the spires here in Bryce reminded her of the beaches in Palawan."

"Really?"

"It didn't make sense to me either. But then she explained that it was because of how vast and endless the view was. She said looking at the viewpoints here reminded her of how she felt whenever she gazed out at the ocean in the Philippines. She felt the same awe-inspiring feeling, like both the rocks and the water could go on forever and ever."

The look Drew flashes me has me both giddy and heartened. It's like he understands just how special it is for me to share these memories of my grandma in this place.

"That makes perfect sense. And it'll be a great tidbit to include when you produce your series about Palawan," he says with a soft smile.

"Maybe." Glancing down at the ground, I'm feeling more hopeful that someday it'll actually happen.

"That's Bryce Canyon for you," Joe says from behind his camera, which is positioned next to Drew and me. "Utterly breath-taking in every sense of the word. It leaves you speechless."

Drew glances at me and winks. "You and Bryce Canyon have that in common," he says softly, so only I can hear.

He leans over and rests his hand on the small of my back for a brief second. Then he winks before his arm falls back to his side, and I'm left gnawing my bottom lip, trying to keep it together.

"Damn, Dunn. Is my hand on your back really all it takes to get you to look at me that way?" he whispers.

I scrunch my face to hide my cheesy smile. "It's just . . . the perfect combination of intimate and unassuming."

"I'll have to do it more often, then."

He taps my back for a quick second once more before turning back to study something on his tablet.

Around us the crew is busy framing shots and going over the shot list for the day. I'm thankful because that means Drew and I can take this moment to share a long bit of smiley eye contact without having to worry if anyone suspects anything.

Until we came to shoot at Bryce, I spent every free evening in Drew's hotel room . . . or he came to mine. We had to make two drugstore runs as a result, and we're nearing the end of our current box of condoms.

It was the single greatest week of sex I've ever had in my life. My thighs were constantly red with beard burn, and I'm operating on some kind of post-orgasm endorphin high I've never experienced before. Rylan and Haley have both asked me multiple times over the past several days why I'm smiling so much. I quickly make up something about being so happy with how the shoot is progressing; then my face inevitably turns red and I squint down at my tablet or phone or whatever I'm holding in my hand and change the subject.

It's a strange turn of events . . . I started out this shoot with a relationship history that would rival these barren desert Utah landscapes. And now I'm on cloud nine smiling uncontrollably because of Drew Irons.

But it's more than our physical connection that endears him to me. Just spending time with Drew is the highlight of my day, whether we're in bed together, sharing a drink at a bar, or grabbing food with the crew.

It's also the fact that it's an absolute pleasure to work with him. We collaborate like two colleagues who have worked together for years.

Tablet in hand, Drew leans over and asks me to review tomorrow's schedule. Then his eyes cut to me. "I'm going to need to make a drugstore run for some . . . supplies."

I bite my lip at his whispered tone, then dart my stare back to the tablet screen, pretending to squint at something. "We're staying at a shared condo for the Bryce shoot. Remember the rules?"

"Oh, right. The 'no sex when we're in a shared living space' rule. I forgot."

I give his arm a playful shove. "Look, I know we were so exhausted when we checked into the condo late last night that everyone collapsed in their rooms and went straight to sleep, but I have a feeling you remember that rule."

"A few days of mind-blowing sex can make a guy forget just about anything."

I fight the smile tugging at my lips. "We gotta be professional. Remember?"

He nods once. "Of course."

I check the time and see that Blaine is late, as usual. "Well, we've been here an hour and Blaine is nowhere to be found. You ready to hike down to the basin and shoot?"

"Ready."

An hour later, we've packed the gear up and hiked the half mile down the nearest trail to kick off the first day of filming the iconic hoodoos that make Bryce Canyon famous. After studying his lines all morning, Drew nails the first several scenes. I smile as he delivers tidbits about how Bryce Canyon isn't actually a canyon—it's a series of cliffs and basins. He's in the middle of explaining how the hoodoo rock spires are made of limestone while walking along the hilly trail when we hear shouting behind us.

"Cut!" I yell, then turn around to see Blaine jogging down the trail over to us.

"Don't worry, everyone! Your superstar is here!" He's grinning wide and decked out in lime-green cycling gear for some reason.

When he makes it over to us, he stops, his eyes zeroing in on Drew. Then he frowns and tilts his head. "What the . . . Why are you guys filming Drew doing the scene?"

"We're setting up the shot," I say to him. "We needed to do something if you're going to show up two hours past call time."

He turns his head and frowns at me like he doesn't quite believe me. I hold my breath. If Blaine figures out that we've replaced him, he'll surely flip out. He may not be willing to consistently put in the work of a show host, but he sure as hell still wants the title and credit.

"Well, I'm here now." Blaine glares at me for a second, then turns around to face Drew, who's standing several feet away. "Can you run through that scene again, Drew?" Blaine hollers. "That way I can see how it goes and then film it myself."

Even from where I'm standing, I can see Drew's jaw tense as he bites down, displeased at Blaine's request.

"Sure thing, man," Drew answers.

For the rest of the shoot until sundown, we film Drew's scenes and Blaine's half-assed attempts. Inside I'm simmering, annoyed that we're wasting all this time filming Blaine when I'm just planning to use Drew's footage.

After the final shot just before sundown, we wrap up.

"That's a wrap!" I call out.

Everyone claps. Drew gives Blaine a high five and praises him on a job well done. Blaine eats it up, beaming while babbling nonsense about artistic expression. Drew nods along with a glazed-over look in his eyes.

Blaine announces he's going to meditate among the hoodoos. I flash him a phony smile and a thumbs-up and follow the rest of the crew back up the trail to where we're parked.

Despite the chill in the air, we're all drenched with sweat by the time we hike back up to the parking lot.

"See you all back at the condo?" I say, wiping the sweat off my brow.

Everyone nods or says yes between gasps for air or gulps of water. Except for Joe, who only seems mildly out of breath. I glance over at Drew, who somehow looks like a fitness model, even though his face is red and covered in beads of sweat.

He walks over to stand next to me while he digs through his pack for the keys to his truck.

"Welp, I'm going to need a shower after that," Wyatt says, his face and clothing covered in sweat.

"That's the annoying part about Bryce," I say. "All the trails are downhill first, then uphill."

"Damn Mother Nature," Wyatt mumbles as he takes off his jacket. "I call dibs on the shower first."

"No way." Joe laughs as he loads his equipment into the van. "You always use up all the hot water. Every shoot I've ever been on with you, you're a hot-water hog. Let someone else go first."

While Joe and Wyatt get into a joking argument about bathroom-sharing etiquette, Drew pivots his body to me. The collar of his long-sleeved T-shirt is soaked in his sweat. His neck and the top of his chest glisten with perspiration. It makes my mouth water.

"You know," he says softly, "the economical and environmentally conscious thing to do would be to take a shower together."

"Behave yourself," I say to him quietly with a naughty lift of my eyebrow.

A playful smirk dances on his lips. Then he winks at me before loading up his truck. When he turns and bends over to haul equipment and toss it inside, my mouth waters once more. All that bulging muscle under that sweat-soaked fabric. It would be heaven to see Drew soaking wet, to run my hands all over his body, to let my mouth wander all the way—

He slams the door shut and spins around to me, the corner of his mouth quirking up into one hell of a sexy smirk. "I wouldn't dream of breaking the rules, Dunn. Even though it would be very fun . . . and very, very worth it. Don't you think?"

A spark ignites in his hazel-brown gaze as he wiggles his eyebrows. Then he softly taps the small of my back with his fingertips. My entire body tingles. He turns away before I can respond. But I already know my answer.

TWO HOURS LATER I'm lying on the bed in my room of the condo rental after a long, hot shower. I should run to the kitchen and scrounge up something to eat . . . but what I'm hungry for isn't food.

What I'm craving is that sexy man in the bedroom down the hall from me, who's probably lying in bed all shower fresh, wearing nothing but those snug boxer briefs that make me go gaga every time I see him in them.

I groan into my pillow, annoyed that for the next week, we can't do anything with each other because we're sharing this rental with everyone else on the crew and I don't want us to get caught.

I sigh, wondering if the raw want for Drew that's simmering inside me is going to dissipate at all over the next few days.

"You know it won't," I mumble to myself.

Just then my phone buzzes with a text. I grin when I see it's from Drew.

Gotta admit, as good as that shower felt, it would have been a million times better with you in there with me.

Smiling, I let out a groan into the bedsheets. It seems I'm not the only one who's got impure thoughts on the brain.

Me: We said no dirty sexting, remember?

Drew: You said it. Not me 😊

Me: You agreed to it 😖

Drew: Argh okay I did . . . but come on . . . tell me you're not aching for some alone time.

I stare at my phone screen and silently admit that he's right.

Drew: Tell me that you don't wish you could have me in your bedroom doing the dirtiest things to you right now.

I bite my lip at just the thought.

Me: Okay yes.

Me: I want that very, very much.

He sends a devil emoji. Just the sight of that smirking purple icon makes me chuckle. And then I think for a second. No one makes the rules but us. Who says I can't break them for one night?

Me: Okay, listen. I'm still not cool with sending naughty photos to each other . . . but you're right about the rule thing. Maaaybe it wouldn't be the worst thing in the world to bend them a bit.

He sends a dead-face emoji, and I cover my mouth as I laugh.

Me: If you wanted to dirty text a bit, I wouldn't be opposed.

He sends three high-fives, and I burst out laughing.

Me: Is that a yes then?

Drew: It's a hell yes.

Me: Then tell me . . . if we were in the same bed together . . . what would you do to me right now?

Drew: It's going to get dirty. Very, very dirty. Are you ready for that?

Me: HELL YES!

Drew: I'd kiss you softly at first, teasing. It would start slow and light, then get harder and more desperate.

Drew: You'd barely be able to catch your breath.

My chest flutters and my breathing starts to pick up. Just the thought of kissing Drew has me in a tizzy already.

Me: And then?

Drew: And then I'd strip all your clothes off.

Drew: I'd ask you to get on the bed, on all fours, facing away from me.

My eyes go wide. I think I know exactly where this is going, and holy hell, do I love it.

Drew: I'd kiss up your legs, so slowly. So gently.

Drew: Sometimes I'd use my tongue.

Drew: Sometimes I'd use my teeth, gently scraping them along your impossibly soft skin.

Soon my chest is heaving as I pant. I'm achy all over with want, wishing this very act could be playing out in my bed right now.

I slide my hand down the waistband of my pajama shorts and touch myself softly, tentatively.

Drew: You're not saying much, Dunn.

I bite back a smile, then type out a response with my free hand

Me: That's because you're making me so hot right now, I can't say anything. I can only touch myself.

He sends a mind-blown emoji, and I grin wide.

Me: Keep going. Don't stop. Please.

Drew: I'd keep kissing up and down your thighs until you couldn't take it anymore. Until your legs are shaking so bad, you could barely stand up. And then I'd grab your beautiful, bare ass, and finally kiss you from behind in the place you want it most.

I let out a breath as I circle my fingers around that very spot he's talking about. I close my eyes, the pressure building and building in my chest, my toes curling, my skin heating, my mouth watering.

Drew: Your legs would finally give out. You'd fall on the bed, you wouldn't be able to take it anymore.

Drew: You'd groan into the mattress, into the sheets.

Drew: And then I'd grab you by the waist and pull your legs up, holding them up with my arms.

Drew: I'd slide in, take you fast and hard.

My jaw falls open as I gasp. Then I clamp my mouth shut once more, reminding myself that I need to be quiet, that there are people in this shared condo trying to sleep, and I absolutely cannot make any noise.

So I close my eyes. I clench my jaw and work my hand along my body, moving in those quick, small circles that I always make when I'm so turned on and orgasm is only a minute away.

My phone vibrates with another text from Drew.

Drew: Are you close?

Instead of trying to type in my distracted state, I use the record option in my text message. "So, so close. It feels so good. *You* make this feel so good," I say in a whiny whimper.

When I send it, there's an immediate buzz in response.

Drew: Fuck, that's hot.

I smile to myself as my body begins to clench. I'd bet a million dollars Drew is in his room right now, working himself up too.

I pant, then moan, then whimper. I'm almost to the edge—I just need one more dirty text.

I do another voice text message saying exactly this in that desperate, breathy tone that drives him out of his mind with lust.

Drew: I'd ask for your hands . . . then I'd pin them behind your back . . . and I'd fuck you until you come all over me, screaming my name until your throat was hoarse.

My hand moves with renewed fury as I quickly skim his words on my phone screen. I'm barely to the end of his text when my body seizes and I'm thrashing through climax. The pleasure crashes through me like a tidal wave. All the muscles in my legs cramp, my back arches, my head falls back, and my phone falls away. I use that hand to cover my mouth, muffling the animal sounds I make as I thrash against the bed.

When I finally come down a minute later, I feel like I've sprinted a race. My lungs are raw and burning, and my heartbeat is through the roof. My chest heaves as I glance at the phone, now at the edge of the bed. I start to wring out my legs and arms, wincing at the immediate soreness.

All that from just Drew's words.

I smirk to myself as I pick up the phone and skim his newest text.

Drew: How was that?

Me: I came so hard.

Drew: Good ☺

Me: You?

Drew: Those breathy voice texts of yours drove me wild. Many thanks.

I snuggle into my pillow while chuckling. When I blink I realize just how heavy my eyelids feel and how drowsy I am.

Me: Nothing is ever as good as being with you physically of course . . . but damn, can you do some damage with texts. That was . . . an experience.

Me: I don't even know how to follow that.

Drew: I do. Eggs Benedict. Best way to refuel after a night like that ☺

I laugh into my pillow.

Me: Mmm my favorite!

Me: You're the greatest, I swear. Goodnight.

Drew: Aww shucks. Goodnight, Dunn.

I have just enough energy to put my phone on the nightstand before I'm sound asleep.

16

WHEN I WALK INTO THE KITCHEN THE NEXT MORNING, I'm greeted with Drew standing at the stove in a T-shirt and gym shorts, his back to me as he cooks. Everyone else is up and milling around at the small dining table and the kitchen island in their pajamas.

I fall onto a stool, my legs and my brain still groggy. Despite the sleep fog I'm fighting, I'm tingling in Drew's presence. Even though he's standing a few feet away and not looking at me, just being in the same room has my entire body on high alert. Every part of me, from the goose bumps on my skin to the pulse between my legs, remembers what his sexy texts did to me last night.

I shove the thought aside while I try to focus on the chatter around me. Wyatt is on the phone with, I assume, his mom, judging by his irritated tone and the fact that he's talking about rosaries and Hail Marys.

"I promise I'm being careful." He tosses his head back and slouches in his chair at the dining table. "Yes, I have a snakebite kit, just in case. Yes, I have sunscreen. Yes, tell Lolo I always have at least a half tank of gas so I don't get stranded in the middle of the desert and die." There's a long pause. "Of course

I'm saying the rosary! I say it every day! Well then, you say it for me if I'm not doing it enough times."

I bite back a laugh as I down a glass of water that Haley sets in front of me. I thank her for the cup of coffee she deposits right after. I catch Rylan smiling down at her phone as she texts. She must be talking to Colton.

Out of the corner of my eye I watch as Haley looks at me, then at Drew, then at me again. I roll my eyes.

While drinking, I inhale the aroma of whatever scrumptious dish Drew is whipping up at the stove. I smile at Joe, who's FaceTiming with his kindergarten-age son and girlfriend.

His son holds up a sheet of paper that he painted on at school.

"Wow, way to go, pal! That looks just like me."

I beam wide while holding back an "aww" sound. Joe's little guy sports a wide grin and a mass of long blond hair, which is tied back into a bun, just like Joe's.

"Have a good day at school. I'll call you again tomorrow, okay?"

"Okay, Daddy!"

Joe's son makes a kissing noise, and Joe makes one in return before they end the call.

"Your son looks just like you," I say to him.

He beams at his phone screen while closing out of the app. "He's way cuter, though."

"My ovaries are exploding over here, Joe," Haley says as she tops off her coffee. "Your son is the cutest and your family should be in a commercial; you're so perfect. And that's coming from a stone-cold workaholic who never, ever wants to have kids."

Joe blushes at Haley's words. "I'm a pretty lucky guy."

Just then Drew spins around. "Who's hungry?"

"Smile, Drew!" Rylan says from the dining table while she aims her phone at him.

Drew grins, and she takes a photo.

"I'm posting this to your Twitter and Instagram right now," she says.

"You're a social media wizard, Rylan," Drew says as he grabs some plates from the nearby cupboard.

When everyone on the crew decided that Drew taking over as host was a go, establishing a social media presence for him was the next most important item on our collective to-do list. Rylan offered to run the accounts for him, which I was more than happy to let her do. Given she's ten years younger than the rest of us thirty-somethings, she's more social-media savvy than anyone else.

Rylan shrugs at Drew's compliment as if to brush it off, but the smile on her face remains. "Your accounts are already a few thousand followers strong."

"Wow, that's amazing, Rylan," I say. "I shouldn't be surprised, though. You have a Twitter and Instagram following that's in the thousands."

She squints down at her phone screen. "I can only take partial credit. Drew, you're still trending in New York from that subway gentleman hashtag from weeks ago. Whoever did that deserves credit too."

I hide behind my mug of coffee while taking a long sip. It's better if the crew doesn't find out about how I creeped on Drew. Haley is the only person who knows, and when I told her about my history with him at the beginning of this shoot, I swore her to secrecy.

Drew's eyes cut to me, the smile on his face taking on a deviant edge. "I definitely owe that person a big thanks."

"What's for breakfast?" Wyatt asks from the table, through a yawn, while running a hand through his floppy jet-black hair.

"Eggs Benedict," Drew says.

My stomach does ten somersaults in the second that he

makes eye contact with me. In this shared space where we have minimal privacy, Drew found a way to make the morning after our text shenanigans special for the two of us even though we can't be alone. My heart flutters. This is one of the sweetest—and most creative—things someone has ever done for me.

"Eggs Benedict sounds yummy," I say.

Drew spins around, a prepared plate in hand. He sets a plate of English muffins, Canadian bacon, poached eggs, and hollandaise sauce in front of me.

His eyebrow lifts the tiniest bit, a gentle gleam in his eye. "I heard this was your favorite."

"It is."

I break the perfectly poached egg yolk with my fork. The bright-yellow liquid spills down the plate. My mouth waters, and not just for the food.

When I take a bite, I hum quietly to myself. It's the perfect bite of richness and fattiness from the egg and sauce, saltiness from the bacon, and carby goodness from the toasted English muffin.

"Damn, Drew," Wyatt moans from the table. Rylan nods along while chewing.

"You think you can work as my personal chef?" Wyatt jokes. "I can't afford to pay you a proper salary, but I can pay you in Hail Marys."

We all laugh with our mouths full.

Drew takes a bite from his own plate while leaning against the granite kitchen island. He chuckles, then swallows, then wipes his mouth with the back of his hand.

"I don't know." He looks at me. "I'm already gainfully employed. Gotta check with the boss to see if she's interested in giving me up."

There's the slightest lift of his brow as he gazes at me. His hazel-brown eyes pin me from above the rim of his orange juice glass as he takes a sip.

"Not a chance," I say, the slightest hint of a growl in my voice that is thankfully subtle enough that I'm sure no one picked up on—other than Drew, judging by the way his eyes dazzle.

I turn to Wyatt. "He's too good of a field coordinator. Sorry, Wyatt."

Everyone chuckles. As I finish my breakfast, I admire just how well Drew has managed to fit in with the crew. He's only known us for weeks and yet he jokes and chats with everyone like they've been friends for years. But he's not just a charmer—he's a genuinely good person with a work ethic that meshes amazingly with every member of this crew. And I feel lucky to be with him.

We finish eating, then run through the plans for the day. Joe and Wyatt are filming landscape shots of Bryce Canyon. Haley and Rylan will assist them.

Haley mentions going over the script for the rest of the Bryce and the Capitol Reef shoots when they're back from filming landscape shots, but I shake my head. "I can do that. I'll be stuck at the computer answering emails and reviewing footage anyway. No sense in bogging you down with that," I say. "You guys should all go out and unwind a little when you wrap up. Explore the tiny towns around here, come back to the condo and take a nap, whatever you want."

Everyone's faces perk up except for Haley's. "You sure? That means you'll be stuck here all day staring at your laptop."

"She'll have help," Drew says from the kitchen sink. He turns around and smooths a hand over the rumpled white T-shirt that's clinging quite nicely to his chest. "I'll be working next to her the whole day."

The corner of Haley's mouth quirks up. "You two, always working so hard. I'm sure you'll make the best of it."

No one else seems to notice the undertone of Haley's comment because they're all rinsing their dishes or walking away to their rooms.

Haley is the last to leave the kitchen, but not before winking at me while Drew is turned around loading the dishes into the dishwasher. I walk up to him and he turns to me, then takes a step forward so that we're nearly touching.

He reaches a hand to my face and tucks my hair behind my ear. "Excited to work hard with you today, Dunn. Extra, extra hard."

A sheet of goose bumps flies across my skin. It's just a few seconds of contact, but I can't help it. Every bit of Drew I can get—his words, his breakfast, his knowing eye contact, his smiles—is enough to send me into a flutter every single time.

"Especially after last night," he whispers. "We're going to have an empty condo. Just you and me—finally."

I go breathless at the memory. "You better be excited. Because once our work is finished and everyone is gone, I'm expecting you to live out exactly what you described to me in those texts you sent last night."

His brow lifts slightly. "You're willing to throw out the 'nothing happens in Bryce' rule you were so adamant about last week? You have a weak resolve, Dunn."

"I tried. I really, really did." I tug at the hem of his shirt, breathless. "I can't help it. You bring out the naughty rule breaker in me."

That cheeky smile tugs at his lips once more. "Let the rule breaking begin."

WORKING SIDE BY side with Drew all morning and afternoon has garnered us impressive results. My inbox count is down to three and we're nearly finished going through the scripts for the remaining episodes.

My phone buzzes with a text from Wyatt.

Wyatt: Just wrapped. Sure you guys don't want to join us?

Me: No, you go without us. We've still got some edits to the script we're working on.

Wyatt: Don't work too hard.

Drew squints at his laptop as he sits across from me at the kitchen table. "Do I have to say, 'For bonus footage, check out our website' at the end of the episode?"

"What's wrong with that?"

"It's kind of . . . unexciting."

I lightly kick his chair. He chuckles and holds both hands up. "It's not an insult to your script writing, I swear."

I narrow my gaze at him in mock annoyance. "What would you rather say?"

"How about, 'Explore even more by visiting our website for bonus footage'?"

"That's cute. Catchy. It even rhymes. Sure, go with that."

He grins and types quickly on his laptop. "We make a hell of a team, Dunn."

"We do."

Collaborating with Drew makes me feel even more confident about the series.

And even if all we do for the rest of the day is work, I'd be one hundred percent content. Because no matter what I'm doing with Drew—flirting, working, fooling around, riding in the car, eating breakfast—it's always the best. Because it's with him.

My phone rings with an incoming FaceTime call. When I see it's my mom calling, I tell Drew to wait just a second.

I answer and see her and Dad sitting next to each other on their living room couch, smiling. They greet me at the same time.

"Hi, *anak*!"

"Hi, honeybun!"

"Hey. Great to see you, guys."

"I know you're busy working, *anak*, but we just wanted to say a quick hi."

Then in their signature adorable style, they ask a bunch of questions in a row without waiting for me to answer.

"How are things going for you?"

"Is the weather holding out? Have you had to use that rain gear I sent you?"

"You're getting enough sleep, right, *anak*?"

"Did you get the extended travel insurance like I recommended, honey?"

I bite back a groan and keep smiling. I have the best, most supportive parents in the world, but they always insist on Face-Timing together and talking at the same time, making it nearly impossible to have a clear conversation.

"Things are good. The weather has been mild so far, perfect for filming. Yes, I'm getting enough sleep. And I didn't need the extra travel insurance, Dad. Work covered everything."

They both mention again how proud they are of me for working on my first series.

"I told all the ladies in my aerobics class about my brilliant daughter's amazing new show and they can't wait to watch it, *anak*."

"Thank you, Mom."

"Apong would be so happy and proud to know that you're filming in Utah. She had so much fun taking you kids on that road trip when you were little. She talked about that vacation all the time."

My chest warms at just how proud and happy she sounds. Dad nods along.

"You're going to knock this series out of the park, honeybun,"

Dad says. "This is gonna be the first of so many big hits for you, I just know it."

I hold in the surprise dedication for Apong Lita that I plan to air with the Needles episodes. I'm dying to tell them, but I know that it'll be a million times more impactful if they see the dedication when they're watching the actual show.

Seeing their excitement has me the tiniest bit more hopeful. If this series goes well, I'll be one step closer to hopefully someday filming a travel series in the Philippines—that would be another surprise for my family. I take a quiet second and wish as hard as I can that this all works out and that someday I can make my island getaway series a reality.

"You're eating enough too, right, *anak*? And sleeping? Do you need me to mail you a care package of vitamins and snacks? I used to do that for you when you went off to college, remember?"

"Promise I'm doing just fine, Mom."

Off to the side, Drew laughs quietly.

"Is someone there with you?" she asks.

"Oh, um, yeah." I pivot the phone slightly so they can see him. "This is Drew; he's the field coordinator on the crew. He's amazing."

I bite my tongue as soon as those final two words go tumbling out of my mouth. I can tell by the way Mom's thick and shapely eyebrows raise that she's caught on to the something extra that rests in my tone when I talk about Drew.

His cheeks are pink as he smiles and tells my parents how nice it is to meet them.

"Your daughter has been a pleasure to work with. The whole crew loves her."

They beam at his praise.

"She gets her work ethic from her mom and her good looks from me," Dad jokes as he points to his short-buzzed gray hair.

Mom swipes her long, wavy, black hair over one shoulder and

laughs as she pats Dad's arm. "Ay, you stop. We both know she looks like me. Her dark hair, those brown eyes, that nose, her tan. That's all me."

"Thank goodness." Dad pulls her close and plants a kiss on her cheek.

"Sorry about them," I whisper to Drew as Mom and Dad playfully bicker about who's the lucky one in their marriage.

Drew shakes his head, still grinning. "It's all good."

"Okay, Mom. Dad. Great to chat with you, but we've got a ton of work to get through still."

"Of course, *anak*. You stay safe, okay? And don't forget to take a break soon. You work so hard, you'll burn yourself out if you're not careful. So nice to meet you, Drew!"

Drew says likewise, and we all say good-bye.

"You look just like your mom," Drew says as I put away my phone.

"Everyone says that whenever they see us. It's my favorite compliment."

I reach my hands up and stretch, groaning softly as I will my stiff body to loosen. My phone buzzes with a text.

Mom: Wow, Drew is so handsome!! Is he single?

I roll my eyes and shove my phone across the table. Out of the corner of my eye I see Drew pop out of his chair and walk over to me. Then he leans down and wraps his arms around me from behind, nuzzling against the side of my neck. A million goose bumps flash across my skin.

"Your mom's right. We deserve a break. We worked pretty hard today," he growls softly before pressing a teasing kiss to my bare shoulder.

"Okay." The word falls out like a gasp as he kisses along that sensitive spot of my skin where my neck meets my shoulder.

He's kicked things off by kissing that spot the last few times we've fooled around. I'm impressed that he's committed it to memory already.

He runs his hands along the sides of my body slowly, firmly. When I turn my head to the side, he captures my mouth in his before I can utter a breath or a word. I run my hand roughly through his hair as our tongues tangle wildly. We stay that way—our mouths glued together, handsy as hell—until Drew pulls my chair back and pulls away from me long enough to scoop me up. I let out a high-pitched squeal, giggling as he marches me quickly to my room down the hall.

He kicks the door shut; then he sets me on the bed, his eyes glimmering with anticipation. "I'm gonna need you naked, Dunn. Now."

"That goes double for you, Irons."

We break into identical grins as we quickly undress.

"I'll never get tired of looking at you," I say, my eyes glued to his Adonis belt.

Then Drew leans down and tilts my head up to look at him with his finger under my chin. "I was just about to say the same thing to you." He ends it with a kiss that sends my heart racing and my breath fleeting.

"How do you want me?" I ask, chest heaving.

"On the bed. On your hands and knees. Facing the wall. Please."

I'm grinning like a madwoman as I maneuver myself on the bed according to his request. A beat later when I'm in position, I feel it. The softness of his lips against the back of my left thigh. He skims slowly, softly up my leg, his hot, wet breath hitting right between my legs, in that spot I want him the most. But instead of giving it to me, his mouth lands at the top of my right thigh, just below my ass cheek. There's a soft scrape that leaves me gasping, then another soft kiss against my skin. He moves down my thigh, then back up; then he's back between my legs, his breath wetting my skin.

"Please, Drew," I whine, my arms shaky as I struggle to hold myself up while those tingles of pleasure make their way inside me.

He grunts behind me and then I feel it—that exquisite softness of his tongue as he makes contact.

My jaw drops and my eyes press shut. It is so, so good.

I gasp. "Fuck, Drew. That's—"

The slam of the front door of the condo jolts me. My eyelids fly open. Drew pulls away and I turn my head around so I can look at him. I start to ask him what that sound was, but then there's a shout.

"Hold on, man! It's gonna be okay!" Joe's voice booms behind the door.

There's the sound of heavy footsteps, then banging at my bedroom door. "Alia! Alia, are you in there?"

I shoot up, kneeling on the bed. Then I glance at Drew. Then I glance at the door.

Shit.

Drew's eyes go wide as he stares at me while kneeling buck naked on the floor. I jump up and run to my bedroom door.

"What's going on? Is everything okay?" I ask.

"We need the first-aid kit," Joe says, his tone breathless and panicky from behind the door. "You have it, right? We can't find it anywhere, and I think Wyatt is having an allergic reaction."

Joe babbles something about Wyatt downing a drink that must have had vodka in it and how he started having trouble breathing as they pulled into the condo parking lot. The hair on my arms stands on end. Wyatt is allergic to vodka.

"His entire face is turning red," Joe says, his voice pitchy with panic. "He's got hives on his chest and he's struggling to breathe . . . or maybe his throat is closing. I—I don't know . . ."

The sound of muffled voices follows.

"There's an EpiPen in the first aid kit, right?" Joe asks me through the door. "I thought you said there was."

"Shit," I mutter to myself. "There is, but . . . You're sure the kit wasn't in the van?" I could have sworn I left it in Wyatt's car. That's where I've always kept it. Unless I messed up something . . .

"We looked everywhere," Joe says, interrupting my frenzied train of thought. "When you didn't answer your phone, I tried calling Drew to ask him if he knew, but he didn't answer."

My eyes cut to Drew, who's tugging both of his hands through his hair, his face twisted in bewilderment. He starts shaking his head and mutters the word "shit," but I put my finger over my mouth.

"Quiet!" I silently mouth to Drew before turning back to the door. "Yeah, um, Drew went out. For . . . supplies."

There's the sound of footsteps fading away from the door, then Joe's voice. I think he's in the living room now judging by how far away it sounds.

Out of the corner of my eye, Drew's brow flies up.

"Supplies? What does that even mean?" he whispers.

I hold my hand up at him. Behind the door there's a thudding sound.

"Get him on the couch," Haley says. "Lay him down."

I throw my shirt and yoga pants back on, then turn my bedroom upside down searching for the first-aid kit.

"I'm looking for the kit!" I yell, hoping they can hear me in the living room. "You need to go out the window," I whisper to Drew as I crawl on the floor and search under my bed.

"What?" he whisper-shouts. "Alia, you can't be serious."

I whip my head up to look at him. "I am serious. Look, there's a balcony outside my window that's, like, six feet above ground. You can jump that, right?"

He opens his mouth, but I cut him off. "They can't see you in my bedroom, not like this. Just jump out, get dressed, and then walk in the house. It'll be fine."

He frowns, his chest heaving with a breath. Then he nods. "Fine."

He yanks on his boxer briefs, grabs his jeans and T-shirt, and opens up the sliding door, shutting it behind him quietly.

My head spins as the seconds pass, and I still come up empty-handed. Then I flip open one of my suitcases and see the first-aid kit tucked underneath a bunch of my clothes. I must have been in such a hurry when packing in Moab that I absentmindedly shoved it in my luggage.

"I found it!" I yell before flinging open my bedroom door and sprinting out to the living room. Wyatt lies on the couch, his chest heaving as he struggles to catch his breath. Haley is crouched on the floor holding his hand while Rylan stands behind him, phone in hand, eyes wide with horror.

"Should I call 911?" Rylan asks, her voice shaky.

"No, I've got this!" I yell. "The EpiPen! I have it!" I fall to the floor, and Haley scoots to the side. "It'll take too long to wait for an ambulance to get here. Joe, help me get his jeans off. I need to give him the shot in his thigh."

Joe nods frantically while pulling off Wyatt's pants and yanking up his boxers.

I zero in on the bare patch of Wyatt's tan skin. With my heart thudding in my ears, I look at the pen in my fist and repeat the instructions I memorized when I bought the pen for this trip.

"Blue to the sky, orange to the thigh. Blue to the sky, orange to the thigh."

I look at the pen in my shaky hand once more to make sure I've got it positioned correctly with the blue end up and the orange end pointed toward Wyatt's leg. Closing my fist around it, I stab the orange needle end into Wyatt's thigh and press it there for ten seconds. I hold my breath, staring at Wyatt, his eyes fading, his breaths shallow. But then after a few seconds, he starts to blink rapidly. His breathing evens out.

"Damn," he rasps, beads of sweat glistening on his forehead. Then the corner of his mouth twitches up. His brown eyes go from cloudy to clear. "Thanks, Alia."

I let out a breath and clutch a hand over my chest. Joe mutters, "Holy shit"; Haley says, "Oh my God"; and Rylan falls to the floor on her knees, cupping her face in her hands.

Haley wraps an arm around her. "I'll go grab an ice pack from the freezer on the back deck," Haley says. "To help him cool down."

Rylan jolts up, a dazed look clouding her normally vibrant face. "It's okay. I'll get it."

She slips out the sliding glass door. Joe leans down, his eyes watery, and pats Wyatt's leg. "You gave us a scare, man."

Color flushes back to Wyatt's cheeks. He still sports that dazed look in his eyes, but his breathing is even now. He reaches up to pat Joe's arm. "No more homemade cocktails for me."

Joe shakes his head, cursing. "That fucking guy. We even told him you were allergic to vodka. He swore it was gin in the bottle. I knew we shouldn't have bought anything from that roadside stand."

I whip my head to Wyatt. "You bought alcohol from a roadside stand?"

Wyatt shrugs. "It was cheap. The guy was selling two-dollar flasks of cocktails. How could I say no to that?"

"Rylan and I told you guys it was a bad idea," Haley says as she readjusts to sit cross-legged on the hardwood floor. "But no. You *had* to buy cheap cocktails from a guy who was operating out of his van, clearly baked out of his mind."

I groan, then shake my head. "Are you fucking kidding me?" I let out a laugh of disbelief, then fall from my knees to my ass. My legs are as heavy as cement now that the adrenaline rush is over.

"Thanks for not calling an ambulance." Wyatt winces as he rubs his thigh where I injected him. "You saved me thousands of dollars in medical bills."

I toss the EpiPen at him, annoyed but relieved. "You and your mom need to say a few more rosaries, praying for intelligence for you. Because holy hell, buying alcohol from the side of the road has got to be the most—"

Rylan's scream interrupts me. All four of us whip our heads in the direction of the sliding glass door, where she walked out just a minute ago. Joe, Haley, and I jump up and run out the door; then all our jaws promptly drop at the sight.

There's Drew, standing in the backyard of our condo rental, wearing only his boxer briefs.

17

D REW LOOKS AT US, HIS EYES WIDE, HIS BROW ALL THE way up to his hairline. Then he folds his hands over the front of his body, covering his crotch.

He reins in his expression to neutral. "Hey, everyone," he says calmly.

"Hey . . ." we all say in unison.

"You scared me, Drew," Rylan says, setting her hand over her heaving chest. "One minute I'm digging through the deep freezer, and the next I look up and see you standing in your underwear. What the . . ."

Joe chuckles. "Yeah, man. What's the story there? I thought Alia said you went out for . . . supplies."

From the corner of my eye, I catch Haley covering her mouth as she tries not to chuckle. I whip my head to her, hoping my glare shuts her up. I'm sure she can figure out what exactly Drew and I were up to while the rest of them were out.

I take the ice packs from Rylan as she gazes with wide eyes at Drew, then shove them into Haley's hands. "Can you take these to Wyatt? Now."

She scrunches her face to keep from laughing but nods and walks back into the condo.

I shoot my wide-eyed stare back to Drew. "Are you . . . okay?"

He purses his lips together, then nods once at me. "I got a little sidetracked while out for supplies." He emphasizes the word "supplies" in a way that makes me want to chuck something at him. "Something was up with my truck, so I was taking a look under the hood and got a bunch of dirt and grease all over my clothes. Thought I'd disrobe in the yard so I wouldn't get anything dirty in the condo. Wouldn't want to risk losing our rental deposit."

I let out a breath, thankful that the excuse Drew thought of is plausible. Joe and Rylan seem to buy it judging by the way they nod along.

"I didn't realize you guys had come back," Drew says. "Sorry about that."

Rylan excuses herself to check on Wyatt. A beat later, Joe lets out a laugh. "Damn. What a crazy day."

He walks back into the house, leaving Drew and me to stand and stare at each other.

"Sorry to kick you out. Of my room, I mean," I say quietly. "It all happened so fast . . . I wasn't sure what to do."

His expression softens. "It's okay. It sounds like you saved the day."

The corner of my mouth tugs up slightly. "What happened? Why didn't you get dressed?"

He rubs a hand against the back of his neck. "I thought it would be a good idea to toss my clothes on the ground first before I jumped down. But they landed in a puddle. And I didn't think it would be the best idea to walk into the house in just my underwear. I was just going to hang back in the yard until I could sneak back in, but then Rylan walked out and saw me."

We both start laughing.

"Well, everyone's seen you now," I say. "Just come inside already."

Smiling, he turns around and walks the few feet to where his soiled clothes sit in the grass; then he follows me as I walk inside.

"I guess we'll have to take a rain check on today," he says softly behind me.

"I guess so."

"LET'S GET ANOTHER sweeping vista of Inspiration Point," I call out to Joe and Wyatt.

They nod and set up for dual shots of one of the most scenic lookout points in Bryce Canyon. Most tourists flock to Sunset Point and Sunrise Point in the park, but the sweeping vista of Inspiration Point makes it my favorite hidden gem in the park. From where we're standing near the very top of this lookout point, the view appears like an endless amphitheater of rugged rock pillars. In the canyon below are thousands upon thousands of hoodoos, fins, and spires. Under the golden sunlight of late afternoon, it's like the rocky earth is on fire in every hue of red, orange, and pink.

"Hell of a view." I hear Drew's voice from behind me.

I twist around and beam when I realize he's not talking about Inspiration Point. The way he's looking at me, I know he's remembering last night and what we got up to.

Last night was two days after the fiasco with Wyatt's allergic reaction.

All the stars aligned and everyone fell asleep early at the condo after a long day of shooting. Then Drew sneaked into my room, and we enacted that very dirty text exchange, shattering my 'no sex in the shared condo' rule.

Totally worth it.

I can't look at Drew too long when my smile is this goofy.

One look at me with this expression and everyone will be able to tell what exactly is happening between us. A grin this cheesy only happens after a night of mind-blowing sex.

So I glance down at my tablet and pretend to scan whatever text is on there. "Inspiration Point *is* stunning," I say, biting my lips, which are fighting to curve upward. "Glad you think so too."

"I'm pretty damn inspired after last night, Dunn," he growls softly before walking off to help Rylan with a lighting issue.

Inside I'm squealing with glee. Just then there's a shout behind me. I spin around, but then see that it's Blaine doing pirouettes in the parking lot.

I grit my teeth, then inhale. This morning when we started shooting, Drew went through his usual routine of demonstrating the scenes for Blaine. But the whole time, Joe and Wyatt were filming everything so that I can edit the footage later and make Drew the focus.

"What the hell is he doing?" Haley says after walking up to me.

"I have no clue."

He yelps, then shouts something unintelligible. The rest of the crew ignore him as they continue filming the panorama shot.

"I guess it's good that ninety-nine percent of the time he's on set, he's out of it," Haley says. "It makes it easier to pull off the host swap."

I nod in agreement. But on the inside, I'm a ball of nerves. I know this is the right thing to do. But still . . . part of me wonders how the execs will react when I show them I've pulled this stunt.

I shove aside the thought and focus on Haley, who's swiping through my tablet to ask me a question about tomorrow's shoot.

When Wyatt and Joe announce they've completed the shot, I walk over and check out the footage. I'm beaming at how well they've captured the beauty of Bryce in this single smooth shot.

"Amazing job, you guys," I say. "That's a wrap!"

Everyone starts moving to pack things up while I run to unlock my car and open the doors for Haley and Rylan so they can load the gear. Heavy footsteps come up around my side.

"I know what you're up to," Blaine says.

I lean back out of the car and twist around to look at him. "What?"

When he glares at me, all the wrinkles in his forehead jump out from the leather-like surface of his skin. He swipes a hand through his blond hair. "You're up to something. I might not know exactly what it is, but I know you're doing something behind my back. And that's bullshit. I'm the star—the priority. So whatever you're doing, it stops now."

Instinctively my stomach drops; then dread follows. But I hold my ground. I don't flinch or look away. I've spent enough years in this industry working alongside men with overinflated egos, just like Blaine. I used to let them intimidate me. I used to clam up and nod along with whatever they were saying because I was young and inexperienced.

It took me years to train myself out of that automatic response. But I finally realized that some men act this way because they have nothing else to stand on. They're often terrible at their jobs or insecure and want to take it out on the nearest person, which sometimes happens to be me. They simply think that because they exist, they're better than me and can talk to me like I'm their unworthy underling.

I've seen people like Blaine coast through life because they just happen to be connected to the right powerful guy who keeps giving them chance after chance, while the rest of us work years for a shot at our dreams.

And I'm sick of it.

I can't revolutionize the entire outdoor TV industry, but I *can* stand up to the one entitled jerk who's hell-bent on making this shoot a living nightmare for my crew.

"You know something, Blaine? I've done more than enough to accommodate your rude and entitled behavior. This entire crew has."

His brow lifts—he's clearly shocked that I've taken such a tone with him. I'm guessing not a lot of people dare to.

"Almost every day of shooting, you've derailed things by throwing a temper tantrum or coming to set hours late or showing up high out of your mind. And I'm sick of it. All I'm doing is trying to produce a series for the network, despite you trying to ruin it every chance you get. If you can't see that, then that's your problem. Not mine."

Blaine blinks and stares for a second, as if he's processing what I've said. Then he squares his shoulders and puffs his chest out before glaring at me once more.

"You should be on your knees thanking me for being on your pathetic little show. It's pure garbage, and the only reason anyone is going to watch it is because I'm the host."

I take a breath and pull the same move of straightening up and squaring my shoulders before I take a step into his space.

"You have no idea who you're dealing with, Alia."

"*You* haven't got the first clue what I'm capable of. I've got more footage on you than you even know—stuff that could ruin you. So don't test me, Blaine. You'll be sorry."

We stand for a tense second staring daggers at each other before Joe's voice interrupts.

"Everything okay here?"

I turn to him standing there with a bag of gear in each hand. His tone is pleasant, but the concern in his eyes is clear.

"Whatever," Blaine mumbles before stomping across the parking lot to sit in the back of the black SUV that he arrived in today. Colton scurries from helping Rylan to the car.

Joe steps closer to me. "What was all that about?"

"Blaine knows something's up."

I quietly explain that Blaine has figured out that we're plotting something without him.

"I don't think he realizes what, though."

Joe shakes his head. "You'd think with all the heavy drugs and the drinking, he'd be oblivious to this. He's oblivious to so much else. What'd you say to him?"

I sigh. "I went off on him about professionalism and decency, then made a thinly veiled threat that if he doesn't back off, I'll leak all of the compromising footage we have of him. That seemed to shut him up."

He chuckles. "Better than what I would have done, which would be stammer, then offer him some shrooms to distract him."

I wince and rub a fist against my forehead. "Maybe that wasn't the best thing to do. It's just . . . it's getting harder and harder to just sit there and endure him, you know? I'm sick of him throwing his weight around. He deserves to be told off."

Joe shakes his head and pats my shoulder. "I honestly can't think of a better way to deal with that guy than what you did."

I glance around at the rest of the crew. "Can you quietly pass on to everyone later tonight that we need to be extra careful about keeping things under wraps so Blaine doesn't find out more?"

"Consider it done."

"Thanks, Joe."

He walks off to continue packing up. I lean against the car and take a moment to collect myself.

"Hey."

I straighten up and see Drew's face twisted in concern.

"You okay?"

I shrug. "Kind of. Not really."

The nerves spinning inside me ease the slightest bit at just the sight of Drew. A cuddle session later tonight should be good enough to rid myself of the remaining stress from arguing with Blaine.

I explain to Drew how Blaine confronted me just minutes ago, and how I pushed back.

Drew rubs his hand over his face. "Shit."

I'm about to ask if he'd be up for meeting tonight, but when I focus on his expression, I'm thrown at how annoyed he looks.

"What exactly did you say to Blaine?" he asks.

"I just told him that he has no right to question anything we're doing because everyone except for him is just trying to do their job. But then he called the series 'stupid' and 'pure garbage,' said we were lucky to have him as host, so I told him he needs to watch his attitude or I'll ruin him with all the footage we have of him taking insane amounts of illegal drugs or berating Colton."

I flinch at how harsh it all comes out when I retell it.

Drew's eyes widen, and I hold up a hand. "Okay, I know that sounds bad, but it seemed to make him back off. I honestly don't think he's going to bring it up again."

For a few seconds, Drew says nothing. He just takes a breath and runs a hand through his hair.

"Jesus, Alia. Way to make things worse."

"What? How exactly did I make things worse?"

"We're already on thin ice with Blaine as it is. His replacement is taking his job right in front of him. If he can tell something is up with us, then maybe we need to just ease his concerns rather than threaten him."

His pointed tone doesn't sit well with me. I suddenly feel like I'm a PA being talked down to by a higher-ranking crew member.

"Ease his concerns?"

"Maybe if you told him he had nothing to worry about or fed him some BS about what a great job he's doing and how irreplaceable he is, he wouldn't be so suspicious."

"Drew, Blaine called this series garbage. That's insulting to me and you and everyone else who's been working so hard. I'm not going to coddle someone who's going to openly insult me and everyone I work with."

Drew rolls his eyes. "Come on, Dunn. You should know better than to let a ridiculous insult like that rile you up. You know Blaine doesn't know what he's talking about."

My skin heats. I can't believe Drew is being so dismissive.

"You've got to be kidding me," I mutter.

Drew closes his eyes and takes a breath before addressing me once more. "Look, we're doing something unprecedented here. We're changing hosts without the network's permission. We're pulling a Hail Mary when we don't have the authority to. We need to be careful with how we handle things if we want this to work."

I cross my arms. "You're right. I should just stand there and allow entitled douchebags to say whatever they like, to disrespect and degrade me and my coworkers. It's always better just to sit there and take it instead of standing up for myself."

"That's not at all what I mean, and you know that."

"Do you know how many times over the years I've had to just sit there and take it from people like Blaine? Self-important jerks who think that their mere presence is a gift from God and that everyone should kiss the ground they walk on even though they treat everyone like crap, with zero consequences?"

Drew starts to speak, but I cut him off.

"You know, Joe came up to me when he saw how upset Blaine made me. And when I told him what happened and how I dealt with it, he didn't criticize me. He supported me—unlike you."

"That's not fair. Of course I support you."

"It doesn't feel like it," I mutter while yanking my hair into a ponytail. "I'm not even asking you to do anything. All I want is your support in this shitty moment. And you can't even give me that."

He tugs a hand through his hair. "Alia—"

"Your attitude is exactly why guys like Blaine get away with being assholes. Because every time someone like you appeases them, you're essentially saying it's okay for them to continue acting like total jerks, mistreating everyone around them. Maybe if guys like you called out guys like Blaine, it would help put a stop to this disrespectful and toxic work culture. Because seriously, Drew, it's exhausting working like this. It's fucking exhausting being told constantly that I need to just smile and endure endless bullshit in order to do my job. And what's even more fucked up is that you—someone who I thought understood me—would rather appease someone like Blaine instead of standing up for what's decent."

When I finish speaking, I take a breath and spin away in the direction of the rest of the crew, ignoring Drew's calls after me.

I thought Drew understood me. I thought he was on my side. I was wrong.

Behind me I hear the shuffle of footsteps. Drew grabs me gently by the arm and stops me, spinning me to face him. "Can we please talk about this?"

I shake my head and yank out of his grip. "I have nothing else to say to you."

I grab random gear bags, chuck them over my shoulder, and load them into my car. Then I jump into the passenger seat. Haley jumps into the driver's seat and does a double take when she sees me sitting there.

"You're not riding back with Drew?" she asks.

"Nope." I fiddle with my seat belt, struggling to buckle it.

"It looks like he wants to talk to you," she says.

I cut my stare to her. "I'm done talking to him."

Haley presses her lips together, clearly shocked by my hard tone. "Okay."

When Rylan hops in the back seat, Haley backs out of the parking spot and heads back to the highway. Rylan starts chattering about a cute thing Colton did. All I can offer is a weak smile. Thankfully Haley keeps Rylan engaged in conversation.

All the while I stare down at my phone, pretending to be focused on something super important while I try my hardest not to cry.

18

GREAT WORK TODAY, GUYS. WE'RE DONE FOR THE DAY,"
I holler at the crew after we finish filming the sunset
shot at Sunset Point in Bryce.

I take in the landscape one last time. At eight thousand feet
of elevation, this lookout point offers views of the endless hoodoos that line the canyon below. I smile to myself when I remember how Apong Lita took so many photos of this spot on her
camera that she went through an entire roll of film, then ran
back to the car so she could load more and take another full roll.

That memory is a needed distraction from how hurt I still am
from yesterday's argument with Drew. We didn't speak the entire night or at all during today's shoot.

Rylan waves to me while standing next to Joe. She sets down
the light stand she just finished folding and walks over.

She holds her hands in front of her, fidgeting. "I know you're
so busy right now, but I was wondering if you have some time,
can you take a look at that online featurette I put together about
Upheaval Dome?"

"I'd love to."

Rylan beams. "Great! I'll run and grab the tablet from my bag
and show you."

I pull out my phone and check the messages I missed while I'm waiting for Rylan.

"Hey."

I whip my head up at the sound of Drew's voice.

"Can we talk about . . . yesterday?" The knit of his eyebrows and the softness of his tone have my chest aching.

"It's not necessary." I look back down at my phone. I'm not in the mood to rehash things. "Let's just focus on work, okay?"

I don't wait for him to answer. I turn around and walk toward Rylan. I take the tablet out of her hand and review the video she's put together.

"Wow, Rylan." I smile at her. "That's really slick."

"Really? I was nervous if the music would sound too over-the-top."

"Not at all. It sets the mood so well. Who's the artist? Did you have any trouble licensing the music?"

She shakes her head. "Colton's cousin's band. A lot less expensive than the music we normally license for videos."

"Seriously amazing work, Rylan. You have such a skill for this."

Still grinning, she thanks me. Haley calls to her from a few feet away, asking for help finding something in the car.

Rylan turns back to me as she walks off. "Oh, would you mind showing that video to Drew? He asked me earlier if he could take a look at it, but we got busy and I forgot. I figured since you guys are riding back to the condo together you could show it to him."

She spins away, and I try my best to rein in my annoyed sigh. I need to be professional, even if I'm still reeling from our argument.

I spot him standing by his truck talking to Joe. Joe turns away to walk back over to Wyatt to help him finish loading up the van. Drew's brow lifts when he sees me. I blink and can swear I see a hopeful gleam in his eyes.

I hand him the tablet. "Rylan wanted your opinion on the Upheaval Dome featurette she put together for the Expedition website."

"Oh. Sure." His shoulders fall the slightest bit. Then he glances up at the sky, where a wall of gray clouds is slowing inching across the sky. "Looks like it's gonna rain." He glances over at me. "Do you mind sitting in the car while I watch this?"

"Fine."

We hop in the car. I wave at Wyatt, Joe, Haley, and Rylan as they pull out of their parking spots and drive away.

I spend a few seconds staring out the window with my arms crossed until I register the silence in the car. I turn to ask Drew why he's not playing the video.

"I fucked up. I'm sorry, Alia," he says. I open my mouth, but he shakes his head. "Just please let me get this out, okay? Please?"

"Okay."

"I was out of line yesterday. I thought about what you said . . . about how the things I said about Blaine's behavior and appeasing him perpetuates shitty behavior from guys like him . . . You're right. I was in the wrong. Instead of arguing with you, I should have listened to you so I could better understand things."

Drew runs a hand over his face. He glances briefly out the window before pivoting his body to me. He rests his hand on the center console next to where my hand rests. His fingers twitch, like he wants to touch me, but he doesn't. His gaze cuts to me once more.

"I hate that I hurt you. And I hate that I was 'that guy.'"

"That guy?"

"The kind of guy who lets a shitty guy's behavior slide just because it's easier than calling him out. My older sisters would get on me about that growing up. How much it pissed them off to see that happen over and over at work and in their personal lives. I vowed to myself I wouldn't ever be 'that guy.' But I realize I've done that a lot in my life—in my career. I mean, I like to think I stand up for what's right and that I step in when someone crosses the line."

My mind flashes back to that first day of shooting at the Delicate Arch when Blaine made that blondie comment to Rylan. Drew called him out immediately.

"But that's not enough. I need to be better," he says, holding my gaze. "I should have been better for you yesterday. I'm sorry that I wasn't."

Inside I soften at the conviction in his voice, at how his gaze doesn't waver. I've noticed that when other people apologize, they can barely look me in the eye. Not Drew. It's like everything in him—his body, his eyes, his words—is working together to demonstrate his sincerity, to show me just how sorry he is. And I believe him. He wants to be better. And that's good enough for me to forgive him.

"I just want to do everything I can to make this series—your dream—come true," he says softly. "Even if it meant putting up with Blaine's BS every now and then, I thought it would be worth it. But I realize now that was the wrong approach."

I clear my throat. "This series means everything to me, and I want to do everything in my power to make it happen, but on the right terms. If I have to compromise my integrity and my self-respect or the crew's feelings for someone like Blaine, I don't think it would be worth it."

"I get that now."

I slide my hand over his. Drew's mouth twitches upward as he looks at our touching hands. Then I lean over and pull him into a hug. Burying my face against his chest, I breathe in his minty scent, which I craved all last night. He wraps his arms around me. A low hum of satisfaction emanates from his throat above me. I feel vibrations against my chest as he holds me tight.

"Thanks," I whisper into his chest. Then I lean back to look at him. "I'm sorry for giving you the cold shoulder all of last night and today. It wasn't the mature way to handle this."

"It's okay. I understand why you did it. I'm not eager to chat with people who hurt my feelings either. However you want to handle things when it comes to Blaine, I'm behind you one hundred percent. But more than that, you're my—"

He frowns as he cuts himself off. He clears his throat, the expression on his face uncertain. "I just mean that you're really important to me. I don't want to ever make you feel otherwise."

I lean back into him to hug him again. "Is it okay to admit that I'm not totally sure what I want to do when it comes to Blaine?"

"Of course it's okay." He kisses the top of my head. It makes me melt into him even more.

"Dude's a kind of weirdo I've never seen before," he says. "Like a weirdo on steroids. And every type of drug known to man. How is he not dead yet?"

I laugh into his chest before leaning back to look at him.

"I've got your back, Dunn." He cradles his palm against the back of my head and my insides go mushy.

I press a kiss to his lips. His tongue tangles with mine. Soon we're panting.

"I really, really like making up with you, Dunn," he says against my mouth.

I let out a breathy chuckle. "Me too. You're excellent at apologizing."

We share another naughty kiss before breaking apart.

"You should watch that video Rylan put together," I say after catching my breath. "She's so excited for you to see it."

Drew bites his lip, smiling before swiping the tablet up from the dashboard of his car. While he watches, I lean back in my seat and smooth out my clothes and my hair. I glance over and see him beaming at the video.

"Damn. This is incredible. Rylan did a hell of a job. And that song." He bops his head along to the acoustic indie tune.

I chuckle. "She was dying to show it to you."

"I mentioned to her when I saw her editing it the other day that Upheaval Dome is my favorite thing we've seen in Utah so far, so that's probably why," he says.

"Really?" I look up from digging through my bag for a hair tie. "We've seen a lot of incredible sites. Canyons that go on and on forever. Rock formations that look like phalluses and mushrooms. Upheaval Dome is the one that takes the cake for you?"

Drew laughs, then swipes his finger across the tablet screen. "Just the fact that we don't know how exactly it was formed is mind-blowing to me. The best guess scientists seem to have is that it was created when a meteor hit Earth millions of years ago." He looks up at me. "But you know that."

I pull down the mirror on the visor. "I remember that coming up when I was researching while writing the script," I say as I gather my unruly hair into a ponytail. I glance at him. "So that's why you like it so much? Because it's a geological mystery?"

"Nah. I like it because it reminds me of you."

I laugh. "Upheaval Dome is an impact structure. So you're comparing me to a destructive meteor that hit Earth millions of years ago and left a devastating mark on the surface. That's smooth, Irons."

He rubs the back of his neck, his smile taking on a timid sheen. "No, I mean . . . it reminds me of your effect on me."

I stop laughing when I notice the tender expression on his face.

"I mean it in the best possible way," he says. "You came into my life like a meteor—both times. The night we met on the subway and then when we met again in Utah. I wasn't expecting it, either time. But seeing you . . . It shook me."

"I shook you?"

He nods. "You're this beautiful and ballsy woman. You had my attention from the get-go, and not just because you're gorgeous. It was the way you carried yourself. You were confident, forward, and bold. You told me what you wanted and when you wanted it—both on our date and when we started working together."

I blush and glance down at my lap. "I thought you were annoyed with me that first day of shooting at Arches. You didn't think I was too demanding?" I let out a shy laugh.

"Not even close. I was in awe of you. Yeah, we argued, but it made me like you even more. It showed me you were willing to fight for your vision and for your crew. Not to mention, you're hot when you're in your element. You command a set with such focus, but you're also kind and approachable. It's a killer combination."

I stammer. I can't even say thank you. I've never had anyone describe how they feel about me in this way.

His eyes are dazzling with an emotion I can't quite nail down. "You've left an impact on me, Dunn," he says softly. "I just know that after this shoot, I won't be able to forget you."

He turns back to look at the tablet screen for a second. The video is paused on a wide shot of Upheaval Dome. The cylindrical formations look like majestic gray mountains on the screen. They jump out from the red-rock background in an abrupt contrast.

When he looks back up at me a second later, his cheeks are red. He leans his head back against the headrest. "Shit. That was a really weird and creepy thing to say." He lets out a breath, then laughs.

I grab his arm so he looks at me, my heart pounding. "It wasn't. It was . . . the best compliment anyone has ever given me."

My head is spinning at what Drew means by what he said. When we started hooking up, we agreed there wouldn't be any expectations for our arrangement—or for us. But he just said he couldn't forget me . . . Does that mean he could want more than this temporary setup?

For a second, I let myself dream about doing this with Drew long-term. Mind-blowing sex. Working together on more projects. Cuddling in bed. Spending evenings after a hard day at work chatting over our favorite drinks. Enjoying his eggs Benedict on a regular basis. I even fantasize about fighting with him because making up with him is so damn hot.

My heart skids in my chest. A new kind of heat consumes me from the inside out. It's different from arousal or that heat I feel whenever we flirt and tease each other.

It's a heat rooted in comfort and longing. It's a heat that makes my chest ache and my heart swell.

I'd really, really love to have all that with Drew—something more than this arrangement.

And that thought jolts me to the core. Because that's the first time I've felt this way about anyone in years.

When I refocus on him, there's an expectant look on his face. It makes me think that maybe, just maybe, he wants something more with me too.

He slides his hand in my lap, where my hand is resting. I take that as a prompt to say exactly what's on my mind.

I clear my throat and silently command my heart to stop beating out of my chest so I can hear myself think and word this very, very important proposal properly. "Do you think that maybe, after this shoot is done, we can—"

His phone blares. I grit my teeth, watching as an impossibly deep frown claims his face. He pulls his phone out of his pocket and I hold my breath, hoping that he'll silence it or turn it off or chuck it out the window, anything to make the noise stop so I can ask him if he actually wants to make things official with us.

When he answers, my heart sinks.

"Hey, Quinn. What's up?" He turns to me and mouths, "My sister. Sorry."

I nod and try to smile.

"Whoa, whoa, whoa, slow down." Drew frowns as he stares straight ahead. "What do you mean . . . ? He what?" Drew closes his eyes and leans his head back on the headrest, then lets out a sigh. "Okay. Yeah, I can switch to FaceTime if you want to put him on really quick, hang on."

He switches to FaceTime, then looks at me. "I'm sorry about this."

"Is everything okay?"

"Yeah, it's fine . . . It's just my sister's husband works overseas a lot and she gets overwhelmed with my niece and nephew, so I told her if she ever needed a breather or they start acting up and she can't get ahold of my brother-in-law to just call me, and I'll try to help out."

I make an "aww" sound before I can catch myself.

"Drew, you didn't tell me you were with someone," Quinn says.

He purses his lips as he looks back at his phone screen. "Yeah, but it's nothing. Just my coworker."

I pull my lips into my mouth as I endure the sting of his words. As he talks to his sister, I quietly absorb the ache of his dismissal and wonder if I read his declaration of affection from minutes ago completely wrong. If I truly meant something to him . . . If I were truly someone special to Drew, someone who he wanted something more—something serious—with, he wouldn't refer to me as "nothing" or "just his coworker."

His sister yells the name Logan. I notice that her facial features are more delicate than Drew's, but they have the same slender nose and sparkling hazel-brown eyes. Her face disappears from the screen, and then a young blond boy appears. He looks like he's in early elementary school.

"Hi, Uncle Drew!" His blue eyes shine. I can't help but smile at just how excited his little nephew is to see him.

Drew beams at him. "Hey, buddy. How's it going?"

Logan chatters about school and how he signed up for T-ball and what his pet lizard ate for dinner. The way Drew listens intently while Logan talks makes me want to squeal. And then my mind automatically imagines Drew cuddling a chunky baby in his arms while he smiles and coos. My chest swells. I swallow and hold my breath until the feeling passes.

"That's good, buddy," Drew says, snapping me out of my daydream. "Your mom told me that you haven't been listening to her lately. She said you yelled at her and called her a bad name. What's going on there?"

Logan's cherub face goes blank. "Um, I dunno." His eyes dart to the side.

"Buddy, I know it's tough right now with your dad gone for work. I know you miss him."

Logan wipes his nose with his wrist as he aims his wide-eyed stare at Drew once more. "Yeah, I miss him a lot."

"That's probably why you're feeling sad and upset, right?"

It takes a second for Logan to reply, but then he says a soft yes while nodding.

"It's okay to get upset sometimes when you're feeling sad because you miss someone," Drew says. "But you have to remember that your mom is working really hard while your dad's away, okay?"

Logan nods.

"She loves you so much, and she just needs you to listen to her. So when she tells you that she needs you to do something, you have to do your best to help her. Can you do that for me, buddy?"

I bite my lip to keep from *aww*-ing out loud again. Watching burly, sexy lumberjack Drew slip into doting-uncle mode is like catnip for me.

Logan pauses for a second, but then nods. "Okay, Uncle Drew. I'll listen to Mom more. I promise."

Drew grins at him. "That's my champ. And remember: it's never okay to call your mom names. Understand?"

"I promise I won't do it again."

"Will you be sure to tell your mom sorry and give her a hug after you finish talking to me?"

He smiles and nods.

Drew promises to mail the gifts he's bought for Logan and his sister soon, contingent upon a good report from Quinn.

Logan's eyes go wide. "I promise, Uncle Drew."

"I gotta go, but I'll talk to you again soon, okay? Love you."

Logan says, "Love you too," and they hang up. Drew tosses his phone on the dashboard of his car and then leans back with a groan.

"Good God. I love my sister and her kids more than anything, but man, it's exhausting dealing with them sometimes." He lets out a tired chuckle, then rubs a hand over his face. "Phone calls like that make me so freaking glad to be on my own. I just have to worry about me and no one else. Thank fuck for that." He lets out a heavy sigh.

Any lingering hope and sentiment I had from a few minutes ago, when he went on about how I've made an impact on his life and how he'll never forget me, vaporizes. He probably meant that as a memory, that his time with me will be pleasant to look back on, but nothing more. Because he just said he prefers to be on his own . . . which means he's clearly not interested in anything serious.

I fix my stare on my lap so he hopefully won't notice the disappointment that I'm certain is painted on my face.

"Sorry, what were we talking about before Quinn called?" he asks.

I glance at him as he scrubs his hand over his face.

Shaking my head, I look out my window. "I forgot. It wasn't important."

He touches my arm, and I turn to him. "You mentioned something about after the shoot. About what?"

His eyes shine with concern. But I know better than to read too much into it. That connection I felt earlier, that hope I thought I felt from him, was probably just the emotional high I was riding after his apology.

I look Drew in the eye. "I . . . just wanted to say that you're an amazing host. You should think about headlining some other show after this series is done."

I hope all the effort I'm putting into keeping my face neutral pays off. I hope he believes what I'm saying.

His stare remains fixed on me. And then he blinks. "Oh. Thanks. Yeah, I don't know. Maybe." Another long moment passes. "That's all you wanted to say?"

I squint down at my phone just to avoid that raw feeling of being stared at by him. "Yup."

Out of the corner of my eye, I see that Drew remains facing toward me. But then after a second, he turns forward and starts the car. He pulls out of the spot, heads straight for the highway, and drives us back to the condo rental.

19

"SO LET ME GET THIS STRAIGHT," HALEY SAYS. "YOU CHICKened out on telling Drew your feelings because he had a cute conversation with his nephew?"

I groan through my sip of coffee as Haley drives us from our new condo rental to Capitol Reef National Park. "When you put it like that, I sound like an asshole."

She shrugs as she focuses on the road ahead. "I'm just repeating what you said to me."

"You're not, not even close. That's not at all what I said."

"Then explain it to me."

If I weren't currently preoccupied with mentally dissecting my and Drew's conversation from two days ago, I'd be enamored with the nearby scenery. Surrounding us is more of that iconic red-rock landscape. Mesas and plateaus dot the highway along the drive to Capitol Reef.

"You don't fool me. I know you're not gawking at the pretty rocks," Haley says.

"I actually am," I say defiantly. "And I'm thinking about the shot list for today. I'd love to get some shots of the Fruita orchards in the park. Can you believe there are more than three

thousand fruit trees in the middle of Capitol Reef? Early set-
tlers planted cherry, apricot, peach, and nectarine trees. And
apple trees. And plum trees. They really liven up this desert
landscape."

From the corner of my eye, I catch Haley shaking her head.
Going on and on about the random orchards at Capitol Reef is a
poor stalling tactic. My best friend isn't going to let me off the
hook that easily. I'm going to have to admit my true feelings
about my last interaction with Drew, and I'm not looking forward
to it . . . because I know just how raw it's going to make me feel.

I turn to Haley, and she shoots me a deadpan stare. "Are you
seriously talking about fruit trees right now?"

My shoulders slump. "He just sounded so sincere when he
said that even after this shoot is over, he could never forget me.
I thought that was his way of saying he wanted to pursue
something . . . serious."

"Is that what you want?"

"I want it if he wants it," I say before draining the last of my
coffee and setting the paper cup in the center console cup holder.

Haley makes a disgusted noise. "Nope. Not acceptable. Since
when are you the kind of woman who lets a man dictate your
wants and needs? Or your feelings?"

I clamp my mouth shut, burning from the inside out because
Haley is exactly right in her assessment of me.

I sigh. "I'm scared of getting hurt, Haley. You know better
than anyone my dumpster-fire dating history."

I don't have to reference my heartbreak with Reid. The way
she looks at me, I can tell she knows whom I'm talking about.

"I told Drew about Reid."

Haley whips her head at me. "You did?"

"It was weirdly easy to talk to him about it. Before, just thinking about talking to anyone other than you about that awful rela-

tionship made me want to crawl under the nearest rock and disappear. But Drew was so supportive and understanding. He didn't judge me. I felt . . . better after being so open with him."

"That's awesome, Alia."

"I guess the fact that I'm so comfortable with him and can talk to him about anything signifies just how much I like him."

"Bingo," Haley says softly, eyes glued to the road. "And that's why you should tell him how you feel. Hiding your feelings isn't good for either of you. You know that."

A sliver of nagging doubt seeps into my brain and takes hold. "I can't. I'm not ready. Especially when he's already said that he doesn't want anything serious."

My old defenses, the ones I spent years developing in order to guard my heart, take hold once more. I'm like a cat crawling up a tree. It's instinctual at this point and impossible to shake after so many years of training myself to make this my natural response.

"He seemed to move on fine from our conversation," I say. "And he hasn't brought it up since then. We've only talked about work. I feel pathetic enough as it is sitting here, spilling my feelings about him to you when there's a very real possibility that he's not even thinking about me in the same way."

Haley turns in the direction of the park. I glance out the side-view mirror and spot the van with Wyatt, Joe, and Rylan behind us. Behind them is Drew in his truck.

"Alia, did he say those exact words to you? He said he wasn't interested in pursuing something serious with you?"

I let out a breath, annoyed at how she's still stuck on this. "After talking to his nephew, he said he was glad to be on his own. He said he was glad that he only had to worry about himself and no one else."

Haley shakes her head. "I don't think that means what you

think it means. To me, it sounded like he was glad he didn't have a kid to worry about. I really don't think he meant you. You should tell him how you feel."

"Well, I think that it's better to just keep things the way that they are between us—casual and uncomplicated—rather than ruin the last week and a half of shooting with uncomfortable conversations about our feelings and expectations."

"It's like I'm in high school all over again," Haley mutters. "The way you guys communicate—two adults in their thirties—is fucking adolescent."

"I'm scared, Haley," I quietly admit. "It makes this feel too real. And if this is real, that means we could hurt each other. It means I could get my heart broken. I don't want that ever again."

Haley sighs before turning to look at me. "I get it. I really do. But is this how you want to live your life? Too scared to share your feelings with the guy you care about?"

I'm kicking around her words in my mind as she pulls into the entrance of the park and stops by the park ranger's station to show our credentials. Now that we're in Capitol Reef, we're officially on the clock and need to be focused for the shoot. I shove aside all relationship-related thoughts as we drive along the main road in the park to our scheduled destination. We make it to a lookout point that offers a sweeping view of the major attraction of the park: the Waterpocket Fold, a sixty-five-million-year-old geological landform that looks like a wrinkle in Earth's surface. It runs for almost one hundred miles and creates a dramatic landscape of rugged cliffs, canyons, natural bridges, and arches.

When Haley groans about her growling stomach, I open the glove box and pull out a packet of gluten-free rice crackers along with a fruit-and-nut bar.

"That's part of my job. To keep you from getting hangry whenever we're on the same shoot."

Haley happily accepts the bag and bar. I start to turn to open the door, but her hand on my arm causes me to turn back to her.

"And it's my job as your best friend to give it to you straight. You always do the same for me, whether I'm venting about guys or family or work. It's why you're my best friend."

"I know," I say quietly.

"Just think about what I said, okay?"

I nod, thankful to have a best friend who never sugarcoats. Her honesty is rooted in how much she cares about me.

We get out of the car just as everyone else pulls up behind us. When they start unloading equipment, I catch a glimpse of Drew hopping out of his truck and walking toward the back. Rylan runs over to him and hands him a backpack containing all the clothes he's set to wear for today's shoot. He smiles a thanks at her and sheds the light puffer jacket he's wearing before unzipping the bag and setting it in the bed of the truck to unpack it.

That movement of him pulling off an item of his clothing captures my attention. Yeah, it's shallow to focus on just the physical aspect of Drew, but it's what I need to do in order to keep things in perspective. And if I can concentrate on strictly the physical, I won't get caught up in emotions so much.

I take a breath and walk over, tablet in hand, to go over the shot list with him.

He slips off his shirt and raises an eyebrow at me. "How do I look?"

"Ridiculously hot. Like always." I keep my tone casual and cool.

"Why do I have the feeling that if you were the one dressing me today I wouldn't be wearing very much?" He pulls a long-sleeved hiking shirt from the pack and slides it over his head.

I bite my lip and try not to laugh. "Because you know me too well. And I think I've made it very, very clear just how much I enjoy seeing you naked."

He leans down to grab one of the boots from the pack, skimming the shell of my ear with the stubble of his beard for a split second. "Almost as much as I enjoy seeing you naked, Dunn."

He straightens back up to his full height and checks the size of the boots before bending back over to slip them on. This time, I let myself giggle.

I go over the schedule for today with Drew, then check the time. "Blaine hasn't shown up yet. No surprise there."

Drew makes a scoffing noise as he pulls on a puffer vest.

"But there's no telling if and when he'll arrive. So if he does, let's just go with the same excuse we've used before. We'll tell him you're demonstrating the shots for him, and then we'll film him like usual. But still, I want to get in as many shots with you as possible."

"Got it. I'm ready." Drew holds his arms out and does a spin. "How do I look?"

"Like you have to ask."

"Aww, shucks, Dunn." A sly grin tugs at Drew's lips.

"It's exactly like you said," I say, my voice low and my eyes still directed at the tablet. If I'm going to keep this conversation in the realm of hot and heavy, we need to at least appear professional if anyone happens to look over. "I always, always prefer you with your clothes off."

I glance at him, wondering if he notices the fire in my eyes. I can feel it in every cell of my body as I speak to him.

Even though we only connect our stares for just a couple of seconds, I can tell just how well I've set him off. A small smile appears on his face; then he leans over, pretending to squint at the tablet screen.

"I think we need to do something about that, Dunn. Tonight."

"Does that mean if I text you later tonight when everyone else is asleep in the condo, you'll answer? And be up for what I want?" The rasp in my voice makes it sound like I'm pleading.

"I'll have my phone on me the entire night. I'd better hear from you."

The low growl of his words sticks with me long after he walks off to Wyatt to get mic'd up for the shoot. I'm left buzzing with anticipation for all the naked things we're going to get up to.

WHEN I WAKE up in my bedroom of the condo, everything is pitch-black. For a moment, I'm in that confused, foggy-headed space where you've napped for way too long and forget where you are.

I sit up and check the clock on my nightstand. It's almost midnight.

"Shit," I mutter to myself.

Rubbing my eyes with the heels of my hands, I let out a soft groan. The entire condo is quiet—that means everyone's asleep. That also means I slept through my rendezvous with Drew.

I swipe my phone from the nightstand and see that two hours ago I missed four texts from Drew.

Drew: Just wanted to make sure we're still on for tonight.

Drew: I'll head to my room and just wait for your message then.

Drew: My guess is that you fell asleep.

There's a sad emoji at the end, then another text.

Drew: Just kidding. You must be exhausted. Sleep well.

He ends that text with a kissing emoji. It makes my heart flutter. I quickly text him an apology and an explanation.

Me: I'm sooo sorry! I only meant to nap for an hour when we came home from the shoot today . . . and four hours later here I am texting you. Can I make it up to you?

I rub my face with my hands, wondering what I'll do now. There's no way I can fall back to sleep after a nap like that.

I glance at my phone sitting on the bedspread. Drew is probably fast asleep now too. Maybe I should just hop in the shower and catch up on emails, or—

My phone buzzes.

Drew: Don't worry. Glad you got some sleep. You've been working so hard.

Me: Sorry if I woke you up.

Drew: You don't ever have to be sorry about waking me. You're the only person I want waking me up right now. Or ever.

I bite my lip, my skin heating at just how much his reply makes me glow.

I try to think of a cool response, but he replies first.

Drew: Are you planning to go back to sleep?

Me: I don't think I can . . . That nap screwed up my sleep schedule for the night I'm afraid.

Me: Would you be up for meeting up now? I know it's late . . .

Drew replies with a gif that's a cartoon mouse nodding excitedly.

Drew: Meet me at the hot tub in the center of the condo complex in ten.

Me: ???

Me: It's the middle of the night.

Drew: And?

Me: You want to go swimming at midnight? When the hot tub is closed?

Drew: No, I don't want to go swimming ☺

My stomach flips.

Me: Oh . . . I see 😊

Me: I don't want to wake everyone.

Drew: Then be extra quiet ☺

Drew: Come on, Dunn. Didn't you ever sneak out when you were a teenager to meet up with your high school boyfriend?

Me: Possibly . . .

Drew: Everyone's dead asleep. I can hear Wyatt snoring through my wall. If we're quiet when we slip out, we'll be fine.

Drew: I'm not going to be able to sleep either with the thought of you awake in your bed, in those sexy tiny shorts you wear to sleep. Let's do something about it.

Drew: Pretend I'm your high school boyfriend. Do it for old time's sake

I bite my lip as I grin, my thumb hovering over my screen while I think about what he's asking me to do. A bit of quiet, sneaky hot-tub time with Drew sounds a million times better than lying in bed battling restlessness the whole night.

Biting my lip, I take a breath and reply.

Me: You've convinced me. Meet you there in 10.

I STAND AT the edge of the hot tub, wrapped in a towel, gazing down at the water. We agreed that I would slip out of the condo rental first, then quietly make my way to the hot tub. Drew would follow a couple of minutes later.

In the dark, even without the lights on, the water glows blue. I rub my hand against my neck, thankful for the higher temperatures southern Utah is experiencing now that it's late April.

I crouch down and touch the water, smiling at how warm it feels. I look up and can barely make out the stack of lounge chairs in the corner. Behind me I hear the soft shuffle of footsteps.

My heart races even though I know it's Drew.

I turn around and see his tall, broad figure walking toward

me with his phone on flashlight mode in hand. In his other hand is a towel.

Now that he's close, I can see he's smiling.

"You came," he says softly.

"I would never ditch you."

Thanks to the glow of his phone, I get a decent view of his body. He's wearing these swim trunks that hang low on his hips. The shadows from the harsh glow of his phone create a million defined lines. My eyes scan above, and I see the hard planes of his stomach and chest. My mouth waters.

"Look at those lines." And then I cup my hands over my cheeks at what a dork I sound like. "I mean, you look nice."

He lets out a soft chuckle. Then he drops his towel and reaches for me, then slowly peels the towel away before tossing it on the pile.

He pulls me against him, his hand with the phone slowly moving along the length of my body.

"You've got some damn fine lines of your own."

Gripping his shoulders, I blush. "I don't know about that."

His hand gives my waist a gentle squeeze before he runs his fingers along my hips; then he cups my ass cheek.

"I'm a pretty big fan of these lines, Alia."

"Those aren't lines," I whisper, my breath ragged. "Those are curves."

He skims my mouth with his. "Call them whatever the hell you want. They're hot."

I lean up, gently pressing my mouth against his in a light, teasing kiss. His tongue slips in my mouth and I moan softly, reminding myself that I need to be as quiet as possible.

He steps back, his hand falling away from me. He turns the light off on his phone before dropping it on top of the towels. With my eyes finally adjusting to the darkness, I observe him as he quickly loosens the drawstring on his trunks and slips them off. A grin splits my face.

"How do you feel about skinny-dipping?" he says, pulling me against him once more.

Closing my eyes, I savor the warmth of his skin against mine. "Is this what you got up to when you snuck out of the house in high school?"

"I wish."

I chuckle softly; then I tug off my top and bottom. "I'm definitely all for being naked in the water with you."

He takes me by the hand and guides me to the edge of the hot tub, where there's a metal railing along the steps.

I grip my other hand on his shoulder as I follow him into the water. The sudden wetness draws a soft shudder from me.

"Here." He steps to the middle, careful to move slowly to keep splashing to a minimum.

Then he turns around and pulls me against him once more. Immediately the warmth from his naked skin on mine has me hot all over.

Now that I'm this close to him, I can make out his face in the darkness just fine. His chest heaves slightly with a breath. And then I feel him harden against me.

He smirks down at me. "Is this okay?"

"Very."

I slide my palms slowly up his torso and rest them at his shoulders. I can just make out his eye color in the surrounding pitch blackness.

"So you got me all the way out here," I say, my voice a hair above a whisper. "What did you have in mind?"

His smirk doesn't budge, even when he raises his eyebrow. "This."

His mouth lands on the side of my neck, and my mouth falls

open. Thankfully I remember that I need to be quiet, so all that falls out of me is a hot, silent breath. I shiver at the feel of his hot tongue teasing that spot right above my shoulder.

"Drew . . ." I whisper-groan, my eyes fluttering at the heavenly feel. It's like a pleasurable, orgasmic, ticklish feeling.

"Yeah?" he says quietly, his mouth on my skin.

Again my brain short-circuits the longer his tongue plays along that patch of skin. Eyes rolling to the back of my head, I let out a soft moan and run my fingers through his hair.

He pulls his tongue away but keeps his mouth against my neck. "This seems to be a very important spot on your body."

I yank his head back and plant my mouth against his, leading him in a hungry kiss. He responds with a low moan and a smile I can feel against my mouth. His hands settle on my waist while I grip his bearded cheeks in my hands.

My head spins trying to process all the sensations around me. His hot skin against my hot skin, the smell of spice from his cologne, the taste of his tongue in my mouth. The hard feel of his muscle against the softness of my hands. How silky and thick his hair is.

We stay in that rapid kissing rhythm, our hands flying everywhere, for what feels like minutes. And then we break apart to catch our breaths. Before I can say anything—before I can think of anything to even say—Drew's mouth lands back on the side of my neck; then he glides a hand below the water.

I gasp once more when he makes contact with my most sensitive spot.

"Shh," he whispers through a chuckle.

I nod and clamp my mouth shut. But the circles he's making with his fingers against me threaten my ability to keep silent. Because Drew's magic touch and even more magical rhythm are going to break me.

I've never been much of a fan of manual stimulation with other men. But Drew? Drew is a master tradesman with his hands. He moves confidently and quickly. His touch is firm but gentle. He keeps a steady rhythm that has me clawing at him and struggling to keep my voice contained to my throat. Right now his hand is delivering untold amounts of pleasure through my body.

The heat building between my legs slowly spreads to my core, then my arms and fingers and toes.

When my chest feels like it's on fire, I open my eyes. Drew's gaze is locked on me. Even in the darkness, I can see that his eyes are dilated and glazed over. His jaw is set tight. I shiver at his carnal expression. He seems to like watching me get all hot and bothered. After a minute, a muscle in the side of his jaw twitches.

"God, you're sexy," he mutters.

I can't help but chuckle softly, my eyes rolling back, my head falling back.

He stops circling, then presses his palm against me. The change in sensation is a delicious shock to my system.

My head snaps up and I gasp. Then he starts those divine circles once more.

My head lolls against his shoulder as the sensations intensify throughout my whole body.

"We have to be quiet," he whispers in my ear.

I press a hand over my mouth to muffle myself.

"Use my shoulder," he growls softly.

Two pants later, my mouth is on the meaty part of his shoulder. A soft, low moan sounds from his throat.

"I love it when you do that," he whispers.

"Do you really?"

"Uh-huh."

Mouth open, I quietly pant against his hot, wet skin. "I just . . . I don't want to hurt you."

"You could never. Bite harder if you want." He speaks in a growled whisper that sets my heart racing.

His fingers pick up speed, and my legs go wobbly. If I were just standing on land while doing this, I'd crumble. But the water helps support me as my knees give.

Through a silent gasp, I clamp down on Drew's shoulder. He lets out a grunt, then a satisfied hum. The pressure between my legs builds and builds. Every nerve inside my body, every goose bump on my skin, goes haywire. One of my hands is tugging at the back of Drew's head, where his hair is the thickest. My other hand is wrapped around his shoulder, clutching at that endless wall of skin and hard muscle and warmth.

There's a flash where he touches me. It's like someone has lit a match inside my body and I'm about to explode. The pleasure and heat building inside me start to give way to that telltale tingle that feels so insanely good, that acts like a signal for what's to come.

A second later, it all comes to a head. Climax rips through me so hard that even the meat of Drew's shoulder can barely muffle me. I start to moan, but then with his free hand, he grips my chin and leads me to his mouth. His hard kiss swallows the rest of my moans and groans. A minute later I'm limp, shuddering against his body. Wrapping my arms around his torso, I collapse. Thanks to the sturdy hold of his arms around my waist and the water, I'm held up.

Closing my eyes, I let out a soft, satisfied sigh. Then I wiggle my feet and stand up when I feel strong enough to. I gaze up at Drew, a smug smirk plastered on his face.

"You good?" he whispers.

"More than good." I give his right hand a squeeze. He chuckles. "We're not done yet, though."

Drew's brow raises, and I push him against the edge of the hot tub.

"Sit up," I whisper.

Smiling, he leans back while gripping the edge, then hauls himself up. Water cascades from his body like a million mini waterfalls. In this sitting position, his impressive length is just below eye level.

I grip him at his base and start with a long, slow stroke. His brow furrows as he clenches his jaw. "Alia . . . you . . ."

"Shh." I cut him off. "Now it's your turn to try to be quiet. See how you like it."

Eyes closed and head back, he grins. After a minute, I speed up and the smile drops from his face. His chest heaves.

"Goddamn," he mutters, swiping my hair out of my face.

He cups my cheek, then leans down to plant an insanely sloppy and tongue-heavy kiss.

"That feels amazing." He groans quietly.

"Just you wait," I say before lowering my head to him.

It's another minute of slow, long slides of my tongue before I hear Drew's breathing grow ragged. Then his breath catches and he runs his fingers through my hair. His thighs tense. I smile to myself and speed up my rhythm.

It ends with him making a fist in my hair and letting out a quiet grunt, then a string of whispered curse words. I lean away from him and catch my breath. He slips back down into the water and falls back against the edge before pulling me into his chest.

He wraps his arms around me and nuzzles my neck. His hot, wet breath flashes across that supersensitive spot to the side, right above my shoulder. Shivers dance across my skin.

"Skinny-dipping with you is my new favorite hobby," Drew says.

I close my eyes, letting his warmth and wet skin engulf me. "Ditto."

We share a minute of silence, Drew's breathing soothing me into a relaxed state I don't think I've ever felt.

"You're not rushing to get back to your room, are you?" he asks.

"No way."

"Wanna lounge with me for a bit?"

Eyes still closed, I nod into his chest. He braces his hands on the edge of the hot tub and pushes himself out. Then he stretches his arm to me and helps me climb out. We walk over to the nearest lounge chair with our towels. He grabs one, then dries me off. My chest flutters at just how gentle and attentive Drew is as he carefully presses the plushy towel all over my skin.

"How does that feel?" he asks, wrapping the towel around me when he finishes.

"Perfect."

I settle on the lounge chair while he dries off; then he cuddles next to me.

"So I gotta know. In addition to sneaking out some nights, what were you like in high school?" Drew asks.

"A weirdo. I'd skip out on homecoming games and school dances so that I could watch documentaries, but then I'd sneak out to meet my boyfriend. I was a super-selective rule breaker."

"That's very you."

"Is it?"

I can feel him nod above me. "You put your energy into the stuff you give a crap about. Everything else can wait."

"I like the way you word that."

"I like the way you live your life."

"I had a handheld camera that my parents bought me for Christmas one year and spent a lot of my nights filming random nature stuff and editing them together into short films. Birds flying, squirrels chasing each other, rainstorms, super-windy days when it looked like the branches were going to fly off the trees. I was kind of a nerd."

"Nah. More like a teenage filmmaker. That's cool."

"My parents thought it was a little weird, but Apong Lita always supported me. She'd tell them off whenever they'd tease me about bringing my camera with me everywhere. She said they were lucky to have an artistic and creative kid who spent my days filming and editing rather than getting in trouble."

"Except for that whole 'sneaking out to meet your boyfriend' detail."

I lean up to look at him. "I never got caught."

He grins, and I settle my cheek back against his warm chest. I close my eyes and cuddle closer into him. Each second that passes, the muscles in my body loosen and relax. I'm aching to spoon with Drew until we both fall asleep. Just the thought of waking up cuddling into his massive chest, all comfy and warm, is heaven.

"So what was high school Drew like?" I ask.

"A jock. I did almost every sport."

"I knew it," I say with a chuckle.

"Did you know I was a gymnast too?"

I twist up. "Really? That's awesome. There were only a couple guys on my high school gymnastics team, and they all got made fun of by our male classmates pretty often. It was so immature."

"My reason for doing it was kind of immature. I figured the boy-to-girl ratio was in my favor since it was mostly female students on the team, and I was a ball of raging hormones."

"God, you're terrible." I giggle into his chest while softly slapping his arm. "Well, I think it's safe to say that high school you with your ladies' man ways would have been way, way too smooth for high school me."

"I highly doubt that, Dunn."

"Don't spare my feelings," I tease. "No way would you have even noticed me. I was glued to my camera, and it sounds like you were glued to the entire girls' gymnastics team."

His chest rumbles softly with a quiet chuckle. "Actually, I had a thing for smart, driven girls like you. I still do, if I'm being honest."

His tone dips low to something more serious. It gives me tingles in my chest all the way to my toes.

"That's sweet, but I don't know if I would have been the kind of girl you'd have snuck out in the middle of the night for."

"You're dead wrong, Dunn. I would have snuck out every night to see you. I would have been the luckiest bastard to date someone like you in high school."

His compliment has me glowing. I tilt my head up once more so I can look him in the eyes when I ask him this question.

"So are you making up for lost time now?"

His mouth quirks up and his gaze doesn't waver when he answers. "Definitely."

In the minutes that follow we say nothing more. We stay holding each other, eyes closed, content in this embrace.

No, we haven't defined what we are to each other. But that's okay. Because what we've said to each other in this moment of shared physical and emotional intimacy is more than enough. We've acknowledged that we're more to each other than just something physical. And that's plenty good for me.

"We should probably head back," Drew says in a whisper.

I open my eyes and gaze up at him. He cups a hand over my cheek, and I nuzzle into him, softly humming. "Just a little bit longer."

"Okay."

Another minute of cuddling passes before we stand up, grab our clothes and towels, and walk quietly hand in hand back to the condo. We don't walk in one at a time this time; we go to-gether. And as we silently and slowly walk down the halls to our separate bedrooms, Drew stops me, pulls me against him, and lays a soft kiss to my lips.

"See you in the morning," he whispers.

"Night-night."

I fall asleep with a smile on my face and tingling all over.

20

T'S THE FINAL DAY OF FILMING AT CAPITOL REEF, AND AS I glance out at the Hickman Natural Bridge, where we're filming our final scene of the day, giddiness courses through me. My very first series is nearly wrapped.

Drew smiles at me from where he stands several feet away, right in front of the awe-inspiring natural arch formation that's one of the most popular tourist draws in the whole park.

That telltale tingle starts in my stomach and sneaks all the way to my chest.

Ever since that night at the hot tub, when we shattered our "no sex in a shared condo" rule yet again, things have felt different in the best possible way. Like an unspoken acknowledgment that whatever is happening between us, we're both on board with it.

"That's one hell of a shot you've set up," Wyatt says to me as he adjusts the setting on his camera. "That arch looks kinda like it's carved out of clay."

"That's exactly what my *apong* said when we visited here," I say, smiling at Wyatt. "She said it looked like a giant shaped the entire arch by hand from a lump of orange-red clay."

I focus on the weathered exterior of the rock, how thousands of years of erosion have given it countless pockmarks and etchings.

"And it kind of looks like someone poured a bucket of brown paint over the arch too, doesn't it?" I remark, almost to myself.

"Damn. Did you get your artistic eye from your *apong*? All I got from my *lola* was her eyes and chin."

He nudges me and I laugh.

"I like how you decided to have Drew start by standing off to the side of the arch and then walk over while he's talking," Wyatt says. "Other outdoor shows always have the host standing right in front of whatever attraction they're filming. It's so boring. Your idea is way better. More visually engaging for viewers."

"I remember Brooke did that in a couple of the shoots I worked with her on. She always said she couldn't stand when the host just stands there and talks."

Wyatt adjusts his Yankees baseball cap so that it's facing in its trademark position of sitting backward on his head. He flashes me a thumbs-up. "You learn from the best. And now you're the best."

I laugh at his glowing compliment. But Wyatt shakes his head.

"Whatever you work on next, whether you're directing or producing, I'd love to be your cameraman," he says. "I don't want this to be the last time we're on a crew together. And I know every single person on this series agrees. We're all dying to work with you again."

"Thanks, Wyatt. That means the world. Truly."

He nods before turning back to his camera. I spend a quiet moment beaming from the inside out. When I glance up, I see Rylan as she runs up to Drew to tuck away an errant tag sticking out from the waterproof hiking jacket that one of our sponsors provided. Then she jogs back over to me, and we wait for Wyatt and Joe to finish setting up the shot.

And then for the first time in a long while, I think about the future. Filming for this series is almost wrapped, and that means that soon, we'll all be headed back to New York. Drew and I won't be able to see each other every day like we do now.

But instead of dread and sadness filling me, I feel slightly hopeful.

Because in this moment I realize that I actually want to give things between Drew and me a proper shot.

My stomach and my heart do a double flip.

I know what this means. This means I have serious feelings for Drew. It means that I've fallen so very hard for him. And I need to tell him.

My nerves go haywire at just the thought. But right now I need to focus on the moment and what's in front of me: wrapping up the Capitol Reef segment of the shoot.

Rylan walks over to me and asks what I think of the outfit she's styled for Drew.

"He looks great," I tell her. "You're definitely getting stylist credit on the series."

Her eyes go wide, right as she squeals and grins. "Really? Oh my gosh, I've been dying for a stylist credit!"

I pat her arm and glance around. "Is Blaine still indisposed?" I ask quietly.

Rylan's face turns serious. "Yes. He's still back at the trailhead with Colton. Apparently Colton said he had a bad trip last night. He hasn't been able to move more than two steps without getting so dizzy that he falls to the ground."

I let out an annoyed huff of breath. Even though I'm glad we don't have to accommodate Blaine for our final shoot of the day, I'm still annoyed at his behavior.

"Poor Colton," I say.

"He says he's quitting after we're done shooting the series."

"Good for him. He's put up with more than enough. If he ever is interested in a PA job, I'd be happy to have him on my crew."

"Really?"

Rylan hugs me so hard I stumble back. Then she covers her mouth with her hands.

"I just know he would love that so much! That's why Colton hasn't considered quitting his job yet—he's afraid he won't be able to find anything good in the industry. But he'll love working for you. He's got an amazing work ethic and he's such an easy person to work with, I promise you."

"I have no doubt. I've seen the way he manages Blaine, and I'm honestly impressed. If he can handle being Blaine's assistant, being a PA will be a walk in the park."

Rylan hugs and thanks me once more before running off to help Haley with the lighting. Minutes later, we're ready to shoot. I look up at Drew, who's standing tall against the brilliant red landscape around him. He's decked out in more designer outdoor gear, including a long-sleeved thermal shirt, lightweight jacket, and dark-gray hiking pants. He stomps one of his hiking-boot-clad feet onto the dirt, kicking up a small cloud of fiery dust. It rivals the thudding of my heart every time I look at him. I can't wait to tell him how I feel . . .

Focus on now.

I catch his eyes. "You ready?" I mouth to him.

A sly smile tugs at his lips. "Always."

"Action!"

Drew runs through his lines smoothly, his charisma evident in the natural way that he speaks and in the subtleties of his presentation: he keeps eye contact with the camera, but it's not the unblinking, unnerving eye contact people tend to have when they're not used to being filmed. There's not a trace of nerves. He talks like he's speaking to an old friend. I hold my breath as I watch him. He's magnetic. Viewers are going to feel like he's their very own tour guide, which is exactly the kind of personal connection I want the host of this series to have.

When he finishes the sequence, I yell cut; then we run through it a handful more times. Then we film him completing part of the nearby trail, and then the closing.

Drew plants himself on a nearby boulder. Behind him the spring sky is impossibly blue, not a cloud in sight.

"That's it for this episode of *Discovering Utah*. Be sure to explore even more behind-the-scenes footage by visiting the Expedition website. And I'll catch you on our next adventure." He ends it with a dangerously wolfish smile.

He holds the pose for three seconds, and then I yell cut.

"That's a wrap on our Capitol Reef shoot, everyone," I holler.

The whole crew cheers. I laugh and tell everyone job well done.

"Now let's see how quickly we can pack it all up," I say. "We're due back in Moab tonight, remember?"

When we rearranged the schedule to fit in the overnight shoot at the Needles, we cut our time in Moab short by a few days to accommodate, then tacked them onto the end of the shoot.

"That's a two-hour drive we have ahead of us," I say, bracing myself for groans. "But at least tomorrow's a free evening for everyone."

To my surprise, Wyatt's the only one who groans in annoyance.

"Come on, man," I hear Joe say. "You're not the least bit excited to be back in gorgeous Moab? I am!"

I chuckle to myself. Joe smacks him on the back. "We've only got a couple more days in the coolest little desert town in the world. Let's make the most of it." Joe spins around to address everyone. "How about we all do drinks tomorrow night?"

I laugh at Joe's undying enthusiasm and say I'm in. Haley, Drew, and Rylan all chime in with their agreement too.

Joe claps a hand on Wyatt's shoulder. Wyatt now looks a tad more heartened at the mention of alcoholic beverages.

"That's the spirit!" Joe sings.

After a few minutes of packing, Wyatt's shocked tone hits my ears.

"Whoa, man," he says. "What happened to your shoulder?"

When I glance over, my eyes nearly pop out of my head. Wyatt is looking over at Drew, who's changing out of the ad sponsor's clothes. He stands bare-chested with his backpack full of clothes at his feet. My eyes zero in on Drew's left shoulder, which is covered in red bite marks.

I choke on a breath. Rylan asks if I'm okay and I nod, babbling something about the desert dust making my throat dry.

Ever since that night in the hot tub when I discovered just how much Drew likes it when I bite him, I let myself go a bit crazy on the meaty parts of his shoulder, much to his delight. I silently scold myself, annoyed that it didn't occur to me in my haze of arousal that one of the crew members might see him changing on set and notice my marks.

I quickly look away and busy myself shoving nearby objects into gear bags. What will Drew say? What excuse will he give Wyatt? He could say that he fell or scratched himself . . . But if Wyatt looks at Drew's shoulder for longer than a second, he'll know for sure that's garbage. You don't get human teeth marks on your shoulder from falling.

My face heats as the seconds tick by. But then I hear Drew's easygoing chuckle. I peek up at him. He's grinning, neck twisted to look at the offending spot on his left shoulder.

"Oh that." He shrugs at Wyatt. "Just had a nice time the other night, that's all."

He slips on a white T-shirt over his head while Wyatt looks on. Recognition flashes across Wyatt's face and he chuckles. He nods at Drew. "Damn. I thought I heard the front door open the other night. Someone's been sneaking out?"

Drew smirks as he pulls on his jacket. "Something like that."

"Say no more." Wyatt holds up a hand, grinning.

Drew grabs a couple of gear bags in each hand, then catches eyes with me. I have to turn away because I'm grinning like a total goober.

A minute later he offers to help me carry more gear to the cars.

"So. We've got a whole day free tomorrow." He glances down at me. "What do you feel like doing, Dunn?"

I glance around and make sure that no one is within hearing distance. "What I'd like to do involves staying in one of our hotel rooms for the majority of the day."

And so I can finally tell you just how crazy I am about you.

I bite my lip, wondering if it's obvious just how much I'm buzzing with bliss on the inside.

A spark flashes behind Drew's eyes. "I'll never say no to more time in bed with you." Something serious and sincere takes over his expression. "But can we do something else too? Like, go out to dinner?"

His request is a surprise, but I can't help the joy bursting in my chest. Perfect timing. Tomorrow night I'll tell him how I feel and that I want to make things official between us. "I'd like that."

The most beautiful smile spreads across his face. It does something strange and wonderful to my heart.

"Then it's a date."

"ARE YOU EVER going to tell me where we're going?" I glance over at Drew in the driver's seat of his truck, trying to keep my drooling under control.

He grins as he drives along the main road in Moab. "It's a surprise. We're almost there, though."

I still can't get over how dapper he looks. When he met me at the door of my hotel room to pick me up for dinner, my jaw dropped clear to the floor. I didn't think Drew could ever look more handsome than the times I've seen him decked out in all that rugged outdoor gear—or naked.

I was sorely mistaken. He's a vision in slate-gray dress pants and a crisp white shirt, the top buttons left undone so I can steal a peek of his gorgeous smooth skin. I've never been someone who goes nuts over a guy in a suit the way others do. But now that I've seen Drew all cleaned up, my stance on men in suits has changed. I'd kill to see him in a tie and a suit jacket now . . . and then I'd strip it off him, piece by piece . . .

"You're staring," he says, the edge of his mouth twitching up into a smile.

"That's because I've never seen you so dressed up. You look incredible."

"That goes double for you, Dunn."

I smile to myself when I remember how he looked at me when I opened the door. His eyes went wide and his mouth dropped as he did a full-body scan of me in the black velvet romper, black blazer, and black heels I chose for tonight. A hungry smirk crept onto his face.

His eyes cut back to my legs, which I'm silently proud of. All that hauling and hiking during these past several weeks have resulted in me gaining some nice tone in my calves and thighs.

"Those legs. Damn."

I bite my lip at his growl, then smooth a hand over the hem of my shorts. I was so excited for a proper date with Drew that I ran to a random Moab boutique earlier and bought a new outfit. "You told me to dress up. This was the best I could come up with. I just hope it's up to the dress code of the place we're going."

Drew turns off the main road and then takes another turn. He pulls into a gravel parking lot near a medium-size, two-story brick house with a dark roof. It looks like a house that's been turned into a restaurant.

"Thought we'd give Desert Bistro a try," he says as he shuts his truck off and unbuckles his seat belt. I smile in giddy surprise at how Drew has planned an intimate and romantic date.

I start to open my car door but he tells me to hold tight, then jogs around the truck to help me out. I thank him as he takes my hand and leads me across the parking lot.

"I didn't pick the best shoes for this," I say as I wobble slightly on the uneven gravel.

"I can carry you if you'd like."

"Don't you dare."

We both laugh. Inside I'm buzzing at the surprise and how easy it is to be with Drew in this environment—in any environment. It doesn't seem to matter if we're covered in dust and sweat, naked in bed together, or on our way to a fancy dinner. It always feels good to be around him.

For a quick moment, I wonder when would be the best time to broach the subject of making things official between us, but I don't want to interrupt the natural and playful flow of our conversation.

Relax. Enjoy the moment. You can talk serious stuff later.

Drew opens the door for me and we step inside the cozy restaurant. When he places his hand on the small of my back, I close my eyes and quietly swoon. It makes me weak in the knees every single time he pulls this move.

When I open my eyes, I take in the interior, which is bright with loads of massive windows. The late-afternoon sunlight bathes the light hardwood floors in a bright glow. Polished wooden tables adorn the open space. Along the walls are framed photos and illustrations of various desert scenes and the iconic red rocks of southern Utah. A handful of woven fabric wall hangings with geometric motifs in bold colors complete the décor.

"I love this place," I say, enchanted.

"You haven't tried the food yet," Drew teases.

I breathe in the aroma of garlic and spices. "It smells amazing in here. I have no doubt the food will be incredible."

A smiling hostess greets us and leads us to a two-person table by a window in the corner of the restaurant. I can see other diners near us, but we're far enough from them that our small table feels private and intimate.

She hands us two food menus and a drink menu.

"Have you been here before?" I ask Drew.

"Nope. I'm a Desert Bistro virgin." He opens the menu.

I giggle into my glass, narrowly avoiding choking on my water. "I can't take how good you look. You should dress up more often."

When he grins, the slightest tinge of pink creeps up his neck and cheeks.

"You trimmed your beard."

"I didn't want to look like the Beast standing next to Beauty all night long."

I scrunch my nose at him, fighting the very cheesy smile that's aching to stretch across my face.

"You're dynamite with the compliments tonight."

He scoots his chair closer to the table and rests his elbow on the edge. "Just speaking the truth. You look insanely good, Alia."

I finally let that cheesy smile loose. "I like that you call me both Alia and Dunn. No one else does that."

"Is Alia a family name? I've never heard it before."

The server arrives, and we order a bottle of white wine.

"It's a weird story. My name was supposed to be Aila, after my dad's grandma, who was from Scotland. But it's such an uncommon name here in the US that the hospital misspelled it on my birth certificate."

"Seriously?"

"Seriously. But my parents ended up liking the sound of 'Alia' better, so they just left it."

"That's an epic name-origin story. I got the name Andrew because it's my dad's middle name."

We're chuckling as the server returns with the wine. He pours us each a glass, and we sip in silence for a few minutes while we look over the menu.

"I won't have to carry you back to the car after drinking this, will I?" he teases.

"Nope. I had a glass of pickle juice earlier, so I'm covered."

He chuckles when I wink at him.

"Do you know what you want to order?"

"The beef tenderloin sounds incredible," I say sipping the crisp wine. "This is the best wine I've ever had, by the way."

"Happy to hear it." He sets his glass down, my favorite sly smile curling his lips.

I glance around the dining room, taking it all in. "It's been ages since I've been out for a proper dinner like this. I usually just order food to go when I'm lucky enough to be near decent restaurants while on location. Or even when I'm home in New York. The long hours we work, I just don't have the patience or energy to cook."

I stop myself when I realize I'm babbling, but when I glance up at Drew, he doesn't seem bothered, gauging by the content expression on his face.

"When's the last time you were taken out for a proper, fancy dinner?" he asks.

I look off to the side, trying my hardest to remember. "I was twenty-five."

Drew almost drops his glass. "Damn, Dunn. How's that possible? A woman like you hasn't been out on a single proper, fancy dinner date in seven years?"

"I'm flattered that you think I deserve to be wined and dined at only the finest establishments."

He winks at me.

"But honestly, that fancy dinner was so awkward. The guy I was going out with at the time was trying to go all out for my birthday. We had only been dating for a couple of months. I told him he didn't need to, but he insisted."

"Wow. He really went for it."

I tilt my head at him. "You haven't heard the worst part. He surprised me by bringing his mom on the date—and I'd never met her before."

Drew winces.

I let out a drawn-out "yeah" in response.

"I'm guessing that was incredibly awkward?" Drew asks.

"You guessed right. It made me feel horrible, honestly. I knew the relationship wasn't going to last . . . I was actually trying to figure out a way to break things off, and then he springs this fancy date on me and also, 'Surprise! You get to meet my mom!' I wasn't going to break up with him when we were out to dinner together, so I tried to be as polite and pleasant as humanly possible, but it was so uncomfortable. His mom kept asking questions about when we were going to get married and how many kids I wanted to have."

"You're joking."

"I wish. She even made a comment about how I needed to get on it because my biological clock was ticking."

"Fuck," he mutters behind his wineglass before taking a sip.

A server walking by whips his head at Drew and frowns at his cursing. We both throw our heads back and laugh. A minute later, a different server stops by our table to take our dinner orders.

"The nerve of her," Drew says while rubbing his hand over his cheeks. "And you just sat there and took that all night? On your birthday?"

I grimace while nodding. "I was young and in my people-pleasing phase. I wouldn't do that now, of course."

Drew reaches over and brushes away a strand of hair that's stuck to my glossed lips.

I take a second to savor the feel of his thumb on my mouth. Then I clear my throat and settle down. "In a nutshell, it was hands down the most uncomfortable dinner I've ever had in my life. The food didn't even taste good. I was so worked up, I couldn't enjoy it."

"Yikes," Drew says, drinking more wine.

"I broke up with him the day after that date. I'm sure his mom hated me."

"She doesn't sound very likable herself."

Drew pours me another glass of wine, and I quietly reflect on how easy it is to joke and laugh with him about anything. I'd never met someone I could be this at ease with before.

"When is your birthday? I don't think I've ever asked you."

"August 12," I say. "When's yours?"

"December 5."

"Ah, that's a really good date to have a birthday, if you're going to have a birthday in December," I say. "Not too close to Christmas, so you don't get screwed out of a proper birthday present. I hate when people give one gift and say it's both a Christmas and birthday gift."

"Well, I did try my very best to make my mom go into labor with me well before Christmas," he says matter-of-factly. I cover my mouth to keep from laughing too loud.

Our server stops by again to drop off a basket of freshly baked biscuits and homemade butter along with the steak tartare we ordered as our appetizer. We dig into both dishes, alternately between bites and making "mmm" sounds.

"I don't know if I ever want to eat steak cooked again after trying this," Drew says.

"Do you think it would be rude for me to flag down the waiter and ask for my beef tenderloin to be left raw?"

Drew breaks into a boisterous, full-body laugh. A couple seated several feet away turns to stare. I feel weirdly proud of causing such a reaction.

"I guess this isn't really the place to let out a loud cackle, is it?" he says.

I wave my hand in the direction of the gawking couple, brushing them off. "Nah, laugh away. You're here to have a good time."

The meal is perfectly timed. The moment we finish our appetizer, a busser promptly takes away the empty plates and refills our glasses. We sip wine for a few minutes before our entrees arrive.

"Mmmm, oh my God," I say after the first bite. "Okay, I stand corrected. This steak is perfect. I don't want it raw anymore."

I hold out a bite to Drew. His eyes nearly roll to the back of his head as he chews. "Wow, that's incredible."

I raise my right eyebrow and shoot him a knowing smile. My eyes drop to my plate.

"What's that look for?" he asks.

"It's nothing." I shake my head, still smiling.

"If you don't tell me right now, I'm going to laugh again and piss off that couple who glared at us earlier."

When I refuse to say anything for several seconds, he lets out a boisterous "Ha!"

"Okay, okay," I say in a loud whisper, trying not to laugh. "God, what a child you are."

He raises his brow at me. "So tell me. What was that look about just now?"

"The way you rolled your eyes eating that bite of steak." I pause. "You make that face a lot in bed."

"Oh." He blushes once more. "I . . . uh . . . wasn't expecting you to say that." He smiles, clearly embarrassed.

I reach out and touch his hand gently. "Don't be embarrassed. It's hot." I hold his gaze, hoping that shows him just how very unembarrassed he should be.

"Okay, no more of that dirty talk out of you," he says while grinning. Then he slices a piece of his duck for me. "Eat this. This should keep you from saying much for at least a minute."

I laugh and chomp down on the fork. "Mmm, yum!" I say with a full mouth.

"Shh," he says, pressing his index finger over his lips. "Focus on chewing."

I giggle while trying to keep my mouth closed. We finish our meal, and the server asks if we're in the mood for dessert. Drew glances at me.

"I'll leave that up to her."

I check the time. "As good as dessert sounds, we'd better get going. We still have to meet the crew at Moab Brewery for drinks. Remember?"

The server nods and collects our plates and starts to turn.

I lean over the table and lock eyes with Drew, careful to keep my tone low. "We can have dessert later. At the hotel."

The server must have heard me because he's chuckling while he walks away.

Drew appears unfazed, though. He doesn't even blink. Only that sly smile remains. "Yum."

The check arrives and I reach for it, but he grabs it from me. "Let me at least split it with you," I say.

Drew frowns at me, looking the most serious I've ever seen him. "No way that's happening. I asked you here; I'll pick up the check."

He winks at me and places his credit card in the sleeve of the pocket with the bill holder. I thank him and take one quiet, deep breath. Now's as good a time as any to tell Drew how I feel about him and how I want us to be more than just a work hookup.

When the server returns after running his card, he signs the bill and we stand up from our table.

"Drew, can I . . ."

He turns away as we walk past the host stand at the entrance of the restaurant and pulls a slim box of matches from a small metal bin sitting on the edge.

He hands me the matchbox. "So you remember tonight after we leave Utah. And me."

I stare at the tiny box in my hand, my heartbeat skidding to a halt as we walk to the car.

"What do you mean by that?"

"We probably won't go out to dinner like this again. Gotta enjoy this while it lasts, Dunn." He speaks while staring straight ahead without looking at me.

"Oh. Right." That's a hell of a way to phrase things. It's like he's acknowledging that this was all temporary . . .

This perfect date will be over soon—and our time together will end. Everything between us will just be a memory.

That thought cracks my heart in half. It's clear as day in this moment that Utah is the end of the road for Drew and me.

As he drives us to the brewery, my throat aches with the urge to say just how much he means to me and how I don't want us to end when shooting wraps.

I even open my mouth, but my nerves take over, leaving my stomach in one massive knot. Why should I even bother? He's already made up his mind about us.

I stay quiet, press my eyes shut, and say nothing. Pursing my lips together, I stare out the window, terrified that if I try to speak, I'll break.

"You're awfully quiet, Dunn."

I take a moment to collect myself, thankful that it's night-time and so dark that he can't see the tears welling in my eyes. I blink them away before I answer.

"Just tired."

He pulls into the parking lot of the brewery and helps me out of the truck once again. And then he flashes that flustered smile. My favorite smile of his, the one that leaves me warm all over.

"One drink," he says. "Then we'll head back to the hotel."

I smile to keep from tearing up again. "Sounds perfect."

21

WHEN WE WALK INTO THE MOAB BREWERY, I'M BLASTED with loud chatter and laughter. I'm immediately jolted by the décor, which is a mix of small-town bar and outdoor-gear shop. There's a raft bolted to the ceiling along with mountain bikes, paddleboards, and other sporting equipment. If I were in a regular happy mood, I'd gawk and laugh. But since I'm on the verge of crying, I frown at the crowd and do a scan for the crew. Everything from the bar to the tables is full. But then I see Joe waving at us from a long table in the corner. I plaster on a smile that I hope doesn't look too fake and make my way over.

"You finally made it!" Joe announces. He pats me lightly on the back. "How was dinner? Super-duper yummy?"

I nod, relieved that it seems like everyone is tipsy enough that they don't question why Drew and I decided to have dinner together before meeting them. The excuse we gave everyone was that we had to go over some hosting stuff for Drew for the rest of the shoot, but that seems especially flimsy, now that I think about it.

Just then Joe gazes right past me and grins.

"There he is! Our superstar. Have a shot with us."

Drew starts to say no, but Wyatt, who's sitting at the other side of the table, points to a line of shots on the table. The plate of lime wedges indicates that it's tequila.

"Come on! You gotta do one," Wyatt goads him.

I glance up at Drew, who hesitates, then relents. Rylan walks up to the table from the direction of the bathrooms.

Her eyes go wide. "Tequila shots are my favorite! Yay!"

She swipes a shot glass, then hands one to me. I down it immediately while everyone else holds out in order to listen to the toast tipsy Wyatt is shouting over the restaurant speaker system, which is playing some country song I don't recognize.

"Hey." Haley walks up to me, her beautifully thick eyebrows knitted in concern. "Everything okay?"

"Everything's fine." I reach for another tequila shot and down it. Wyatt points at me and cheers me on. I turn back to Haley. "Why do you ask?"

She crosses her arms. "Because you walked in here with the biggest scowl I've ever seen a human being make, then proceeded to down two tequila shots when I know for a fact that you hate tequila."

"It's alcohol," I mutter, then reach for a third. Haley grabs my arm and pulls me away from the table and down the corridor by the hallway bathrooms.

She turns me to face her. "I mean it. What is going on with you?"

I open my mouth, but before I can think of some lie to spew to her, all my emotions from the evening collide inside me. My lip trembles and my eyes water, and then I let out the most pathetic cry sound I've ever made in my life.

"I like Drew, Haley. Like, I really, truly like him. Like, I'm legitimately falling for him. I think I might be . . ." I drift off and sniffle before I say what I'm too scared to verbalize.

Haley's expression softens. "You love him, Alia. That's amazing. Why are you so sad about it?"

"Because." My voice breaks before I can say more. "He doesn't feel the same way. He doesn't feel the same way, and it's my fault because I made those ridiculous rules in the beginning for us to follow when we started hooking up, about how this was all supposed to be just a good time and nothing more—nothing serious—but that's total garbage because now I want something serious with him. But he doesn't want it with me."

Haley squints at me, probably trying to make sense of my snotty babbling. Then after a second she sighs and rubs my arm. "Alia, I love you, but screw this bullshit."

I open my mouth and nothing but a croak comes out.

"Just tell him how you feel," she says.

I shake my head. "I can't. He just handed me a box of matches as we left the restaurant and said something weird and cryptic about how things between us aren't going to last past tonight so we'd better enjoy it while it lasts."

Haley squints at me like she's trying to make sense of my babbling. She rubs my arm in a caring gesture. "Forget about the matches. Are you one hundred percent sure that's what he said? It sounds like you've had a lot to drink and maybe you misunderstood what he meant . . ."

I shake my head and step away, wiping my nose on my jacket sleeve as I walk away from her and back out into the dining area. I don't have the energy to rehash everything for Haley. I opt to head straight for the bar instead of heading back to our table where I'll have to see Drew, and I just can't right now. My heart will explode.

I sidle up to the bar and wait for the bartender, who's frantically pouring beers, to notice me. Just then there's a hollered shout that echoes through the brewery.

I turn to the entrance and see Blaine, his arms raised, shouting while grinning. Most diners stare at him with confused looks on their faces. A few laugh as he starts high-fiving random people. I squint at his outfit of black leather pants, no shirt, and a suede jacket with loads of long fringe, then roll my eyes.

Next to him stands Colton in a rumpled, plain, gray T-shirt and jeans. His youthful face boasts the telltale signs of exhaustion: there are bags under his eyes and his skin is extra-pale. He spots me when he looks around, then walks over, leaving Blaine to continue high-fiving bewildered strangers.

"Hey." I pat him on the shoulder. "You okay?"

He shrugs, then looks at me. His expression slides from exhausted to concerned. "Are *you* okay?"

I swallow and shake my head. "Yeah. Just . . . kind of a rough night."

"You and me both," he mutters. "I'm fed up with Blaine."

"Your reserve of patience is much deeper than anyone else I know, Colton." The bartender comes over, and I request a bourbon for me and ask Colton what he wants. He asks for a beer.

"Thanks," he says, leaning on the bar top while running a hand through his mess of red hair. "I really, really need that."

Just then Blaine starts running between tables while whooping.

"I'm sorry he's here," Colton mumbles. He shakes his head as he looks away from Blaine and back to me. "Rylan was texting me the time and place for drinks, and you-know-who happened to see my phone. He insisted on coming."

Colton looks so downtrodden, I want to hug him. The bartender drops off our drinks, and Colton takes a long sip.

"It's okay. You don't need to apologize," I say to him. "Blaine is going to do whatever the hell he wants, no matter what anyone tells him. Unfortunately."

Colton nods, his eyes downcast.

"You should go over and say high to Rylan." I point to the table just as Blaine shouts, "God bless you all!" before running over to the far end of the restaurant, where a mountain bike hangs from the ceiling as part of the outdoorsy décor. He jumps up a few times and tries to grab the front tire. A huge-muscled dude wearing a black shirt walks over to him, shaking his head. Blaine scrunches up his face in disappointment before disappearing into the crowd.

I roll my eyes and nudge Colton. "Ignore him. He's on the security guy's radar now. Go see your girl."

His smile is genuine joy and relief. "Thanks, Alia."

He walks off, and I spot Rylan flashing that giddy grin she always displays when she sees Colton. She pulls him into a hug, and I let a small smile slip. At least one couple in this brewery reciprocates romantic feelings for each other.

I take a long sip from my glass, leaning my back against the bar. To my left is a couple exchanging sweet kisses between sips of beer, and to my right is a guy cheering while watching some sporting event on one of the TVs above the bar. I'm contemplating getting an Uber back to my hotel room when I hear Drew's voice near me.

I turn and see that he's standing at the bar, right next to the sports fan.

"I'm flattered, but no, thanks," he says to someone on his other side whom I can't see. There's a high-pitched chuckle that follows. I lean to the side a little and see a pretty woman with light-brown hair grinning up at him.

"Look, I'm sure a guy like you has girls lining up around the block wanting to buy you a drink," she says in a teasing, high-pitched voice. "Let me at least be your first drink of the night."

I shake my head and close my eyes, focused on finishing the rest of my drink so I can leave. The sports fan cheers once more, and I try my hardest to tune in to his nonsensical sounds just so I don't have to listen to Drew get hit on.

The woman hitting on Drew lets out a cute giggle. "I see. You make a lady work for it. I can respect that."

My blood boils and I bite down so hard, my temples immediately throb. Even though I know I shouldn't, I peek over at them once more. She's running her perfectly manicured hand along his forearm . . . the forearm that I held on to just a couple of hours earlier when he helped me walk through the gravel parking lot to the restaurant.

My chest aches. I can't do this. I can't stand here and listen to the guy I'm in love with get chatted up. I throw back the rest of my drink, set the empty glass on the bar, and attempt to walk in the direction of the bathrooms without Drew seeing me.

I take a step forward, but sports guy jumps out of his stool and raises his arms in the air while screaming something unintelligible, then backs into me. I'm thrown off balance and fall right into Drew's back.

He spins around and steadies me with both of his hands on my arms. His eyes go wide. "You okay?"

"Fine," I mutter, annoyed that sports guy hasn't even said sorry. "I got in the way of that guy's enthusiasm."

I nod to the sports fan, whose eyes are still glued to the TV screen. Drew glares at him while I glance over at the woman next to him, who's scowling at me now. I try to shrug out of his hold, but he turns me to face him.

"Hey. What's wrong?"

I guess I'm not hiding my dejection very well. It's probably written all over my face.

"Nothing. I'm just trying my best not to interrupt your drink date."

I pin the woman next to him with an unblinking stare. After a second she looks away, rolls her eyes, then sips her drink.

Drew frowns. "What are you talking about?"

"We're not together, Drew. You can accept a drink from whoever you want." A dizzy spell hits from the hard liquor I shotgunned a minute ago.

"Alia, I'm not here to do that. Why would you think that?"

"Because dinner's over and we're done, right? That's why you gave me the matchbox from the restaurant—to remember you and this night when this is all over, right? So drink with who you want and fuck who you want." I jut my chin at the woman next to him, who's now staring at me with her mouth open. "Including her. You'll get some free alcohol out of it too. Win-win."

I wince internally at my hard tone. I hate how mean I sound . . . but downing all those shots and that glass of bourbon is making it impossible to keep myself in check. All the thoughts and feelings I've been hiding over the past few weeks are finally spilling out of me.

Drew's jaw tightens at my harsh words.

With his hands still on my arms, he turns to address the woman. "Sorry, but I'm not interested in drinking with you or sleeping with you. You're better off hitting on some other guy."

She makes a disgusted face and mutters "your loss" before walking off.

I brace myself to endure Drew's angry frown and whatever harsh words he has for me—I deserve them. But when he turns to look at me, it's concern that paints his face. "Alia. I would never even think about another woman while we're together. Why would you say all that? Why would you think that we're done? That's not what I meant. And that's not at all why I gave you the matches."

Tears burn my eyes and my lips start to tremble before I can even answer. I yank out of his grip. "I gotta pee," I mumble before stomping off in the direction of the bathrooms.

I'm at the wall on the far side of the bar, right in front of the hallway by the bathrooms, when I feel a soft hand on my shoulder.

I spin around and see Drew standing there, tenderness laced through his features.

"Please talk to me."

The sound of his soft tone makes me break. Tears fall from my face a half second later, and I can't even blame it all on the alcohol. He's about to see what a mess I truly am.

"I like you, Drew." I sniffle. "I really, really like you. I mean, yes, you're amazing in bed, but I like *you* too. I have feelings for you. Really deep and mushy-gushy feelings. Our date tonight was the most perfect date ever . . . I don't want it to be just a memory or the last time we ever have dinner together." I sniffle. "Every day my feelings for you have gotten stronger and stronger. It doesn't matter if we're just chatting in the car or working a fourteen-hour day together; it's always the best day because I get to be with you. And I just . . . I don't want it to end."

I pause to catch my breath from all the crying and babbling. My vision is blurry through the tears, but I can still make out Drew's form in front of me. Then I blink a few times, and he comes back into focus. And then I'm speechless. Because instead of the dread or shock I expect to see on his face, all I see is the most beautiful smile.

"Dunn. I don't want it to end either. And I feel the exact same way about you."

My mouth falls open. "You do?"

He grins. "Absolutely. How could I not? You're incredible."

My heart squeezes itself into a tiny, hopeful ball.

His gaze locks onto mine. Around us people are laughing and shouting and drinking, but it all becomes muffled. All I can see and hear is Drew.

He scoops my hand in his. "I've never felt this way about anyone before. It's never been this good. Ever. You get me in a way that no one else has. You helped me work through my stage fright. I'm the host of a show because of you. I never, ever thought I'd feel comfortable in front of the camera, but I am now. Because of you. You're beautiful, funny, hardworking, brilliant, talented, and the most supportive person I've ever known. I'm in awe of you. I feel like the luckiest bastard in the world to have a second chance with you after I blew my first one when we met two months ago."

I let out the breath I've been holding ever since he started talking.

"And that stuff I said after dinner about enjoying it while it lasts? I just meant going out to a fancy dinner, because while we were at Desert Bistro, you said you hardly ever went out to restaurants. That's all."

"Oh." I feel so unbelievably silly.

He shoves his free hand in his hair, like he's both happy and flustered. "Look, I was going to wait until our last day of shooting to say this to you, but now's as good a time as any. I want things to be official with us, Alia. I want you to be my girlfriend. And I know it might be complicated because our work schedules are insane and we travel constantly, but I don't care. I really think this—we—could work. I want to be with you."

He leans down and kisses me. It lasts only a second, but it's more charged than any physical thing we've done up to this point. Because right now, the meaning behind his words is loud and clear. He cares about me. He wants to be with me. His words, his actions, his feelings, his everything, makes that clear.

I run my hand up his chest, unable to control the grin on my face. I'm suddenly thankful that from this angle, we're hidden by a giant floor-to-ceiling wooden beam. I want this moment for just us and no one else to see.

"I want all of that too, Drew. Every single thing."

The smile on his face turns giddy right before he pulls me

into a kiss so sloppy and rabid, I think I might pass out. When we break apart, I'm lightheaded and it's not because of the alcohol.

"It's official, then. We're together," he says.

"Exclusive. Boyfriend and girlfriend. Whatever you want to call us."

"We should probably celebrate. At the hotel. Now."

I let out a chuckle. "Sounds perfect. Let me run to the restroom first, though."

I start to walk away, but he pulls me gently by the arm against him as he kisses me once more. I playfully smack his arm, then walk down the darkened hallway to the bathroom. I'm about to walk into the women's restroom when I hear a yelp. I stop and glance up but don't see anything. There's a giant cowboy statue next to the door of the women's restroom. Maybe someone on the other side bumped into it?

"Blaine, I said stop."

All the air leaves my body at Rylan's panicked tone.

"Come on. You look so pretty tonight. I just want to show you how much I appreciate the hard work you've been doing this entire shoot." Blaine's slimy tone causes all the hair on my arms to stand on end.

"Please let go of me."

I step forward and around the statue. My stomach turns at the scene: there's Blaine cornering Rylan against the wall, gripping her arm so hard, I can already see her skin turn red.

"Get the hell away from her," I say.

Blaine whips his head around to me, frowning. "Get lost. This isn't your business."

I step closer to him and shove him. He lets go of Rylan and stumbles back.

"Fuck you. It's absolutely my business."

I turn to Rylan, who has tears in her eyes. She immediately starts rubbing her arm. It makes me rage on the inside.

"Are you okay?" I ask her.

She nods. "I came out of the bathroom and he cornered me," she mumbles, staring at the floor.

I whip around to Blaine, who's standing a few feet away, his face twisted in anger. And then I snap. He's angry that I interrupted him trying to force himself on Rylan.

"You are fired," I growl.

Blaine's eyes go wide. "What the— You can't fire me! We still have two more days of shooting!"

"I don't give a shit." I step in front of Rylan so she doesn't have to look at Blaine while he freaks out. She must be shaken to the core after what he tried to do to her. "You are a disgusting predator, and I'm not putting up with you a second longer. You're done."

I expect Blaine to shout more obscenities or even threaten to have me fired after he talks to his buddy Byron at the network. What I don't expect is for him to scoff, then walk up to me, the vilest evil smile plastered on his face.

"Your bullshit, worthless series is ruined without me," he says. "You realize that, don't you?"

I grit my teeth and straighten up my posture. In my heels I meet him eye to eye. I refuse to let him intimidate or taunt me right now.

"We'll manage just fine without you. Your stand-in, Drew? All those shots he spoon-fed to you because you were too high or hungover to do your job? We can use all of those and make him the host. We don't need you, Blaine. We never needed you."

He takes a breath, his too-tan face reddening. He shakes his head. "Drew's saving your ass, huh? No surprise there given the shitty job you've done. Tell me, Alia. Who'd you have to screw to get this show? I mean, you're a pretty girl. That's obviously how you got this job." He lifts an eyebrow at me. "That might be a nice way to make things up to me, you know."

I take a deep breath at his repulsive words while keeping my eyes on him. Behind me I hear Rylan gasp. I know exactly what Blaine's trying to do. Whenever a guy like him makes a comment like that to a woman, he wants one of two things: to make her feel worthless and small or to make her cry.

I pause for a beat, then rest my hand on Blaine's shoulder. His eyes widen, like he's surprised I'm touching him. And then a split second later, I shove my right knee square in his nuts.

He drops to the floor like a sack of bricks. Judging by the deafening scream he lets out, he wasn't expecting my response.

"Assault!" Blaine yells between wheezes as he writhes on the floor. "You bitch! That was assault!"

My heart thunders in my throat at the adrenaline rush. Behind me I hear heavy footsteps. I turn and see Drew, a worried look on his face.

"What the . . ."

His brow flies to his hairline as he stares at Blaine.

"That wasn't assault, you creep. You were threatening her and she defended herself," Rylan says as she comes up behind me to stand on my other side.

I turn to her and check on her arm as my heart pounds against my rib cage. My throat squeezes at the red mark. "That's probably going to bruise," I say. I grab her hand in mine, hoping it's a comfort. "We'll get some ice on that."

She nods. I take a breath, then explain to Drew how Blaine had Rylan up against the wall as he groped and harassed her, and how the subsequent event led to him squirming around on the floor. His eyes go from wide to angry. He glances down at Blaine. "You piece of shit," he mutters.

Then he turns to Rylan and asks how she is.

"I'll be okay," she says softly.

Just then Wyatt saunters in, probably in need of the bath-room. His eyes bulge at the scene in front of me.

"Damn . . . What did I miss?"

"I'll explain in a minute," Drew says, his gaze fixed on me. He cups my face in both hands. "Are you okay?"

I nod, closing my eyes for a second at the warmth of his palms.

"You're such a bitch," Blaine mutters, still rolling around on the floor.

Just then Drew's face reddens and his jaw clenches. His hands fall away from me and he turns around to Blaine. Then he crouches down to help Blaine off the floor.

"Thanks, man," Blaine says, still heaving for air.

Drew aims his stony expression at Blaine; then he punches him in the gut. Blaine falls to the ground gasping for air once more. Then Drew hunches over him.

"If you so much as breathe in the direction of Alia or Rylan or anyone else on this crew, I'll end you. You will stay the hell away from everyone. Understand?"

All Blaine can seem to do is wheeze and nod.

"Whoa," Wyatt mutters behind me. I turn and fill him in on what happened in the last few minutes. His drunken expression sobers quickly when he soaks it all in.

When he turns to Rylan to see if she's okay, I pull my phone out of my clutch and dial Colton. I don't have the energy to fight the crowd back to our table and then loudly explain what has happened. He answers on the second ring, and I explain every-thing.

When I hang up, I glance over at Drew, who's still standing over Blaine, like he's a guard keeping watch over him. He fishes his phone out of his dress pants pocket. "I'll call Joe and tell him to settle his tab so we can all leave."

"I'll call Haley and tell her the same."

Just then Colton comes running over to Rylan and hugs her. "Are you okay?" The way Colton's voice trembles makes my heart ache. "I was talking to Joe and Haley at the table; I wasn't paying attention. I should have—"

Rylan shakes her head. "It's no one's fault. Other than Blaine's."

When I hang up after talking to Haley, I notice Colton's pale face turn red. He walks over to where Blaine's rolling on the floor. "I quit, asshole."

His chest rises as he glares at Blaine; then he walks back over to Rylan and hugs her. We all walk back into the main area of the bar to our table. Haley runs over to the burly security guy to report what happened; he glares in the direction of the bathrooms before stomping over.

"We should call the police too. To report him." I turn to Rylan. "Is that okay with you? Reporting what he did?"

Rylan pauses for a moment. Colton squeezes her hand.

"It's okay. Whatever you want to do, we'll support you," he says.

She nods. "Yes. I want to report him."

Drew calls the police, and I walk over to Rylan and give her a hug while we wait for them to arrive.

"We're all here for you," I say to her.

22

WATCH AS THE POLICE CAR PULLS AWAY FROM THE PARKING
lot of the Moab Brewery with Blaine handcuffed in the back.
Then I turn and walk to the far end of the building, where
Rylan is standing with Colton. He hugs his arms around her.

Everyone else is milling around the parking lot trying to figure out who's sober enough to drive.

"How are you feeling?" I ask her.

She hugs her arms. "I feel . . . weird. Unsettled."

"You're really brave for what you did."

"I don't know about that."

"You absolutely are, Rylan. It takes courage to report a creep
like Blaine."

"He's probably going to post bail and get out," she says softly.

"Maybe. But we'll make sure he doesn't get away with this. I
promise."

Everyone gathers round and echoes their support for Rylan.

A gust of cool, crisp, evening desert air whooshes around me.

"I just hope this doesn't mess up the series," Rylan says.
"Blaine is buddies with one of the executives. They might be
mad that I reported him to the police. And it could be bad publicity for the show."

"Don't even worry about that," I say. "Tomorrow I'm calling HR. I'll file a report and fill them in on everything. And when I present the show to the execs, I'll tell them everything that happened. Blaine's not going to get away with what he's done."

As confident as I sound, I'm still riddled with doubt. The television industry isn't known for being especially progressive when it comes to handling celebrities who harass people and abuse their power.

"And honestly, they'll probably be more pissed at me than anyone because I fired Blaine without asking them first," I say.

Just then Wyatt chimes in. "We all stand behind you one hundred percent on your decision."

Everyone voices their agreement with Wyatt.

Drew looks at me. "We've still got a series to finish—your series," he says. "Once everything is filmed and edited, you're going to present it to the execs and they're going to fall in love with it. They're not going to care about Blaine and his bullshit after you've blown them away."

"And if for some reason they do, we'll support you," Haley says. "Every single one of us will tell them just how horrific Blaine was and that you didn't have a choice but to fire him."

Rylan, Joe, and Wyatt reiterate what Haley says. My eyes water; I am completely heartened at how much they support me.

Drew steps up to me and pulls me into him. "You don't have a single thing to worry about. Promise."

I cuddle into his chest and whisper, "Thank you." When we pull away, everyone except Haley is staring at us with surprised looks on their faces.

Oh shit. With that affectionate embrace, Drew and I just outed ourselves to the crew.

In the chaos of this evening, I didn't even think about it . . . I just needed Drew's comfort so badly.

"Well, um . . ."

Drew shuffles next to me as I stammer. "We have an announcement to make," he says.

Wyatt turns to Joe. "You owe me twenty bucks."

Joe rolls his eyes before digging into his pocket, pulling out cash, and slapping it into Wyatt's palm. Haley bursts out laughing.

"What was that about?" I ask.

"We figured you two were together. We had a bet going on whether or not it would come out before shooting wrapped up," Wyatt says.

"Oh . . ." I drift off and catch Rylan smiling at us.

"You two make such a cute couple," she says. Colton nods his agreement.

I let out a scoff of disbelief, then glance up at Drew, who's sporting a flustered grin.

Wyatt levels a stare at us. "Look, I know I was in the middle of having an allergic reaction at the condo in Bryce, but even I figured out what was going on." He looks at Drew. "You were in your underwear, man. Come on."

Drew and I let out dual flustered chuckles. "Why didn't you say anything?" I ask.

Joe shrugs. "We figured you guys wanted to keep things private."

"I can finally do this now." Drew scoops my hand in his. "And this." He leans down to peck my lips.

"I honestly had no idea until I overheard Wyatt and Joe talking about you guys the other day," Rylan says.

"Me either," Colton says.

Haley tilts her head at them. "That's because you both are so sweet and innocent and uncorrupted by life."

We all chuckle, then disperse to walk to our cars. Drew and I stop at his truck before getting in. Drew shoves his hands in his pockets and looks at me.

I let out a chuckle of disbelief. All the adrenaline drains from my body, leaving my limbs feeling heavy.

I blink and fight back a yawn. "Well . . ."

"That was . . ."

"I honestly have no words to describe this night."

Drew lets out a breath, then steps closer to me. "Me either. We don't have to talk the whole rest of the night if you don't want to."

"Can we stay in the same hotel room? I mean, now that everyone knows, we don't have to sneak around anymore. I could really use a cuddle after tonight."

This time when he smiles at me, I can see his whole heart in his eyes. "That sounds perfect, Dunn."

"I THINK I'M all packed," Drew says as he crouches on the floor of his hotel room near his suitcase.

I sit up in bed and smile up at him. The bedsheet falls from my bare chest.

Drew raises an eyebrow. "Now that's a view I could get used to seeing every morning."

I bite my lip and smile. "When we get back to the city, I'll try to make that happen for you."

After the last two days of filming in Moab, we're finally wrapped on *Discovering Utah*. Today we're headed home to New York with Drew and me embarking on a whole new adventure: a relationship.

Drew walks over to the bed and bends down to kiss me. "Too bad we're not on the same flight. You sitting in the seat next to me would make enduring a long flight a hell of a lot nicer."

My heart races at the soft growl of his voice. I press another kiss to his lips. "At least we'll both be in New York for the foreseeable future—in the same borough even. Maybe while I'm hunkered down editing the series over the next few weeks, you can stop by and visit me to make sure I'm taking the appropriate number of . . . breaks."

He grins. "I can do that."

I check the time. I've got a little more than an hour left before I'm due at the airport with the rest of the crew. "I need to pack. My room looks like a tornado hit it."

"Fine." Drew leans back up to stand at his full height, groaning in mock disappointment.

I hop out of his bed and throw on my clothes from yesterday. I'm pulling my shirt over my head when I feel Drew's massive arms wrap around me from behind.

"I don't mean to sound like a total softie, but I'm gonna miss you, Dunn."

He kisses the side of my neck. I close my eyes and take a breath to steady myself. If I'm not careful, I'll end up back in bed with Drew, and we'll both miss our flights back to New York.

"I like it when you're a softie. I'm going to miss you too." Reaching behind me, I run my fingers through his hair.

Then I turn around and give him a proper kiss.

"Text me when you land," I say through a gasp as I pull away from his mouth.

"I'm not getting in until after midnight," he says, his mouth on my neck once more.

I yank at his T-shirt. "That's okay. You can stay over at my apartment. I owe you after spending the last two nights in your hotel room."

His expression softens. "You still doing okay?"

I melt on the inside at the question. He's asked it every day since what happened with Blaine.

"Yeah, I'm okay," I say softly. It's the truth. I've been so busy focusing on the series and my new relationship with Drew that I haven't had a lot of time to stress about Blaine.

He hugs me tight against him.

"I haven't heard anything from the network execs so far, so I'm guessing Blaine hasn't worked up the nerve to go to Byron. Yet," I say.

Drew shifts and looks down at me.

"I'm just nervous about how it'll all go down when we're back."

"What do you mean?" Drew asks.

"I mean . . . other than kneeing Blaine in the balls the other night at the brewery, I think I did everything right. I emailed Brooke and called the head of Human Resources at Expedition the day after everything happened to let them know what went down. And I helped Rylan file a report with HR. I just wish . . . I just wish that was enough."

"You don't think that's enough? Alia, the whole crew has yours and Rylan's backs. We'll all make HR reports when we get back. You don't have to worry." Drew's eyebrows knit in concern.

"I know that, but honestly . . . given that our executive board is all straight white males who have never experienced a day of sexual harassment in their lives, it makes me wonder how this will all go. When I explained the situation to the execs and then told them I had a backup plan ready to go, they didn't seem convinced."

"They'll be convinced when you show them the first episode after you edit it," Drew says.

I shake my head. "Blaine's agent is pals with Byron. And yeah, Blaine is the one at fault, but sometimes that doesn't matter when you're connected to the right people."

Drew's expression goes hard for a second; then it turns thoughtful. "We'll figure out something. Blaine won't get away with this. I promise."

Despite the knot of anxiety in my chest, the way Drew stares at me, unblinking and with conviction in his eyes, I feel heartened again. When I look up at him, there's the faintest ping in the center of my chest. His eyes shine bright, like there's something behind them I've never seen before.

It's a whole different rush of emotions that flood me in this moment. The intensity has me almost shaking. I could tell him I love him right now . . .

But I nuzzle into his warm and broad chest and hold back. I don't want to say it just yet, not when we're about to leave each other. I'll tell him tonight at my apartment when we're together again.

We kiss again, and then I pull away and head for the door.

"Have a safe flight, Dunn. I'll see you tonight."

I walk out of his room and head to mine, then spend the next hour trying to pack up all my belongings. When I finish packing, I realize I never finished my tuna sandwich from yesterday. I wrinkle my nose at the thought of it stinking up my room and how unpleasant that will be for housekeeping when they come to clean. I grab it and quickly run it to the trash on my floor.

When I turn in the direction of my room, a sharp, low voice halts me dead in my tracks.

"You know why the hell I'm here."

Twisting my head around, I try to see where the voice is coming from, but there's no one in the hallway. There's the sound of a deep chuckle. My ears prick.

Slowly, I walk in the direction of the sound. I stop short when I reach the corner of the hallway on the opposite side of the floor from where my room is.

And then I see it. From my angle, I spot the broad spread of Drew's shoulders. In front of him stands Blaine.

My stomach curdles. I dart behind the wall and freeze so they can't see me.

"I have a bone to pick with your little girlfriend," Blaine spits out. The hateful way he says it makes my skin flash with fire.

"That's not happening," Drew says calmly.

There's a moment of tense silence when neither of them says a word. I hold my breath. Then Blaine finally speaks.

"Then how about a goddamn apology for sucker punching me the other night? Fuck, that hurt," Blaine whines.

I expect Drew to refuse, to tell Blaine to get the hell out.

But he doesn't. Instead he does something I never in a million years thought he would do. He laughs.

The lightness of his voice makes my skin crawl.

"Okay, man, I'm sorry," Drew says. I can tell he's smiling too. "But you know how it is. You're there with your girl; you gotta put on a show. I couldn't bitch out."

There's another second of silence before Blaine cracks a chuckle.

"Okay, okay. You got me there," Blaine says.

"Truce?"

"Truce."

I hear a soft clapping noise. They must have just shook hands . . . but why? Why is Drew all of a sudden interested in being pals with Blaine? My brain spins with confusion. After everything he said about Blaine . . . After what he said to me that night and earlier today . . . The way he comforted me, that look in his eyes that made me believe that he was behind me one hundred percent . . .

"Look, man, we're all about getting a good lay."

Drew's voice sounds so foreign right now. He doesn't sound like himself, like the sincere, sweet guy I know. He sounds like a douche-bro who's trying to impress someone.

My head goes foggy and I flash back to that day standing outside Reid's office. My ears ring . . . all I can hear is him telling outright lies about me over the phone.

She's fucking crazy.

She's practically obsessed with me.

I need her gone ASAP.

We're all about getting a good lay.

The words blur together in my mind until Drew's and Reid's voices start to sound the same.

Blaine speaking pulls me back to the present.

"That's what you did with Alia, isn't it?"

The slimy lilt to his voice when he says my name makes my skin crawl. I bite down so hard, my jaw feels like it's going to break.

"How'd you guess, man? That was my plan all along. String her along this whole shoot, and then ditch her," Drew says. "How could I not? She made me host. I've been dying for a break like this for years. And I mean, sorry it cost you your job, but hey. It's a cutthroat business, right? You gotta take the opportunity when it presents itself."

Blaine scoffs. "That's some brutal shit right there."

"Tell me you wouldn't have done the same for a job you've always wanted."

"You got me there."

My head spins faster and faster as the truth of Drew's words is revealed. I was just a means to an end—a way for him to get the hosting job he always wanted.

Hot tears burn my eyes. Seconds later I hear Drew speaking again.

"When the work is done, I'm done," he says. "I can't handle anything serious. I'm not wired that way. I like the chase, the fucking, then I'm gone. Just like you, right?"

Just like Reid.

My heart plummets all the way to the pit of my stomach; my breath lodges in my throat.

Blaine's taunting laugh hits my ears. I think I might vomit.

"That's cold, man," Blaine says. "Even I don't have it in me to make a girl fall in love with me and then drop her."

A laugh that doesn't sound like Drew's echoes against the walls. My throat throbs with the urge to sob, but I hold it together.

"Then what's your style?" Drew asks. "I gotta know how the great Blaine Stephens gets those notches on his belt."

My heart bottoms out completely, and my legs ache with the urge to run away. I can't stand here and listen to this a second longer.

This isn't the Drew I know and love.

But maybe the Drew I got to know wasn't the real Drew at all.

My eyes water as I let the thought soak in. My Drew was a facade. The real Drew is a jerk who talks about me like I'm a conquest and a rung on the professional ladder.

He's just like Reid. How could I be so foolish?

I run back to my room with tears in my eyes. Then I splash cold water onto my face and force myself to stop crying. I gather all my luggage, check out of the hotel, and meet everyone as they stand in the parking lot by the cars.

"We ready to go?" Wyatt asks as he loads luggage into the van.

"Yup!" Rylan answers.

Wyatt and Joe hop into their van while Haley, Rylan, and I jump into the car I rented. I start the car and head straight for the airport without speaking a word. The whole way, Rylan chats about how Colton is moving to New York at the end of this month. Haley peers back periodically to chat with her.

"You're awfully quiet," Haley says to me.

"I don't have a lot to say at the moment," I say quietly.

Haley reaches over to pat my arm. "Someone's missing Drew."

Rylan lets out an "aww" sound.

I don't say a word because if I do, I'll fall to pieces. And I need to keep it together long enough to get through security and board the plane. Thank goodness I'm sitting next to Haley and not anyone else the entire flight. I'm going to break down. I know I am, and Haley is the only person I'm comfortable enough to do that in front of.

And that's exactly what I do. Through baggage check and security, I keep my composure.

But the moment I fall into my seat on the plane, I start to tear up. My phone buzzes and I glance at the screen.

Drew: Hey, Dunn. Miss you already. Can't wait to see you to-night.

The tears in my eyes turn angry.

Me: Don't bother.

Fury commands my movements as I swipe my thumb across my phone screen and block his number. Then I turn off my phone and stare out the window through teary eyes. There's a tap on my arm. I twist around to see Haley's face painted with concern.

"Shit . . . What happened, Alia?"

She hands me a packet of tissues. I blow my nose and then tell her the whole awful story.

23

IT'S BEEN TWO DAYS SINCE WE'VE BEEN BACK FROM UTAH, Alia. What are you even doing?" Haley says as she stands in my office.

I don't glance up at her as I sit at my desk. I keep my eyes glued to my computer screen and focus. I've got fifteen minutes until I present the first-episode cut of *Discovering Utah* to the Expedition network execs.

"I'm trying to work," I say.

Haley walks over and plops her tiny frame on my desk. "You and I both know that presentation is stellar. You could have given it yesterday in your sleep. And you know that's not what I'm asking about." She studies me with those deep-brown eyes. "Are you okay? In the two days that we've been back, you haven't done anything other than edit in your office and then edit at your apartment."

"And find a therapist," I add, eyes still on my computer.

Haley sighs. "Yes. And that. I'm really proud of you for it. I just wanna make sure you're okay."

It didn't take long after unloading on Haley during the flight for me to realize that I needed some help. Next week I have an appointment with a therapist to talk about what happened with Drew—and my entire dating and relationship history.

I can't just bury the pain from an awful breakup and hope it magically goes away, like I did with Reid. The trauma from the way things ended with him resurfaced with Drew. This time, I need to actually process my pain, anger, and feelings of betrayal instead of shoving them deep inside me and letting them fester for years and years.

I finally make eye contact with Haley. "I'm not okay. But I will be." I check the clock. Eleven minutes till presentation time.

"Are you sure you don't want to talk to Drew?" She flashes that same concerned expression that she did when I quietly sobbed to her on the plane ride back from Utah.

"I have nothing to say to him."

Drew is the host of the show and that means in all the hours of editing that I've done over the past two days, I've had to watch clips of him again and again while I edit. Sometimes it's a comfort, to be reminded of the person he was . . . how happy he made me. But then the unforgivable words he spoke to Blaine resurface, and I'm broken all over again.

"Don't you think you should at least talk to him?" Haley says, bringing me back to the present. "He's the new host of your show."

"Are you serious right now? Don't you remember what I told you? How he betrayed my trust to Blaine, of all people?"

I try my best to keep my composure, but my eyes water anyway.

She leans over and hugs me. Despite how annoyed I am at her right now, I return the hug because I definitely need it.

"I'm not trying to make excuses for what he did . . . I honestly can't even begin to fathom why he would want to hurt you like that," Haley says. "All I'm saying is that if you talk to him, you could tell him off or whatever to help you get a tiny bit of closure. That's all."

I sigh, then pull away. She hands me a tissue so I can blow my nose.

"I don't have the energy for that. I just want to move on. And I want to nail this presentation."

Haley nods once at me. "You will."

She reaches into my purse and pulls out my makeup bag to touch me up.

"Better?" I ask.

"Much. You're going to kill it. I told you that charcoal shift dress with a black blazer would make you look like a sleek corporate shark."

I laugh at her phrasing. She hops off my desk and walks to the door. "Drinks tonight?"

"Yes, please. Thanks, Haley."

She tells me to knock 'em dead before leaving my office. I save the last of my work on my laptop, and I am about to head to the conference room when my office phone rings. I answer it.

"Alia?"

The sound of Drew's voice makes my stomach fall to my feet. "Drew?"

"I've been trying to get ahold of you since I landed back in New York." He sounds breathless, like he's been running all over the city looking for me.

My chest squeezes at the sound of his voice. It's like a weird sort of muscle memory. My body isn't used to being angry with him, so it's still fondly remembering all the amazing things he made me feel.

"I blocked your number," I say sternly.

"Why? Tell me what I did to make you cut off all contact with me. Please, I'm going out of my mind here."

I bite the inside of my cheek. I absolutely will not cry. "Did you honestly think I wouldn't find out?"

"Find out what? Alia, please—"

"All those horrible things you said about me in the hallway at the hotel the day I left, Drew! To Blaine, of all people!" I glance up through the glass walls of my office. Thankfully no one in the cubicle farm seems to have noticed my shouting because everyone is fixed on their computers.

There's a long pause on his end of the line. "Crap . . . Alia, I'm so, so sorry you heard that. That wasn't part of the plan. But he just showed up and I had to think fast—"

"What the hell are you talking about?"

He stammers for a few seconds. "What I mean to say is that I was planning to tell you that night I landed back in the city about what happened with Blaine, but then I got your text telling me not to bother and you blocked me, so then I couldn't—"

The reminder on my email sounds. Five minutes until the presentation.

"Drew, just stop."

"Alia, please just let me explain."

"Listen to me. I'm only going to ask you this once, and I need you to tell me the truth. Did you tell Blaine that your plan was to string me along for the shoot, then dump me? That all you wanted was the hosting job? Did you tell him you were all about the chase—the fucking—and that was it?"

His sigh echoes against my ear.

"Yes, but I swear, I didn't mean it like—"

"Stop. Don't say another word. I have exactly one minute until I have to leave my office to pitch the series and I need to get this out."

Haley's words from minutes before sound in my head.

If you talk to him, you could tell him off or whatever you need to tell him to help you get a tiny bit of closure.

But I'm not going to tell Drew off. That won't make me feel

any better. What I will tell him is the truth. Yes, it's going to hurt, but it's what I need to do to move on from him—from us.

"You made me feel like Reid made me feel all those years ago—used and worthless. Because I thought you cared about me. The way you acted while we were in Utah, so protective and loving, it made me fall for you so hard"—I swallow to keep my voice from shaking—"I love you, Drew. I was going to tell you that the night you got back from Utah, the night you were supposed to stay at my apartment."

I pause for a quick breath, continuing before Drew can interrupt me.

"And even now that I know what kind of person you truly are, I don't regret loving you. Because the person I was when I was with you, that was one hundred percent me. I gave you all of me, and I'm proud I was brave enough to do that. I've never, ever done that with anyone else. But I did it with you. And my only regret is that I didn't figure out your true self sooner. Because you didn't deserve me."

I hang up before my voice breaks. Then I tilt my head up, grab a tissue from my desk, and dab until I'm certain no tears will fall.

And then I stand up, grab my things, and walk out of my office and into the conference room where all six executives and Brooke sit at the table, waiting for me.

"GOTTA SAY, ALIA. This is a pretty risky move." Byron peers over the top of his glasses at me.

I'm standing at the front of the room, the white wall behind me illuminated with the ending shot of the first episode. It's Drew standing next to the Delicate Arch, his dazzling smile on display. At the top of the image is the *Discovering Utah* title in fiery-red block letters, an homage to the landscape of the state.

I open my mouth to address his comment, but another exec, Peter, speaks up. "I like it." He grins. "A lot. Drew's a natural." He spins his chair to Byron. "I was never a fan of that Blaine guy anyway."

The other execs murmur comments along those lines. I hold my breath, silently telling myself not to interrupt the soft rumbles of positive feedback.

Brooke winks at me. My racing heart settles when I look at the confident expression on her face. She cleared today in her schedule to sit in on my presentation to support me, and so I would have one friendly face in the audience.

She turns to the execs. "I think what Alia managed to do on this shoot is nothing less than a miracle. She had a truly horrible and unprofessional host who made it impossible for anyone to do their job, but she found a way around it. On her own. Without going over budget and without pestering any of you to hold her hand. How many other showrunners or producers can you say that about?"

She looks pointedly at Byron, whose clean-shaven cheeks redden.

"That's a good point," Peter says.

I flip the screen to show a screenshot of Drew's social media accounts. "Drew has a solid following on both Instagram and Twitter. Rylan put up teaser photos and video clips during the shoot to entice viewers, and it received a strong response from the public."

I point out the thousands of views and likes each of Drew's Utah posts on social media have received. Impressed murmurs follow.

"And I know that Drew doesn't have the follower count that Blaine does. But I do think the combined follower count he has online isn't anything to discredit, especially since his engagement is significantly higher than Blaine's."

I show a comparison of stats between Drew's and Blaine's social media accounts. Drew's figures are triple Blaine's.

"I'm confident Blaine's follower count will continue to fall once the network releases a statement explaining that he was fired due to sexual misconduct," I add.

"The press release from the network addressing Blaine's official firing and the assault he committed went out this morning," Brooke says. "Since then he's been dropped from all of his remaining sponsors. That reality show he signed on to do in the fall has also axed him."

Peter sighs. "Blaine's lawyer is threatening to come after us for not paying out the remainder of his contract—after he deals with the court hearing for the assault charge in Utah."

Nerves start to swirl at the bottom of my stomach, but I take a breath and address the room.

"That's not surprising given Blaine's entitled and lazy behavior that persisted for the whole shoot," I say. "But every member of the crew gave statements to HR attesting to Blaine's behavior, which often involved excessive alcohol and illegal drug use that impeded his performance on the job so much so that Drew had to serve as his stand-in for the entirety of the series—in addition to how he sexually harassed and attacked Rylan. I kept track of the dates and the incidents of everything in a spreadsheet that I sent to both HR and legal. And I requested a copy of the police report filed in Moab, which documents the worst of his conduct, and have given that to HR to circulate to our media contacts. All of that would void any claim he would have to compensation."

It takes a moment for everyone to soak in what I've said, but once they do, they seem more settled. I catch Byron crossing his arms. He's frowning, but I can't quite tell if it's because his choice of host turned out to be horrific or if it's because he's thinking about something else.

When he turns his frown on me, I decide, screw it. "I remember what you said to me when I first pitched this series to you, Byron. You told me I needed to take more risks. Well, this is my kind of risk taking. I fired the host because he attacked a crew member—and I did it without the approval of you or anyone else at the network because it was the right thing to do. And then I put a series together with my field coordinator, who happened to be natural on-camera. That's a hell of a risk too. And I'm proud of it."

A tense silence follows for a few seconds. And then Byron holds up his hands. "You're right. I'm sorry for what Blaine did. Truly. I think it's safe to say I'm done putting my hands in all things production and talent related."

I almost choke at how openly Byron admits his shortcoming. The rest of the execs nod along with him.

Peter looks at me. "You clearly know what you're doing. We're all on board with your risk-taking move, Alia. The show with Drew as the new host is a go. Go ahead and continue editing the twelve episodes we planned. We'll start promoting it at the end of July for a fall airing—if you think you can get us the episodes by then. That's about two and a half months away."

I smile. "I can absolutely do that."

"And anytime you have any more ideas you want to pitch, come straight to me," Peter says. "I know we still have to see how the show does ratings-wise when it airs, but I have a good feeling about it. You clearly have a talent for this content. And we need more stuff like this at Expedition."

I thank him, then thank everyone else. They all compliment me as they leave the room. When it's just Brooke and me in the room, she hugs me.

"Oh my God!" I sputter.

She holds me by the shoulders, her ruby-red lips stretched in a smile. "You nailed it, Alia! I knew you would!"

"I just . . . I can't believe they actually went for it . . . I mean, I'm so freaking happy they did; I honestly don't even know what I would have done if they didn't, but . . ."

I pause from babbling to take a breath.

Brooke squeezes my shoulders. "I'm so proud of you. You've blown everyone away."

I'm in the middle of thanking her when Haley comes running into the conference room. "Drop whatever you're doing and watch this. Now."

"Don't you want to know how the presentation went?"

Haley shakes her head. "No. This. Now."

I almost laugh at her insistence. But when I look at the video playing on her phone, my jaw drops. It's Blaine standing in the hallway at the hotel in Utah.

"Haley, what is—"

"Just watch it," she orders.

It takes a second for me to hear what he's saying, but after a moment it all registers. It's the conversation Drew had with Blaine that I overheard.

Brooke stands off to the side of Haley and me, her eyes bouncing between us in confusion.

Haley waves a hand at her. "I'll explain in a minute, I promise."

"Then what's your style, man?" Drew asks. "I gotta know how the great Blaine Stephens gets those notches on his belt."

This is the moment I ran off. On the screen, Blaine pauses to glance around, like he's checking to make sure no one is around to hear him.

"Exactly what I did with that sweet little thing Rylan. I compliment them at first on set. Let them know I like what I see. Then I after a while I move in for the kill."

"The kill?" Drew's tone is hard.

"Yeah, man. Just like I did that night at the brewery." Blaine laughs. My skin crawls. "I know she was playing hard to get. They always do. Girls like that want you to chase them. They say they want you to leave them alone, but I know what's really up. No means yes, right?"

My breath quickens. So does my pulse. Blaine is detailing in his own words how he attacked Rylan.

"So that's exactly what I did—I went after her. I waited till there was no one else around, and I could get her in a quiet corner by the bathroom. And then I let her know just how hot she was making me."

"Huh." I can tell by the way that sound falls out of Drew's mouth that he's livid.

My mind spins as I make sense of what I'm hearing. This whole conversation, Drew was pretending to make amends with Blaine. It was all a setup to get him to admit what he did to Rylan on video.

The memory of being with Drew that morning before flying back to New York flashes in my mind. I remember hugging him so tight, telling him how nervous I was that the execs would side with Blaine because he was in the power position since he was connected to Byron.

"And how did you do that? How did you let her know?" Drew's voice in the video pulls me back to the present. There's a tinge of anger lacing his words that Blaine doesn't seem to pick up based on how he's grinning and chuckling.

"Oh, you know, I touched her arm, led her back behind the bathrooms so we could have some privacy."

"She wasn't into it, though," Drew says quickly.

"Maybe not at first, but I have a way of turning things around. If only that bitch Alia hadn't interfered."

I flinch at Blaine's insult. There's a low exhaling noise that bursts from Drew that makes my eyes widen.

"Is that why you grabbed Rylan's arm like that?" Drew asks.

Blaine shrugs. "A lot of girls like it rough. They just don't know it at first."

My jaw drops just as Brooke says, "Oh my God."

And then the screen goes blurry for a second. There's a shuffling noise followed by a loud slam. Then all I hear is breathing.

The image on the screen steadies. I make out Drew's arm pressed against Blaine's chest. Blaine wheezes.

"You're a piece of shit," Drew growls through the breath he heaves. "You're a goddamn predator, and you're going down."

And then it all clicks in my brain. Drew did this to help me. This video is irrefutable evidence of Blaine's behavior in case I needed it if the execs tried to challenge me. Thankfully they believed me and trusted my handling of everything . . . But the fact that Drew went through all this to secure this extra evidence against Blaine blows me away.

The video cuts out. Then Haley taps the screen. That's when I notice the thousands of likes and retweets and views of this video.

A few comments with the #subwaygentleman hashtag catch my eye.

> Damn. Good on the #subwaygentleman for calling out this predator. Fuck @blaine_stephens. Dude deserves to rot

> Hell yeah @drewirons aka #subwaygentleman! This is exactly what we need more of—men willing to call out other men on their rapey behavior!

"So he . . . didn't betray me," I say softly. It's like I'm in a daze trying to process the ninety seconds of video I just watched.

Haley shakes her head. "It's obvious now that he just said all that stuff to goad Blaine into admitting what he did to Rylan. He wanted to get it on tape as proof. Oh, wait." Haley turns her phone back so she can see it. "He wrote a caption with the video." Her eyes go wide. "You need to read it."

I squint at the phone.

Just in case there are any defenders of that disgusting sack of crap @blaine_stephens, here is proof of his harassment and the assault he committed on my coworker. Yes, this was a setup. He admitted to my face what he did with no remorse whatsoever. He laughed like it was a joke. And he bragged like assaulting someone is something to be proud of. And then he had the gall to call our showrunner a derogatory name for defending the woman he targeted. He deserved to lose his job with @ExpeditionNetwork and he deserves to lose every sponsorship and job opportunity he's been given.

My head feels like it's whirling in a million frenzied circles as I process Drew's Instagram post.

"When did he post this video?"

"This morning," Haley says. "It's been trending all over Twitter and Instagram. Rylan was the one who forwarded me the link. She told me that Drew called her earlier today and explained he had a video of Blaine confessing what he did and asked if she'd feel comfortable posting it to expose him. After she watched it, she said she was one hundred percent on board."

He was probably going to tell me all this when he called me today . . .

"I was wrong . . . He tried to tell me . . ."

Haley squints at me. I explain how Drew called me before the presentation and how I talked over him to go off on him and to tell him I love him.

"Whoa . . ." she mutters.

My brain finally catches up. This means Drew's loyalty for me never wavered. It means that his feelings for me are true. And it means that I need to find him immediately and try to make things right.

Brooke holds up a hand. "I'm sorry, but what is going on?"

Haley turns to her. "I swear, I'm going to fill you in." She spins back to me. "You and Drew need to talk. Now."

I nod and smack her phone back into her hand, then hug her before darting out of the conference room. I jog to my office, grab my purse, and sprint down the hall in the direction of the elevators.

As I smack the buttons a dozen times, it occurs to me that I have no idea where Drew lives. I know he lives in Brooklyn, but I never asked his address. I start to dig my phone out of my purse. Maybe if I call him on my way out of the building, he can give me his address, and then I can sprint over there and we can talk and make all of this right . . .

The elevator on the far side dings and begins to open. I dart over to it and stop dead in my tracks. "Drew."

It's the first time I've seen him in the flesh since Utah, and for a long second, all I can do is stare. He's not an image on a computer screen that I've been looking at for hours and hours—he's the real thing, standing right in front of me in the elevator, and he's ten million times more divine in person. His hair is mussed, and he's shaved his beard. Now it looks more like a well-grown five-o'clock shadow. He's wearing jeans and this plaid, casual button-up that is rolled up along his perfect forearms. He looks like a hot lumberjack who got a trim at the barber. The very definition of ruggedly handsome.

His brow is wrinkled all the way to his hairline, and he's gazing at me like he can't believe he's seeing me.

"Alia." The way he says my name sounds breathless. I wonder if he sprinted to get here too.

His dazzling hazel-brown eyes fall down the length of my body. "Whoa . . . you look amazing."

"Thanks. Listen, I—"

A boisterous crowd of suits walks over to the elevators.

One of the older men laughs and looks in our direction. "You going up?"

"No," I bark at him, then jump into the elevator with Drew. The doors shut and I hit the emergency button, which stalls us.

"What are you doing?" Drew asks.

"We need to talk now, and I don't want anything or anyone interrupting us. I just saw the video you posted."

"You did?"

I nod. "I was taking the trash out at the hotel before leaving for the airport and overheard you with Blaine. I only heard part of the conversation . . . I had no idea what you were planning to do. That's why it hurt to hear what you said. I thought you were telling him how you really felt about me. And honestly . . . as weird as this might sound, hearing you say all that triggered me. It reminded me of what Reid did to me all those years ago, how he lied about me and betrayed my trust."

Sadness shines in his eyes as he nods.

"I'm so, so sorry, Drew. I should have let you just explain yourself."

I sniffle, trying to hold back tears.

"It's okay. I owe you an apology for what I said. I didn't mean any of it, not a single word. I was just trying to think of something I could say to him to get him to admit what he did. And I understand why you were upset . . . You had no idea what was going on, plus the trauma of your relationship with Reid . . . Honestly, if the same thing had happened to me, I would have reacted just like you did." He rubs his hand along the back of his neck. "It all happened so fast, that day at the hotel. I was walking to get ice and then out of the blue I saw Blaine wandering the halls. He wanted to confront you, and something clicked in my head. I thought that this would be the perfect opportunity to get proof of what he did, in case he or anyone tried to go against you or Rylan." He shakes his head. "So I took him aside, put my phone in the front pocket of my shirt, hit record on my camera, and tried to make him think that I was on his side."

"It worked," I say. "You got him to admit what he did on video."

He sighs. "I wanted to tell you. I didn't want to release it without you knowing. But then when you sent that text and then blocked my calls, I went out of my mind trying to figure out what I did wrong. And then when we talked this morning, it all clicked. And that's when I called Rylan to post the video on social media and hoped you would see it—so you would see that I never meant to hurt you . . . even though I did. And then I thought screw it, I should just run over here to try and explain everything to you . . . I don't know why I didn't think to do that sooner. I've just been such a mess these last couple of days without you . . ."

His face twists like he's in agony. I squeeze his hand again and step closer to him. "It's okay. Situations like this are always messy. There's never a neat and clean way to expose someone horrible."

The lump that's been lodged in my throat ever since leaving Utah eases. Everything is out in the open. Now for the next part—the most important part.

"Drew, I meant what I said on the phone earlier. I love you. So much. I know that we just met two months ago, and I have a lot of work to do on myself . . . I'm gonna start seeing a therapist to talk about my relationship trauma with Reid. I think it'll help me move on . . . so I'm in a better, healthier place for my next relationship." I swallow, taking a much-needed moment to calm my nerves. "I've never felt about anyone the way I feel about you, Drew. And I know that most people would think it's too soon . . . And you probably aren't totally out of your mind like me and fall in love after knowing someone for weeks, but that's okay because I just want to be with you and . . ." I pause to calm my frenzied heartbeat. "Can we please start over?"

A hard swallow moves along his stubble-covered neck. "No way am I starting over with you."

All the breath leaves my body. My hand loosens around his, but then he pulls me against him.

"I don't want to start over because I'd rather pick up where we left off. I love you, Dunn." A grin stretches across those gorgeous lips of his. "And if we both love each other, there's no reason to start over. We can move straight ahead."

My eyes well up, but this time I'm grinning so wide my cheeks ache. And then he leans down and kisses me. I lose track of the seconds, the minutes, the time, the place. Kissing Drew feels like coming home. I don't ever want to stop.

When we finally break apart, I'm still grinning.

I cup his scruffy cheek with my hand. "So that means—"

Just then the elevator doors squeak open. When we twist around to look, there's a maintenance guy in coveralls standing right in front of the doors . . . and a small crowd of people standing behind him. The loud guys in suits look on, confused expressions on their faces. Behind them stand Haley and Brooke. Both of them go from frowning to grinning once they see it's us in the elevator.

Coveralls guy frowns at us. "The elevator doesn't seem broken."

"Oh, um, sorry about that," I say, my face heating. "False alarm."

I'm still hugging Drew by the waist when I answer him. Despite how shocking it is to have an audience, I grin wide. I don't know if I'll ever be able to stop smiling around him.

Coveralls guy rolls his eyes and walks away.

"Uh . . . can we get in the elevator, then?" the loud suit from minutes ago asks.

Drew starts to stammer something, but then Haley walks over.

"This elevator is spoken for. You're better off taking the stairs. Or wait for the next elevator," she says to him. Then she turns to us. "You guys made up?"

Drew and I nod at her. She beams at us. I look up at Brooke and see an amused smile on her face.

She glances at Drew. "Andrew. Good to see you."

"Hey, Brooke. Likewise."

And then I suddenly realize how odd this all must look—two crew members all over each other in the elevator at work. My hands fall from Drew as I turn to face Brooke.

"Sorry, Brooke . . . I . . . I, um . . . This probably isn't the most professional behavior in the world. Crew members pairing up during a shoot, that is." I let out an embarrassed chuckle.

She holds up her hand. "You don't have to justify anything to me. That's how Greg and I met, remember?"

I nod, remembering how she's now dating the subject of her current series.

"Finding romance is quite a feat when you're on location. I would know," she says. "Enjoy yourselves."

I let out a breath, relieved. Drew peers down at me while wiggling his eyebrows before he scoops my hand into his once more.

Haley walks up to the elevator, a knowing smile on her face. "You two heard Brooke. Enjoy yourselves."

She presses a button, and the doors close once more.

Drew glances up at the floor numbers that are positioned at the top of the elevator. "Looks like we're headed for the basement."

"No one ever goes to the basement," I say. "That's where all the utility stuff is."

Drew smirks at me. "Haley's a genius. That gives us sixty floors to enjoy ourselves."

He wraps his arms around me, tugging me close against his body. I bite my bottom lip, my heart pounding. But behind all this excitement lies contentment. All that uncertainty and struggle and anticipation of the last several weeks have brought us here. Despite everything, Drew and I are finally, officially together. I've never been so happy.

"Does this mean we'll finally get to live out my fantasy of you having your way with me in an elevator?"

I tug at the buttons on his shirt. "Possibly. I've got a pretty good idea of what we can get up to."

He grins, his heart in his eyes. "I'm all yours, Dunn."

Epilogue

One Year Later

L AST SHOT OF THE DAY, GUYS," I HOLLER ACROSS THE PRIS-
tine white beach we're set up on. "Let's see if we can nail it."

Drew glances up at me from where he stands several feet away. "I think I can nail it."

Rylan runs over to Drew to straighten out the short-sleeved button-up he's wearing, restyle his hair, and dab away the few droplets of sweat on his forehead.

She finishes and runs back over to stand by me.

"Excellent work, Ms. Stylist."

Rylan beams wide. "Thanks."

I turn around and check that the rest of the crew is ready. Wyatt and Joe flash me a thumbs-up from their cameras. Haley looks up from the tablet to nod at me. Off to the side Colton stands with a boom mic.

I look back at Drew and wink. "Action."

Today is the last day of shooting for *Hidden Gem Island Getaways: Philippines*. Tomorrow we start our journey back to New York.

I still can't get over that I'm shooting my second series. When *Discovering Utah* aired last fall, it was an instant hit. It received the highest ratings of any new series debuting in the fall for

Expedition TV. The network immediately approached Drew and me to film another show. And that's when I pitched my other dream. This time I went big, though. I proposed a series where each season we focus on a different ocean region. The network was all for it, signing us for three seasons. In a few months we're headed to Micronesia. After that, we're hitting up little-known beaches in the US.

Curling my toes in the sand, I watch my boyfriend nail his lines for the last scene that we're filming today on Jomalig Island. There's not a hint of hesitation when he looks at the camera. The stage fright that held Drew back from his hosting dreams is under control now. He insists it's because I set him at ease—and that I'm the only person he ever wants to host for.

During this six-week shoot, we've been island hopping all over the Philippines. We've hit Palawan, Seco Island, and Romblon Island. Every time we set up, I get that same flash of warmth in my chest. Apong Lita would be so excited to see her favorite beaches featured on this series.

I swallow back the emotion in my throat when I remember how Mom cried happy tears after watching the Needles episode of *Discovering Utah*.

"Oh, *anak*. That was such a beautiful dedication. Apong would have loved it. Absolutely loved it."

And when I told her and Dad that I had just gotten the go-ahead from the network to film an entire series in the Philippines, they were just as thrilled and emotional.

"Apong Lita is smiling down on you," Mom said, sniffling. "She is so, so proud."

Even my dad, who hardly ever cries, got teary. "We couldn't be prouder of you, honeybun."

When I think back on their reaction, I get a lump in my throat. I focus back on filming. I was able to recruit everyone from the Utah crew for this series, and hopefully they can all join Drew and me next season and the one after.

Even though it's been a year since we've all worked together, our dynamic is the same as it was in Utah.

"Jomalig Island is the very definition of a hidden gem," Drew says as he walks along the beach. A small wave kisses the sand, hitting his feet. "It's got the gorgeous golden-sand beaches and crystal-turquoise water that everyone loves, without the crowds of other touristy areas."

Drew goes on to mention how vacationing here is a must for travelers who prefer a relaxed, more local experience.

Then he stops walking and turns to look at the sparkling-blue ocean before focusing back on Wyatt's camera. "I know this won't be my last visit to this incredible island. Thanks for joining me on this episode of *Hidden Gem Island Getaways*. Can't wait to explore our next hidden gem with you again soon. Until next time."

"Cut! That's a wrap!"

Gentle applause from the people watching us nearby makes me smile. I take a moment to glance at the water. My second series is officially wrapped.

Drew walks over, wraps his arms around me, and presses a kiss to my lips.

"So did I nail it?" he asks, his voice soft.

The butterflies in my stomach swarm. "You always do."

His smile widens, and he kisses me again. It doesn't matter how many times Drew gives me those soft little kisses. They'll always make me flutter from the inside out.

He's made it a habit to do that every day at the end of filming. It's a fun little routine we've carved for ourselves. Spend several hours shooting, behaving like consummate professionals, then at the end of the day when we wrap, we let ourselves act a little like boyfriend and girlfriend.

"God, you two. Get a room," Haley whines in mock disgust.

I roll my eyes and toss my hat at her; she catches it and puts it on her head.

Drew walks off to help Colton put away equipment while I help Wyatt pack up.

"So how many Hail Marys is your mom doing in preparation for our journey back to the States?" Haley asks Wyatt as he zips up gear bags.

"Only three. She's easing up a bit, I think."

Joe chuckles as he finishes breaking down a tripod, then wipes the sweat off his brow. "Well, they're out of vodka at the resort, so you at least don't have to worry about that," he says, patting Wyatt on the back.

"We should definitely have a celebratory drink tonight, though," Wyatt says.

Just the mention of alcohol has me on high alert. I'll have to be extra-careful.

Haley elbows my arm. "What do you say? A drink before we head back to our beach huts and pack up for the journey home tomorrow?"

She turns to ask Drew, Rylan, and Colton, who are walking over to us.

"We're in," Colton says, grabbing Rylan's hand. They give each other a smile that makes me grin despite the nerves firing inside me.

"I'll definitely join you guys," I say. "I probably won't drink, though. I'm feeling pretty dehydrated after working in the sun all day. Best to stick with water, I think."

I keep my tone light to make sure no one suspects anything. When we finish packing everything up, we head to the hut where the hosts at the small resort we're staying at are serving dinner.

Drew walks up to me and wraps his arm around my waist as we walk. "You doing okay?"

I try my best to smile and nod and not let on that anything is on my mind. "Just excited to go home."

"Me too, Dunn." He kisses my temple.

It's the truth. I do feel great. There's just that one thing hanging in the back of my mind . . . and I won't be able to deal with it until we're back home.

I shove the thought aside and breathe in. The aroma of garlic, fresh-caught fish, and sauteed veggies hits my nose as we walk into the hut. As if on cue, my stomach growls.

"Hope you're hungry," Drew says while peering at the table, where a giant pot of meat, veggies, and rice sits.

"I'm starving."

STANDING IN MY bathroom, I stare at my phone, which is sitting on the edge of the sink. One more minute left.

Ever since arriving home from the airport late last night, I haven't been able to focus—not until I ran to a drugstore this morning and bought a pregnancy test. And now I have to wait sixty seconds to find out if my and Drew's lives will change forever.

My heart races in my chest as I count the seconds. Even though Drew and I aren't married, we've been committed to each other ever since the day we declared our love in the elevator at Expedition TV, just over a year ago. He moved into my apartment a few weeks later. The only reason we haven't made things legal between us is because we've been so busy with work this past year with the success of *Discovering Utah*. We haven't even had time to take a weekend trip together. But we did agree that someday we'd like to get married and have kids . . . It's just that things might be happening a bit sooner than expected.

Drew's keys jingle in the door. I contemplate waiting in the bathroom and looking at the results myself and then telling him, but I decide not to. We should look at it together—because we're in this together.

I fling open the bathroom door just as he kicks off his shoes. He smiles at me and holds up a bag of takeout. "You said you were craving soft pretzels with cheese sauce so I grabbed some on my way home from meeting with my agent. No Brie, though," he teases.

"Thank God. Ever since I saw that guy taking bites out of that wheel of Brie cheese the day we met on the subway, I can't stomach the stuff."

"I had to make a convenience-store run for Snoballs too. I thought I had more left."

"You did. But I ate them all."

Drew frowns at me, clearly confused about why I devoured his Snoball stash when I previously couldn't stand them.

"Um . . . hormonal changes can cause changes in your taste buds."

"What?"

I pause, clearing my throat. "I have to tell you something."

I try to fold my hands in front of me to appear calm. Instead I end up fidgeting like a nervous wreck.

Drew's eyebrows furrow. "What's wrong?"

"Um, well . . . I've been feeling a bit off these past few weeks, and I thought it was because of all the traveling, but then I missed my period and . . ."

Drew's eyes go wide. My breath lodges in my throat. Instead of babbling more nonsense, I grab his hand and pull him into the bathroom. Then I point to the pregnancy test, which is facedown on the edge of the sink.

"Are you pregnant?" he asks, his voice soft.

"I don't know. I wanted to wait to find out until you came home."

He turns to me and smiles. "Well, let's see, then."

I take a breath and flip it over. When I see two solid pink lines, my mouth opens. "Holy shit."

My heart leaps out of my chest as I look at Drew. Because in addition to grinning the biggest grin I've ever seen him make, he's also tearing up.

He drops the takeout bag on the floor, then pulls me into a hug.

"Holy shit, Dunn. We're gonna have a baby."

The way his voice shakes as he holds me makes me tear up. We hold each other while sniffling for what seems like minutes. Then Drew's arms loosen around me and he leans away. He grips me gently by the waist, his eyes glued to my stomach.

"This is the best news. Ever."

"You're not nervous? I mean, you're an awesome uncle, but you always joke about how much of a handful your niece and nephew are and how happy you are to give them back to your sister when you've spent the day with them. You won't be able to do that with our baby."

"Of course I'm nervous. But I'm way, way more excited. It'll be different when it's our baby. I'll get overwhelmed, I'm sure, but I won't want to be away from our baby. Or you. Ever."

I have to plant my feet firmly on the floor so that I don't collapse while I swoon.

"How are you feeling?" he asks.

"I'm so happy, but I'm a little scared too. I've never been pregnant before. I don't know what to expect." My mind races. "And I don't even know how I'm going to balance traveling and work when the baby comes."

Drew blinks, like he's thinking about what I've said. Then he grabs both of my hands in his and squeezes. "I get that. I mean, I don't one hundred percent know what you're going through . . .

I'm not a woman. But you're the most talented producer at Expedition, Alia. You made yourself a star with *Discovering Utah*. You're going to do it again with *Hidden Gems*. Everyone loves working with you. The network will fall over themselves to accommodate you and whatever you need while you're pregnant and after you have the baby. I'll make sure of it."

All the nerves and uncertainty plaguing me a minute ago are fleeting. Because I just remembered I have the most amazing partner, who will be with me every step of the way.

"A baby and two insanely busy careers are going to be one hell of an adventure."

When he shakes his head, his smile doesn't budge. "This is the best adventure I could ever go on, Dunn. Because it's with you."

His eyes well up, which make mine well up. I lean up and kiss him. Then I wrap my arms around his neck and pull him against me so tightly that I can feel his heart beating against my chest.

"So damn smooth, Irons."

Acknowledgments

First and foremost, a gigantic thanks to Stefanie Simpson, my amazing friend, for reading this book when it was barely past a first draft. You were encouraging and enthusiastic, and it made all the difference in the world. I love you, lady.

Thank you, Bella and Tessa, for blessing me with your TV production expertise and answering all my random questions.

Thank you, Steph Mills, for putting me in touch with Tessa and for your wonderfully encouraging emails.

Lauren Maxwell, a million thanks to you for helping me navigate the New York City subway via Instagram DMs. Someday I will visit and you can show me the ropes in person.

Skye McDonald, thank you for helping me properly set the scene of a busy subway car ride.

Thank you, JL Peridot, for your pep talks and your friendship. You always cheer me on when I need it most. You're a gem.

Thank you to the best agent, Sarah Younger, and the best editor, Sarah Blumenstock.

Thank you so, so much to Vikki Chu for designing yet another stunning book cover. You always bring my books to life in the most beautiful way.

Huge thanks to my husband, Alex, my favorite hiking buddy on the planet. Our road trips to Utah inspired this book. There's no one in the world I'd rather get lost in the desert with.

Thanks to my family and friends for supporting me, loving me, and being proud of me.

And thank you to everyone who buys and reads my books. I know I've said this a million times before, but it means the absolute world. Truly.

One more thing: The National Park Service and the show *Rock the Park* were inspirations for this book. NPS employees and volunteers work diligently to preserve so many beautiful lands while also making them accessible to the public. If you're able, visit a national park or monument. It's a great way to support the NPS while also observing the beauty and majesty of the land around you. If you can't make it out to your nearest national park, watch *Rock the Park*. It's a fun and engaging program that showcases all that the national parks have to offer.

Don't miss

Simmer Down

available now from Berkley Jove!

OCEAN AIR HAS A FUNNY EFFECT ON ME. MAYBE IT'S THE salt.

I inhale while driving along the lone main road in southern Maui. The briny moisture hits my nostrils, coating the back of my throat and lungs. I wince at the slight burn. A handful of breaths and I wonder just how close I am to reaching my daily allotment of sodium. Leave it to a food truck owner to view everything around me—including oxygen—in terms of food.

But that's how all-consuming food truck life is. It's my work, my thoughts, the air I breathe. It seeps into everything. I've only been doing this a year, but that's one of the first things I've learned.

I shove aside the thoughts of saline air. Instead I run through my mental checklist like I do every morning while navigating the slow-moving traffic to my parking spot near Makena Beach, one of the most popular tourist spots on Maui.

Chicken *adobo* wings are chilling in the fridge. Check.

So are the papaya salad and fruit salad. Check.

Pansit is freshly made as of this morning and ready to dish up. Check.

A fresh batch of vegetable oil sits in the fryer, ready to heat. Check.

Waiting for the oil to warm should give me just enough time to prep everything for the day. Check.

For a split second I'm smiling, satisfied at the menu I've put together for today with a shoestring budget and limited supplies. Everything's ready to go. The garnishes, the utensils, the napkins, the whiteboard with today's menu written on it. Check, check, check, and . . . damn it.

I groan while gripping the steering wheel. I forgot the menu board at the commercial kitchen where I prep the food every morning. Again. I sigh, my cheeks on fire when I think about what an amateur mistake I just made. That means I'll have to recite the daily specials and prices in addition to the standard menu items to every customer who comes to the window to order, an annoying and unprofessional act.

I shake my head, disappointed that I've tainted the workday before it's even started. It's only marginally worse than my typical mess-up with the menu board. I wince when I remember how I almost always forget to display it until after sliding open the window, which signals that I'm open for business. And when I remember it, I spin around, usually knock over a rogue sauce bottle or metal bowl, scurry out of the truck, prop it up at the front, and run back inside. That's when I typically trip up the stairs while customers gawk. It's like the cherry on top of a hot mess sundae, a dead giveaway that despite all my planning and all my checklists, despite my year of hard work, long hours, and on-the-job learning, I don't belong in this food truck world.

I slouch in the driver's seat as I begin to deflate. No other food truck I've been around seems to struggle with the basics like I do. A whole new checklist slides to the front of my mind. My very own life checklist that I never, ever thought I'd have.

I'm twenty-nine years old and struggling to make a living

in the most popular tourist destination in the Pacific Ocean. Check.

I started a food truck business with zero food truck experience. Check.

I mistakenly thought that all my years working in high-end restaurants would be all the prep I needed to run a food truck. Check.

I share a condo in Kihei with my mom—a condo that was meant to be my parents' retirement haven. Check.

A familiar sinking feeling hits, one I haven't felt in weeks. It's a heavy dose of doubt mixed with good old-fashioned insecurity, reminding me just how out of my element I am.

Another lesson I've learned? Life doesn't always care what you have planned. Sometimes it pulls the rug out from under you and takes one of your parents with it, leaving you and your only living parent under a mountain of medical debt, your savings ravaged, and with zero viable options on how to dig your way out. So you and your mom pick up where she and your dad left off. You take the used food truck your dad bought because it was his and your mom's dream to run their own food truck in Maui during their retirement. You put the only professional skills you honed—your cooking and restaurant skills—into fulfilling your dad's last wish. You put your heart and soul into that food truck, cross your fingers, and hope for the best.

I silently recite my other checklist, the one I mentally skim in my head each day, whenever I need a reminder of why I'm here and why all the struggle is worth it. It's the one checklist I'm eternally grateful for.

My mom is alive. Check.

I get to see her every day. Check.

Even when I mess up, I'm fulfilling the promise I made to my dad. Check.

I focus, crossing my fingers around my grip on the steering

wheel, hoping for a good day. I hope I sell out during today's lunch service. I hope that weird grinding noise that emanates from this rickety truck is just a fluke, and not a sign that I need to replace the brake pads, something I can't afford. And I hope the gas in the tank is enough to last me until the end of the week, because I can't afford that either.

With every new concern that hits this mental checklist, worry bleeds into my gratitude. I sigh, gazing out my window at endless palm trees and sand, homing in on the soothing crash of the waves. At least I can count on the stunning beauty of Maui to put me in a pleasant mood most days. My heartbeat slows, my jaw relaxes, and my hands loosen around the steering wheel.

Soon the road transitions from smooth pavement to pockmarked concrete. I pull into that perfect semicircle of dirt overlooking the ocean that I just happened to stumble upon back in December. Once again, I'm grateful. For the last three months, this has been Tiva's Filipina Kusina's go-to parking spot. Because of that, we have a steady flow of customers from Big Beach, which means a reliable income most days. Which means we're that much closer to being out of the hole.

As I turn off the engine, I fix my gaze on an unfamiliar silver food truck situated right next to where I normally park. I climb out and walk over, zeroing in on the Union Jack flag decal that rests on the left side of the window. Over the window reads "Hungry Chaps" in bold black letters. On the right side of the window is a cartoon image of a plate of fish-and-chips and some half-moon-shaped pastry.

I sigh. Hungry Chaps must be a new addition to the island food truck circle. They must not be aware of the unofficial policy of not encroaching on another truck's territory. I practice a smile and stroll to the closed window of the truck. It's my turn to offer a friendly welcome and a polite explanation of Maui's unspoken food truck etiquette to this newcomer, just as the established food trucks did for Mom and me when we first started. The rules are simple: no parking in spaces that other trucks have occupied long term, and no parking too close to another truck unless you have their permission.

Living on an island makes competition fiercer—there's only so much space to begin with. When we first started out, we couldn't find regular parking and had to drive all over the island from open spot to open spot. It was impossible to build a customer base that way, never having a consistent location where people could easily find us. It meant months of unsteady income, which meant we were barely breaking even.

I knock on the cloudy glass window. A lightly tanned face pops up from behind the counter. The window is so smeared that I can barely make out the person.

"Hi there! Do you have a sec?" I say.

"Absolutely! Just a moment," an English-accented male voice answers. I smile. His accent sounds a lot like that of my uncle, who lives in London with my auntie Nora. I wonder if this guy's from London too.

A thud sound and the clang of metal dishes crashing to the floor echo from inside the truck. Out of the corner of my eye, I see a man exit from the back.

He strolls up to me, kicking up clouds of dirt with his heavy steps. He's a tall, sun-kissed drink of water with honey-hued hair cropped close to his scalp and a few days' worth of dark blond scruff on his cheeks. I tilt my head back to get a proper look at his face. That's a new one. I'm nearly five feet ten inches, and my neck is perpetually sore from having to peer down at people. But this guy has to be pushing six feet three inches, maybe even six four.

He looks familiar, even though I know for sure I've never

seen him before. Probably because he looks like a hybrid of Michael Fassbender and Zac Efron. In other words, impossibly good-looking.

He flashes a smile at me, and I promptly forget what I was going to say. Instead I respond with what I assume is one of the dopiest grins I've ever beamed at another human being.

"So nice to finally meet you," he says.

"Oh, um, thanks," I stammer, thrown off at how friendly he is to me, a complete stranger.

When he blinks, it's like I've been dazzled by the shiniest peridot gem. His eyes boast the most perfect shade of hazel green I've ever seen. But it's more than just the color leaving me tongue-tied. There's a genuine kindness behind them I don't often see when I make eye contact with someone I don't know. The way he stares catches me completely off guard, like I'm the only thing worth looking at in the surrounding area. It's impressive, considering the landscape is the very definition of breathtaking with the nearby lush green hills, cloudless blue skies, and multitude of palm trees. Not even the expansive lava field across the road, which appears practically endless as it stretches all the way to the horizon, seems to capture this guy's attention. Even I stop to gawk at it at least once a day.

I let my gaze linger on his eyes a second longer than what is considered polite. My stomach flips. I could fall damn hard for eyes like that.

For a fleeting moment, the Neanderthal part of my brain takes over. An image of me under him appears. Those hazel eyes pinning me, those thick lips stretched in a smile. A slight shake of my head erases the decidedly dirty thought like the drawing on an Etch A Sketch. What in the world is wrong with me? A friendly greeting from a handsome man shouldn't send me into an X-rated daytime fantasy. I silently scold myself. This is apparently what eighteen months of self-imposed celibacy will do to a woman.

He sticks his hand out and I shake it, appreciating the firm yet gentle gripping method he employs. I'm so used to men offering weak handshakes that feel like a dead fish in my hand. But I dig this guy's style. He doesn't automatically assume I'm too weak to make his male acquaintance.

When he lets go of my hand, he looks back at his truck. "Apologies, I didn't think you were coming for another hour."

"What do you mean?"

He points his thumb at his truck. "It's all ready for you. Just be careful when you walk in because I tripped and knocked over a few metal bowls on the way out here." He runs a hand through his hair. "Afraid I'm still getting used to navigating my tall self within the confines of a van. Sorry, I mean 'truck.'" He holds a hand up. "I can assure you, everything is up to code."

I squint up at him, thoroughly confused. "That's great, but why are you telling me all this?"

"Well, I thought you'd like to know. You're the health inspector after all."

"Oh . . . no, I'm . . . I run a food truck."

I point to my truck, which is parked behind his. He pivots his frown to it, narrowing his stare, like he's just now noticing the giant food truck parked nearby.

"You're not the health inspector?"

I shake my head, hoping the movement comes off as good-natured and not dismissive. "Sorry, I'm not."

A long moment of silence passes where he takes another long look between me and Tiva's truck. I count to ten before the silence starts to turn awkward. New guy is clearly confused. Best to use a gentle, cheery approach when I inform him of the unofficial rules he's breaking.

I clear my throat. "I know this is probably awkward timing, but, um, you're not actually supposed to park here."

He whips his head around to me. A glare replaces his confused frown from before, and it is downright lethal. My mouth goes dry. It's a struggle just to swallow.

Silently, I remind myself that he's the newbie. He's just confused, and some people get annoyed when they're confused. I just need to explain myself, and then he'll understand. I power through the awkwardness permeating the air between us.

"See, I've had this spot for the past several months, and it's kind of an unspoken rule on Maui that food trucks don't park this close to each other if they're not in a parking lot or at an event. And seeing as I was technically here first—"

He turns around and walks back into his truck before I can finish speaking. My jaw hangs open in the salty ocean breeze. Did he seriously just do that?

I stand for several seconds, arms dangling at my sides, processing the moment. Maybe he's embarrassed and needs a bit of time before he moves his truck. I can certainly understand. I've made plenty of mortifying mistakes while learning the food truck ropes. This morning's menu mishap is small beans compared to the time I lost the credit card reader and could only take cash for a handful of days, or the time I mistakenly filled the sweet chili sauce bottles with sriracha.

I fold my arms across my chest, waiting for the engine to fire up. But nothing happens. Just more clanking sounds from the inside of his truck. I check my watch and see that a full minute has passed since he walked away from me. The longer I stand out there alone, the clearer it becomes. That midsentence exit wasn't embarrassment; it was a dismissal—of me. He's not going anywhere.

Heat makes its way from my cheeks all the way down to my

chest. The whole time I was standing here, trying to be nice, he was disregarding me. I march up to the truck and pound on the cloudy glass window.

"Can you please move your truck?" I ask.

I catch his silhouette walking back and forth inside the truck, blatantly ignoring me. Steam levels my insides. What the ever-loving hell is this guy's problem?

I pound on the window with both hands. Politeness isn't working. It seems this newbie is in need of a harsher welcome. "Hey! Listen, you're in my spot."

This time when he walks out of the truck to meet me, he plants himself a foot away, resuming that killer glare from minutes ago.

"Maybe you couldn't tell by the way I've been ignoring you, but I don't care what you have to say," he says.

His irritated tone combined with the melodic English accent throw me off-kilter. I didn't expect to be arguing with a hot James Bond soundalike today, and it's messing with my head.

"Um, what?" I stammer.

"Oh, bloody hell. Do you really need me to explain? I'm not moving."

"Excuse me?" My voice hits that shrill register whenever I'm shocked and pissed at once.

"For fuck's sake," he mutters, glancing up at the sky. "I don't have time for this."

"Well, make time." My hard tone verges on a bark. "You're new here, right? I'll explain. I'm Nikki DiMarco. I run this food truck, Tiva's Filipina Kusina, with my mom, Tiva."

I almost mention that it's her day off, but I catch myself. Impossibly hot dickhead probably doesn't care about the details. Pursing my lips, I let the momentary embarrassment wash over me.

He deepens his scowl, and I'm jolted back to our confrontation. I point behind me to the rusty white food truck bearing Mom's name in bold red letters. Underneath the text is an artist's rendering of a plate of noodles and *lumpia*. He glances briefly at my truck, then back at me.

"Like I was trying to say before, you're not supposed to park right next to a competing food truck," I say. "It's kind of an unspoken rule here."

It's a struggle to keep my voice steady, but I want to be the calm, rational counter to this guy's angry petulance.

Crossing his arms, he shrugs. "Let *me* explain something. I'm Callum James, and I don't care. I'm staying right here."

Those arresting hazel-green eyes peer down at me. Funny, I used to think of green as a cheerful, enlivening color before this stranger turned hostile. Now green will forever be associated with "obnoxious" and "jerkoff."

"I don't know who the hell you think you are, but what you're doing isn't cool. At all," I say.

He smirks. The nerve of this jackass.

"Is something funny?" I say through gritted teeth.

He shrugs, letting his hands fall to his hips. Even through the loose-fitting T-shirt he's wearing, I can tell this prick is cut. It's obvious from his thickly muscled arms that are covered with ropelike veins, from the broad spread of his shoulders.

It's a quick second before that smirk widens to a smug smile. "'Isn't cool at all?' Did you honestly say that?"

The rough, guttural register of his voice sends a sheet of goose bumps across my skin. Soft yet lethal. Like a bad guy in an action movie whispering threats to the main character who's tied to a chair.

He chuckles before letting his gaze fall along the length of my body. Is he seriously checking me out right now? A deep, seconds-long inhale and exhale is the only way I can cope.

I will not punch this douchebag in the face.

I will not punch this douchebag in the face.

I chant the silent mantra in my head while gritting my teeth.

"Hey," I bark. "Are you kidding me? Eyes up here."

His shoulders jolt slightly at my demand. At least he has the decency to look embarrassed. But a beat later it melts from his face, leaving behind a steely frown. He takes a single step forward, leaning his head down toward me. "Listen, petal. I don't care one bit if you think this is 'uncool.'"

When he makes air quotes with both hands as he says "uncool," I swallow back fire. The bastard called me "*petal*." Where the hell is this guy from, *Downton Abbey*? Who the hell calls anyone petal anymore?

I open my mouth to unleash a tirade of expletives and "how dare you," but he cuts me off.

"I have just as much right to park here as you do. I'm not doing anything illegal, and I'm not moving. Get over it."

He spins around and saunters behind his food truck, leaving me standing there with my jaw on the ground, my fists clenched, and nothing to say.

How the hell did this happen? How was this guy able to shift from charming stranger one minute to insufferable bastard the next? How did he just destroy years of island food truck etiquette in minutes? How did a complete stranger leave me a mess of frustration and outrage?

The window of his truck slides open, and a man with a younger, friendlier version of the hostile stranger's face sticks his head out.

"Are you all right?" he asks in that same melodic English accent, his own hazel-green eyes glistening with concern.

At least this one's polite. I slap my hands on the metal countertop lining the window. His shoulders jerk up. "I'd like to speak with that ball of sunshine you work with."

His eyebrows jump up his forehead. "Um . . ." He twists his head back. "Oi, Callum!"

Callum walks up to the window, still sporting that sour, unfriendly expression on his face. Does this guy suck on lemon wedges before engaging other human beings?

When I wag my finger up at him, he doesn't even blink. The polite one does though before flashing him a panicked look.

"You want to defy local food truck etiquette by being a complete asshole? Fine."

The words punch out in a firm, steady tone. My fuck-off tone. Callum's disrespectful attitude is the last straw in my already shit-tastic morning—in my already shit-tastic life. I can't take one more thing working against me right now. So I won't.

"From this moment on, I'm going to make your life a living hell." I tilt my head to the side. "Deal with it."

In the split second after I speak, all I see are his eyes. Strangely, they still read kind, and it's enough to make me question for the briefest moment if I've been too harsh. But his brow furrows, his nostrils flare, and his mouth twists into the tightest purse I've ever seen. Never mind. If he were truly kind, he wouldn't have met my politeness with outright dickishness. I spin around and march back to my truck.

"Bloody hell, what did you say to her?" the polite one asks as I walk the six feet back to the other side of the clearing.

The only tidbit I hear before I'm back in my truck is Callum barking the name Finn. Judging by their resemblance, I'm guessing they're brothers. And Callum would do well to listen to his little brother Finn next time, as it might keep him out of trouble. Too late now though.

I tie on my apron and start prepping for lunch. Sunlight shines through the open window, illuminating the blade of my knife as I chop heads of cabbage. The adrenaline from our fiery exchange is a surprise source of energy. I shred the whole tray in half the time it usually takes.

All he had to do was show one ounce of courtesy. But no. He wanted to start a war. With a total stranger who was perfectly polite to him until he played dirty. A total stranger who's been through hell this past year and a half, who is tired of ducking from the constant stream of curveballs life chucks at her.

As of today, I'm done ducking. I'm fighting back.

He wants a war? It is motherfucking on.

Photo by Daniel Muller

SARAH ECHAVARRE SMITH is a copywriter turned author who wants to make the world a lovelier place, one kissing story at a time. Her love of romance began when she was eight and she discovered her auntie's stash of romance novels. She's been hooked ever since. When she's not writing, you can find her hiking, eating chocolate, and perfecting her *lumpia* recipe. She lives in Bend, Oregon, with her husband and her adorable cat, Salem.

CONNECT ONLINE

SarahSmithBooks.com

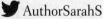 AuthorSarahS

AuthorSarahS

Ready to find
your next great read?

Let us help.

Visit prh.com/nextread